BETRAYER OF WORLDS

Larry Niven AND Edward M. Lerner

BETRAYER OF WORLDS

TOR®

A TOM DOHERTY ASSOCIATES BOOK

New York

BETRAYER OF WORLDS

Copyright © 2010 by Larry Niven and Edward M. Lerner

All rights reserved.

A Tor Book
Published by Tom Doherty Associates, LLC
175 Fifth Avenue
New York, NY 10010

www.tor-forge.com

Tor® is a registered trademark of Tom Doherty Associates, LLC.

ISBN 978-0-7653-2608-9

Printed in the United States of America

0 9 8 7 6 5 4 3 2

CONTENTS

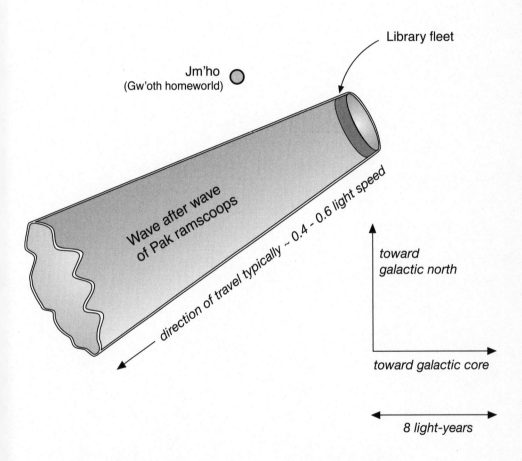

BETRAYER OF WORLDS
INTERSTELLAR SETTING

NOTES

1. Worlds not to scale
2. Distances as of Earth date 2780
3. Distances as viewed in galactic (nonaccelerated)
   reference frame—no relativistic effects

DRAMATIS PERSONAE

HUMANS

Roland Allen-Cartwright
  New Terran mercenary captain (Pak campaign)
Sigmund Ausfaller
  Defense Minister of New Terra (and head of the secret intelligence service); Earth expatriate
Alice Jordan
  Sigmund Ausfaller's deputy; Sol system expatriate
Beowulf (Bey) Shaeffer
  Starship pilot and adventurer; stepfather of Louis Wu; location unknown but presumed in Human Space
Enzio Walker-Wong
  New Terran mercenary captain (Gw'oth campaign)
Carlos Wu
  Physicist and all-around genius; Louis Wu's biological father; location unknown but presumed in Human Space
Louis Wu (aka Nathan Graynor)
  Earthborn adventurer, recruited by Nessus into the Citizens' cold war with the Gw'oth

ARTIFICIAL INTELLIGENCES

Jeeves
  Shipboard AI on early human interstellar colony ship Long Pass; *also, various New Terran clones and derivatives*
Voice
  Illegal Citizen AI derived from a Jeeves; AIde to Nessus

CITIZENS/PUPPETEERS

Achilles
>*Minister of Science; aspires to head the Experimentalist Party—and thereby become Hindmost*

Baedeker
>*Hindmost; head of the Experimentalist Party*

Clotho
>*Radical supporter of Achilles; captain of stolen starship* Remembrance

Nessus
>*Senior agent/scout of Clandestine Directorate*

Nike
>*Deputy Minister of Foreign Affairs, hence Director of Clandestine Directorate; Experimentalist; former Hindmost*

Thalia
>*Scout; General Products Corporation representative to Jm'ho (effectively the Concordance Ambassador to the Gw'oth)*

Vesta
>*Nike's senior aide and longtime protégé*

GW'OTH

Bm'o
>*Tn'Tn'ho (dynast) of Tn'ho, the preeminent city-state on the Gw'oth home world of Jm'ho*

Ng't'mo
>*An 8-plex group mind (i.e., a Gw'otesht-8 ensemble), in service to Bm'o*

Ol't'ro
>*A 16-plex group mind (i.e., a Gw'otesht-16 ensemble); leader of the breakaway colony world of Kl'mo*

Rt'o
>*Counselor to Bm'o*

Sr'o
>*Lead mind within Ol't'ro*

WUNDERLAND

1

The jungle was eerily quiet.

Hugging the uneven ground behind a thin screen of greenery, Nathan Graynor peered over the precipice to where a dirt road followed the narrow, undulating floor of a steep-walled canyon. The suns, one yellow and one orange, were high overhead. Anyone glancing up from the road toward either ridge would only see glare.

The perfect time and place for an ambush.

The day was cool and a breeze blew steadily. Still, sweat trickled down Nathan's face. Nerves, he told himself, knowing that was at best a half truth.

With the barrel of his laser rifle, he nudged aside a frond for a clearer look. (The fern was green, clearly terrestrial. Across the rugged gorge where the second group of rebels hid, the red-gold vegetation was as plainly native.) Ruts and potholes scarred the primitive road: no obstacle for antigrav vehicles, but scarcely navigable for anything with wheels.

He wasn't afraid, not exactly. Fear would have required truly believing that this was happening, that he was here.

Life had been that way, surreal, since the missile punched through *Clementine*. The emergency restraints in the pilot's couch had saved him. Everyone else aboard died when the ship broke apart. Resistance fighters reached the wreckage first. Deep in shock, unquestioningly, he had gone with them.

He took small, measured sips from his canteen. He took deep, cleansing breaths. When neither calmed him, he looked skyward for serenity, at the birds and their native equivalents soaring effortlessly in the thermals that rose from the plain. That didn't work, either.

In the Resistance camp he had drawn plenty of sideways glances. The rebels didn't fully trust him—yet here he was. Maybe they had chosen not to leave him behind unguarded. Maybe, finally, they felt comfortable with him. Or maybe they wanted to see if he would bolt into the jungle given the chance. (Would they have let him go? He didn't think so.)

One way or another, his presence here was a test.

A faint droning drifted Nathan's way, and hints of metallic clanking. Over the plain below, in the far distance where jungle still hid the road, a cloud of brown dust now hovered.

Their target approached.

The aristos controlled space around Wunderland more completely every day. Nathan—and even more so, his former crew—had learned that the hard way. Snoopersats might intercept even the briefest radio whisper. And so from Nathan's left, where Logan, the leader of this guerrilla band, lay hidden, the most basic of signals: a soft avian trill.

Get ready.

Nathan whistled an acknowledgment as best he could, not knowing what he tried to imitate. More "birdsong" to his right and from across the gorge. The guerrillas wore camouflage over their improvised armor; even with their whistles to guide him, he spotted no one. Seven answers in all, including Nathan's own.

The crossfire would be deadly.

Reviewing what had passed for training—mostly "If it reflects, don't shoot it" and "If you see them, assume they see you"—Nathan raised the laser rifle to his shoulder. (There had been a lesson, too, on improvising explosive devices from household chemicals. Making bombs scared the hell out of him, and he tried his best to leave that knowledge theoretical. Seeing his hands shake, others had built the explosives now hidden in the ravine far below.) Through the scope he followed the barely-a-path across the rocky plain below. Not-quite trees swayed where the road entered the lower jungle.

The first vehicles emerged: tractors, cargo floaters, flatbed trucks. Civilian vehicles, all. People jammed the truck beds, balanced precariously on the sideboards, plodded alongside on foot. Another few minutes would bring the caravan into the canyon. Into the trap.

Birds circled high overhead, indistinct against the suns' glare. Their presence, perhaps, signified nothing.

In his mind's eye they were vultures.

Cranking up the magnification Nathan saw more women and children than men. Everyone kept glancing fearfully over their shoulders. He saw a few dogs and even a sway-backed horse. Here and there people clutched hunting rifles, but that didn't make them the enemy. Who would venture into this wilderness unarmed?

He zoomed closer still, examined weary faces. Half the adults looked *old*. Boosterspice was plentiful, if pricey; to look old meant you were poor. Most men's chins were stubbled, but of asymmetric, pointy-on-one-side/close-cropped-on-the-other beards, Nathan saw not a one. Only Wunderland's aristos sported those ridiculous, high-maintenance affectations as symbols of indolence and leisure.

This couldn't be the rumored garrison resupply convoy. Nathan waited for the call to stand down. Instead, from his left, a brief chittering.

On my signal.

Madness! These were civilian refugees. Poor farmers by the look of them and of their vehicles. Why the tanj ambush *them*? Nathan cleared his throat.

"Quiet!" Logan hissed.

For the first time since getting stranded, Nathan wondered if one side was any better than another.

Be honest, he chided himself. The second time. The first time was when two guerrillas marched a third, her face bruised, the cloth badge of the Resistance ripped from her blouse, out of camp into the jungle. Only the men, their expressions grim, had returned.

Nathan had chosen to believe they had sent her away. These people had pulled him from the wreck, whisked him away before Internal Security arrived. He owed the guerrillas everything, from the shirt on his back to his very life.

Now he wondered if he could live with the debt.

As the hum of engines swelled, Nathan's mind churned. Join in the slaughter? Never. Stand by, doing nothing, and watch? How was that better?

There *had* to be another way. A warning shot to scare off the civilians? No. The laser beam between plain and cliff top would point back at him. That woman vanished into the woods outside camp . . . Nathan had a pretty good idea how the Resistance treated sympathizers. Or—

Probably no one was looking *up*. Nathan raised his rifle and fired. With a squawk a bird stopped its circling. Gravity here was scarcely half that to which Nathan was accustomed, and the bird, cut almost in two, fell in slow motion.

Splat went the carcass, just ahead of the caravan.

The people on foot turned and ran, zigzagging, back toward the trees. Engines raced. Vehicles jerked into reverse or turned off the road to circle back. Maybe he had saved a few—

Crash! A tractor and a truck collided, blocking the way into the jungle.

"Now!" shouted Logan.

From both canyon rims guerrillas opened fire. Laser beams, silent, scythed down three men before anyone below noticed. Then: screams. Curses. More bodies crumpling. Chaos.

It was a massacre, sickening—

Sudden motion *behind* the slaughter. Sleek and sharklike, three antigrav gunships burst from the jungle, their charge spookily silent. Laser cannon blazed bloodred. As the gunships neared, their railguns let loose.

The guerrillas launched their only two surface-to-air missiles. One hit. Trailing smoke, its engine stuttering, a gunship arced down, down, down. . . . It smashed—*boom!*—into a cliff face, and the ground shook. Across the gorge two men more brave than sane ("If you see them, assume they see you!") kept firing. The remaining gunships spewed their own missiles.

No one could have survived those blasts.

"Fall back!" Logan shouted.

At least Nathan, his ears ringing, decided that was the order. He was already slithering backward, away from the precipice and deeper into the jungle, as quickly as he could.

He had done what he could for the refugees. The thought offered no comfort.

The caravan was doubly bait. The militia had used civilians to entice the Resistance. The guerrillas, just as callous, had attacked the refugees to lure an aristo patrol into reach.

Blam! Blam-blam!

More missiles. The ground slammed Nathan, flung him high into the air. He came down stunned. Through the underbrush, backlit by explosions, he glimpsed a profile. It loomed over him, well over two meters tall. What with the low gravity, most Wunderlanders were gigantic.

One of the guerrillas. Cody something. Was he here to help Nathan or kill him?

"Come on," Cody growled. Maybe he hadn't seen Nathan warn the refugees. "Time to go."

As Nathan struggled to his feet, another blast bounced him off a tree trunk. His left arm and some ribs snapped. And something molten had spattered his camo. It ate through the cloth, through his body armor. The bellow of railguns swallowed his scream.

Cody sprayed first-aid foam over the hole in Nathan's vest and his side went numb. The Wunderlander helped Nathan to his feet and together they staggered into the jungle.

A YELLOW OVAL GLEAMED on the sloping roof. Not a sun, Nathan gradually decided. The glow of a lamp, reflected on . . . what? How long had he been staring at the glow and why were his thoughts so fuzzy?

He looked around. He was flat on his back on one narrow cot among many. All the cots were filled, most by people wearing bloody bandages. He remembered the jungle being eerily quiet. Now that dubious honor belonged to this . . . ?

First-aid ward, he decided. In a futzy *cave*. Geological time later, he figured it out: body heat. Snoopersats would zero in on any camp this size in the wild.

He didn't remember getting here. Cody had carried Nathan out, then.

Had anyone else among the guerrillas made it? Nathan sat up, the better to check the other beds. He noticed his cast before trying to put any weight on that arm.

But he had forgotten about the ribs and the burn. He gasped. The one person standing—a medic?—was tweaking the flow rate on a drip bag. She turned her head. "Be with you in a minute, soldier."

Drip bag. Cast. Bloody tanj bandages! Blurry though his mind was, it hit Nathan: this was medieval. He should be asleep, oblivious, within a computerized cocoon dedicated to healing him. But did the guerrillas even have autodocs? He couldn't recall seeing any.

He had felt fine until he sat up. Now all he felt was the throbbing in his side. Pain was so . . . archaic. Finagle, he couldn't remember when autodocs came into general use. Well before his time, and he was 130. He didn't know how to deal with pain. No one did anymore. His head spun and his breathing raced—

"Careful." The medic, her sweat-dark hair gathered in an untidy bun, caught Nathan as he toppled. She helped him lie back down, then squirted something into his IV. "Here's a little something for the pain."

"Wait," he said, a moment too late. Maybe that tardiness was no accident. The first wave of relief kicked in and it felt familiarly wonderful. "How much of this stuff have I . . . ?"

He drifted off before finishing the question.

ACROSS THE WORLDS of Human Space, people disdained the Wunderlander aristos. Running a blockade to deliver medical supplies to freedom fighters was noble. Running a blockade to sell medical supplies? That dimmed the luster, but it was still in a good cause.

Wasn't it?

Things were less black and white viewed up close. Wunderland's civil war, like all civil wars, was nasty. It sundered families. It offered no quarter and expected none. It recognized no civilians, no innocents, no neutral parties. Benefit of the doubt was a scarce commodity—

A nonexistent commodity once you'd bled DNA all over a wrecked blockade runner.

Through a drug fog Nathan struggled to make sense of things. He had not set out to be a smuggler, any more than he had set out to be a master chef, a mechanic, a pilot, or any of the other things he had been. No career, no hobby, no marriage could last for a century. He had had honest, if mercenary, intentions buying a share of the med shipment. Joining *Clementine*'s crew thereafter was simply prudent, just protecting his investment.

He had deluded himself, of course.

A respite from the dull routine yet another career had become? Of course. A way to get beyond Paula Cherenkov dumping him? Running the blockade was that, too.

Sinking back into hazy oblivion, Nathan confronted a harder truth. He ran—still—from far older demons.

2

The trail had gone cold long ago.

Cold trail: a carnivore's metaphor. A human's metaphor. Nessus was neither.

"Nessus" was a label of convenience, something humans could pronounce. His true name—given enough pairs of vocal cords to enunciate it properly—sounded like an industrial accident set to waltz time. Or so, at least, a human had once described it. A long time ago . . .

Humans had called Nessus' kind Puppeteers before, more than a century earlier, they had withdrawn from Human Space. More often than humans realized, a few Puppeteers returned. The galaxy was a dangerous place and humans made excellent cannon fodder.

Cannon fodder: another human metaphor. Nessus had spent much of his life among humans, when even a day among aliens did not speak well of him. No sane being left Hearth, separated himself from the herd. By setting hoof on Wunderland, Nessus was, by definition, *insane*.

He had learned to embrace insanity. The full measure of his madness was that he had even come to *like* humans.

Perhaps insanity—and a well-chosen human agent—might once again avert disaster for the trillion and more Nessus had left behind.

NATHAN WENT UP and down the aisles of the hospital ward. He emptied bedpans, took routine med scans, distributed water, and dispensed pills. His duties distracted him from the tightness in his side, where the burn had healed badly, and kept him busy and his conscience clear. The work kept him, without killing anyone, in the good graces of the Resistance.

"Hey, Big Nate."

As the only one vertical, Nathan was taller than these Wunderlander giants. Under the circumstances, you found humor where you could. "Hi, Terry. How are you doing today?"

A chain of wet coughs: fluid in the lungs. "Just great, Big Nate. You can't tell?"

Nathan patted the man on the shoulder and moved on to the next patient. He topped off the water pitcher sitting on the floor beside her cot. "How's it going, Maeve?"

"You tell me," Maeve said. She had a stern face, the kind that seemed locked in to a scowl, but that was only a guess. She had little reason to smile.

Nathan waved his scanner over her. Indicators lit, mostly green. He paged down and saw more green. "I'm no doctor, but I'm guessing you'll be out soon." With only one kidney.

"Uh-huh," she said. "I'm ready for a pill."

Hadn't she heard him? But of course she had. The "doctors" here couldn't properly treat half of what they encountered. Instead, they drugged their patients to the eyeballs. "It's too early," he lied. Because you don't want to end up like me.

And because the fewer painkillers I dole out, the more I can keep for myself.

By the time the doctors had released Nathan, he'd been hooked. He could get drugs here. Irony of ironies, lots of these meds had been salvaged from *Clementine*. He recognized the batch numbers. Drugs flowed from the government to the black market to the Resistance. If the two sides could manage to trade, tanj it, why couldn't they *talk*?

Maeve grabbed for his sleeve. "It's time, Nathan. I know it is."

"Nice try." He extended his arm. Years and light-years away, when he had had a bit of money, he had indulged in a wrist implant. Clock, calculator, compass, and more . . . the implant was, pitifully, the most valuable thing he still owned. He would have sold it for drugs, but nobody here had the skills to remove it intact.

Maeve peered dubiously at his wrist, but had no way to know he had set back the time. The pitiful ruse—and more, his reason for it—shamed him. "See you later then," she said.

"Right." He stepped to the next cot. "How are you feeling, Richard?"

By shift's end, Nathan's hands were shaking. Hating himself, he slipped into the dense shrubs not far outside the cave. There was little privacy in any guerrilla camp, he had found. Many used this thicket for a bit of quick sex.

A tryst wasn't *his* purpose. He had liberated three painkillers during his last shift; now he popped two into his mouth.

The night was warm, the outside air untainted by antiseptic and fear. He plunged deeper into the wild, lay down beneath a flowering shrub, and drifted off. . . .

NATHAN'S CHILDHOOD MEMORIES were so deeply repressed he expected never to recover them all. Still, flashes came to him: in dreams, in therapy—

With drugs.

Falling asleep one night in his own bed, his own room. His parents had been strange that whole week. Anxious? He hadn't understood it. Neither did his sister, and she was almost six. She usually understood everything.

Awakening in—well, he didn't know where. Not his bed. Not his room. Not his *house*. Getting up, rubbing the sleep from his eyes, and staring out the window. Nothing was familiar.

Mommy and Daddy, gone. A friend of theirs, looking *so* sad. "I am your father," he kept saying. And he kept calling them Nathan and Tweena—pleading, insisting, finally *screaming* over their howls of protest. Tears streaming down all their faces. "Those are your names. You must remember them for your own safety."

Confinement inside the new house until they could recite much more than their new names without hesitation—and without tears.

In time, Nathan's original parents reappearing. And how they had changed! Mother, who had always been so happy and carefree, seeming—Nathan was a long time putting a name to the look—haunted. Mother crying about the strangest things, as though the hue of the sky or the length of the day could be wrong. But First Father had changed the most. He who had once towered over everyone had somehow shrunk to Mother's height.

By then Nathan had gotten old enough to notice who had skin like bronze and slanted eyes. He and Tweena did. New Father did. Mother and First Father, the incredible shrinking man, did not.

Old parents and new, when they thought no one was listening, talking about other times and places. About wondrous adventures. About terrible adversaries. About implacable forces out to get them all. Black holes and space pirates were somehow among their more normal experiences. Nathan working up his courage—he was about ten, then. Asking them, old parents and new: who were they *really*? The only answer was an awkward silence and Mother looking terrified.

As soon as Nathan could, he had run away.

THE MEMORY STORM PASSED.

Nathan emerged from the bushes into brutal clarity. He was a druggie, a fugitive, and flat broke. Everything he had saved over a lifetime had gone down in flames. He was trapped on Wunderland. If the aristos caught him, the *best* he could hope for was years of hard labor in a reeducation camp.

First Father's adventures—and Nathan, almost despite himself, believed those whispered, overheard allusions—usually ended in triumph.

Nathan wondered: Would *he* ever measure up?

THE HUMAN CROUCHED behind the clear wall. The ceiling, not fear, explained that posture, for Nessus had constructed the isolation booth to Earth norms. He had forgotten how tall Wunderlanders stood.

"This is outrageous!" the man said, flushed with rage. He turned a full circle in the tiny cylindrical booth, whether seeking an exit or someone to confront. He found neither. He poked at his pocket comp, swore as he found that comm was jammed, and put away the device. The main thing visible beyond his cell wall was a floor-standing mirror. He glowered at that. "Release me immediately."

"In good time," Nessus answered from behind the one-way glass. He spoke fluent Interworld in a throaty contralto. He could as easily have imitated a burly human male—or, for that matter, a string quartet. That he chose *this* voice was no accident. Women trusted it and men as reflexively lusted after it. Either way, it gave him an edge. "I apologize for the low ceiling. Feel free to sit."

The Wunderlander remained standing, haughty despite his stoop. His uniform, gauche with buttons and piping, epaulets and insignia, could have graced a Gilbert and Sullivan operetta. His chin jutted out, and the spike of his aristocratic beard left a waxy streak on the clear material of the tube. "I demand that you release me."

"Major Buchanan, you are in no position to demand anything." Nessus let that sink in. "I will, however, release you. After we finish, of course."

"Swine," Buchanan growled. "I'll tell you nothing."

Yes, you will, Nessus thought. This was hardly his first abduction. "You must realize that I intercepted you between transfer booths, and yet you did not comment." It meant human authorities here had learned to do the same. The insurgents would avoid the system, and that might explain why Nessus had not spotted his true quarry yet.

Or else the one Nessus sought had moved on to another world entirely, the trail grown colder still. . . .

Nessus denied his raging pessimism. "You presume that my intervention must have triggered some alarm. You are sure that system diagnostics must be running even now, that Internal Security"—for which Buchanan was a midlevel cog—"will locate this booth and come bursting through my door. None of that will happen."

Buchanan scowled but said nothing.

"In fact," Nessus continued with a self-assurance he did not feel, "the last notice the transfer-booth system took of you was when you teleported home this evening. When someone does look for you—tomorrow, perhaps?—they will believe you walked out your front door."

Sweat had begun to bead on Buchanan's forehead. He glanced around, seeming to notice for the first time that his cell was no ordinary transfer booth. "Why am I here?" he asked.

Concession enough: Buchanan *would* cooperate.

Many times, on many worlds, Nessus had pried the information he needed from those loath to offer it. This foray into Human Space was no different. His need was as great as ever—and the methods he used as distasteful as ever. But as always, they worked. They had led him across Human Space, from Home to Fafnir to Earth and now to Wunderland.

And with each day away from Hearth and herd, the pressure on Nessus grew.

Something would motivate Buchanan's cooperation. Coercion? Bribery? Trickery? One of them, although Nessus did not know which. Yet. He did know that he could not continue for much longer in this manic state. Mind-healing catatonia would crash down on him, sooner rather than later.

He needed answers *now.*

Bribery worked. Before whisking Buchanan, by now sweating profusely, back to his home, Nessus had the identities of mob leaders across Wunder-land. He had suggestions how to contact them.

If Nathan Graynor had indeed come to Wunderland, someone in the criminal underground should know.

3

Nathan shuffled from the cave mouth, nodding to the sentries. The wounded never stopped coming and he was exhausted. Before he could sleep, though, he needed a pill. Pills.

He passed the quickie thicket (a couple noisily occupied within) to plunge deeper into the jungle. He retained just enough dignity not to want to be seen at his worst: feeding rumors to Silverman, the camp's black-market supplier, in trade for a few more pills.

Nathan followed his customary route, wondering if tonight was the night the perimeter patrols shot him anyway. Both suns had set and the jungle was dark. Walking slowly until his eyes adapted, he made his way downhill to the rendezvous: a massive granite boulder in a clearing unequally bisected by a weed-choked stream. "It's Big Nate," he whispered. The patients' nickname for him had stuck. "I got off shift a bit late."

That wasn't Silverman beside the boulder. Nathan froze.

"Come no closer," the thing said in an incongruously sexy feminine voice.

A shiver ran down Nathan's spine. He *knew* what that thing was . . . didn't he?

The creature was about Nathan's height, but there any resemblance to a human ended. The alien stood on three legs, its single hind leg complexly jointed. It wore only a broad sash from which pockets dangled. Its two tiny heads capped long, sinuous necks. Each head, flat and triangular, had a mouth, one ear, and one eye. Its torso (pale, but by starlight Nathan could not guess at a color) was vaguely reminiscent of a wingless, featherless ostrich. A broad dome, covered by a dark mane indifferently braided, perched between the alien's broad shoulders. At least Nathan decided to call shoulders those muscular bulges where the necks joined the torso, for mouths and necks apparently did double duty as hands and arms. Those head-and-neck assemblies reminded him, inanely, of sock puppets—

And suddenly Nathan knew what a wondrous manifestation this was. He almost forgot his craving for drugs. "You . . . you're a Puppeteer."

Heads swiveled, and for a moment the alien looked itself in the eyes. "We were often called that. I am Nessus."

Puppeteers! Nathan had studied them in college. Their presence in Known Space had always been limited, the locations of their worlds a secret. They had controlled an interstellar trading empire. Then, only a few years before Nathan's birth, the Puppeteers had all disappeared from Known Space.

And yet here one stood. . . .

Nathan said, "I thought the Puppeteers ran from the explosion"—a chain reaction of supernovae—"at the galactic core." The radiation would sterilize this part of the galaxy. In twenty thousand years or so. A Puppeteer couldn't be too cautious.

"And so most of us have. Some of us still have business to complete."

As do I. For want of a pill Nathan's skin crawled. "I was expecting to meet . . . a man."

Heads bobbed—up/down, down/up—in alternation. "The criminal element has been most helpful in my investigation. They indicated where I could find you."

Nathan trembled. *These* tremors had nothing to do with his craving for a pill. "You've mistaken me for someone else."

Again, Nessus looked himself in the eyes. "No mistake, Nathan Graynor. Your stepfather's exploits are famous. I find myself in need of his talents. As I could not find him, I have come to you."

Nathan's hands began shaking uncontrollably and he jammed them into jumpsuit pockets. He couldn't have been older than eight the time he overheard his fathers discussing Puppeteers. They could not have known he was behind the sofa. Still, everything was very circumspect and cryptic. No story or context, just hints and insinuations.

Only the moral was clear. Puppeteers keep their word, but you don't always get to see the fine print in time.

Kind of like a deal with the Devil.

"We do not have much time," Nessus said. He trembled, too. "Help me to find your stepfather and I will remove you from this place, this misnamed Wunderland."

And if Nathan declined?

Whether or not Nessus so intended, he had given the "criminal element" reason to suspect Nathan might be important—and they would be correct.

A live blockade runner to make an example of? The aristos would love nothing better. Even now Silverman must be digging up information about how Nathan came to this camp. How long before Silverman sold out Nathan for an Internal Security reward?

It was too awful to think about. "How did you get past the patrols, Nessus?"

A neck bent briefly downward and straightened, pointing. Nathan noticed a thin disc resting on the packed dirt of the path. The Puppeteer stood on the disc, not on the path itself.

Nessus said, "This device and another like it transported me directly here. Think of them as open transfer booths. Untraceable, of course."

"One of your . . . minions brought it?" Who better than the black market to smuggle something into a Resistance camp?

"For a princely fee."

History said Puppeteers were cowards. Nathan believed it. Who but cowards fled perils twenty thousand years removed? But cowardice was a way of life for Puppeteers, not an insult. What of the opposite label?

Nathan said, "Trusting the criminal element, sneaking into an armed camp. Forgive me, Nessus, but those actions seem insanely brave."

"If I were not insane, I would never leave home." With one head, Nessus plucked at his braids. "But even the craziest among us cannot handle an alien world for long. So, decide. Will you assist me?"

The aristos would hunt Nathan forever and he had no way off this planet. Of *course* he wanted in! The catch was, he had no clue where his father was. Either father. He had had no contact with his family for decades.

And if he had known? As much as he resented—had sometimes hated—his parents, they hid for a reason. He would not sell them out. Certainly not to an insane alien.

"I guess you don't know," Nathan said. "There was an accident a few years after I left Home. Everyone died."

Nessus plunged a head deep into his mane, twisting and tugging convulsively.

The Puppeteer was terrified! That fear might come only of standing here, exposed and alone among aliens, his manic bravery at low ebb. Nathan sensed more was involved.

Who the Finagle *were* his parents? What had they done? What drove them to abduct their own children? From whom did they hide? And what service could any of them possibly provide to draw a Puppeteer out of hiding?

With a shudder, Nessus lifted the head from his mane. With both heads held high, he fixed his gaze on Nathan. "Take his place."

Nathan blinked. "Doing what?"

"It may be dangerous," Nessus said, scraping at the disc with a forehoof. "You will be compensated well. I can reveal no more than that."

More dangerous than the middle of a civil war? "How well?"

"Extraction from this place. Wealth, commensurate with your success. And excuse my indelicacy . . . a cure for your addiction."

If Nessus knew that much about him . . . "Why would you *want* my help?"

"You are Louis Wu, the son of Carlos Wu, among the most brilliant minds of Earth's many billions. Your mother was born Sharrol Janss. Beowulf Shaeffer, your stepfather, was an adventurer and explorer without peer. He was of great service to my people more than once. He skimmed the surface of a neutron star and lived to tell of it. He traveled to the galactic core and discovered that it had exploded. He . . ."

Louis! An explosion of memories, like fireworks in the brain. His name from the distant past. And those astonishing disclosures about his family. Accompanying Nessus was a way to recover it all.

Nessus was still speaking. "There is another condition. Things that you will see cannot be revealed. Your memories will be edited before I return you to Known Space."

"Edited," Nathan—no, Louis!—repeated.

Something warbled softly in Nessus' sash. "A proximity alarm. Whatever you decide, decide quickly. Twenty seconds after I leave, this stepping disc will explode."

"Edited *how?*"

Nessus thrust a head into a pocket—and vanished.

Twenty seconds! Nineteen. Eighteen. Seventeen.

The count ticked down in Louis's mind. His heart pounded.

Fourteen. Thirteen. Twelve. Eleven.

He stared at the circle on the ground. You arrive in Wonderland down a rabbit hole. You don't leave that way.

Nine. Eight.

From downstream: a noise, indistinct. Probably a perimeter patrol. What would the Resistance leaders think of finding him near an exploded alien device?

And how *big* an explosion? *Run,* he told himself. His legs were rooted to the spot.

From two short paces away, the disc stared back.

His stepfather—the infamous Beowulf Shaeffer!—trusted Puppeteers to keep their word. All the words. Including the words in the fine print.

Six. Five.

Beyond that disc were truths he had sought all his life. His past. His roots. If he did not go, could he live with himself?

Four. Three. Two.

Louis stepped—

NEVERLAND

4

Nessus flicked into the isolation booth aboard *Aegis*.

Tonguing his transport controller again, he reappeared on a disc outside the booth on the reflecting side of the one-way glass. Shuffling off the disc he caught a glimpse of himself: twitchy, disheveled, wild-eyed. The manic state into which he had worked himself had all but dissipated.

At any second Louis might arrive.

Nessus was almost too drained to care. Courage and caution—madness and sanity—must balance. Escape into catatonia would no longer be denied. Half a deck away, his cabin was too distant to attain. His heads darted between his legs. His knees started to buckle. . . .

Had he reconfigured the booth's stepping disc? If not, Louis would flick out!

Nessus shook with fear. How could he not remember how he had left the booth disc configuration! Only one way: he was too near complete collapse to function. Checking the transport controller would do nothing useful. He would only wonder anew in a moment.

Somehow Nessus withdrew his heads from between his legs. He grasped the stepping disc by its rim and lifted it from the deck. The disc slipped from his teeth; he overbalanced and stumbled backward against the hull.

Nessus braced himself with his hind leg; his hoof scraped paint from the wall. He gripped the disc again and heaved. His hind leg, straightening, pushed him away from the wall. The disc tipped up, up . . . and over. It crashed to the deck, dark side up. Upside down.

Control settings and address modes no longer mattered. With its active surface flush against the deck, safety interlocks rendered the disc inert.

Nessus bleated to himself, the double-throated glissando edged with hysteria. He could have engaged the same failsafe circuits simply by remaining on the disc.

Louis flicked into the isolation booth.

Nessus collapsed. Eyes squeezed shut, heads pressed against his belly, he squeezed and squeezed the fleshy ball of self until he could scarcely breathe.

Until the only sound in the universe was the muffled beating of his hearts.

WHAT THE . . . ?

A curved, clear wall. Louis turned, squinting against sudden brightness. He was inside a capped cylinder. It had no door! The room beyond was all but empty. He saw only a floor-standing mirror, a dark circle on the floor, and a leather-covered hassock.

Slowly, the hassock swelled and contracted. Swelled and contracted. Breathed? Nessus, apparently, with his heads and legs curled under his torso.

"Nessus! Let me out! Nessus! Someone!" And a few seconds later, a bit plaintively, "Anyone?"

The only response was painfully loud echoing inside the little booth. The "hassock" did not stir.

Louis pounded the clear wall with his fist—once. The wall was *hard*. "Tanj it, Nessus! Let me out!"

Once the echoes trailed off: silence.

What did he know about Puppeteers? Not much. Louis studied the "hassock." By starlight he had been unable to discern color. Nessus (as much as Louis could see) was off-white with scattered patches of tan. His mane was a darker brown.

Behind Nessus, the wall held a slight curve. On every surface, recessed handholds (well, mouth holds). A ship, then. The room was big: this was a cargo hold.

For three months his first thought upon waking and his last thought at night had involved getting off Wunderland. About getting—somehow—to a ship. A bitter laugh bubbled out of Louis. Be careful what you wish for.

He kept looking around. Anywhere but the mirror. Anywhere.

The fleshy mass looked as tightly clenched as ever. Would he know when Nessus began to recover from his fear? Shouting accomplished no more than it had before.

Depression settled over him like fog. Nathan or Louis, what did it matter? He was a druggie, a danger to himself and useless to anyone else. Face it. Face what you are.

He turned, finally, toward the mirror. A hollow-eyed figure stared back. Louis began to shake. "You promised a cure for my addiction!" he screamed.

Nessus did not stir.

Louis slumped against the side of the booth. He was trapped until Nessus recovered from his panic attack.

It looked like the cure would be going cold turkey.

TIME PASSED. Nessus didn't move.

Louis switched to studying the walls beyond his cell. Standing on tiptoe he noticed a broad scratch in the curved gray wall behind Nessus. Those long gray curls on the deck beside him were peels of paint.

A long disused synapse fired: General Products hull. A Puppeteer would choose nothing less.

Back when Puppeteers had traded in Known Space, General Products Corporation was the core of their commercial empire. More than anything else, GP sold spaceship hulls. No one knew how a GP hull was built or of what it was made, only that the indemnity if one failed was enormous. (Another childhood memory: his fathers talking. Evidently, GP hulls were not *quite* impregnable. But the piddling little surface-to-air missile that reduced *Clementine* to a flaming ruin would not have scratched a GP hull.)

The price of indestructible hulls soared after the Puppeteers withdrew from Known Space. The GP hulls left behind had been reconfigured mostly as warships, top-of-the-line cruise ships, and yachts for the super-rich. The largest model GP hull, a sphere roughly three hundred meters in diameter, was used to transport whole new colonies. The tramp freighters Louis generally flew—as often as not working for his passage—were scruffy, human-manufactured ships.

Louis had flown only once in a GP hull. He remembered that GP hull material was transparent. That light passed through was a feature. You painted whatever parts you wanted opaque.

Recalling obscure history, like studying every seam, scratch, and dent on the unreachable walls, was a distraction. So what was he distracting himself from? The quaking in his limbs, of course: harbinger of the seizures destined to come.

Tired of looking at Nessus, unwilling to face the mirror, he began yet another survey of the room.

Through the scratched-clear swath behind Nessus: motion. Something drifting. Seaweed? And . . . bubbles? And something else—

An eye! Enormous!

Captive of a comatose alien, in a tiny prison, aboard an alien ship, beneath the sea, with Finagle knew *what* nosing about outside. Trapped without food or water, without as much as a chamber pot.

He needed a pill! He needed an escape from the miasma of fear and doubt and mind-crushing depression. His hands shook and he broke into a sweat. His head buzzed and spun, and he kept expecting to vomit. Instead, his bowels let loose. *Then* he vomited, all over himself. A moan bubbled out of him as the seizures began.

Nessus did not stir.

LOUIS WOKE TO AN UNBELIEVABLE STENCH, his nose centimeters above a puddle of vomit, urine, and excrement. His limbs were contorted and his joints screamed. His neck was on fire and his head pressed against the booth wall at an unnatural angle. Only the narrowness of the cylinder had kept his head from flopping into the filth. *His* filth.

For now the seizures had stopped. He unfolded himself and stood. It felt like he had been beaten by a team of experts, had been detoxing for days. His wrist implant showed he had been trapped for only three hours. Almost a day, though, since his last pill. Black despair crashed down on him.

Nessus remained a tightly wound mass.

"Nessus!" No response. "Nessus, you useless piece of . . ." Louis trailed off. A hint of clarity had returned. Might a Puppeteer take offense at an insult?

He did know they were cowards. "Fire!" he screamed. Nessus twitched and Louis dared to hope.

The twitch faded away.

Because despite everything, shreds of sentience must lurk in that rolled-up mass. If Puppeteer ships carried anything capable of combustion, they would brim with fire detectors and suppression equipment. There would be fire alarms, and they would not sound like hysterical humans. Nessus wasn't buying it.

Louis tried to take heart from his failure. Shouting "fire" had involved more forethought than anything else he had done since stepping aboard.

No door: he must be in a teleport unit. The circle on the floor beside Nessus: was that what Nessus called a stepping disc? Had the circle by the resistance camp been that dark, Louis could not imagine how he would have seen it. That disc had been the color of—

He scraped aside some of his filth with a shoe. *That* color.

Of course: he had flicked from one stepping disc to another. Craning his neck, he saw most of the cylinder's cap was the same light color.

Hmm. Another stepping disc affixed to a clear ceiling. That disc shimmered.

He reached up and brushed his fingertips lightly over the ceiling disc. It had a film of some sort, he decided. A molecular filter. Something to admit oxygen and remove carbon dioxide. Three hours in this little enclosed space—without fresh air he would have died by now.

Too bad the filter didn't remove the stink.

Finagle! Here he stood between stepping discs and he had just now thought about any of this? Add confusion to his withdrawal symptoms.

How did Nessus control the discs? He had plunged a head into a pocket just before disappearing from the jungle. A device in his pocket, then.

Louis had no such device. He clasped his hands behind his back, pretending not to notice their renewed shaking. Maybe the discs also had built-in controls, underneath or out of sight along an edge.

Top and bottom discs were almost flush with the cylinder sides. Louis could scarcely force a finger between disc and wall, but he sensed a slight recess in the edge. There might be controls within, but even if he found them, he could not see what he was doing.

With which disc would he experiment? Not the one that kept him breathing, even if he could manage to detach it. He'd have to try the disc on which he stood.

How could he upend it?

That disc in the jungle had been a bomb. Blind experimentation might explode this one. He would try it anyway. It wasn't as though he had a lot of choices.

He'd have to get above the disc.

He set one foot against the wall, set his back against the other, and raised his other foot. Slowly he climbed. The creep upward, pressing hard against the walls, made back and leg muscles scream. Like rock climbing, he told himself. Never mind that this cylinder is as slippery as glass; the fall couldn't really hurt him.

From maybe twenty-five centimeters above the floor, he reached around his hips, toward the floor. He jammed all four fingers into the gap at the edge of the disc—and one foot slipped. He cracked his head as he splashed into the filth.

He tried again with the same result.

Nessus didn't hear or didn't care.

With feet spaced a bit farther apart, Louis managed on his third try to stay suspended as he forced the fingertips of his right hand into the gap. The disc lifted, breaking suction with a disgusting slurp. Then it slipped from his grasp and he fell.

The shakes got him again. Louis lost track of how many times he made the attempt. Finally he had the disc angled upward at about twenty degrees. With his back and leg muscles trembling from strain, he crept higher, wondering if he could possibly climb high enough to set the disc on its edge.

He couldn't.

The disc slipped and fell. Wham! He slammed onto the disc, the breath knocked out of him. But not before he had glimpsed the disc's underside in the mirror. The disc's bottom was dark, like the circle outside the cylinder.

That circle, presuming it was a stepping disc, was upside down. If it operated at all, transferring there would teleport him *into* the deck. Doubtless Puppeteers built fail-safes to prevent that.

Surrendering to the shakes, Louis let depression wash over him.

ANOTHER BOUT OF SEIZURES and hopelessness passed. Nessus had yet to stir.

The Puppeteer did not respond to Louis's shouts. Not to "Help!" (disinterested in helping another?) or "Fire!" (what harm was there in trying again?) or the more general "Danger!"

Danger, if anything, curled up the Puppeteer even tighter. Too vague, Louis decided. By this stage in his terror, Nessus must be beyond anything but hiding from an undefined danger.

There was a germ of an idea here. Louis chewed his lower lip, trying to coax out the thought. Suppose some peril loomed against which Nessus *could* take action? The hull was indestructible, but *Nessus* wasn't. What about a big explosion alongside the hull?

An emergency restraint field had saved Louis during *Clementine*'s crash, but only because he had been in the pilot couch. Would even Puppeteers equip cargo bays with emergency restraints?

"Submarine approaching!" Louis shouted. "Nessus! Torpedoes in the water! Nuclear warheads."

Shuddering seismically, Nessus unfolded. His necks writhed like serpents. His heads swiveled, searching everywhere for danger. "Torpedoes?" he bleated, leaping to his hooves.

"My mistake. Just some fish," Louis said.

Seeming not to hear, Nessus galloped for the hatch. The cargo hold echoed with the clops of his hooves.

"No torpedoes!" Louis screamed.

Nessus skidded to a halt partway out the hatch. One head plucked at his mane. "No submarine?"

"No," Louis answered, as firmly as his shakes allowed. "Now get me the tanj *out* of this cell!"

5

An alert lamp pulsed. A timer began counting down the final hour. The moment Nessus had anticipated—and dreaded—was at hand. Louis Wu would emerge soon from the autodoc.

And then Nessus must judge whether the man was up to the challenge.

Beowulf Shaeffer was the one Nessus sought. Needed. Shaeffer was special. A neutron star, the galactic core explosion, a black hole, an entire solar system of antimatter: he had survived encounters with them all—only to be undone by some mundane accident.

Unless, of course, Louis lied.

As often as Nessus had found it expedient to lie, he did not doubt that someone else might. Especially when a simple lie might extract Louis from a dire predicament.

And yet: maybe the luck of Beowulf Shaeffer *had* finally run out.

Nessus had thought a great deal in recent years about luck and unintended consequences. He continued to fret, worrying and plucking at his mane, as the autodoc countdown reached ten minutes. Five. Two.

Nessus sidled onto a stepping disc he had set onto the deck. This autodoc was monstrously large, too bulky for anywhere but *Aegis'* main cargo hold. Big as befit the autodoc's unique capabilities.

Shaeffer had hidden himself well. Too well. Nessus had surreptitiously hired private investigators and criminals across the worlds of Human Space. None of his minions had found any trace of Shaeffer, either under his own name or any alias Shaeffer was ever known to have used. Not for decades.

Dead? Concealed beyond hope of discovery? Nessus could live with either. Better those than the final possibility: that Nessus was too late. That another had already found Shaeffer.

For Nessus was not the only Puppeteer familiar with Shaeffer's extraordinary talents. . . .

. . .

BRIMMING WITH ENERGY, bursting with life, Louis woke.

Scores of readouts, all in the green, shimmered in the clear dome that hung scant centimeters over his face. A 'doc, of course. He had been too weak to get in unaided. Nessus had had to help.

"Ship's gravity is higher than Wunderland's," Nessus had offered while guiding and pushing from behind.

A fact, perhaps, but not the essential truth. Exhaustion and the shakes had defeated Louis's solo attempts to climb into the intensive care cavity. That, alas, he remembered clearly. Of the dreams that followed, he recalled only bits and fragments. Only enough to be certain that there *had* been dreams, that the autodoc had been exercising his engrams, maintaining memories for a brain otherwise too inactive, or too drug-addled, to do it for itself.

Nessus' polite fiction made the Puppeteer seem less alien.

None of the controls were where Louis expected them. Was this a Puppeteer 'doc? He found a panic button and slapped it. The dome began to retract.

"Ah, you are back," Nessus said. The Puppeteer stood far across the room. "Do you feel better?"

Better? The burn scars had vanished from Louis's left side. He raised a hand for study and it was rock-steady. His fingers, splayed, showed no hint of tremor. He didn't sweat and he wasn't nauseous or dizzy. There was none of the anxiety and depression that had all but crushed him between pills, no crawling-of-the-skin portent of seizures waiting to strike him down.

Feel better? Finagle, Louis felt *terrific.*

Sitting up, he grabbed the unfamiliar jumpsuit that lay draped across the bottom of the 'doc. He didn't want to think about the disgusting state of the clothes he had worn aboard.

"I feel much better, Nessus. Thank you."

"There is much to talk about."

Time now to reveal the fine print? Louis tried and failed to care. Even the air, spicy and exotic, rich with some Puppeteer scent, shouted that he was on an adventure. Stepping out of the 'doc, he felt agile and light on his feet. He dressed quickly, while Nessus studied his hooves. "Where are we going, Nessus?"

"To begin, a world called Hearth."

"I never heard of it."

"Nor have you heard its true name." Nessus sang something evocative of oboes and French horns, of cellos and harps.

A few bars, no more, but the music sent shivers down Louis's spine. The chords spoke somehow of home and belonging. And he realized—

He had no idea of the way home! To *any* home, to *any* world on which he had ever set foot. Earth, Home, Fafnir, Wunderland: he could remember neither their positions nor the pulsar landmarks by which to locate them. More than exercised, his engrams had been . . . examined. Pilfered.

"You've tampered with my brain!" Louis roared. The Puppeteer seemed alien again. No, more than alien. Worse than alien. Monstrous. "You wanted to *use* my mind. Are you crazy?"

Even as Louis protested, a calmer part of him chided. He was at Nessus' mercy. He had *put* himself at Nessus' mercy. So never mind the immaturity of losing his temper—and where had *that* come from?—this behavior was dangerous.

Nessus dipped one head into a pocket of his sash. (Preparing to vanish again, trapping Louis in this cargo hold to reconsider his behavior?) "It was necessary," Nessus said with his other head. "But consider, Louis. You knew your memories would be altered before your return. This is before your return."

Fine print.

Louis tamped down his rage, trying to think with his mind instead of his hormones.

After the confusion that was his childhood, memory was a fixation. An obsession. Memory was the sole, gossamer link to all that had been taken from him. He clung to the bits he *did* remember. Throughout his adult life he had studied countless tricks and ploys, learning to learn.

And so he recalled verbatim what Nessus had warned. *Things that you will see cannot be revealed. Your memories will be edited before I return you to Known Space.*

The imprecision of *before* was the least of Louis's problems. Nothing in Nessus' words limited memory editing to what Louis saw while on this trip! Louis could be returned to Known Space as a vegetable, and Nessus would have kept his bargain.

And Louis had been too addled even to notice. Compared to that failure, the physical weakness from which he had been delivered paled to nothing.

If he survived this adventure, Louis vowed, he would never take drugs again. He would think before he acted. He would be more deliberate in everything he did. If he survived—

No.

He would be more deliberate beginning *now*. Without Nessus' help, Louis would never get home. "Explain what I am to do," he said.

NESSUS LED THE WAY to *Aegis'* tiny relax room. Fresh-from-the-autodoc euphoria would fade soon enough; when it did, Louis would realize he was ravenous. And Nessus wanted a drink bulb of warm carrot juice. No matter that his biochemistry could extract little nourishment from any terrestrial food. He found the beverage soothing.

His spirits *needed* soothing.

Louis looked all around as they walked, peering down cross corridors and peeking into the occasional open hatch. He bounded more than walked, scarcely able to contain himself—until he skidded to a halt.

Louis gaped at a darkened hatch window. He touched a cheek, still staring, as though convincing himself the reflected image was truly him. Hard living and a recent lack of boosterspice had started him down the path to looking his true age. "I . . . I look *young*. Maybe twenty."

Nessus had hoped Louis would not make that discovery so soon. It only added to the necessary explanations. "This particular autodoc also rejuvenates."

"A Puppeteer 'doc, then."

"We prefer Citizen." Nessus extended a neck briefly, pointing down the corridor, and resumed walking in that direction. Warm carrot juice sounded better and better. He said, "But this is not a Citizen autodoc; in fact, Carlos Wu built it. Yes, Louis, your father. It is the most advanced autodoc ever built by your people or mine."

Most advanced failed to do the unit justice. Carlos had accomplished something truly revolutionary. Nessus knew for a fact this autodoc had rebuilt Sigmund Ausfaller after the man had had half his chest blasted away. It rebuilt Ausfaller a second time from a heavily irradiated, all-but-carbonized husk. And Ausfaller claimed this autodoc had once rebuilt Beowulf Shaeffer from a severed head.

That was why Nessus had custody of the precious device, why the Hindmost had agreed to allow it off Hearth. *Aegis* carried copies of Hearth's largest medical libraries. Had he located Carlos, Nessus would have pressed the human to reprogram its nanites to also heal Citizens. Alas, that effort must be undertaken without benefit of Carlos's genius. Just as far more pressing concerns must be addressed without benefit of Beowulf.

"How did you come to have the 'doc?" Louis asked. "Citizens, I mean."

"For complicated reasons, Carlos and Beowulf had to abandon it." Yet another incomplete truth. "It was later acquired, at great expense, from criminals." A huge lie.

They came to the relax room and Nessus motioned Louis inside. As Louis piled a tray with foods from the synthesizer, Nessus brooded about the many falsehoods this autodoc had evoked.

He had once spent most of a year searching Fafnir for the autodoc. To complete the search Nessus had had to ignore an urgent recall to Hearth and then lie about why he had been detained. The wonder was that he had ever found the device. Shaeffer had hidden it underwater, off the coast of a tiny, nameless, and unpopulated coral island.

Many years later, so that Nessus could deliver the autodoc to Hearth's scientists, he had invented a fable about a Fafnir crime syndicate offering the autodoc for sale. The story served a second purpose, because crooks did not give receipts. He had needed an explanation for some of the General Products wealth he had redirected. Always for the benefit of Hearth and herd— as *he* perceived it.

Louis gave his complete attention to a plate of potatoes and seared meat. He paused before tackling a cheese omelet. "Then why doesn't it look like the 'docs I've used?"

"It was a prototype, Louis. Your father was short and he had sized the autodoc for himself. When it came under Citizen control, we replaced the intensive care cavity." Longer, wider, and deeper, the cavity would now physically accommodate any human, even the tallest Belter or Wunderlander. Someday it would be reprogrammed to handle a Citizen. "And a good thing, too. You are taller than Carlos."

Louis twitched. "When I was young, my . . . stepfather was *much* taller than Carlos. Somehow they became the same height. Did that have something to do with this autodoc?"

"Carlos and Beowulf have complicated stories. Beowulf, of course, was a—"

"The history lesson can wait." Louis pushed away his tray. "I'm still waiting to hear what you expect me to do."

A padded Y-shaped bench was the main piece of furniture in the relax room. Suddenly too tired to stand, Nessus half collapsed onto it. Merely to describe this mission would take all his strength.

A trill to the ship's computer authorized its Voice to respond to Louis—with limited access to data. Man and machine could continue to talk when, very soon now, *he* must hide in his cabin. A second trill evoked a hologram. From the corner of an eye Nessus saw Louis blink.

Five globes now hung over the relax-room table, each sphere marking a corner of an equilateral pentagon. Four of the worlds showed large blue oceans and skies flecked with cloud, their continents lush with farm and forest. Earth-like, Nessus knew—even though Louis would no longer fully appreciate that—except for their necklaces of artificial suns. These planets flew free of any star.

The fifth world was of similar size, but there any similarity ended. No artificial suns orbited this world; it blazed with its own light. Only scattered small parks interrupted continent-spanning cities. Beholding Hearth, his hearts skipped beats.

"The Fleet of Worlds," Nessus said.

"The glowing world, that's Hearth. That's your home."

"Yes." The home of all Nessus held dear. "The Concordance holds sway on Hearth and its Nature Preserve worlds."

"Hearth is different," Louis muttered to himself. He stared at the image, considering. "No sun. So the Puppet . . . Citizens are taking their *worlds* away from the core explosion?"

"Our worlds are safe and familiar." Nessus moved a neck in sinuous waves, the gesture encompassing the ship. "Sane beings do not fly *this* way."

"So, they travel in normal space." Louis pondered some more. "No matter how safe the worlds are, what dangers loom in their path?"

A minute, no more, and Louis had focused on the essential problem. He was his fathers' son—in quickness of mind, at the least. Nessus permitted himself a moment of hope. "That is the question, of course."

"What am I to be, then," Louis asked. "An advance scout? Expendable?"

"More than a scout, certainly. A problem solver. I like to think not expendable, because I will accompany you."

"You went to a great deal of trouble to find my fathers. I don't believe you would do that for some theoretical danger. What has you scared more than usual?"

Nessus replaced the Fleet with another image: of a five-limbed creature scuttling about an ocean floor. In human terms, the being somewhat resembled a starfish crossed with an octopus, or perhaps five tube worms fused together at their tails. One "worm" directly faced the camera, revealing the limb to be a hollow tube, its aperture slowly pulsating. From deep inside the hollow, past rings of sharp, closely packed teeth, eyes and less obvious sensors peeked.

He said, "It's a Gw'o, no bigger from tip to tip than the length of your arm."

"It doesn't look scar . . ."

Louis trailed off as Nessus, with another tone burst, replaced the holo again. Now an industrial complex sprawled across a plain of ice. An upwardly curved track, an electromagnetic launcher, hurled a ship into the sky. The vessel lit its fusion drive and raced away. Except for running faster than real time, the video was untouched.

Nessus said, "The Gw'oth broke through the ice of their ancestral ocean less than two Earth centuries ago. Before that, their technology was stone tools. Now they have fusion and hyperdrive."

"Two centuries," Louis echoed.

If Nessus had done his edits properly, Louis would no longer remember Earth's orbital period. That memory should be gone, along with every other memory that could conceivably point his way home without Nessus' help.

Nessus said, "We recently discovered that the Gw'oth have established a colony in the Fleet's path."

PREVENT A WAR.

Louis ran laps around the passenger deck, his rejuvenated body demanding *action*. Compared to his father's (!) autodoc, boosterspice was scarcely a step beyond exorcisms and leeches. Louis seethed with wonderment and unwonted energy.

And more than a trace of worry. Had he not just gotten *out* of a war?

The worry could wait. Nessus said they had a long flight ahead of them.

Louis picked up the pace, his boots pounding the deck. He was young again! He had so much energy to burn off.

And less wholesome urges to fight off. Some dark recess of his mind demanded pills, something to take off the edge. The body could be cured. Had been cured. Bad habits? Those, he would have to break.

He began running flat out. The jumpsuit wicked away sweat as fast as he produced it. Nanofabric? The cloth was yet another wonder of Puppeteer tech.

If the energy of youth and the challenges before him could not distract him, free him, nothing ever would. Voyage far beyond Known Space. Prevent a war between the frighteningly advanced Puppeteers and a whole new alien race. He had embarked, surely, on an adventure to rival anything even the infamous Beowulf Shaeffer had ever endured.

("Too bad you won't remember it," taunted that part of Louis still craving a pill. Too bad you'll never be able to tell your father what you've done.)

Louis ran and ran, till sweat rolled down his face and his chest heaved—

To the second star to the right and straight on till morning.

FROM THE COMPARATIVE SAFETY of his locked cabin, Nessus listened to unending thuds. The footfalls came faster and faster as Louis burned off his excess energy, or sublimated his innate aggression, or worked up his nerve. Would Louis succeed? *Could* Louis succeed? Nessus had his doubts. Not even Beowulf Shaeffer had been Nessus' first choice.

If only Carlos Wu's autodoc healed minds half as well as it healed bodies.

At his best, Sigmund Ausfaller was exceptional. His innate paranoia found connections no rational mind could. His brilliance found opportunities amid the direst of circumstances. In the years Nessus had known the man, Sigmund had had adventures to rival anything even Beowulf Shaeffer had accomplished. And so Nessus had abducted Sigmund, his memory, like Louis's, stripped of all knowledge of the location of Human Space.

But Sigmund was broken. His last adventure had left him adrift in deep space in the crippled stub of a ship. Sigmund was half mad when help finally arrived. He was too scarred, mentally and emotionally, ever again to set foot aboard a spaceship.

Louis would have to serve.

6

Louis sat in the copilot's crash couch, a drink bulb of Kona coffee in hand and a plate of scones at the ready. Whatever complaints he might have, the repertoire of *Aegis'* synthesizer was not among them.

The couch where Louis sat could have been purchased on any human world. Almost certainly it had. Everything else on the bridge—the control consoles, the pilot's couch, even the padded rim of the hatchway—looked half melted. Corners and edges must be unnecessary risks. A person could bang his knee.

He savored a bit of scone. ("Substituting one appetite for another," an inner voice mocked.) Ignoring the scorn, he took his time chewing. When the subtle flavors had faded, he called out, "Voice. Show me one of the Gw'oth ensembles."

The holo that popped up was disgusting: a Gordian knot of flesh, writhing and pulsating. The Gw'oth came in every color of the rainbow, and in infrared Louis could not see. Hues and patterns changed in real time for reasons he could not fathom.

"A Gw'otesht, sir," Voice intoned. "Specifically a Gw'otesht-16. As this ensemble is configured, it is optimized for four-dimensional simulation."

Voice was the shipboard artificial intelligence. Amid technological marvels from stepping discs to the programmable nanofabric of Louis's jumpsuit, Voice was an anomaly. Nessus had acquired a human crash couch; he could as easily have purchased a far more capable AIde on any human world. He hadn't. Why not?

Because cowards do not build their possible successors. Interesting that Nessus would use even an out-of-date AI. . . .

A puzzle for another time, Louis decided. He said, "And other ensembles, entailing different connectivities, suit other problems. So an octuple wherein each Gw'o uses three tubacles to connect to three other Gw'oth would tackle 3-D problems. Static modeling of molecular bonds, for example."

"A Gw'otesht-8. Indeed, sir."

Louis smiled at a crazy notion: an English butler had taught Voice its mannerisms. "Call me Louis, please. And these biological computers drive the Gw'oth's rapid advancement?"

"Yes, Louis."

"And yet they disclosed this information." Louis stopped, frowning. "Or did they?"

A long pause ensued. Voice consulting with Nessus about what information could be disclosed? "A previous scouting mission penetrated the Gw'oth computer networks. This imagery came from a Gw'oth data archive."

Puppeteer spies: not a surprise. But scouting seemed like a dangerous undertaking. How many Puppeteers would run the risk?

Louis asked, "Was Nessus there?"

"Indeed, Louis."

"Voice, show me those mission reports."

Another pause. More consultation?

"Keeping busy, I see." Nessus stood just outside the bridge, half in, half out of the hatch, one head held high and the other low. Ready to flee in any direction?

"Yah." And you don't like the direction my studies are taking me. Why?

"Are you ready to take a break? I thought it was time that I share some more of your family's history," Nessus said.

Louis gestured at the Puppeteer-friendly crash couch. "I'm all ears."

NESSUS' MANIC-DEPRESSIVE CYCLE had him holed up in his cabin. Again. He responded, sometimes, to questions.

With the bridge to himself, telling himself he was bearing the long flight better than Nessus, Louis set out to relax. He sprawled across the copilot's couch, sipping from a drink bulb. His latest coffee experiment involved a Tanzanian blend. His notepad lay on the console ledge, the visible page half filled with pen-and-ink sketches. The threat of war did not impress the laws of physics. Like it or not, the long flight to Hearth left more than enough time to savor *and* study.

Not just anyone could relax on the bridge of a starship. Few objected to the speed of hyperdrive: a light-year every three days. Hyperspace was another matter entirely. Less-than-nothingness lurked just beyond the ship's hull. Instruments revealed nothing about the space behind space. Theoreticians disagreed on what hyperspace was.

On commercial starships, passengers turned to liquor, pills, and sex— to anything that helped them forget or deny or ignore where they were. Or weren't. Semantics dealt poorly with the situation. The bridge displays, had they looked outward, would have shown less than nothing. The Blind Spot, pilots called the phenomenon. For many people, the wall surrounding a window or active view port seemed to come together. It was as though the port—and whatever it purported to show—did not exist. For other observers, the mind blanked out entirely. People had gone mad staring into the Blind Spot, forgetting where—and even that—they were.

He tried to forget having thought of pills.

The ancient race of Outsiders, from whom humans and every other known starfaring race had purchased hyperdrive shunts and instantaneous hyperwave radio, priced underlying theory separate from the designs. The designs, without explanation, were expensive enough.

Only it was no longer every known race. The Gw'oth had evidently invented hyperspace technology independently, from observations taken in flight. Surreptitious observations, apparently. Nessus was less than forthcoming about why Gw'oth had been aboard a Puppeteer ship.

So much for a break from study and worry.

"Voice," Louis said, "resume instruction." A holo popped open, text and images scrolling past at a quick-skimming rate. From time to time Louis would insert a hand into the holo, speeding or slowing the scroll rate with a gesture. A virtual tap-tap would open auxiliary displays with related information.

More often, the same tap-tap would lead to an apology from Voice. "I am not authorized to provide further information." Nessus, who perhaps could, was not responding.

From time to time Louis spared a glance at the pilot's console, into the clear sphere from whose center radiated short lines. Only in details did the Puppeteer implementation differ from the instruments with which he was familiar. Perhaps the mass pointer's purpose was too straightforward to permit more than one fundamental design.

Each line in the sphere pointed toward a nearby star. The longer the line, the stronger the gravitational influence, proportional to mass over distance squared. What passed for piloting in hyperspace was keeping the desired line pointed at you.

A trained dog could do the job, except that the mass pointer only responded to a sapient mind. AIs could not operate a mass pointer, either. The Outsiders priced explanations for that, too, above what anyone would pay.

When a line approached the surface of the sphere, you changed course or returned to Einstein space. The mathematics of hyperdrive, to the degree anyone understood it, had issues with gravitational singularities. Wait too long and—

Well, what would happen was one of those topics about which the "experts" perpetually disagreed. Except this: you would never be seen again.

Just as Louis might never see home again?

He glanced yet again at the mass pointer. Logically, a peek every day or two more than sufficed. Stars were days apart even at hyperdrive speed. Only logic could not dispel the gnawing doubt that a real universe, a place of heat and light and matter, still existed. Logic had no answer for the need to reactivate a view port, despite the less-than-nothing that would stare back at you. And so, logic be damned, for their own sanity pilots dropped out of hyperspace every few days just to see the stars.

When had *he* last seen a star?

He pressed the intercom button. "I'm going to take us back to normal space for a while." He gave Nessus a chance to disagree. A *short* chance. "In five. Four. Three. Two. One. Now." Louis flicked on the view port. Amid infinite blackness, stars blazed, diamond bright. To starboard, a nebula glimmered.

The universe still existed. A bit of the tension he had not admitted to having drained from his body.

Which of these stars were in Known Space? Not knowing made his skin crawl. ("You'd like to think it's that, and not the pills you still crave.")

The 'doc had ejected Louis's wrist implant—lest its built-in comp hint at the way home? Not knowing how long he had been in the 'doc, he could not even venture a guess how far they might have come since Wunderland.

Maybe *none* of these stars warmed any world known to humans. Before retreating to his cabin, Nessus had told Louis which star to steer by. After that way station, there would be another, and another, and another.

The longer Louis traveled, the more unlikely a return to home seemed. Whatever *home* meant. He did not lack candidates.

FIRST THERE WAS HOME, the world on which Nathan had grown up. And from which he had fled as soon as he could.

Next came Fafnir, from which the Graynors had emigrated. Fafnir, unlike Home, permitted group marriages. Nathan had traveled from Home to Fafnir, hunting for his past—but to a suspicious eye, the Graynors in the public archives on Fafnir were not the Graynors *he* knew. Not to mention that the Fafnir version of the family had included a second woman.

His family must have had a second wife to pass itself off as the strangers in the holos. Who was she? *Where* was she?

Fafnir was a water world, with one small continent and lots of coral islands. Its gravity was mildly oppressive. Its day lasted only twenty-two standard hours. (Twenty-two, he remembered. The meaning of *standard* eluded him.) And if that was not enough, plenty of Kzinti—like eight-foot-tall erect tigers—had remained behind after their Patriarchy lost yet another war and ceded the planet to human settlers.

Not exactly Earth-like.

Home was supposedly the most Earth-like of the human-settled worlds. Its active plate tectonics had produced several continents. It had all-but-standard gravity and a day more than twenty-three hours long. Even parts of the biosphere were Earth-like. Some mutated native pathogen had wiped out the first batch of settlers.

For all that, his mother often hid indoors, shaking and muttering, with every curtain tightly drawn. If Home gave her panic attacks—flat phobia, in the vernacular—how could she have grown up on Fafnir?

Obviously, she hadn't.

Mother's flat phobia suggested she (and all the "Graynors"?) were from Earth. When Nathan finally made it to Earth, he understood. Eons of evolution could not be denied: Earth looked, smelled, and *felt* like home.

A DNA sample might have told local authorities who he was. Nathan had tortured himself for months: Should he try to find out? Suppose Earth was his birth world. He had been taken away as a child, surely innocent. But his parents . . .

If his suspicions were correct, they had gone to extraordinary lengths to escape. To hide. But why? From whom? Were they criminals or refugees?

His imagination failed him. Not knowing, he would not risk setting the authorities back on their trail.

And while Nathan waffled, he had met Paula Cherenkov. And lost her. And fled his own misery to Wunderland. And found new miseries.

And become Louis Wu, champion of—and not-quite-prisoner to—the fabled Puppeteers.

THE RUSH OF MEMORIES made the hunger for drugs that much worse.

The more information Nessus doled out—and the more old memories that stimulated—the clearer it became: Louis's family had been driven into hiding. Now it gnawed at Louis that he had added to their pain by abandoning them.

What if he *did* make it home? Would Nessus have left intact any memory of Louis's personal history?

Voice had not noticed Louis's distraction. "Freeze display," Louis snapped. He would have to go back to pick up the thread. He jiggled his drink bulb. All but empty. He strode briskly to the relax room, telling himself it was only for coffee—

And the tanjed synthesizer refused to make painkillers. Not, anyway, unless Nessus entered an authorization.

Louis told himself he only wanted to know if he could get pills. His addiction wasn't broken unless he had a *choice* to lapse.

Knowing himself for a liar, Louis went to his cabin in the hope of sleep.

7

Insanity ebbed and flowed. Right now insanity was at low tide, and it was all Nessus could do not to hide in his own belly. He had rallied sufficiently merely to cower in his cabin, monitoring Louis through reports from Voice and widely strewn sensors.

The shipboard AI was yet more insanity, but without Voice for company Nessus might long ago have succumbed to catatonia. The farther the Fleet of Worlds raced from the little corner of the galaxy humans so arrogantly called Known Space, the more grueling these solo trips became. After 135 years of steady acceleration, more than thirty light-years farther.

Earth years and light-years. After so much time spent away from Hearth, Nessus even thought in those terms. He even, sometimes, found himself thinking in *English*.

Baedeker had insisted Nessus take along an AI—no matter that AIs were strictly prohibited by Concordance law. Not even Clandestine Directorate was to know.

Humans had long used AIs, even back to the old, stolen colony ship from whose embryo banks New Terra had been settled. A copy of Jeeves, the colonists' primitive AI, was unlikely to go rogue during this trip.

A most unusual Hindmost, Baedeker.

The first time he and Nessus met, Baedeker was only an engineer at General Products Corporation. He and Nessus had, in a completely un-Citizen-like manner, almost come to blows. And now they were friends. More than friends. At times it seemed they could become—

That was another matter that did not bear thinking about so far from home.

"What is Louis doing?" Nessus asked Voice.

"Examining the geometry of the situation, sir." An explanatory holo opened.

Nessus studied the star map, centered on the Fleet. Suns and worlds were not to scale, of course, or none would have shown. Twenty light-years in the Fleet's wake: Jm'ho, home world to the Gw'oth. Eleven light-years ahead: Kl'mo, the aliens' newest colony.

Predators' jaws, waiting to close.

The crooning, chanting, murmuring crowds of Citizens on his cabin wallpaper had lost their power to calm. The redolence of herd pheromones endlessly circulating through the ventilation system no longer eased his loneliness. He pawed at the cabin's deck, the lure of catatonia stronger than ever. "And what does Louis have to say about that?"

"He wonders why the Concordance would choose to fly the Fleet into such a dangerous neighborhood."

Because every challenge we overcome only reemerges as a newer, even bigger challenge. *That* answer would beget even less welcome questions.

"I will go speak with him," Nessus said.

"Very good, sir."

NESSUS FOUND LOUIS in the relax room, nursing a drink bulb, slowly circling another instance of the star map. Half-empty plates covered the small table, waiting to be recycled. The notepad beside the plates showed a doodle of a Gw'o.

Nessus settled onto his padded bench. "What do you think?"

"I think your people should reconcile with the Gw'oth."

"Assume others are pursuing that course and that they fail. What are the Fleet's risks?"

"The Fleet is doing half light speed?"

That was information Voice would not have divulged. With lots of suppositions, Louis might have reached that conclusion from estimating the red shift of the Nature Preserve worlds' suns. This was the son of Carlos Wu, all right. "Close enough."

"They need only to scatter stealthed objects in the Fleet's path. At those speeds, even a small mass would become a potential planet-buster." Louis frowned. "You had to know that."

"It is why you are here." Nessus plucked nervously at his mane. "Your suggestions?"

"I gather the Fleet passed safely by"—Louis pointed into the holo—"Jm'ho. Why expect trouble when you pass the new Gw'oth colony?"

Nessus looked himself in the eyes. *Because we are cowards,* the gesture said. *We worry because there might be a problem.*

That was an easier answer than the whole truth.

"Why would they care, Nessus? Here *we* are, breathing the same air, comfortable with the same lighting and room temperature. Hearth must be like Earth or Home. The Gw'oth evolved in frigid water beneath a permanent roof of ice. It's not as though either species would covet the other's worlds." Louis squeezed the last drops from his drink bulb and ordered another. "Unless you've given the Gw'oth a reason to distrust . . ."

"*We* have no reason to trust *them*. The Gw'oth developed hyperdrive in secrecy, inside their water-filled habitat module, while aboard our ship." *Our* could be misconstrued as Citizen. Louis had no need of the more complicated details. "They took their habitat to hyperspace without warning— from inside our ship. Do you know what that did?"

"Give me a minute." Louis paced a bit, brow furrowed. "Ships wrap themselves in a normal space bubble to protect the crew from hyperspace. The hyperspace shunt carries with it everything inside the bubble. So if the Gw'oth bubble was any larger than this habitat . . ."

"Among other things, it carried away most of our ship's hyperdrive shunt." *And cut the General Products hull itself in half.* Nessus was not about to reveal a way to destroy the supposedly impregnable hull. "The remaining crew barely survived long enough to be rescued."

A crew, at that point, of only two. Sigmund Ausfaller was insane, all but comatose, by the time rescuers arrived. He had preserved Baedeker in medical stasis.

"But *why*?" Louis asked.

"The Gw'oth did not say."

Even within Clandestine Directorate, that was the only answer. Unofficially? Baedeker had his suspicions. The Gw'oth had surreptitiously learned the secret of hyperdrive. They must also have tapped into discussions they were not meant to hear—such as Baedeker advocating the execution of Gw'oth allies lest they bring home Concordance secrets.

Louis considered. "But the Gw'oth know the Concordance has its own ships. That puts their worlds equally at risk. It brings to mind something from Earth history. Atomic bombs, as horrible as they were, turned out to be stabilizing. No one dared start a full-out war. Mutual assured destruction, I think people called the balancing act. MAD, for short. Surely neither the Fleet nor the Gw'oth would be foolish enough to make first use of planet-busters."

Mutual assured destruction. That was madness indeed! That was why the Concordance had hidden for so long from—everyone. But New Terra knew the Fleet's location, and now, too, so did the Gw'oth.

"What defenses does the Fleet have?" Louis asked.

Until New Terra went free, only secrecy had been needed. And little else had been possible. Few enough Citizens could scout. There would never be enough Citizens able to crew a navy!

Since New Terran independence, the Fleet had steadily deployed sensors and weapons: lasers, particle beams, guided missiles. Since the rise of the Gw'oth the pace had accelerated. Without crews, and unwilling to use AI, inflexible automation had to operate everything. In far too many scenarios, the Fleet's defenses could only blast away without hesitation at any possible threat.

"Nessus? I can't understand the danger without knowing how the Fleet would defend itself."

A nasty toxin waited in the relax-room synthesizer. Louis would be in his father's autodoc when *Aegis* neared Hearth and authentication codes were given. Voice would be turned off. Nessus would take *no* chances with compromising the Fleet's defenses, inadequate as they were.

"I am not prepared to discuss that." Nessus felt little less programmed than Voice.

With a flick of a hand, Louis banished the star map. "Then how am I to . . . never mind. I'll leave that alone for now. Maybe the Gw'oth don't even want to attack. The world they settled may simply be a good choice for them. Its location along the Fleet's path doesn't prove anything."

"They may believe they have a reason," Nessus conceded.

And yet for all Baedeker's antipathy toward the Gw'oth, he had never, even as Hindmost, taken action against them. MAD had prevailed.

"A reason?" Louis finally prompted.

"There was . . . friction in our early contacts."

Much more than friction, if Baedeker's plans for the Gw'oth had been overheard. But the Gw'oth had greater cause to fear the Fleet.

"What *kind* of friction?"

"Not important." Nessus shuddered. "This is. In recent years, the Concordance has faced one danger after another. The times being so extraordinary, the Citizens have entrusted governance to the Experimentalist Party. What you would call politics now comes down to competition among the—"

"*Politics?* You brought me here to meddle in Puppeteer politics?" Louis's eyes flicked to the synthesizer.

Nessus fought his own self-destructive urge: to hide. "Did you ever wonder why Beowulf Shaeffer undertook such dangerous missions? No, I do not change the subject."

Reluctantly: "Sure, I've wondered."

"The first time, skimming the surface of a neutron star, because a Citizen scientist and scout coerced Beowulf into going. The same scout hired Beowulf for a journey to the galactic core because he had survived the first trip."

"*You* are a Citizen scout."

Nessus had not been far from the scene, but neither had he been responsible. He certainly was no scientist.

"He calls himself Achilles." And Hearth had yet to recover from the chaos unleashed when his second hiring of Shaeffer encountered the galactic-core explosion. "Achilles is a politician now, not a scout. An ambitious politician."

"Is there another kind, Nessus?"

"While Experimentalists rule, the contest for power comes down to a competition among radical ideas."

All too often, crazy ideas, for not only scouts were insane. It took a special sort of madness to aspire to responsibility for the herd, rather than to submerge oneself within the herd. And among the few who aspired even to be *the* Hindmost . . .

Would Louis serve a society whose entire political class—by definition—was crazy?

The crazy-scariest possibility of all was that Nessus might have failed to find Beowulf Shaeffer because Achilles had found Shaeffer first. Trouble followed Shaeffer and Achilles both.

Nessus said, "Achilles aspires to guide the Experimentalists, and hence to become Hindmost of us all. As Minister of Science he has the public ear. He campaigns on taking 'all necessary measures' to end the Gw'oth threat."

With a sigh, Louis looked away from the synthesizer and the drugs he was too proud to request.

Nessus waited.

Louis said, "The Gw'oth are too smart *not* to have stealthy ships or probes watching the Fleet. Whatever they overhear they can transmit home by hyperwave radio. And apparently what they're overhearing is threats."

Nessus stood, tottering on trembling legs. Of *course* the Gw'oth secretly followed events on Hearth, just as squadrons of stealthy Concordance probes ringed the Gw'oth worlds. "I fear, Louis, we are giving the Gw'oth a reason to decide they must strike first."

"It would still be mad. . . ." Louis paused to gather his thoughts. "What if there is a message in *where* the Gw'oth put their settlement? Ice moons with oceans are common enough."

"Of course there is a message! A threat. They put themselves in the Fleet's path."

Louis shook his head. "I suspect that it's more than that. They could scatter planet-busters into the Fleet's path from ships. They don't need to establish, or expose, a colony to make an attack on the Fleet."

"Then what are you saying?"

"If the Gw'oth established colonies as distant from Jm'ho, but in other directions, your people would never have encountered them. So maybe the meaning of the new colony, of this Kl'mo, is that they want the Concordance to know the extent of their capabilities."

"Why would they want that?"

Louis began pacing. "To demonstrate that they are dispersed, that you cannot hope to find all their colonies. That if war should come, some of *them* will survive."

"And we, bound to our Fleet of Worlds, will not." Nessus shuddered, marveling that he did not collapse in terror. Even hindbrains and trembling flesh must know some disasters are too cosmic to flee. "War remains madness, but mutual destruction would no longer be the outcome. *That,* you are telling me, is the message."

Louis laughed bitterly. "My entire military career was one skirmish in which I almost got myself killed, and from which I became an addict. Yet somehow you expect me to penetrate the grand strategy of genius aliens I've never met."

Almost certainly you already have, Nessus thought. You have Beowulf's quick mind and love of the strange. You have Carlos's brilliance. You have the human heritage of aggression and war.

All Nessus said was, "That is why you are here."

Only, it soon turned out, he had been preparing for the wrong crisis.

NO MAN'S LAND

8

Amid chaos and ruin, light-years from Hearth, alone but for the ragged sounds of his own breathing, Achilles stared.

Debris floated all around him. Some things were recognizable and more were not: bits beyond counting slashed—or melted and recongealed—from every part of the ship.

But no stretch of the imagination could still call *Argo* a ship. It was a hulk, nothing more. Here and there ragged edges of onetime decks clung to the hull. The last wisp of air was long vanished from the vast, cavernous expanse. Life support, communications, propulsion, artificial gravity, sensors: all were gone. The flotsam that cargo and bulkheads and ship's systems had become endlessly rebounded, in eerie silence, from the hull or one another.

His spacesuit recycled almost without loss; it could sustain him for years. A stasis field froze time; it could sustain him forever. For what? No one knew where he was, and Pak warships would be converging on his location. His hearts would stop from fright and conditioned reflex when the Pak arrived to claim their prize. Until that ignominious end, he had only his memories to occupy him. Bitter memories.

Once again his plans had gone horribly awry. . . .

ARGO POPPED INTO NORMAL SPACE.

Flat displays and holos sprang to life all around Achilles. He kept lips and tongue on the hyperdrive actuator while his other head swiveled to survey the readouts and imagery.

"Target acquired," his copilot called. Roland Allen-Cartwright sat across the bridge. He was a large man, swarthy, with close-set eyes. "Call it three light-days."

"And?" Achilles prompted.

"I'm looking at a squadron, twelve ships, about half a light-year distant. Big ships. Receding from us. And the usual background radio chatter."

White-hot fusion flames streamed behind the twelve ramscoops, shouting their presence and course. Achilles had chosen his quarry from light-years away. By no known science could *Argo*'s reactionless thrusters be detected from similar distances.

Then again, he did not know what the Pak knew. Yet.

Any ramscoop accelerating toward *Argo* would be less obvious. Any ramscoop coasting toward *Argo* would be nearly invisible. To infer an approaching ramscoop required subtle modeling, element by element, of ripples in the tenuous interstellar medium, or triangulation of faint neutrino sources. Both methods entailed significant uncertainties. Both methods took time.

Or he could take more active measures.

"One radar ping," Achilles ordered. If any ships lurked nearby, waiting to pounce, he meant to know *now*. The ping would not forewarn his quarry, three light-days distant. Before radar's light-speed crawl ever reached that ship, *Argo* would strike.

"Ping sent," Roland said. Seconds passed. "Nothing."

Minutes passed before Achilles released his grip on the hyperdrive control. "What is the target ship doing?"

Roland frowned at his instruments. "It looks like there is a big free-floating snowball out ahead of it. So collecting water, I would guess."

Hearth sweltered from pole to pole in the industrial waste heat of its trillion inhabitants. The home world had not seen snow in ages. In simpler times Achilles had encountered snow on human and Kzinti worlds. In more recent, more troubling times, in the "rehabilitation" camps on Nature Preserve One, he had made a far more intimate acquaintance with snow. He did not like snow.

At maximum acceleration *Argo* would match normal-space velocity with the isolated Pak ship within half a day. The hyperspace jump to the Pak's position would take even less time. "Prepare your people, Roland. At this time tomorrow, we attack."

"DID I ACTUALLY SAY *ATTACK*?" Achilles asked.

He was past caring that he talked to himself and starting to wonder when he would begin answering. His words were muffled by the ball of flesh into which he had wrapped himself, his necks between his front legs and his heads pressed tight against his belly. How long had it been since he last unclenched? Wearing a pressure suit, he need never loosen to catch a breath.

He unwound anyway. The white-hot flame of a ship, or ships, decelerating toward him would be his only warning of death's arrival, and the only functioning long-range sensors were his eyes. He would circumnavigate yet again the transparent hull, from which most of the paint had been seared away.

A bit of the drifting flotsam bumped his flank. He arched a neck for a look—

At the severed arm of Roland Allen-Cartwright.

Achilles' heads whipped back between his legs. As his mind retreated into the troubled past, his last coherent thought was that he needed more dependable human hirelings.

"DROPPING FROM HYPERSPACE in three," Achilles announced over the intercom. "Two. One. Now."

On the main bridge display, stars appeared. So did a Pak ramscoop, its fusion drive blazing. It was but ten light-seconds away.

"Missile launched," Roland called. "Locked on target."

View ports went blank automatically as Achilles popped *Argo* back to hyperspace.

The missile carried a neutron bomb armed with a proximity switch. Achilles doubted even Pak technology could fend off a nuclear attack launched from out of nowhere.

Three minutes later *Argo* returned to normal space.

There was no need for a second missile. The Pak ship was adrift, its fusion flame extinguished. Instruments detected not a flicker of ramscoop field or a whisper of comm.

The neutron flux from the bomb would kill everyone aboard within a day. Then Roland and his cronies could search the derelict at their leisure.

WITH A FINAL PRECISE wriggle of lip nodes, Achilles eased *Argo* into position slightly ahead of the Pak derelict. He set the autopilot to maintain their position.

"Two miles and a bit," Roland said, standing. "Close enough."

"Be careful," Achilles answered.

He pretended not to hear the snort as Roland left the bridge. You had to make allowances for beings willing to run dangers for you. No one could still be alive where Achilles' crew was headed, but that did not preclude dangers. Beginning with a ship-to-ship transfer at almost half light speed.

Capture of a Pak vessel was momentous, and Achilles had coiffed himself for the occasion. Gold chains and strands of jewels glittered in his mane. Curls and braids and waves, each artfully dyed, were piled high above his cranial dome. He took a moment to straighten a braid. No one aboard, alas, could appreciate his resplendence.

The Pak vessel, imaged by stern-mounted infrared sensors, loomed in the main bridge holo. Achilles' overall impression was of a great length of pipe. The flared bow hinted at the magnetic field that had—until the neutron-bomb blast scrambled things—projected far ahead to sweep up interstellar hydrogen. Small tanks ringed the aft end. The ramscoop field gathered too little hydrogen for propulsion until the ship, feeding its fusion drive with onboard fuel, got up its speed. The fat torus amidships was the crew compartment.

On the main console, a status lamp began to blink: a cargo-hold hatch opening. Roland's voice came over the intercom. "We're leaving now."

On an internal security camera Achilles watched ten figures in space-suits leap from the open hold. On external IR sensors he watched them jet on invisible puffs of compressed gas toward the slowly tumbling Pak ship. He had *Argo* to himself.

A monument to the arrogance of genius, the Pak vessel held his eyes. In interstellar space, with neither planetary nor solar magnetic fields to protect you, the radiation would slowly kill you—and that was while you stood still. The faster you moved, the deadlier things became, with every stray atom and molecule coming on like cosmic rays. Ships needed shielding, and lots of it, for protection.

A ramscoop field, by sweeping up the atoms and molecules that came sleeting at a ship, did double duty as shielding. Pak were too sure of their technology, too certain of their ability to improvise around any problem, to backstop the ramscoop field with simple, foolproof, massive shielding. Why carry all that dead weight?

Even without the deadly blast of the neutron bomb, the Pak on that ship were doomed the moment their ramscoop failed.

But the ramscoop field was also deadly. Magnetic fields intense enough to deflect molecules moving at near light speed also induced massive electric currents. Crewed ramscoops had to warp the magnetic field around the habitat module. If that force-field bubble ever wavered, the magnetic flux would kill everyone.

It took arrogant brilliance to fly such ships—much of it, clearly, deserved. The Pak had crossed tens of thousands of light-years in ships like this.

The salvage party had shrunk to ten tiny dots. Sending one person would have sufficed, if that one carried a stepping disc. But if, against all logic, any of the Pak had survived? Achilles had refused to permit stepping discs on the first visit.

"Your status?" Achilles radioed.

"About halfway," came Roland's voice. "*Argo* still looks huge, I'm happy to say."

Because it *was* huge, a #4 hull, the biggest that General Products made. Most #4s were cargo ships, hauling grain from the Nature Preserve worlds to Hearth. Achilles needed a ship this big for quite another reason: to carry home his prize. Once his hirelings confirmed that everyone aboard the ramscoop was dead. For now, in its position just in front of the wreck, *Argo*'s girth and impenetrable hull shielded the humans from the sleet of interstellar gas and dust.

Achilles continued to watch, anxiously, as the ten tiny hotspots closed the distance to the Pak ship. Closer they crept, and closer, and closer . . .

He began plucking at his so carefully styled mane. The madness of the moment asserted itself. It was *so* tempting. He could close the cargo hatch and jump to hyperspace. With minds of their own, his heads reached for the console—

"I wouldn't do that."

Achilles twitched, his heads whipping around toward the unexpected voice.

Roland stood in the entrance to the bridge, a stunner in hand. "You're not going to abandon my people. Move away from the console."

Achilles stood from his crash couch. "You did not trust me."

Roland laughed scornfully. "Why would we?"

Meaning capture of an alien ramscoop struck very close to home. Achilles changed the subject. "Do I have other unannounced company?"

"Just me." Roland laughed again. "If you choose to believe that."

That was the problem with criminals and mercenaries. The attitudes and aptitudes that made them useful also made them unreliable. Long ago and far away, Beowulf Shaeffer had been a much more dependable tool.

Moving slowly, lest he get himself stunned, Achilles set a display to show the bridge security camera. Roland was nowhere in the picture. Achilles waved a head at the camera. His double in the image remained at work at his console.

Argo's security sensors had been compromised.

"So who is about to board the Pak ship?" Achilles asked.

Roland leaned against a console shelf, far across the bridge from Achilles. Too bad the human did not take a proper seat. Had he settled into any crash couch on the bridge, Achilles could have immobilized him with the crash-protection force field. Maybe the human knew that.

"Nine," Roland said. "All but me. The tenth suit was empty, a balloon on a string, towed along so you wouldn't suspect anyone had stayed behind." He managed to look apologetic. "Our mission cannot succeed if you get cold feet. Hooves. Now move to the center of the bridge."

With its heater on, an empty suit looked no different to infrared sensors than an occupied suit. Clever.

Backing up as directed, Achilles pointed a head at the main display. "They are almost at the ship."

Still standing, Roland reached for the copilot's console. "Then let's watch."

ROLAND'S DEPUTY, a dour and sturdy woman named Tabitha Jones-Calvani, led the salvage party aboard the derelict. "It's not pretty in here," she reported.

Helmet cameras told as much. Corpses floated about, contorted, dotted with lesions. Even knowing what to expect, Achilles felt nauseous.

The Pak were humanoid, although shorter than humans. Their leathery skin was like armor. Their limbs were heavily muscled, and their joints enormous to take the strain. In death, many hands curled like claws—with wicked talons protruding.

These were born warriors.

"No, it's not pretty," Roland answered. "Take it slow and be safe."

Achilles could only agree. He watched the humans fan out to search the ship. They remained sealed in their spacesuits, and their boot magnets let them walk despite the lack of gravity.

Here and there, as the intruders proceeded, they found Pak belted to their stations. Panels were removed, racks extended, and components scattered about. Cabling snaked everywhere, looking improvised. Achilles managed to respect their doomed efforts to survive, wondering what they thought to construct that could change—anything.

"Approaching the bridge, I think," Tabitha said. "The bow, in any case."

"Take it slow," Roland repeated.

Helmet lamps sent bright spots skittering about, revealing more bodies and scavenged equipment. The camera through which Achilles looked wobbled as its wearer sidestepped yet another floating corpse. The body was frozen, its mouth agape, in a final paroxysm.

"Poor bastard," someone muttered.

"He would kill you if he could," another answered.

"How many bodies did—?" Achilles stopped. Something in the image had changed. In an open equipment bay: a bit of red glow, where all had been shadow before.

Screaming began. It was unworldly, inhuman. All around the camera's suddenly spasmodic point of view, images writhed and jerked.

"Finagle!" Roland shouted. He nodded at a console, at external sensor readouts. "The ramscoop field is back up. Without a crew bubble."

Too late, they knew what the dying Pak had been up to. Setting a trap. Everyone on that ship was as good as dead. Achilles galloped for the hyperdrive control.

There was a hiss like an angry swarm of purple pollinators: Roland's stunner. It was a warning shot, and Achilles backed away from the console. His legs tingled from the near miss.

"We can save them!" Roland yelled, standing at the midrange comm console. "If I can kill that field quickly."

The communications laser was powerful enough to cross a solar system. Up close it was a fearsome weapon. It might destroy the repaired field generator, or the power plant that fed it, without killing all the humans aboard. At the least, it would kill with merciful quickness.

Roland reached for the transmit button and—

The second Pak trap snapped shut its jaws.

9

The Fleet of Worlds had once held *six* worlds. On one of the six, then known simply as Nature Preserve Four, a few million humans had faithfully served the Citizens. As farmers, factory workers, eventually scouts: grateful humans did everything they could for their benefactors and mentors. They knew themselves to be descended from an embryo bank recovered from a derelict ramscoop found adrift in space. There had been, they were taught, no clues aboard to the location of the ship's point of origin.

And then those servants discovered the whole truth: *Citizens* had attacked the ancient ship when it risked finding Hearth.

The chain reaction at the galactic core had just been revealed, and the Fleet of Worlds had just cast off its tie to Hearth's ancestral star. Death lunged at the herd from behind. Unknown perils lurked in their path. At that, the worst possible moment, as Citizen society strained and sanity crumbled, the servant humans had rebelled.

And so Nature Preserve Four, renamed New Terra, had won its independence. It now flew ahead of the Fleet—a world of unwitting scouts. The New Terrans were too few and too weak to confront their former masters. And most were also too cautious, their culture having been modeled on their masters' society.

Earth authorities, if they should ever learn the fate of the lost colony ship, would have a more forceful reaction. Nessus had spent many years— if often in hiding—on Earth and its colony worlds. He did not doubt humanity's wrath.

But fits of bravery were not the only form of Nessus' madness. He had come to *like* humans. When Achilles conspired to reclaim New Terra, hoping to govern there as viceroy for the Concordance, Nessus had brought the humans a champion: Sigmund Ausfaller. And so New Terra had kept its freedom. And so, for long years, Achilles had lost his.

The next time trouble came to this part of the galaxy, it was the Gw'oth who first spotted it. They and Sigmund, as much as anyone, had saved everyone.

Even the Fleet.

It did not matter, in a way, that in saving everyone else Sigmund had been broken. He would have refused to take sides between Gw'oth and Citizens anyway.

Nessus never intended Louis to know any of that.

And then, this time by Nessus' choice, *Aegis* dropped again into normal space. A recording awaited him on a remote hyperwave radio buoy.

A foreboding message from New Terra, sent by Sigmund Ausfaller. . . .

AUSFALLER.

It was a name from Louis's troubled childhood, a name overheard when his parents were unaware he was in earshot. The boogeyman personified. Louis didn't know who Ausfaller was, not exactly, but he had a pretty good idea *what* Ausfaller was. An evil genius. A raging paranoid. An obsessive. An ARM, an agent of the United Nations military.

The one who had chased Louis's family across the stars and into hiding.

And now Louis had a face to put with the name.

An altogether ordinary-looking man, thickset and middle-aged, looked out of *Aegis'* main bridge display. He had a round face, with dark hair and eyes. He wore a jumpsuit that, aside from its programmed color choices, looked the twin to what Louis wore. Ausfaller could be any bureaucrat, on any world—

Until you looked into those piercing, haunted eyes.

"Voice, replay the message," Louis said. His impression was that the message came via a relay of buoys. The direction of the ship's hyperwave-radio beam—if he could figure out how to access that information— would tell him nothing.

"Nessus," the message began, Ausfaller's brow ominously furrowed, "we have a situation. My sources say you are away from the Fleet. I neither know nor ask what your purpose is. I only hope that whatever you're doing has you closer to the action than we are here. Call when you get this. You'll be put through to me, day or night. Ausfaller, out."

Louis studied the frozen final frame, considering. Ausfaller spoke strangely accented Interworld. And there was a bit of hesitation at times, as though he was out of practice. Odd.

Day or night? That phrasing suggested Ausfaller was on a planet. But hyperwave didn't work inside a gravitational singularity. Laser or regular radio links from a habitable planet took hours to reach the edge of your solar system, where instantaneous hyperwave began to work—unless your planet was nowhere near a sun.

Louis glowered at the holo. "What are you up to, Ausfaller? Why do you know about the Fleet?"

Nessus sidled onto the bridge, nervously plucking at his already unkempt mane. He had retreated, shaking, to his cabin upon first seeing the message. "When Sigmund Ausfaller says something is a situation, worlds tremble. Let us see what he knows."

"Putting through the call," Voice said.

"Louis, you are about to learn things you will not take back to Known Space." Nessus shifted his weight from hoof to hoof. He seemed about to say more when the comm display changed. Ausfaller again, looking very tired.

"Nessus, thank you for responding. It appears our old friend Achilles is away on a mission of his own." A curl of the lip showed that *friend* meant anything but. "If whatever he's up to is sanctioned by Clandestine Directorate, they are not admitting it. I've asked." (Ausfaller named names with whom he had checked, all from Earth's mythology. Louis wondered what *that* was about.) "And the disturbing thing is—" Ausfaller paused. "Who is that with you?"

"My name is Wu. Louis Wu."

"I invited Louis to help me on my business," Nessus said.

It had taken perhaps a minute for Ausfaller to notice Louis. Even doing the math in his head, approximating like mad, Louis was certain: *no way* was Ausfaller on a planet among the Fleet of Worlds. A hyperspace relay beyond the singularity of *five* clustered terrestrial worlds had to be well over a light-minute away from any of them.

Suddenly, it was painfully obvious.

Louis muted the connection. "Another world. A human world, apparently, and they don't speak Interworld. Why did you need *me*?"

"Not all humans are created equal," Nessus said. "As your quick mind demonstrates."

"Very well," Ausfaller eventually resumed. "I'm pleased to meet you, Louis."

Ausfaller had not reacted. Because Wu was a common name? No, Louis decided. Because Ausfaller had not allowed himself to react. He was, undoubtedly, trained *not* to react. He would surely have had more to say if Nessus had included a random party in the conversation.

You and I will talk about what you did to my family, Louis promised himself. Ideally when I can reach out with more than words.

Nessus unmuted the connection. "All right, Sigmund. Tell us what you find disturbing."

"It starts with a band of New Terran criminals unaccounted for. Some of our worst, I'm afraid. Out of sight for about a third of a year, now."

"Criminals and Achilles unseen at the same time?" Nessus said, "That is a tenuous connection at best."

The round-trip comm delays gave Louis's mind ample time to churn. New Terra was a human world, obviously. This Achilles sounded like a high-ranking Puppeteer official, and Sigmund was keeping tabs on him. As secretive as Puppeteers were, Nessus did not seem surprised. Why not? Ausfaller doling out the bad news: because he knew that too much misfortune too fast would send a Puppeteer into shock.

"For one, there is the leader of these vanished criminals. Roland Allen-Cartwright." Ausfaller permitted a flash of anger to show. "He was one of my best people—and, it turned out, a sociopath. I booted him out of the Office of Strategic Analyses, but he had learned very special skills first."

Office of Strategic Analyses. That had to be government doublespeak, like the United Nations giving its massive security apparatus the innocuous name of Amalgamated Regional Militia.

A spy agency, Louis guessed. "What ARM dirty tricks did you teach your bad apple?"

Another delay. Ausfaller refused to take the bait. "The relevant skills for now are how to probe security systems for vulnerabilities. I didn't have my own computer network in mind."

"What did he get into?" Nessus asked.

But Ausfaller was still talking. "Too late, audit software found anomalies that triggered an intruder alert. Someone with far more computer savvy than me would have to give you the details. How isn't the important part. The thing is"—and Ausfaller glowered—"Roland hacked into the sealed archives of the Pak War."

10

Achilles woke screaming. Something tugged at his leg!

His shouts echoing in his helmets, he saw that the tether he had tied just above a forehoof had gone taut. He lived in fear of the tether coming loose, of drifting out the yawning hole that a cargo-hold hatch no longer sealed, into the deadly hail of relativistic interstellar muck.

He forced himself to stop shouting, to breathe slowly and evenly. Gradually his hearts stopped pounding. The battery-powered lights he had rigged scarcely managed to ease the gloom, and shadows moved ominously whenever anything—himself included—shifted in the zero gravity.

He had been alone before. Solitude did not bother him. Much. But *this* solitude was different. He was light-years from any help, his predicament unknown. Other Pak ships would come to investigate the unexpected energy release of the neutron bomb. He wondered how long he had before they arrived.

He had exactly that long left to live. . . .

FLARE SHIELDS HAD ACTIVATED almost before Achilles noticed the bright green light. An instant later there was a flash of orange, as quickly vanquished, then blue, then normal shipboard illumination again. He screamed at Roland, "Get us out of here!"

The human stood, cursing, dueling with lasers with the not-so-dead Pak ship. "Flare shields are holding," he called out. "It's just another automated defense, like the ramscoop field. Probably also triggered by our people going aboard. I'll have it off in a minute."

Achilles sidled toward the pilot's console. The shield blocked the visible light from solar flares. The hull itself would stop the particle flux from even the biggest flare or coronal mass ejection. The shield adapted automatically to ambient light—not all flares were equally hot, hence their color distributions varied—but that did not mean it was agile enough to adjust to—

Another blaze of color, this time fiery red. It seemed longer than the last flash. Then blue again. Then, not any light Achilles could see, but a sensation of heat. Infrared. "Visible" meant something different for every species, and General Products hulls were transparent for all its onetime customers.

"We have to get out—" A stunner blast to the deck made his hooves sting.

"A few seconds more," Roland snapped. "The ramscoop field is down now."

The flare shield could not keep up with these frequency jumps. Why should it? There was a sensation of light *behind* Achilles' eyes—ultraviolet?—then that bright green again, then heat. So *much* heat! He dove for the pilot's couch.

Roland screamed and—

Discontinuity.

Vacuum! Achilles was shrieking, his chest in agony. He had to spew the air from his lungs before they exploded.

Except for dim emergency lamps, the bridge was dark. Something struck him high on a flank. He turned, still soundlessly screeching. It was floating debris, one chunk among countless many, nondescript in the gloom.

It, or something like it, may have saved his life.

The pilot's couch had a stasis-field generator. Inside stasis, time stood still. Nothing could harm him. Had some bit of flotsam not nudged the control, he would have stayed inside, unaware, as the field protected him from the vacuum.

Until, inevitably, more Pak came to investigate.

The gushing from his lungs was weaker now. He was freezing, and yet he thought he could feel his blood starting to simmer. The bridge seemed even darker than a moment ago. A few emergency lamps were lit, and shadows moved unsettlingly. With an eerie distant warble, faintly heard by sound conduction through his body, the last gases erupted from his lungs.

He was drifting!

He lunged at a padded neck rest of the pilot's couch, biting it so hard that his jaw throbbed. His body kept moving, until it gave a tremendous yank on his neck. Somehow he managed not to scream. To lose his grip was to die.

With his other head he tore open the pouch at the base of the couch and extracted the emergency pressure suit. Any other vacuum gear aboard, unprotected by the stasis field, would likely be in tatters and shreds—even if he could find it before his blood boiled from the vacuum.

He got a head, gasping, into a helmet and tongued a control. Air spewed. He felt a bit less muddled. Wriggling into a pressure suit floating in the dark, battered by debris, was the hardest thing he had ever done. With the last of his strength, he sealed the suit's seams. The roar of air in his helmets fell to a whisper. The suit heater kicked itself on.

And then, his chest heaving, Achilles blacked out.

STEEPED IN DREAD, Achilles jetted about the dead hulk. He used his compressed air sparingly, with no way to refill the propulsion tanks.

After overloading or outwitting the flare defenses, how long had the Pak laser cannon blasted *Argo*? He could not tell. The pressure suit's chronometer had, like him, been frozen in time inside the stasis field, and he had not found a functioning clock amid the wreckage. But for a long while, surely. Long enough to sear most paint from the hull. Long enough to cut decks and overheads and bulkheads into scraps. Long enough to melt the hinges of the cargo holds' hatches. Long enough to dissipate the massive debris field that must have sprayed out when the first hatch blew.

So how long? Until, Achilles supposed, the Pak ship's deuterium tanks ran dry.

He raged, then, at the unfairness of life. He raged at the Gw'oth, the threat—and opportunity—who had brought him here. He howled at party leadership that was Experimentalist in name more than in deed, too timid to empower him, and even louder at the bungling Hindmost who ruled but refused to *act*. He cursed his New Terran minions, deservedly dead for their incompetence, and at Pak too stubborn to die before setting their cunning traps.

He raged, above all, at injustice, and at everyone who had ever hindered him, and that he would die here, never having achieved the recognition he deserved. *He* should be Hindmost.

Exhausted, his throats raw from screaming and his exposure to vacuum, Achilles finally slept.

CONSCIOUSNESS RETURNED. Clarity of a sort slowly followed.

His one slim hope was to cross over to the Pak derelict, scavenge parts for a hyperwave radio and something to power it, and cross back before he fried. *Argo*'s hull still served as a radiation shelter. If he called for help, a rescue ship from the Fleet might reach him before the Pak.

The thought of a spacewalk made Achilles ache to withdraw into a catatonic ball, but that innate flight reflex only guaranteed tragedy. He forced himself around and around the hull, searching everywhere through the clear wall for the Pak ship. And when he failed to find that ship—drifted, who knew where, while he hung insensate in stasis—he *did* collapse.

He barely managed to tie a tether before clenching himself into a ball of despair.

11

"Let me share a bit of history," Ausfaller said. "It will save time."

An alien starship, a ramscoop, had plunged into Sol system in 2125. Its pilot had spent most of his life traveling from his home world, somewhere near the galactic core. He was looking for a long-lost colony of his own kind, responding to an ancient distress signal. The lost colonists had evolved, over the eons, into humans.

"I *have* taken a virtual tour of the Smithsonian," Louis said at one point. As in: don't treat me like an ignoramus. "I saw the pilot's mummified body, recovered from Mars. I know he found a Belter prospector in a singleship and told the Belter his story, that his name was Phssthpok."

"Good," Ausfaller said. "I've been off Earth for a long time. That's more background than the ARM had made public in my day. What else?"

"The aliens call themselves Pak."

"More like this." Ausfaller rearticulated the name while popping his lips. "It takes a bony beak to say it properly."

Whatever, Louis thought. That will be useful when I have a bony beak. "They're essentially early hominids, *Homo habilis,* I think, except that the adults can morph into another life stage. If they eat some plant that didn't grow properly on Earth, which is why the ancient colony failed, they become protectors. Protectors are ruthlessly obsessed with protecting their bloodlines and they're scary smart."

"What else," Ausfaller prompted.

So am I a schoolboy to be tested on my lessons? Louis wondered. "The Belter was exposed to that Pak plant. Tree-of-life, was it called? He became a protector. Probably to protect his own family, he killed Phssthpok and disappeared. End of story." Louis paused. "There hasn't been any Pak War. People would have noticed."

Another comm delay, and then Ausfaller smiled wryly. "You think? If you are who I suspect you are, Louis, you grew up on Home."

"Yah," Louis conceded. His parents were less well hidden than they had supposed. Why hadn't Ausfaller come after them?

"The first colony on Home failed, didn't it? A suspected plague." Ausfaller did not pause for an answer. "Jack Brennan, that Belter turned protector, was responsible."

Louis started. Home's history went back only a few centuries. Of *course* he had studied the lost colony while in school—only the collapse of that first colony was mysterious. Plague was just a guess. No pathogen had ever been found. No human remains of that era had ever been recovered, either, only cremated ashes. It seemed the original colonists had gone mad.

A later group of settlers, expecting to arrive at an established colony, instead found every building had been blasted or burned to the ground. That was in an era before hyperdrive; the new colonists were on their own. By the time they had established themselves, the charred and weathered ruins were all but beyond study. The plague—or whatever had happened—never recurred.

That the ARM kept secrets did not surprise Louis. Still, a human protector would *protect* humans, wouldn't he? And while Brennan attacking Home—if, for some strange reason, he had—might fairly be called a protector war, it would not be a Pak War.

Louis felt Nessus watching him. Gauging him? "All right, Sigmund. Why would Brennan attack Home colony?"

Ausfaller grimaced. "The plague was a variation of the virus in tree-of-life root. It's the virus that triggers the life-stage change in adults. I believe Brennan set loose the virus on Home to raise an army of protectors."

Louis remembered something else from that long-ago virtual tour of the Pak exhibit. "Tree-of-life doesn't affect Pak until they're old enough. Why did the virus affect the younger colonists on Home? Remember, *no one* was left."

"If I'm right," Ausfaller said, "Brennan engineered his virus to kill everyone too young or too old to change. Without descendants to protect, the new protectors would lose their will to live—or they would adopt a bigger cause. Brennan's cause. A war against the Pak."

A *world* exterminated to build an army. Louis felt sick. "Against a follow-up Pak fleet?"

"That's our best information," Ausfaller said. "If so, it worked. But, as you said, you would have noticed a Pak War. And, no doubt, you would have noticed any survivors of that war, whether Pak or human protectors. That sounds to me like the two sides fought to a draw. And to the death."

And a few years later, a colony ship arrived and found no trace of plague. Because Brennan engineered his virus not to survive without hosts?

Horrific as were Ausfaller's speculations, Louis found himself believing. "It was bizarre enough that Nessus drafted me to help—"

"Our business does not concern Sigmund," Nessus interrupted.

But Ausfaller's business must concern Nessus. Every minute spent listening in normal space was a minute that, spent in hyperspace, would have brought *Aegis* about two million kilometers closer to the Fleet.

How had this started? A New Terran criminal had broken into archives of a Pak War. Why was that an emergency for Nessus? Why was Achilles interested?

Ausfaller resumed his history dump. Voice would be recording; Louis only half listened, trying to see the bigger picture. No one knew exactly when the Lost Colony fell, but it was around 2400. Close to four centuries ago. A battle to the death then between Pak and human protectors could hardly be cause for alarm now.

Louis broke into the recitation, even though it would take Ausfaller a while to notice. "So there's been another Pak invasion, this one threatening the Fleet or New Terra. That's the archive this Roland broke into."

"The new Pak advance threatened both our worlds," Nessus said, "but it has since been deflected. They are going around us. Sigmund, I do not understand your alarm."

"I'm almost there," Ausfaller said. "There is a final bit of background to cover. Brennan's cold-blooded slaughter on Home was not an isolated event. On the Pak home world, they had developed whole institutions around childless protectors needing a reason to live. If you convinced yourself you served the whole Pak race, you might get past losing your descendants. Phssthpok spent his life hunting for Earth because *he* had become childless.

"One such institution was the Library, the fail-safe repository of Pak knowledge. Whenever clan rivalries got out of hand and civilizations fell, the Library helped the survivors rebuild. Lots of childless Pak ended up serving the Library.

"After Phssthpok set out, some Pak explorer discovered the leading edge of the radiation erupting from the galactic core explosion. Pakhome is near the core, and Pak don't have hyperdrive technology. Everyone who could get onto a ramscoop did. Everyone who didn't have a ship did his best to steal one. Once the ships were gone, everyone left behind fought over the dwindling resources with which to build more.

"So you're right, Louis. Pak hordes came toward the Fleet and New Terra. And yes, the Pak fleets were deflected away from our worlds, in what I called the Pak War, although Nessus glossed over a lot."

Glossed over what? Nessus was plucking at his mane again, Louis noticed, just as he had noticed that the Puppeteer did not want Louis to mention the Gw'oth. Meanwhile Ausfaller worried about Achilles' disappearance, while Nessus worried about Achilles' feud with the Gw'oth. And the New Terran spy gone bad, this Roland fellow, broke into Pak War records before vanishing, presumably in league with Achilles. Round and round the clues went, the Gw'oth surely somehow at the heart of things.

"That's about it," Ausfaller was saying. "Picture thousands of childless Pak, the keepers of an ancient Library. Safeguarding knowledge on a doomed world no longer gives them a reason to live. But if they could carry away that knowledge . . ."

Taking a long swallow from a drink bulb of coffee, Louis tried to take it in. Thousands of childless protectors and an ancient Library—they would need a lot of ships. Protectors *with* family would take those ships if they could. Could even thousands of Librarians have prevailed against a world of desperate refugees?

Not without help. Not without, like Brennan on Home, ruthlessly slaughtering whole clans to turn surviving protectors into allies. Either there was no Librarian fleet or . . .

"There's an enormous armada of Librarians, isn't there?" Louis said. "It's carrying the best of Pak technology. Your bad apple knows everything *you* know about the Library, and he's leading Achilles right to it."

Louis glanced at Nessus. None of the fine print committed Louis to keeping Puppeteer secrets. "And Achilles will use whatever Pak technology he can steal against the Gw'oth. And to make himself Hindmost—if he doesn't get everyone killed first."

Nessus bleated like a bagpipe that had been dropkicked.

A few seconds later, long before Louis's speculation could have reached him, Ausfaller said, "I fear that Achilles is going after the Library, hoping to use Pak technology to take on a nearby species called the Gw'oth. He means to make himself Hindmost."

Two minutes later, Louis had the satisfaction of watching Ausfaller twitch in surprise.

A RARE, CREAMY SOLID WHITE, his elaborately coiffed mane resplendent with gems of Experimentalist Party orange, achingly handsome, Nike looked at Nessus from a recorded message.

Nessus had spent much of his life trying to impress the charismatic politician, to earn Nike's trust and gain his favor. To get into Nike's *life*. Too late, Nessus had come to understand the essential truth about Nike: Nike's main purpose was to help himself. By then Nike had turned crisis into opportunity, and emerged as Hindmost.

Experimentalists remained in power, but Nike's reign had ended. He now served where his talents most benefited the Concordance: at the rear of the Clandestine Directorate. At that task, he was brilliant—and Nessus' superior.

"Achilles *is* away," Nike was saying, his voices rich with undertunes. "That was never a secret. He was personally overseeing an experiment involving planetary drives, reporting from onsite."

The Concordance had bought its planetary drives ages ago from the ancient race of Outsiders, and Citizen scientists still had only an incomplete sense of how the devices worked. About all Nessus understood regarding planetary drives was that they harnessed staggering amounts of energy. Purposefully destabilized, they became destructive beyond imagination, able to shatter whole worlds into shrapnel. As the Pak had learned.

You experimented with the technology, if at all, far from the Fleet.

Once outside the Fleet's gravitational singularity, reports submitted by hyperwave could have been relayed from—anywhere.

And that, once Nike got to the point, turned out to *be* the point. Sigmund, once more, was on to something. Achilles' underlings had covered for his absence for much of a year. They had no idea where Achilles had taken a ministry ship—

Or why he had stopped communicating.

12

Had there been life before *Aegis*? Truly? Louis found that harder and harder to believe. Only the occasional craving for painkillers reminded him of such a bygone era—and he was happy to feel those particular urges fading away.

As Ausfaller had hoped and Nessus dreaded, *Aegis* was the ship best positioned to hunt for Achilles. *Best positioned* did not mean close. Here was more fine print to Louis's arrangement with Nessus. No end date! Gw'oth, Pak, psychotic Puppeteer politicians, paranoid émigré spies . . . Nessus could involve Louis with anything.

Next time—if there was a next time—Louis would negotiate more wisely.

He spent his waking hours poring over the information Ausfaller had hyperwaved. Technological civilizations flattened by relativistic planet-busters, for no more reason than that they lay along the Pak's path. Interrogations of the Pak prisoner Ausfaller had briefly held. Memories, guesses, and surmises from Ausfaller's long-ago reading of ARM files. The Puppeteers' own horrific weapons demonstrated—Nessus was more evasive than usual on the specifics—to convince the Pak fleets to change course. Wondering if Achilles' attempt to seize the Library would provoke the Pak to turn back toward worlds Louis had never seen.

Worlds he nonetheless felt increasingly bound to protect.

But it was the long-range surveillance files, showing wave upon wave of Pak ramscoops, that seized Louis's imagination. With the imagery greatly accelerated, the all-but-static ship deployments became a hypnotic dance. In that deadly choreography Louis read conflicts of every scale, from skirmishes to full-blown battles, of clan alliances made and betrayed on the fly. It made him ill to watch—and he could not look away.

Awful truths seeped into his consciousness. The Pak were *bred* for warfare. Why would they hesitate to squash an alien race when they so freely attacked their own? If Ausfaller was to be believed—and Nessus, at the least, did—Pak had been at each others' throats for eons.

And Louis and Nessus were hurtling into this particular hornets' nest. Alone.

"What are we supposed to do when we get there," Louis finally asked Ausfaller.

"Improvise," Ausfaller had said. Something in his demeanor—or perhaps it was only Louis's subconscious—added: If you're half the man your fathers are, you'll find an answer.

LOUIS STUDIED a vast and orderly arrangement of white-hot sparks, ringed by widely spaced, more distant sparks. Those outliers, Louis decided, were patrols to guard the main group's flanks. In space or in the jungle, some principles of warfare must be universal.

Aegis had just emerged from hyperspace, behind what the Fleet's best instruments suggested was the tail of the Pak migration.

"Your thoughts?" Nessus probed.

Louis walked around the holo, considering. "If there *is* a Library fleet, this would be it. It's more than big enough to take on the wave just ahead, and yet it's not accelerating. The Library fleet would defend itself, but it wouldn't pick fights. There's no purpose in being a Librarian without living clans to use the Library. And loitering at the back of the line makes it less likely clans would attack the Library for its resources."

And maybe the Pak War prisoner, Thssthfok, had only been messing with Ausfaller's head. How do you interrogate a prisoner that much smarter than yourself?

"My conclusion, too," Nessus said.

Suppose these were the Librarians. Then what? There was no sign of Achilles, and no response to Nessus' hyperwave broadcasts.

At least they had been able to use hyperwave. If the Pak had had hyperwave capability, they would have had hyperdrive, too. They wouldn't be taking millennia-long flights by ramscoop.

"Voice," Louis asked, "how large a volume does this last wave of ships occupy?"

"About a hundred cubic light-years."

"Too large a volume to search," Nessus added. Hopefully? "Perhaps this is the time Sigmund is wrong."

Louis kept pacing. No matter where he moved, all he saw was the same precise central array, ringed by the same patrol ships. Hmm. "Nessus, I'd like a closer look."

"How much closer?" Nessus pawed nervously at the deck.

They were eighty light-days from the nearest ramscoop. "Five jumps, just a few light-minutes each. We'll stay only long enough for Voice to get a new image."

"Proceed."

Louis sat at the copilot console and took *Aegis* through a series of hyperspace micro-jumps. Each reemergence into normal space slightly expanded the view in the main display. "That should do it," he finally said. "Jumping us back to our original distance."

At that announcement, Nessus ceased his anxious pawing but said nothing.

The naval formation looked stable to Louis. "Voice. Take all the views since we got here. Normalize the images to a constant size, as though viewing the central formation from a single place. Orient all images the same way. Superimpose them, if you can, ship upon ship."

"That will take a few seconds," Voice replied.

Nessus sidled toward Louis. "What are you looking for?"

The nearer to the ramscoops they jumped, the more recent the light *Aegis* sampled. Time travel, of a sort. "Wait for Voice," Louis said.

"Here is the composite image you wanted," Voice said. A new holo popped up.

Image superimposed upon image, the sparks that marked the central fleet were blinding. The patrol ships, circling the main formation, followed short, dotted arcs. To one side of the main array, three arcs took starkly different courses.

Louis reached into the holo, a fingertip at the spot toward which three ramscoops were converging. He said, "*There* is where we'll find Achilles."

ACHILLES ATE AND DRANK indifferently, floating at random to the limit of his tether. In the beating of his hearts, in the random nudges of drifting wreckage, in the recurrence of hunger, in the coming and going of sleep and dream and catatonia, time passed. He had nothing to do but wait. He had nothing to wait for but extinction.

Death would be quick. The Pak would come, and his hearts would stop in fright.

Once he had had the choice of waiting in stasis. In a moment of clarity, he had taken apart the field generator and hurled its components into the void. The Pak whom Ausfaller had once captured had not known about stasis fields. Achilles would not let an enemy acquire the technology from him.

The tether pulled Achilles up short yet again, and he looked himself in the eyes. He had aspired to rule worlds, and now the limit of his domain was this short range of salvaged fiber-optic cable. He had been a great scientist, and now his only tool was the pressure suit that kept him alive. He had traveled among the stars, and now, other than dim readouts in his helmets, starlight would be the only illumination for the rest of his miserable existence.

Why wait for the Pak? He could end everything now. True, his pressure suit would not open in a vacuum, or allow him to turn off life support, but it could not stop him from piercing the fabric on some jagged bit of debris. Or he could slip his tether and jet from the shelter of the hull. Radiation would kill him slowly, but the suit's life support, unable to save him, had ample drugs to ease his passage.

He drifted in and out of sleep, considering the possibilities. To be or not to be.

Motion!

Not floating debris. That he no longer noticed. And his helmet lights had been off for—well, he did not know how long—but long enough. His eyes were fully adapted to starlight. He could hardly have missed the approach of a fusion-drive ship.

Voices!

Voices, he understood. He was talking to himself again without knowing it.

He listened to the voices for a while, wondering why he did not sound like himself and why he muttered so softly. As long as he was feeling curious, he wondered a bit more about the odd sense that he had seen something moving.

The motion came from *outside* this hulk, in the form of stars eclipsed. A ship!

He tongued the radio controls in his helmets. The muttering became the beautiful, musical speech of another Citizen.

". . . Vessel *Aegis*. Please respond. Repeat. This is Concordance vessel *Aegis*. Please respond. Repeat. This is—"

"Here!" Achilles shouted, harmonics pulsing with need. "I am in here! Here!"

"*Aegis*. Please respond. Repeat. This—"

The hail, obviously recorded, cut out. "I am sending in a human with a stepping disc," the voices said. "You are safe."

PROMISED LAND

13

Achilles cantered onto the bridge, glanced at the main display, and sneered. "I suppose you think we owe them apologies."

Nessus dismissed the image of the Pak derelict, then stood from the pilot's couch. He tried to make allowances, but it was hard. Maybe if Achilles had shown any sympathy for the New Terrans he had sent to their deaths. . . .

No matter how Nessus tried, he could not justify the unprovoked attack on the Pak. The aliens had turned away from the Fleet many years ago. In a few more years, even the alien rearguard would have passed. Why draw their attention now?

Achilles had quickly put behind him the horrors of his ordeal. His coat, off-white with patches of tan, had been brushed until it glowed. His brown mane was replete with braids and curls, freshly woven with orange garnets. Rather than wear a standard shipboard utility belt, he had synthed an ornamental sash decorated with full Ministry of Science regalia.

By asserting his status, Achilles must hope to commandeer *Aegis*.

"I suppose," Nessus answered cautiously, "that provoking the Pak is a dangerous activity."

Achilles stood tall, his hooves set far apart. *Un*ready to run: the stance of dominance. "The Pak crew of that ship is dead, not provoked, and with knowledge from the Library we can eliminate the Gw'oth as a threat. We will take what I came for and be gone before other Pak can respond."

One unstated assumption piled on another in that speech, Nessus thought. Whatever technology Achilles sought might never have existed aboard this specific ship—or at all. The information might be aboard and yet undecipherable, expressed in an unfamiliar clan dialect or extinct language. The information might have been destroyed in the attack, or the repositories—what was the human term?—booby-trapped by the Pak crew before they died.

Achilles was never one to admit to doubt or uncertainty. Or to hesitate to gamble with the lives of others.

Still, could pillaging make these circumstances any worse? Probably not. And if Achilles' mad adventure *did* turn the Pak attention toward the Fleet, Pak knowledge might even the odds.

Nessus sang, "If Louis agrees to the attempt, and I am convinced it does not put my mission at risk, I will act."

"And what is that mission?"

"That is a matter for the Hindmost to disclose." *I have powerful friends.*

"You never had any imagination," Achilles sang, his undertunes rich with derision. "That is why you remain a scout and I am a minister."

Yet I command a ship while you wear a convict's stun anklet, Nessus thought, *and that device will remain on your foreleg for as long as you are on my ship. I need only to trill the proper chords and you will topple like a tree in a storm.*

And because Louis Wu is no fool, we saved you.

"If Louis agrees," Nessus repeated, "and I am convinced the effort can be undertaken safely, we will see."

And anything Louis recovers from the Library will be delivered to Baedeker, not Achilles.

THE OUTER HATCH of a Pak air lock loomed in Louis's heads-up display, the image relayed from a camera in the nose of a remote-controlled, thruster-impelled Puppeteer probe.

The probe's usual purpose was refueling. A stepping-disc/molecular-filter stack would transfer deuterium from any convenient ocean into *Aegis'* tanks. Today, its nose cone removed, the stepping disc stripped of its filter, the probe would deliver Louis straight to the derelict's air lock. *Aegis,* with its impenetrable GP hull, held station just ahead of the Pak derelict to block the sleet of relativistic interstellar muck.

Aegis would jump to hyperspace if anything unexpected happened. Louis could not expect Puppeteers to wait long for Louis to step back. If Achilles was at the helm, not at all.

"Ready, Louis?" Nessus asked.

Louis rechecked his spacesuit's readouts. "Yes." *Ready as I'm going to be.*

Nessus and Achilles had argued about whether to attempt a boarding. At least Louis inferred an argument, the conversation sounding to him like hopped-up squirrels shut in a grand piano. Voice had said he was not allowed to translate.

Nessus had left the decision up to Louis. Boarding might activate the ramscoop field or other, unknown, defenses. That the deuterium tanks on the derelict had run dry was pure speculation.

Unless someone recovered whatever part of the Library that ship carried, ten men and women would have died in vain.

Flashlight-laser in hand, its aperture narrowed to a lethally thin ray, Louis stepped from a cargo hold on *Aegis* to the probe—and into zero gravity. His boot magnets snapped to the probe fuselage.

No ramscoop field—yet. He would have been in agony, the magnetic field inducing massive electrical currents, in full-body spasm. He detached the stepping disc and stowed it in the sling across his back.

Even up close, the hull, aside from a few slightly discolored patches, seemed unmarred by *Argo*'s lasers. It wasn't GP hull material, so what the tanj was the ship made of?

The air-lock controls were intuitive enough. Laser in hand, Louis said, "I'm going aboard."

"Acknowledged," Nessus said.

The air lock cycled and Louis saw a few dim lights inside. His suit sensors reported atmosphere. No artificial gravity. Batteries or fuel cells for emergency circuits, he told himself. Too little power for gravity or the ramscoop field. His skin crawled.

Bodies floated everywhere. The Pak were short, their proportions and enlarged joints making them caricatures of the human form. Most wore only vests covered in pockets. Their leathery skins were blotchy with radiation lesions and the mottling of decay. Putrefaction looked well advanced. Sealed in his suit Louis could smell nothing, but his gorge rose in his throat.

The New Terrans in their spacesuits were contorted, frozen in their final convulsions. Two looked like they might have snapped their own backs. One floated on her back, limbs askew, a red-brown film coating the inside of her visor. One glance inside at death's rictus and Louis shuddered.

"Everyone is dead," he said to break the eerie silence.

"As expected," Achilles replied. "Are the computers intact?"

Computers were why Achilles was there—and why these men and women died. Capture a Library ship and, it stood to reason, you captured much of the Library. Computerized knowledge was compact—the hundreds of ships would be for mutual protection, not cargo capacity.

"A minute," Louis said. A minute of silence to honor *your* crew, slaughtered on *your* watch. He turned slowly, taking everything in with his helmet-mounted camera. "I'll ask again. Should I send back the bodies?"

"Funerals are not a New Terran custom," Nessus said. "To judge by these images, returning the dead would bring no one comfort."

A few deep breaths steadied Louis's nerves. "I'll look for computers." He circled the air-lock-level deck, the thud of his boots and his too-fast breathing the only sounds. He saw nothing promising. It all looked—alien. Few objects exhibited a clear purpose. Or maybe they had too many purposes, multiuse items sharing common components. Here and there he found open cabinets, circuits and modules floating at the ends of spidery cable bundles.

Placards with squiggles labeled the hatches, but he could not read them. By trial and error he found a stairwell. "I'll check another deck."

He kept searching, wondering if he would recognize an alien computer—and what would trigger a booby trap. The salient fact about Pak was that they were *smart*. Smarter, by far, than human. Could he anticipate their thinking?

With each hatch Louis approached, his nerves grew tauter. The trap that killed the New Terrans had not triggered immediately. Maybe opening *this* door would rearm the trap.

Why hadn't the ramscoop field come on the moment Achilles' crew boarded? Why wait?

The Pak who set the trap might have hoped other Librarians would recover this ship. If so, the trap would have to decide whether boarders were Pak. Louis chewed on that theory as he kept searching. Humans and Pak were distant cousins and the humans wore spacesuits. Maybe the recognition logic had been fooled for a while.

Maybe. But no one could mistake a General Products #4 hull for a Pak ramscoop. No, the ramscoop trap was intended to strike after invaders came aboard. No matter how thoroughly an attacker's ship was destroyed—and *Argo* had been reduced to a useless hulk—the ramscoop-field trap would capture useful data in the form of dead boarders and their gear.

"Do you recognize any computers yet?" Achilles asked impatiently.

No. Do you? Louis kept the sarcasm to himself. "Not yet."

"What about weapons?" Achilles persisted.

Because this was all about weapons, something to use against the Gw'oth. If they didn't find Pak computers, maybe useful technology would be lying around already weaponized. "No," Louis answered again. He walked slowly, studying racks of exotic equipment, to a soft *thump* whenever a boot magnet snapped to the deck.

Working aft, he had reached the engine room. The massive magnetic coils could not be part of anything else. He had yet to see anything that looked like a computer.

Something tickled the back of his mind.

"Louis, finish your sweep of the derelict so we can leave," Nessus said.

How tempting that was! Louis could declare himself done, set his stepping disc on the deck, and reboard *Aegis* in an instant. Still, he hated to admit failure. "Soon, Nessus," he equivocated.

Computers could be tiny, and storage exceedingly dense. The Pak computers might be anywhere, in any of the unrecognizable gear around the ship. How would he know?

Because in any library, there are lots and *lots* of files.

Louis stomped forward a deck, his boot steps echoing in the stairwell. He opened a hatch to an equipment closet and stood staring at the photonics racks within. "I think I've seen this same physical configuration again and again. Can anyone confirm?"

"Perhaps," Achilles and Nessus said, almost in unison.

Anyone solicited Voice, too, to offer an opinion. Louis's suspicions about Puppeteer attitudes toward AI had been correct. Nessus had directed Louis not to mention Voice.

"Confirmed," Voice said on a private channel. "So far you have passed eighty-seven racks of that exact physical layout. No other configuration is nearly as common."

"This must be it." Louis took the stepping disc from its sling. He set it on the floor and it floated off.

The racks ran floor to ceiling, and he could not jam the stepping disc beneath. "Tanj! The frame uprights look fused in place."

"Cut out a rack," Achilles ordered.

The oxyacetylene torch in Louis's tool pouch might work—or chopping at the ship might trigger an intruder response. Louis had no better suggestion. "Can you pull me out remotely?"

"If you are on the disc, yes," Nessus said.

With his left boot clinging to the deck Louis pinned the stepping disc with his right boot. The disc itself adhered to neither the deck nor his boot. Carefully he shifted his left boot onto the disc—and started drifting. The boot magnets were too weak to grip through the disc.

He used emergency suit patches to fasten the disc to the deck and his boots to the disc. "Watch my helmet camera. If I move suddenly, pull me out."

He tried to ignore how contorted the corpses had been, how pain-crazed their faces. If the ramscoop field activated, would sticky patches hold despite his own spasms?

He lit the oxyacetylene torch. Directly beneath the blue-hot flame, a spot glowed on an upright. There was no smoke, no scorching, no hint of melting. He applied the flame to the ceiling and deck with the same lack of effect.

With a sigh, Louis extinguished the torch. Decks, bulkheads, the equipment frames: they were probably made from the same impervious stuff as the hull.

"It must be *twing*," Achilles said. "A programmable Pak structural material. There will be handheld tools to soften it. Search the engine room."

"What do these tools look like?" Louis asked.

"I don't know." Achilles sounded pained by the admission. "I had that information aboard *Argo,* but the computers, like everything else, were destroyed."

"Do not comment," Voice said. "Nessus has not told Achilles we have the same files from Sigmund."

On Louis's heads-up display a small hand tool shimmered. He said, "I'll see what I can find." He peeled the patches from his boots and tromped off. In the engine room he quickly spotted a tool that matched the image still on his HUD but took other items to avoid suspicions.

Then Louis experimented. The proper tool, with its one dial turned all the way up, its handgrip tightly squeezed, sliced an interior bulkhead. In minutes he had detached a rack of suspected computer gear. He floated it above the stepping disc—and pictured it crashing to the deck on *Aegis.* "Turn the cabin gravity way down wherever you're going to want this."

"Done," Nessus said. "Ready to receive."

It took Louis eight hours to cut loose all the suspected computer racks, or memory banks, or whatever they were, and teleport them, one by one, to *Aegis.*

Finally the last rack was delivered. Louis stepped through, bone weary, right after. He intended never again to set foot aboard that death ship.

14

It would be best not to abandon an intact General Products hull for the Pak to reverse-engineer. On that much Achilles and Nessus agreed. But could they destroy it? That was the core of the matter, and the bridge echoed with their disagreement.

The impudence of the scruffy scout enraged Achilles. *He* was Minister of Science!

Achilles knew several ways to destroy General Products hulls—all closely held secrets. Simplest was antimatter, if you could find enough. They had none.

Without antimatter, you needed subtlety.

At its most basic, a General Products hull was a single, nanotech-built supermolecule. An embedded fusion power plant massively reinforced the supermolecule's interatomic bonds. At very close range, and with extremely good aim, you could overheat the power plant with a high-power laser. Or, if you knew the details of the embedded software, a laser could reprogram the photonic microprocessor that controlled the power plant—right through an intact hull.

When these vulnerabilities surfaced, General Products had enhanced its designs. Antimatter remained a threat, for basic physics could not be denied, but the other hazards had been vanquished. In late-model products, thousands of heat pipes fanned out from the embedded power plant. Using the entire hull to disperse energy made overheating the power plant all but impossible. The extensively rewritten controller program resisted alteration. Finally, alternating layers of waveguides and mirrors encapsulated the power plant, to deflect and divert even the attempt to access the embedded controller.

Achilles had had *Argo* built in a brand-new hull. Nessus, whether from sentiment or laziness, kept flying *Aegis* long after its hidden vulnerabilities became known. He was a fool.

If Achilles had been as careless, almost surely Pak lasers would have destroyed his hull during that endless instant he had spent frozen in stasis. He would *still* be in stasis, eternally adrift in the interstellar void. . . .

"There is another way," Nessus insisted. "The Gw'oth way."

Baedeker, not yet Hindmost, not yet even in politics, had had the opportunity to end the Gw'oth menace before it began. Instead he allowed the Gw'oth aboard his ship to learn the secrets of hyperdrive. In secret the Gw'oth built a hyperdrive shunt inside their habitat module. When they activated their shunt, the protective normal-space bubble carried off Baedeker's own shunt—and with it the middle of his General Products hull.

"The Gw'oth split a hull," Achilles rebutted. "The end of the hull containing the power plant remained intact. The loss is the same whether the Pak find a reinforced piece or a reinforced whole."

Nessus looked himself in the eyes. "So we carry off the hulk's power plant."

That was—madness. "Holding *Argo*'s severed power plant against our hull is like toying with a hydrogen bomb. If the power plant destabilizes, the shock wave will atomize us."

"The Hindmost says the power plant will not destabilize."

Baedeker was a fool, and Nessus a bigger fool for listening. "Then I must speak with him."

Baedeker *and* Nike joined the hyperwave consultation. They were rivals of Achilles, and of one another, for the hearts of the Experimentalist Party. Apparently they had united for the moment against him.

Radio waves creeping between Hearth and the edge of the Fleet's gravitational singularity added two minutes' delay each way. While they exchanged civilities, Achilles studied his adversaries.

Baedeker was burly. He wore his mane tightly woven in characterless braids, its array of precious stones extensive but mundane. His mane, naturally a pale yellow-brown, had been dyed a rich gold. It clashed with his sash of office.

The coiffure, like its wearer, was unfit for a Hindmost.

Nike was petite, his pale tan hide without spots or other markings. His tawny mane sparkled with gemstones and filigreed gold chains, but no more brightly than his eyes shone with ambition.

He resembled the Hindmost he once had been—and schemed to be again.

"You asked for a consultation," Baedeker began.

"Thank you, Hindmost." Using the title galled Achilles. Nike had waived such formalities among ministers and scouts. Not Baedeker. "I question using the so-called Gw'oth method to destroy what remains of *Argo.*"

"A decoupled hull power plant *will* shut down," Baedeker insisted. Undertunes and subtleties of posture reminded that he had once been a senior engineer at General Products.

"Really?" Achilles warbled skeptically. "Has someone tested extracting a power plant using a hyperdrive jump? How many times?"

The gibe drew silence. Emboldened, Achilles continued. "If you are mistaken, we will lose everything we might have learned from the Library."

Nike leaned toward the camera. "You mean: we will lose *you*."

"Are we humans, to embrace danger?" Achilles sneered.

His voices dripping with sarcastic harmonics, Nike sang, "Those crazy enough to leave Hearth must be crazy enough to protect it."

"Achilles was only vulnerable when he presented his heel," Nessus added. "Where did I hear that?"

"Enough!" Baedeker spread his hooves, straightening his necks assertively to glower down on the camera. "Questing for secrets of the Library was never Concordance policy. That you made the attempt, Achilles, will be addressed when you get back. And lest there be any question, Nessus remains hindmost aboard *Aegis.*"

Take orders from *Nessus*? Achilles trembled with fury but said nothing.

Baedeker went on. "Our objective remains to avoid provoking the Pak. Nessus, you must destroy *Argo*. Nothing can connect the lost Pak ship with the Concordance."

"And if the attempt to destroy *Argo* also destroys this ship?" Achilles chanted. If *Aegis* sails forever through hyperspace, its crew bloodstains on the walls? He resisted the need to paw at the deck. There was nowhere to run.

Baedeker and Nessus exchanged meaningful glances. "If that happens," the Hindmost sang, "we will honor your sacrifices."

. . .

FROM TWO DECKS away Louis heard without understanding another acrimonious round between Nessus and Achilles. They sounded like orchestras tuning up, and whistling teakettles, and cats on whose tails someone kept stomping. Argument that heated had to involve unpalatable choices. Then, if Louis's ears could be trusted, at least two more Puppeteers weighed in: a hyperwave consultation.

He synthed a meal while waiting for the dispute to end. Eating slowly, he finished still waiting. He synthed some brandy.

He got out his notepad and began sketching nothing in particular. But every drawing he started turned into some horror from aboard the Pak ship. Someday, maybe, he could exorcise a few demons this way. It was too soon and he ripped those pages from the book.

"Louis," Nessus finally called over the intercom, "please join me on the bridge."

Louis dumped plate, drink bulbs, and utensils into the recycler. He found Nessus alone on the bridge. Achilles must have lost this round.

"Ah, Louis. I require your services as copilot."

"Of course." Louis took his seat. "Will Achilles be sharing piloting duties with us?"

Frostily: "No."

"To Hearth, then?"

"Not just yet. We have cleanup to do first."

Not a characterization to which Achilles would have taken kindly. Louis supposed that was the source of the quarrel. "The Pak derelict?" he guessed.

"Yes. Lest clues remain of Citizen involvement, Achilles had planned to detonate a second nuclear device aboard the Pak ship. He lost the bomb, like everything else on *Argo.*"

"I don't suppose this ship carries a nuke."

For an instant, Nessus looked himself in the eyes. "Only in a manner of speaking."

Louis considered. "Ah, the fusion drive."

"Correct. While you hold the drive flame on the wreck, I will keep my mouths to the hyperdrive controls."

Ready to jump at the first inkling of danger. "And Achilles disapproved of that plan?"

Another look-himself-in-the-eyes moment. (An ironic laugh, Louis decided the gesture signified.) "No," Nessus said, "he and I found something more . . . fundamental about which to disagree."

No need to worry about that, Louis decided, until he survived this escapade. "While the main drive fires, our aft sensors will be blind. I'll need a probe with remote sensors. Ideally something expendable."

Expendable made Nessus twitch. Still, he lipped and tongued his console and two holograms opened. The first holo was a computer graphic showing *Aegis,* the Pak wreck, and a streaking dot to represent a newly launched probe. The second image showed the view from the probe itself.

Nessus said, "I have launched a short-range probe and linked it to your left joystick."

Louis positioned the robot craft for a side view of the derelict, then returned his left hand to the propulsion controls. With thrusters, he nudged *Aegis* to within a hundred meters of the derelict and aimed the ship's main drive straight at his target. "Ready when you are."

With mouths muffled by their grips on hyperdrive controls, Nessus said, "Proceed."

White-hot fusion flame spewed from *Aegis'* stern. The plasma, splashing and searing, engulfed the Pak vessel. Bow thrusters strained to offset the force of the main drive. *Aegis* bucked and thrummed with the contending energies. The Pak ship drifted under the pounding of the plasma stream.

Louis's hands danced. He balanced forward and reverse thrusts, maintaining the slight separation between ships. He fine-tuned his aim with attitude thrusters. Cabin gravity and inertial dampeners masked all but the occasional faint quaver.

It was like riding the whirlwind or surfing a tidal wave. Louis laughed in exhilaration—and again at Nessus' startled, one-eyed glance.

Not even *twing* could long absorb such vast energies. The hull began to glow a dull red. Fire must rage within, all-consuming. The hull waxed a brighter red, then turned orange, then, with the first hints of yellow—

The derelict split like overripe fruit. Glowing gases—the final remains of bodies, supplies, equipment, everything—sprayed out.

And faster than Louis could say "go," his external displays went blank. They were in hyperspace.

As quickly they returned. "Head for *Argo,*" Nessus ordered.

"And once we're there?" Louis wondered aloud. He didn't think a fusion drive could scratch a GP hull, let alone destroy it.

"Then," Nessus said, "things become interesting."

.   .   .

USING ATTITUDE THRUSTERS in short, gentle pulses, Louis positioned *Aegis*. Radar echoes marked the remains of *Argo*. He matched his course to the hulk's stately tumble, then edged closer.

Aegis had been built in a General Products #2 hull, a slender cylinder about one hundred meters in length. *Argo*, with its GP #4 hull, was a sphere more than three hundred meters in diameter.

"Steady," Louis muttered to himself. "Steady." With glacial slowness, *Aegis* crept into the gap once sealed by cargo-bay hatches. The opening was a tight fit. Like stuffing the pit back inside an olive, he thought inanely.

Radar also showed flotsam adrift inside. As he brought *Aegis* to a halt at the center of the vast, empty cavern, something clanged against the hull and bounced off.

"Piece of cake," Louis lied. "Your turn."

Nessus sat astraddle the Y-shaped pilot's couch. He began systematically scanning *Argo*'s interior with a comm laser, a ghostly green dot tracing closely spaced, parallel arcs around the ship. Despite interstellar darkness, it took image enhancement to detect the laser beam's faint reflection from the transparent GP hull.

"What are we looking for?" Louis asked.

"Your aiming point."

Another tanj Puppeteer secret, then. Like why shining light through the transparent hull served any useful purpose.

The faint green dot returned to where scanning had begun and the survey repeated. Partway through a third iteration, the sweep stopped. As the green dot expanded into a small, even fainter circle, Louis sensed a shimmer. Something *within* the hull wall.

"There." Nessus lifted one head from his console. Straightening that neck he pointed at the ethereal circle. "Take up position with our bow pressed firmly to that spot."

"How precise do we need to be?" Louis asked.

Nessus plucked at his mane. "Very."

The AI aboard remained a secret from their sullen guest. For now, Achilles sulked in his cabin; he would not necessarily remain there.

"Voice," Louis tapped into a console comp, "watch this."

Louis dragged a copy of the dim visible-light image over the radar image. He inserted a fingertip into the composite holo to mark reference points— scraps of deck still clinging, here and there, to the hull—and finally to Nessus' mysterious green spot.

Hands back on the console, Louis typed. "Can you guide me to the laser-designated target?"

"Yes," flashed on the screen. The display blanked, clearing question and answer.

To the all-but-subliminal accompaniment of Voice's flashed course corrections, Louis nudged *Aegis* forward. There was a thump as hulls collided, inertial dampeners absorbing the impact.

"We bounced," Voice flashed.

It took four tries, but finally Louis hit the target dead on, with just the right momentum and gentle thruster pressure. *Aegis* clung like a remora to a shark—only attached from the inside.

Louis glanced across the bridge. "Whatever you need to do, do it quick."

Nessus seemed even more manically wild-eyed than usual. His mouths clutched the hyperdrive controls!

On Louis's console every instrument blanked out—except one. The mass pointer flared to life, blue lines radiating from its center to show nearby stars. As abruptly they dropped to normal space. A few seconds later, radar picked up a debris field. *Argo* had broken apart!

Louis knew it was useless to ask why.

Something clattered off *Aegis'* hull and Nessus flinched. "We are still here," Nessus said, his voice giddy with relief. "Once again, Achilles was mistaken."

15

Louis tossed and turned, afloat between the plates of his cabin's sleeper field. He had too much pent-up energy, and too much on his mind, to sleep. The tension between the two Puppeteers was palpable, and Louis did not relish the long trip to Hearth.

As he reached for the touchpoint to collapse the sleeper field, his doorbell chimed.

He did not *have* a doorbell.

If Louis had had eyes and ears in his hands, he would not knock, either. A Puppeteer could easily imitate a doorbell chime. "Who is it?"

"Nessus," came the soft answer. "May I enter?"

A second surprise. Nessus had never visited Louis in his cabin. "A moment." Louis dressed hurriedly, even while doubting Nessus would care about human nudity, and unlatched the hatch. "Please come in."

Nessus quick-stepped through the doorway. He backed into a corner and, twitchier than usual, closed the hatch behind him. "We must speak."

Louis said, "You first."

Nessus pawed once, nervously, at the deck. "I have instructions for you, Louis, matters you are not to discuss while Achilles remains aboard."

Had the Puppeteer had a onetime lapse in his Interworld skills? "While Achilles is around."

"No!" Nessus fixed Louis with a two-headed stare. "As long as he is on *Aegis*. Achilles is a highly skilled technologist and I am not. Some of our supplies or seemingly innocuous shipboard devices might be altered to serve him as sensors. We might fail to notice."

"Bugs," Louis translated. "Cameras and listening devices."

"Exactly."

"I see." Louis leaned back against a wall, frowning, thinking it through. "So you gamble in telling me this now."

Nessus looked himself in the eyes. "I gamble that bugging a human was not his priority. That, and that not even Achilles can easily bypass the biometric hatch lock I have activated for your cabin. The sensor pad outside your door is presently in setup mode. Press your hand to the pad to complete its initialization. Within your cabin, at least, you will have privacy."

From Achilles, perhaps. How many sensors had Nessus planted? He could have enabled the lock long ago. Louis asked, "What are my instructions?"

"To begin, no interaction with Voice outside this cabin."

"I don't understand."

"All of us, in our own ways, pick and choose among rules. It would be impractical to testify against Achilles if my own . . . shortcuts . . . became known."

Shortcuts like an illicit AI. Nessus had just volunteered that he could be coerced! He needed Louis's cooperation, obviously. But was this revelation a token of trust, a sign of desperation, or a subtle reminder that Louis was expendable?

The one certainty was that Nessus revealed nothing without premeditation.

"What else, Nessus?"

"Codes for you to memorize." Nessus plucked at his mane. "I take another shortcut."

"What sort of codes?"

"Galactic coordinates and control sequences for emergency communications. Clandestine Directorate maintains its own network. If something should happen to me"—with one mouth, Nessus twisted and gnawed on a tress deep within his mane—"use them."

"And don't reveal them to Achilles."

For a moment, Nessus stopped tugging at his mane. "If something happened to me, who but Achilles would be responsible?"

Finagle, Nessus was *serious* about this. Louis held out his pocket comp, activating the unit with his voice- and thumbprints. "Go on. What are the codes?"

Nessus dictated long strings of digits and still insisted Louis memorize the information. He already had a head full of transfer-booth addresses, totally useless information. This data was no harder to memorize.

And, hopefully, equally useless.

After Louis correctly recited the codes enough times, Nessus went on.

"Next, no discussion with Achilles of our mission or how we happened to find him. For your own safety, Louis, you have never heard of Sigmund Ausfaller, Beowulf Shaeffer, New Terra, or the Gw'oth. And you are unaware of any nonstandard autodoc we might carry, for Baedeker believes it embodies advanced nanotechnology that could be misused. If Carlos Wu should be mentioned, Wu is an exceedingly common human name and Carlos Wu means nothing to you."

"I suppose I won't be discussing those subjects with you, either."

"Not while Achilles is on this ship. Not until engineers I trust have scoured it for sensors."

That did not leave many topics. "Tell me this, Nessus. I can understand Citizens taking human names to interact with us, for yourselves and your ships. But why mythological names?"

"You will not be offended?" Long pause. "Humanity's enduring myths speak essential truths about you. We find them fascinating."

"And the name you picked must speak an essential truth about you."

Nessus plucked at his mane and said nothing.

Nessus definitely sounded mythological, but it was too obscure for Louis. Maybe Voice would know, if he would admit to it. On the other hand . . .

Achilles. The legendary warrior favored of the gods, all but invulnerable. The loner who sulked in his tent to protest his share of Trojan booty. *Argo* was little better. It was the sailing ship aboard which Jason and a band of adventurers sought to plunder the Golden Fleece.

"What do our shipmate's choices say about *him*?" Louis marveled.

Nessus put a mouth to the door latch. "If ever you find yourself in doubt whether to share information with Achilles, remember your own question."

LOUIS RACED AROUND *AEGIS.* He circled decks. He ran from bow to stern and back again, scaling and descending stairways three steps at a go. When mere speed palled, he flung himself to the deck to do push-ups, then jumped up and ran some more. He tumbled and shadowboxed and chinned himself from handholds recessed into the ceiling. Then he started over.

The flight to Hearth would be a long one.

It already was.

Nessus and Achilles could not share a room without arguing. That they *did* argue was plain, even though, not speaking Puppeteer, Louis could only guess about what they disputed.

Still, setting aside musical embellishments, Louis knew scattered words from his studies. Gw'o and Gw'oth were not Puppeteer terms. Neither was Jm'ho, the Gw'oth home world, nor Tn'ho, the leading city-state, nor the Tn'Tn'ho, its monarch.

So some quarreling was about policy toward the Gw'oth. Nessus had admitted to such differences even before Achilles set hoof aboard.

Only now it meant more to Louis. Now he knew *two* Puppeteers, and he could compare.

There were similarities, of course. Nessus and Achilles shared the well-known caution of their kind, carefully skirting door frames and furniture. They had many mannerisms in common. Virtual companions in the digital wallpaper accompanied both along the ship's corridors, and pungent scent wafted from the air vents wherever they trod. That they were here at all, far from Hearth and herd, marked both as—Nessus' term, not Louis's—insane.

And yet the longer Louis shared the ship with them, the more different the Puppeteers seemed.

Nessus discussed; Achilles decreed. Nessus fretted before sending Louis into danger; if Achilles felt remorse for his lost crew, he had yet to show it. Nessus came across, somehow, as a bit daunted by his responsibilities. Achilles was smug about his authority and insistent about his prerogatives.

Louis stopped shadowboxing to resume his dash about *Aegis*. Other than consult with Voice in his cabin, exercise was one of Louis's few outlets.

Any more time in that tiny room would make Louis scream.

Not to mention that what little Voice would reveal about New Terra also made Louis want to scream.

New Terra, until recently, was a world of slaves. That had to be why Nessus erased Louis's ability to find Known Space. Louis could not show the New Terrans the path home.

(But Ausfaller was from Earth! Did Nessus trust *Ausfaller* not to show the way? Or had Ausfaller, too, had his memories altered? It pained Louis to suspect he and the ARM had anything in common.)

And that was why Louis's memories would be purged again before he went home, lest he lead an expedition to New Terra and the Fleet. Beings far braver than Puppeteers would fear humanity's retribution if the Puppeteers' crimes were to become known.

Raiding Pak ships. Consorting with Puppeteers. Whole human worlds unsuspected. A corner of Louis's mind regretted the stories he could never tell his fathers.

Chest heaving, legs aching, Louis eased his pace to a lope. He ended his cool-down routine at the relax room, synthing a drink bulb of iced tea. He drained it and got another.

He had weeks left on this trip. He could not spend that long running, speculating, and raging inwardly at ancient injustices. Gw'oth, New Terra, and his own past were off-limits.

The Pak and their Library were not.

Suddenly ravenous, Louis ordered a five-course meal and several bulbs of wine. Imagining ways to crack open the Library would take his best efforts.

IN THE BARE CONFINES OF HIS "CABIN"—nowhere aboard this tiny ship befitted his stature as a cabinet minister—Achilles brooded.

He had much about which to brood:

—The criminal ineptness of his New Terran hirelings, and the peril into which they had carelessly plunged him.

—Baedeker and Nike conspiring against him. How convenient for them if that dangerous maneuver with *Argo* had eliminated their mutual rival.

—Nessus' insolent refusal to acknowledge Achilles' stature, or obey his orders, or even explain how *Aegis* had happened upon him.

—The daily indignity of Nessus ruling aboard this ship.

—The utter humiliation of wearing a stun anklet, as if *he* were some common criminal.

—Locked cabins and storerooms, and whatever petty secrets Nessus hid therein.

—The uncertain future of the Pak artifacts *he* had had the genius to pursue.

—The thinly veiled threats of a trial when he returned to the Fleet.

Achilles circled his tiny cabin, stomping. Nessus: *stomp!* Nike: *stomp!* Baedeker: *stomp! Stomp!*

His enemies stymied him at every turn. They had persecuted him for far too long.

Rule over an arcology had been within his bite until Nessus—a lowly neophyte scout!—had denounced him. Banished to serve as a scout himself, Achilles had distinguished himself and returned to Hearth in triumph.

But he had returned too late. *Stomp!* Nike, become Hindmost, had already surrendered New Terra to rebellious humans. *Stomp!*

If only the trampling of cushions could ease his rage.

He, Achilles, found a way to force the humans back into servitude and the Fleet—with New Terra itself promised as his reward. But when Nessus and Sigmund Ausfaller forged some unnatural alliance with the Outsiders, Nike reneged. *Stomp! Stomp!*

The New Terran government had already surrendered! When Achilles in his righteous wrath would smash his defiant subjects, Baedeker struck. Literally, *struck*: put a sharp hoof through Achilles' cranium!

He woke directly from the autodoc into a second exile, this time at hard labor on Nature Preserve One. Many years passed before he was deemed "rehabilitated"—and by then *Baedeker* had become Hindmost.

So now Baedeker imagined *he* would exile or incarcerate Achilles? Never again!

But for the vile conspiracy against him, Achilles could have been Hindmost. *Stomp!* He would have been Hindmost. *Stomp!* He deserved to be Hindmost. *Stomp! Stomp!*

His turn would come.

He had followers among the masses. And, more helpful at this juncture, he had minions throughout the government, especially at the Ministry of Science. Loyal, well-placed minions.

They would attend diligently to the orders he sprinkled in innocuous-seeming messages to ministry personnel.

16

A man-tall equipment rack, one of eighty-seven from the Pak derelict, occupied the center of a small workroom. Plasteel spars and mounting brackets held the rack firmly in place. Meters, gauges, and analyzers cluttered two workbenches. Cables and adjustable power supplies covered a third. Wall-mounted cameras continuously recorded. Copper sheets lined the walls, hatch, deck, and overhead lest emissions interfere with any of the ship's systems.

Clutching a Puppeteer transport controller, Louis admired his handiwork. A touch would rematerialize the rack in a cargo hold three decks away, for he had mounted the Pak artifact over a stepping disc. That hold was empty, its gravity turned off. Drop from hyperspace, open the hatch, and the rack would blow away. . . .

So why did he hesitate?

He had stolen this—whatever it was. He had destroyed the derelict to cover his tracks. To break into the Pak archives was not only the logical next step, this time it was his idea.

He hesitated at a memory: of a face frozen in agony, of a visor filmed with blood.

Gritting his teeth, Louis extracted a random circuit module.

Naked-eye inspection revealed nothing. Scans yielded structural details but not meaning. Replacing the module, he inspected a second component with the same lack of enlightenment. He sampled a random scattering of modules across the equipment rack, and then systematically examined the three top tiers. Every scan and measurement went into his pocket comp.

The most common components were densely packed, three-dimensional matrices. Almost certainly memory arrays. And it was read-only memory, the bits permanently encoded as atomic substitutions in otherwise pure, defect-free, crystalline-silicon lattices.

Ausfaller's prisoner had spoken of Library knowledge scribed on metal pages. Pak could bomb themselves back to a stone age—and supposedly regularly did—and the Library would survive. Of course that was before the Pak fled the core explosion. The equipment Louis had recovered seemed to offer similar permanence with greatly improved portability.

It was a start. Louis latched the workroom door behind him and called it a day.

WHAT ABOUT THE CIRCUITS that weren't memory arrays? Access circuits, Louis guessed. Or mechanisms for decompressing compacted data. Or error-correction apparatus, for not even Pak engineering could prevent cosmic rays from inducing random errors. Or security mechanisms. Or—

Why speculate? Louis went to his cabin and uploaded his findings to Voice. Voice, too, failed to deduce anything useful. Louis returned to the workroom.

Three fat stubs of insulated copper cable, their ends burnished like mirrors, protruded from the bottom of the rack. The remainder of the cables had been lopped off during the stepping-disc transfer between the Pak ship and *Aegis*. To Louis the wiring looked like a power hookup. Wearing an insulated glove, he unplugged the cable stubs. The copper terminals beneath looked suitable for connecting power.

"Time for the smoke test," he muttered, straightening his improvised cables. He had had to synth alligator clips for quick disconnects. Nothing in *Aegis'* parts bins had sharp teeth.

He ran cables from the rack to one of his power supplies.

According to Nessus, Citizens had an adage: nothing ventured, nothing lost. Louis thought of that as he made the final connection.

No smoke.

Better yet, no pain. Louis released the breath he had not known he was holding.

LEDs now glowed in the rack. On his power supply, a virtual needle jittered about a simulated dial before settling at a modest output level. His RF receiver showed a new low-energy carrier signal.

The Pak equipment was ready to talk.

·　·　·

HEADS CRANING, Nessus circled the test setup in Louis's workroom. "I am impressed."

"Thanks, but there is much left to learn." Louis summarized his experimentation over the past several days.

Too often those techniques were trial and error. Nessus managed not to flinch. "You have not gotten us killed. That is commendable."

"Now watch." Louis tapped the touchpad on one of his bench instruments: a network analyzer interfaced to a human-model pocket computer.

Gibberish flooded what had been an empty display. Nessus recognized characters from Interworld, but most of the symbols were unfamiliar to him. Text reached the bottom and the image began scrolling.

Louis said, "When the rack powers up, it broadcasts a short sequence of pulses. Identifying itself? Asking for a command? Whatever it is, I took it as an instance of an input/output protocol. It took some . . . effort, but now I can elicit responses. Parts of the format appear to function as an index or address. When I vary that part of the message, the rack replies with different information."

Nessus caught the hesitation. Maybe he *had* flinched. Trial and error? Madness!

"That said," Louis continued, "there is less here than meets the eye. The raw data stream from the box is clearly binary, but after that? Your guess is as good as mine.

"All data transfers have lengths in multiples of ten bits. Supposing that the Pak encode characters in ten-bit blocks, I assigned symbols to the 1024 possible values. I used Interworld characters for the most common bit patterns until I ran out. After that, the marks are computer-assigned squiggles.

"Presumably we're seeing Library data. But what does it mean? I can't say."

The workroom hatch opened and Achilles came—stomped—in. His heads swung in opposite directions, glancing about the workroom. "You cannot read it." He spoke in Interworld, adding a sprinkle of undertunes surely meaningless to Louis.

But not to Nessus. Achilles had gibed: *I* know all that happens here.

The Library might hold secrets to mitigate the situation with the Gw'oth. If so, the sooner the knowledge could be obtained the better. And Achilles, after his rogue assault on the Pak, would surely step off this ship directly into prison. He might as well do something *for* the Concordance first.

"Perhaps," Nessus said, "Louis will allow you to assist him."

Achilles raised his left foreleg. "Perhaps I will, if you first remove this ridiculous, insulting anklet. You control the ship. Where am I going to go?"

LOUIS WAS A FAIR MECHANIC: he understood what things could do. But how they did it? For that he needed help, and Voice remained, most of the time, off limits. Nessus was less technical than Louis. That left Achilles.

Achilles was brilliant.

Louis had queried at random into the Pak archive, hoping to find message formats that did *something.* He was far from a theory what any of it—query or response—meant.

Achilles pored over the responses, comparing inputs and outputs, and occasionally encountering long, identical data blocks in the responses. That was sufficient hint for him to derive the addressing scheme within the Library message format, and the representation of digits.

They had translated their first Pak binary codes.

Achilles used the newfound numeric characters to define fundamental dimensionless constants, physical parameters independent of units of measure. (A few, like the ratio of rest masses of fundamental particles, Louis understood. Most, like something Achilles called the gravitational coupling constant, Louis did not.) Achilles used those numeric values to locate what had to be discussions of specific topics in physics. Citizen knowledge of those physical constants hinted at the content of nearby Pak text. Mathematical relationships implied additional meanings. Citizen translation software, until then without a point of departure, began to contribute.

"I need more data," Achilles complained.

Louis retrieved a cargo floater and moved two more racks of Pak gear to the shielded workroom. By the time he had braced the new racks in place and supplied them with power, Achilles had already begun identifying physics terms. Even among the first scattered snippets of Pak science, things he read—and Louis usually could not—made Achilles trill.

Pak and Puppeteer science had evidently reached enough similar conclusions about the universe to constitute a Rosetta Stone of sorts. Most terms Achilles encountered many times over, for the Library saved the discoveries of all clans, across countless cycles of collapse and rediscovery.

Concepts Achilles expected to find in proximity sometimes were not. He pondered that incongruity for a while, softly chanting to himself. "Ah," he finally said. "Active links." He suggested condescendingly that Louis might be able to work out the command formats that would follow such hyperlinks.

While Louis experimented, Achilles isolated simple two-, three-, and four-dimensional data structures in the data streams. He declared them flat, holographic, and animation images. Often he was right. Labels within the images suggested a few more physics terms.

Achilles was still dealing with half-recognized, ill-defined phrases scattered across a sea of untranslated data when Louis had his *Eureka!* moment.

17

The waiting was the hardest part.

Nessus cowered, burrowed deep within a nest of soft cushions, as, in the ambiguous safety of hyperspace, *Aegis* crisscrossed the Library fleet. Again. He had come to his cabin to sleep, but sleep, as it had for days, eluded him. With one head he gulped warm carrot juice from a drink bulb; with the other he tugged and twisted at a mane already stirred beyond further disarray.

Almost as hard as the waiting was Achilles' gloating. Amid the clamoring by his faction for new Experimentalist Party leadership, keeping Achilles far from Hearth became the lesser evil. To the Hindmost, anyway. As Achilles had surely calculated when he advocated this mad scheme.

And so, as Achilles had urged, *Aegis* had reversed course. They could have been back on Hearth by now. Instead they leapt about the fringes and into the interstices of the Library fleet, siphoning knowledge.

Achilles grew more arrogant and insufferable by the day.

The extent of Achilles' influence had taken Nessus by surprise. He promised himself things would be different when he reached Hearth with the proof of Achilles' latest crimes—even as he worried political maneuvering might save Achilles yet again.

Especially if, as looked likely, Achilles returned with the knowledge of the Pak. Success had a way of excusing wrongs.

"Five minutes," Louis announced over the intercom. He was on the bridge.

"On my way." Nessus reluctantly uncurled and stood.

At the clatter of hooves, Louis glanced up from his console. "You look tired."

The twitchy drug user on Wunderland was gone, become someone on whom Nessus increasingly relied. It was hard to remember he had recruited Louis in desperation. Not every surprise was for the worse.

"I can rest on Hearth," Nessus said. And you, Louis, look as haggard as I feel.

Louis smiled. "One minute to dropout." Lips moving silently as he counted down the final seconds along with the timer, he took the hyperdrive controls, "And . . . now."

Nessus' heads swiveled frantically as an arc of instruments and displays returned to life. From readings of magnetic fields and the light of fusion exhausts: no ramscoops within two hours' flight. From the radio backdrop: no diminution of message traffic to suggest any change in behavior among nearby Pak.

"We're safe," Louis said reassuringly. He said much the same each time they emerged to normal space. "We're still stealthed, and even the closest Pak are too distant to see us optically."

"In theory."

"Lots of radio traffic." Louis leaned back in his couch. "Not a surprise. These Pak are librarians. Of course they keep studying and indexing their archives. Even if they weren't librarians, what else would they have to do?"

Hunt for alien intruders sniffing at their flanks, Nessus thought.

"They must be constantly accessing files and adding hyperlinks to enrich the archives," Louis went on. (Nessus had heard it all before. Beowulf Shaeffer was a talker. Like stepfather, like stepson, perhaps. More likely, amid the insanity of this mission, Louis really spoke to reassure himself.) "With archives spread across the fleet, following hyperlinks usually involves inter-ship traffic. Quite possibly none of them know at any given moment which ramscoop has the nearest copy of the file they want. They have to broadcast their requests. It's why *Argo* intercepted so much radio traffic among the ram-scoops."

That realization had turned *Aegis* around. That and spotting the potential of the hyperlinks. Both Louis's insights.

"Ready to deploy the buoy," Achilles called over the intercom.

"Acknowledged," Nessus responded.

"There it goes."

The cargo-hold hatch opened; over an external camera Nessus watched the comm-relay buoy recede.

The buoy's tumbling retreat was somehow a metaphor for the convoluted path that had brought them here.

Triggering a hyperlink requested the transfer of related data. Clicks, Louis called the download requests, the origin of the term lost in human computing history. So read through the salvaged archives, eliciting and recording the wireless download requests. Broadcast the recordings to Library ships. Siphon up the radioed responses. Use the salvaged equipment to administer the Pak comm protocols and decrypt responses.

Scan newly retrieved data for new hyperlinks and repeat.

But in the time a radioed *click* took to reach a Pak ship, that ship might spot them. As quickly as a radioed response could reach them, so might a Pak laser beam. They had Achilles' experience to prove Pak lasers could outwit or overpower General Products' solar-flare shields.

So: buoys.

"Buoy online," Louis announced. "Radio comm tests . . . all pass. Hyperwave comm tests . . . all pass. Onboard computer tests . . . all pass. Power output . . . nominal."

"Hyperwave uploads completed from . . . twelve buoys." Nessus stared at his comm panel, hoping he had miscounted and sure he had not. He hurriedly scanned the upload logs. "Buoy six reported a ramscoop on approach and self-destructed." That made three losses.

"Cargo-hold hatch secured," Achilles reported.

Louis leaned toward his flight controls. "Returning to hyperspace in three. Two. One."

The view ports became soothing pastoral scenes.

Nessus trilled in relief. Another foray among the Pak in which they had not been ambushed.

How long could their luck last?

LOUIS SQUIRMED ON the copilot's crash couch, yawning.

If he wasn't so tired, he supposed he would wonder if they were accomplishing anything. No one had the time or energy to sift the incoming data. Maybe, once they finished here, during the long trip to the Fleet of Worlds.

On Hearth, scientists were salivating for a look at the Pak Library. They, too, had to wait. The highest bit rates that hyperwave transmitters could push through at this distance, even while drawing the ship's full power, scarcely handled speech and short text messages.

Coffee and adrenaline notwithstanding, Louis could hardly keep his eyes open. He thought fleetingly of stim pills—and recoiled. He would *not* travel down that road again.

Instead, stifling another yawn, he reviewed the ship's path.

Aegis raced back and forth across the Pak fleet. Safety lay in speed, in disappearing before any of the Pak could spot them.

Success also lay in speed. Every passing moment carried the telltale gamma-ray pulse from *Argo*'s nuclear attack deeper into the Library fleet. Just as surely, the surreptitious probing of the Library revealed itself to Pak intrusion detectors. Unusual patterns of queries, Louis guessed. Whatever the reason, suspicions spread at light speed among the Pak. More and more ramscoops ignored clicks from the buoys. More and more buoys self-destructed, magnetic fuses denying hyperwave transceivers to the ramscoops swooping to investigate.

Yawning again, Louis reached for another drink bulb of coffee. Had *Aegis* not turned back when it had, the opportunity to ransack the Library would have been lost. Achilles had been correct about that.

So Louis and Nessus hyperdrive-hopped *Aegis* ahead of the warning broadcasts. In time, awareness of intruders would reach the last of the ramscoops. At that moment the expedition's ability to pull information from the Library ended.

Or earlier, if their luck ran out.

It could happen so many ways. A Pak warship changing course or speed while *Aegis* was in hyperspace. Departing hyperspace a few seconds too soon or too late. Something he lacked the imagination even to consider. . . .

Keep your mind on your work.

Nessus was a bedraggled, insomniac mess, struggling more each day to maintain manic-crazy bravery. Achilles, after living through one encounter with the Pak, seemed permanently crazy-brave. Unless, as Louis increasingly sensed, Achilles was simply crazy.

As stressful as Louis found jumping about the Pak fleet, he had his pride. He could *not* suggest retreat before a Puppeteer did.

The moment approached to emerge from hyperspace into another cluster of Library ships. "Dropping out in five minutes," Louis announced over the intercom. "Ready another buoy."

He tried not to notice the tremor in his hands.

18

Achilles passed the homeward flight first in gloating, then in boredom, then, as Nessus, churlishly, continued to deny him access to the bridge controls, in fits of rage.

He had promised himself glory—and surely he had earned it. Despite jealousy and so many enemies conspiring against him, he would have everything. He would trample all who had opposed him. He would take his revenge for past indignities.

If this interminable flight ever ended.

He counted the days. He circled his cabin and, when that grew old, paced the corridors. If his meandering took him to one specific passageway more often than to any other, he deemed that coincidence.

And yet—

Doubts gnawed at him. Others had snatched success from his jaws before. His foes would stop at nothing to cheat him again.

So how would he return to Hearth? In triumph? Or to another banishment?

Pak had warred among themselves for eons. Where better than in the Pak Library to find technologies with which to squash the Gw'oth? Who better to install behind all other Citizens than the genius, the visionary, who delivered that great prize?

And yet—

Enemies always and everywhere beset him. They would bleat like lamed calves about trivia. That he had redirected *Argo* without authorization. That he had misled authorities. They would accuse him of risking war with the Pak.

And yet—

He had loyal servants on Hearth. Powerful servants. Well-placed servants.

Either to appease those supporters or to keep him apart from them, Baedeker and Nike had bent to Achilles' will. How that must have galled them! To maintain consensus within the party councils they had had to allow *him* to go claim the Library. With that treasure he would wrest from their undeserving jaws the greatest prize of all. A new Experimentalist consensus must come. It must make *him* Hindmost.

And yet—

His foes would stop at nothing.

Then neither would he.

LOUIS SQUINTED, bleary-eyed, into a slowly scrolling excerpt from the Pak Library.

The data dump contained a bewildering assortment of text layouts; flat images, both color and monochromatic; holographic images; animations; and simulations. He had suppressed any display of the underlying raw data, for the dataset formats came in an even more dizzying variety of dimensionalities and structures. Hyperlinks in green, red, and yellow pointed to related materials known to be aboard, known *not* to be aboard, or of as-yet–indeterminate presence.

Merely to skim the surface was to know beyond doubt that the Library was *old*.

Most of the math was beyond Louis. Most graphics tantalized more than they taught. Most of the text remained without translation. The scattered translatable passages were painfully succinct and they often defied Louis.

He remembered Ausfaller's comment about terseness. Pak protectors spoke in words or short phrases; their minds filled in the blanks faster than complexity could be articulated. It seemed their written language followed the same concise pattern.

So Louis caught only glimpses of meaning—and those hints fascinated him. He forgot for shifts at a time to eat, drink, or sleep, dictating comments whenever anything made an impression on him. His annotations might make things the least bit easier for the scientists on Hearth. Or they could have a good laugh at his ridiculous speculations.

"Your diligence is commendable," Achilles said.

Louis discovered his eyes were closed, his head resting on arms folded across a cluttered workbench. He opened his eyes and sat up. "It's something to do."

Achilles walked into the workroom, hooves clicking on the deck. He wore a utilitarian belt with deep pockets rather than his customary sash of office. "The trip *is* tediously long."

"There is more than enough in the Library for two to look at."

"Indeed." Achilles looked about the room, as though wondering where to begin. He peered at the still-scrolling display beside Louis, at the benches piled high with equipment, at the three racks of Pak archive still braced in place. Necks moved sinuously as he peered into one of the racks.

"See something?" Louis asked.

"I do not know. Something that struck me as I thought back." Achilles straightened, raising a head to survey the benches. "Ah, there." He found a flashlight-laser, checked that the beam was dialed to full dispersion, and shone the light into the gap between two adjacent component tiers. He sidled around the rack, flashlight in a mouth, projecting the beam into gaps between modules and tracing bundles of fiber-optic cables. "Interesting." He went back to the top to survey more systematically.

"What is it?" Louis finally had to ask.

"Just engineering curiosity." Achilles knelt for a closer look at the deck-level tier of components. The head without the flashlight stayed high, its lone eye focusing on Louis. "The Pak designers took a fascinating approach to coupling optical fibers."

Long before Achilles finished his methodical examination, Louis lost interest and went back to his own studies. After a while he paused scrolling to admire images he had encountered of Pak space elevators. Hyperlinks, their subject matter often unintelligible, lay scattered throughout the accompanying text. Some links might have been about materials and orbital mechanics. The link about the tether itself was coded red. A pity: something strong and lightweight enough for a tether stretching to geosynch was the roadblock to building space elevators.

Louis could read the Pak numbers, though. *Twing* still awed him, and *twing* was like wattle and daub compared to the stuff of Pak space tethers. The bits of automated translation suggested the tether material even blocked neutrinos. That had to be in error.

Louis unfroze his display to resume skimming. A label he clearly misunderstood hyperlinked him into material about energy generation. Fission, maybe. Something about dampening fields? It made no sense to him. He retraced his steps and went on skimming.

A creepy, two-throated yawn right in Louis's ear.

Louis blinked and turned around. "I guess you finished inspecting the equipment."

"Yes. It is less interesting than what you are studying." Another double yawn. "Perhaps I will not stay too much longer. Before returning to my cabin, I think I will try to learn a bit more about *twing*."

Louis nodded and resumed skimming. He noticed Achilles open display windows across the workroom. He did not notice when Achilles left.

The next day, hunting for a multimeter probe that had fallen behind a workbench, Louis wondered where he had left his flashlight.

NERVES FRAYED. Tempers flared. Minds recoiled from the less-than-nothingness just outside the hull. For everyone's sanity, drops to normal space came more frequently.

The closer they came to Hearth, the more messages Achilles found queued for him on hyperspace relay buoys.

Grumbling mightily, Achilles labored over ministry reports and requests. He sent responses via the same relays. After several iterations, Nessus agreed to schedule daily quick drops to normal space.

And (it amused Achilles) so Nessus sealed his own doom.

"NORMAL SPACE IN FIVE MINUTES," Nessus called over the intercom.

"Acknowledged," Achilles said. The improvised sensor readouts in his cabin showed Nessus was on the bridge and Louis was in the engine room. All very normal for one of *Aegis'* daily check-ins.

In the privacy of his cabin, Achilles had put on a pressure suit. He had one helmet already sealed. Now he sealed his second helmet. He reviewed the suit's gauges and indicators. All systems nominal. All tanks and expendable supplies were maxed. He ran the self-test programs. All tests passed. He checked and rechecked his cache of supplies: radio beacons, fuel cells, medical-emergency stasis generators. The time until rescue would pass in an instant.

"Two minutes," Nessus called.

Achilles' hearts pounded. Just two more minutes!

His loyal servants waited for *Aegis* to emerge from hyperspace, the time and place finalized in innocuous code words within the stream of ministry business. The ministry had many ships. . . .

He—with the Library—would return in triumph to Hearth. None would presume to oppose him. He would be Hindmost, master of everything he deserved.

"One minute to dropout."

And his enemies would pay for their insolence. The Gw'oth would be put in their place.

Achilles took a pocket computer from his desk. The crucial command had already been lipped into the touchpad. When the moment came, he had only to squeeze. . . .

"Three. Two. One. Now."

The cabin wallpaper switched from rolling meadow to starscape. Achilles bit down on the touchpad.

Nothing happened!

He pressed again. Nothing. He set the computer on the desk and rechecked the command sequence: perfect.

A loose connection, perhaps. Stuffing the computer in an outside pocket, Achilles rushed from his cabin.

"DID YOU LOSE SOMETHING?" Nessus intoned coldly.

Achilles had put on a pressure suit. His heads probed deep within a utility space that gave access to the hull. Shuddering, he backed up and turned. He winced when he saw what Nessus held in his mouth. "Where did you get that?"

With his free head, Nessus gestured toward the open access panel, to where a glob of putty clung to the hull. "I got it where you left it. Where *my* surveillance equipment recorded you installing it."

Achilles lunged.

Nessus snatched back what he held: a pocket computer wired to a flashlight-laser. Laser case and computer were mottled with the putty from which he had extracted them. He flung the death trap behind him, sent it skittering down the corridor. The melodies of his outrage required two mouths.

"You are sickly clever," Nessus sang, harmonics ringing with disgust. "*Aegis* is an old ship, and you know its vulnerability. So deactivate the embedded power plant and let air pressure blow the unreinforced hull to dust. You 'somehow' manage to get into your pressure suit in time. Your supporters collect you from the wreckage, and the ship's computers, and the lore of the Pak, and—oh, how sad—also the twisted, vacuum-bloated bodies of your shipmates.

"I do not much understand technology, Achilles, but I understand *you*. Killing me would not satisfy you. Ousting Baedeker would not satisfy you. But if Louis and I die because this hull fails? Then you could blame some imaginary delayed effect from how we destroyed *Argo*. You would take me from Baedeker and blame *him* for the 'accident.' Sick."

Nessus gestured again at the access panel. "The shutdown sequence must be coupled into the hull here at the power-plant controller. If I truly understood the twisted nature of your thinking, you would come *here* to set your trap. And so you did."

Achilles' eyes darted like a trapped animal's. "Yes!" he raged. "And you all deserve whatever—"

"Stand back." Louis, holding a stunner, emerged from around a bend in the corridor. Likely he understood none of what had been said. Tones of voice had summoned him. "Against the wall."

Achilles sidled backward.

"Politics? Extenuating circumstances? Past traumas?" Nessus summoned into his voices all the disdain he felt. "Throughout your career much has been rationalized. Even Baedeker excuses your excesses, so shamed is he by the violence you forced him into.

"But no longer, Achilles. No longer. Nothing can justify cold-blooded, premeditated murder." Merely to sing those chords made Nessus ill. The herd protected, it did not prey on its own. "You have gone too far. Too far! Your friends will shun you. Your opponents will revile you. You *will* be punished."

Nessus added in Interworld, "Louis. As we discussed."

Achilles pushed off the wall and spun on his front legs. As he lashed out with his strong hind leg, the stunner crackled. He toppled, his body rigid, still wild-eyed, at Nessus' hooves.

Nessus looked downward with repugnance. "You will return to Hearth in stasis. Hope that the herd has mercy on you."

COLD WAR

19

Storms raged across the perpetually shrouded skies of Kl'mo. Lightning flashed and thunder boomed. Gales lashed oceans and continents alike. Unending rain pummeled the barren land, patiently breaking rock into dust. In millions of years, perhaps, something would take root in that soil.

Far beneath the chaos, hugging a zigzag of hydrothermal vents, tranquil, extended the watery domain of the Gw'oth colony.

The trek to settle this new world had been long and arduous. Sr'o would be content never to leave the watery depths again. But what were the chances?

She hoisted a rock half as long as her tubacle. The serenity, she thought, was some sort of metaphor. She did not entirely understand metaphors or, for that matter, the humans who used them. Before the migration, fleetingly, she had met a few humans: traders from New Terra. She had never seen a Puppeteer or, thankfully, a Pak. She knew *of* the aliens of course, from Ol't'ro's memories—

The Gw'otesht, many in one, survived all, remembered all.

A guard scuttled up to take the rock from Sr'o. "Permit me, Your Wisdom."

She hated being called that, least of all here in the new world, but to chastise the guard would only reemphasize her status. The change from a tradition-based society to a science-based one was already revolutionary; too many colonists could not at the same time overcome the habits of life in a dynastic autocracy. Perhaps the new generation would learn.

Presuming that the colony lasted that long.

"Thank you," Sr'o answered mildly, arching a tubacle in search of a stone small enough that her solicitous protectors might permit her to move it.

She toiled, one among a crowd, at constructing yet another small residence. The traditional stacked-stone building was not for her personal use, any more than the fives of other buildings in whose construction she had, however symbolically, contributed, for *she* lived apart in the colony's great metal stronghold. The physical labor was its own reward: a task with an end to it. A respite.

More often, when Sr'o needed physical release, she joined those working in the fields among the creepers, sponges, and sessile worms. Kl'mo's native biota thrived in the rich chemical plumes upwelling from the hydrothermal vents, but the life transported from Jm'ho—the ecosystem upon which the colonists depended for their survival—continued to struggle. Despite constant, labor-intensive interventions, the transplants grew sicklier and sicklier.

And she, although the lead biologist of the colony, had yet to discern why.

Oh, she could maintain the tiny biosphere of a ship indefinitely, or any number of the little, self-contained habitats with which the inhospitable worlds of the home system had been settled. Grafting an ecosystem into an existing ecology? That was something else entirely. And the problems kept getting worse. One of the colony's many imbalances was between small predators and Gw'oth spawn. Too many mouths, immature and voracious, to feed. . . .

Sr'o lifted and piled bits of rock, hoping at least in this small way to contribute to making the colony successful. The task busied her tubacles—but not her thoughts. Her mind remained trapped in the critical puzzle: whatever nutrients were insufficient, or too abundant, or toxic to the transplants. Isolating the exact difficulties, subtly different for each species, involved slow and painstaking research. Until they solved their problems, the colony needed nutritional supplements from Jm'ho and breeding stocks of new varieties of—well, everything—to reinvigorate the still-fragile ocean-floor ecosystem.

Your Wisdom? She hardly felt wise.

A second guard jetted over to help Sr'o. *You are too important,* his solicitousness declared. *We cannot allow you to injure yourself.*

At the unwelcome reminder of her responsibilities, the tips of her tubacles flared an anxious red. At the first hint of a mood shift the rest of her protectors swarmed, pushing aside her fellow workers. She willed herself to be calm until the chromatophoric cells along her tubacles faded to a less apprehensive yellow-green.

But the harm had been done. The colonists among whom she had toiled flattened obsequiously, and in that uncomfortable pose they sidled away. "We will work more carefully," one murmured, *his* skin quickly shading all the way into far red.

"No one did anything wrong," Sr'o answered. "Pardon my distraction."

Her apology did no good. The polite fiction of equality had been wholly shattered. Her burdens were hers, and she must learn better to bear them. She would set a few more stones into place, then leave.

She was given the time to emplace only one.

"Two ships are entering the solar system," announced the transceiver stowed deep inside one of her tubacles. "Both have radioed the expected call signs." Unstated because it was obvious, the interruption also meant: *Come. We must meld.* Even if, as Sr'o believed, the arrival was the expected supply ship and its escort, the colony had little margin for error.

As the protective squad formed up around her, Sr'o swiveled a tubacle and surveyed those with whom she had been toiling. Those who depended on her. "I must attend to other matters," she announced.

No one argued.

SR'O JETTED DEEP into the colony stronghold, tubacles trailing, guards lagging a respectful distance behind. As she approached the heart of the building, friends/colleagues/alter-egos converged from other corridors, exchanging only terse greetings. Why bother with the clumsiness of words when soon they would be a single mind?

Then she was inside the melding chamber, one among many. Ten. Twelve. Fourteen. Fifteen. Sixteen. The guards, waiting outside, sealed the chamber. The doors would only open from the inside.

Sr'o, trembling, extended the first tubacle. Lr'o took up the limb, and the eye and heat receptor within went dark. The ear within went all but deaf, sensing only the beating of two hearts.

The tubacle probing within Sr'o's own found its mark.

A jolt like the shock from an electric hunter-worm coursed through her mind. There was a flash, indescribable, and from the recesses of her mind unimaginable insights beckoned.

More! She must have more! Switching to ventral respiration, drifting, she extended her remaining tubacles. She groped all around her and felt probing in return. Limb found limb, aligned, conjoined . . .

Ganglia meshing!

Feedback building!

Heart pounding!

Electricity surging!

We will take over. The command echoed and reechoed in Sr'o's mind. Her own feeble thoughts, ephemeral and trivial, faded. . . .

Ol't'ro, the group mind, had emerged.

OL'T'RO CONSIDERED:

The cargo ship, transmitting all the appropriate call signs, with its proper escort. It carried urgently needed supplies from the home world, Jm'ho.

The hegemony of Tn'ho over the nations of Jm'ho.

The origin of that dominance: Ol't'ro's collective intelligence—and the flow of new technology it had engendered—harnessed to the ruthlessness of Tn'ho's rulers. In every generation, the Tn'Tn'ho was more cruel, more controlling, more ambitious, than his predecessor.

The awe, fear, jealousy, and disgust with which most Gw'oth viewed group minds like Ol't'ro.

The rage when Ol't'ro demanded release from their gilded cage.

Breaking free. Escaping Jm'ho in ships that Ol't'ro's own genius—and their daring among Puppeteers and humans—had made possible. Fleeing with a few trusted allies, free thinkers, from the certain and terrible enmity of cast-off masters.

A new home established far from Jm'ho. A home past the Fleet of Worlds, beyond New Terra, to complicate any attack should the refugees be discovered.

The colony's increasingly inadequate food supply. (A hint of protest, *our people are loyal,* surfaced from the unit Sr'o.)

And so, circling around to where Ol't'ro had begun: the timely arrival of aid.

The swiftness with which Tn'ho's rivals—not necessarily Ol't'ro's allies—had sent that aid. A welcome outcome, and yet . . .

Another interruption bubbled up from the depths of the gestalt. It was less than thought, more than memory. An insinuation: *I suspect.*

Er'o was four generations departed, his many-times-transcribed engrams grown faint. Only the most profound influences, the most deeply inscribed lessons, persisted so long after bodily death. Influences like the human, Sigmund Ausfaller. The lesson that paranoia was a survival trait.

But *what* did Er'o suspect?

Any direct assault on Kl'mo risked retaliation by the survivors, and it took only one ship and one survivor to forge a fearsome kinetic weapon. Impact by a ship moving at relativistic speed could kill everyone on a planet.

Yet any overt attack also risked provoking the humans and Puppeteers whom a war fleet would pass en route. And a physical assault risked killing Ol't'ro, the very source of Tn'ho's preeminence, when the goal was to reenslave them.

If the Tn'Tn'ho would have his revenge on his rebellious subjects, what might he attempt?

A second insinuation: *A reward?*

What reward might the Tn'Tn'ho lavish upon vassals willing to betray Ol't'ro and their colonists?

Think like Sigmund Ausfaller, Er'o's remnant urged.

A direct assault was imprudent and the people were loyal. But the colonists must eat. . . .

"Divert the approaching ship," Ol't'ro ordered themselves, preparing to dissolve the meld. "Impound it. Let nothing and no one disembark."

20

Stars shone diamond bright in *Aegis'* bridge display.

From heads held low over the pilot's console, the better, if need be, to escape into hyperspace, Nessus watched the slowly approaching starship. It was a big vessel, longer and far broader than *Aegis.* A General Products #3 hull.

The trills and arpeggios of the newcomer's name were lyrical, evoking bucolic companionship and gentle breezes, fetlock-high meadowplant tickling one's legs, and a cloudless sky overhead. It did not translate well to Interworld. *Contentment* must suffice for Louis.

But things more fundamental than a label were at issue. Achilles had nearly killed Nessus and Louis! The sooner they got Achilles off *Aegis,* the better.

"Twenty kilometers, Louis," Nessus called over the intercom. "Closing speed is ten kilometers per hour."

"I'm ready," Louis answered.

"This is the Concordance starship *Aegis,*" Nessus radioed.

A holo opened to reveal a familiar figure. His eyes were a deep, clear blue. He was slender, with a neatly coiffed mane. Vesta, longtime aide to Nike.

"Hello, Nessus," Vesta sang, his voices a forceful contralto. "We are ready to receive your . . . package."

"Greetings, Vesta. I did not expect to see you here." What did the appearance of Nike's protégé mean?

"The Hindmost has his prerogatives."

Nessus muted the ship-to-ship connection. "Louis?"

Louis was monitoring from a terminal in Achilles' cabin, where Voice would be translating. "Of course, I don't know Vesta. Do you trust him?"

"I know him. He has long served the Concordance."

"That's not what I asked."

How did one explain the nuances of Experimentalist politics to a human, even one as perceptive as Louis? Or the shadow of doubt cast over everyone who had passed through Scouting Academy while Achilles was hindmost of its faculty, secretly nurturing a cult of personality. Planting the seeds of future rebellion.

Was Vesta among Achilles' acolytes?

"Nessus?"

"The Hindmost trusts Vesta." Nessus had no other answer to offer, and it ignored that Baedeker had had to accept even Achilles into his cabinet. To be Hindmost bestowed neither infallibility nor unlimited power.

"I guess that will have to do," Louis said.

Nessus unmuted the ship-to-ship connection. "Vesta, we are ready, too."

"Transmit when you are ready." Vesta appended a fifteen-digit stepping-disc address.

"Proceed," Nessus directed Louis. And in a moment Achilles, still in stasis, was teleported to the waiting ship for trial on Hearth.

NESSUS SET COURSE FOR NEW TERRA, and Louis could not help noticing: the Library remained aboard *Aegis.*

Whatever the Hindmost believed, it seemed that Nessus had doubts about Vesta.

ACHILLES LAY STUNNED, crumpled onto the deck in ignominious defeat. The next moment the corridor vanished and he was in an unfamiliar room . . . he did not know where. Not anyplace he knew aboard *Aegis.*

The stunner blast still held him voiceless and immobile. Only his thoughts were free to roil, his rage to mount. After far too long, his limbs began to tingle. Breathing became less labored. "Where am I?" he wheezed.

"Safe for now, Excellency," familiar voices sang from behind. Vesta!

Achilles stood and turned, his legs trembling. Surveying the room, he saw many overstuffed cushions, a deluxe synthesizer, a desk and computer. Mouth holds in the walls and ceiling. Another ship, then. Not a hindmost's suite but a comfortable cabin.

Vesta stood with heads bowed respectfully, unable to meet Achilles' gaze. A medical-emergency stasis generator peeked from a pocket of Vesta's sash.

"Where am I?" Achilles asked again, this time with stern grace notes.

Vesta wilted further. "At Nessus' report, Baedeker ordered that a ship be sent to bring you . . . to justice, he called it."

Achilles piled cushions and settled himself. "And instead, where do we go?"

"We must return to Hearth, Excellency, as I was ordered." Vesta plucked at his mane. "We share this ship with two squads of Clandestine Directorate security personnel."

Achilles stared. "You have failed me."

"Softer, Excellency," Vesta pleaded. "Guards wait in the corridor."

Guards who must not know Vesta's true allegiance. "Does Baedeker suspect you?"

"I do not believe so. When Baedeker indicated that a senior official must . . . accompany this mission, I endeavored to complain more vociferously than other candidates." Vesta looked himself in the eyes. "He thought to spite me for resisting."

Accompany this mission. Achilles translated without difficulty: bring the criminal home in disgrace. He pictured Baedeker, the fool, the incompetent, gloating.

"You have failed me," Achilles repeated coldly.

"But the actions you have commanded are all well under way! Our progress is excellent."

How would that matter if *he* were to be banished? "Failure has its price."

Vesta cringed. "I will do better, Excellency. On Hearth, with the resources of your many followers, I will find—I will *make*—an opportunity."

21

A sterile, storm-battered continental interior was the last place Sr'o wanted to be. Far from the ocean, it was the best place to do what so urgently needed to be done.

"Suit check," she ordered, although her status-lamp array showed yellows across the board. Buoyant within her hard-shell suit, she nonetheless felt claustrophobic and clumsy. The heavy enclosure held her to the cabin deck. The water she respired carried the taint of lubricant.

She, two technicians, and two guards sidled around one another, checking fittings and external readouts. Someone's tubacle brushed her dorsal region, arching to examine her equipment from above. At every stride, craning and twisting as they performed their inspections, the water droned with the soft whines of exoskeleton motors.

Pk'o: "All yellow."

Kt'o: "All yellow."

Her bodyguards: "Yellow." "Yellow."

And finally, Sr'o herself: "All yellow. We will proceed."

The five of them clanked into the water lock. The inner hatch closed behind them. Exoskeletons held them erect as the water drained. Even afloat within her hard-shell water gear, simply to imagine the onslaught of gravity made Sr'o sag.

Before the migration she had often worked above the ice of Jm'ho. She understood gravity. She had experienced gravity. The crushing, unbearable weight here was nothing like that. Not even humans or Puppeteers would choose to live here. That was among the reasons Ol't'ro had selected this planet.

The last of the water vanished into its holding tank and the egress lamp flashed yellow. The outer hatch irised open. With Pk'o leading the way, they crept from their aircraft down a shallow ramp to the barren ground.

A motorized cart with all their gear waited on the rain-slippery packed clay. With exoskeleton motors shrieking in protest, they clambered aboard the cart to ride to the waiting starship.

As lightning flashed overhead and thunder roared, Sr'o wondered what they would find.

WITH EVERY CLUMSY STEP of her metal-shod limbs, Sr'o kicked rich silt into the water. A lush profusion of sponges and sessile worms carpeted the cargo-hold deck. Motile worms and scuttlebugs, creepers and little clawed hunters of every imaginable kind, swam and scurried and peered out of the luxuriant growth. Everything glowed with health, so fertile and vigorous that Sr'o yearned to rip off her pressure suit, and pull the delicious water through her gills, and feast.

Instead she and her technicians did a full battery of tests with every instrument they had brought. Everything checked out perfectly.

"Are you satisfied?" the captain asked, still irate at the unexplained diversion so far from the ocean. Or perhaps what offended him was the armed escort ship circling above the landing site. Or the armored guards ceaselessly scanning the hold. Or Sr'o's own skeptical behavior.

Sr'o waggled a tubacle apologetically, but her suit made a mockery of the gesture. Ol't'ro had ordered that everyone remained suited for the inspection.

"We came to help," the captain snapped. "When can we make our delivery to your colony?"

Ol't'ro had been *so* certain of tampering. Had they ever been wrong about something so important? Sr'o could not remember such an event.

Or did she merely delude herself? Perhaps settling so far from Jm'ho was a mistake.

A trace of memory from the last meld, and an even fainter Er'o remnant chided, *I suspect.*

What more could she test or question? "Where did you obtain your cargo, Captain?"

"The deep vents at the north end of Gk'ho trench."

"Excellent." The northern trench was a remote wildlife preserve, deep within Gk'ho Nation. Sr'o could not have named a better place from which to take samples and fresh stock. And the Gk'Gk'ho was no friend of the Tn'Tn'ho.

Subvocalizing into a microphone planted deep within a tubacle, Sr'o radioed a private question across the crowded hold. "Pk'o. Can you determine the origin of the cargo?"

"A moment." Pk'o scuttled, his suit clanking, its exoskeleton motors droning, to the equipment cart. Their scans and readings flowed wirelessly into its onboard computer, and it took the technician a while to survey the data. "Almost certainly the Gk'ho wildlife preserve," he radioed back.

"Good," Sr'o responded. "You can start packing up our gear."

"I would like to get the cargo delivered," the captain said, "and the crew needs some time off the ship before we go home."

Sr'o could not bring herself to give the authorization. She raised a tubacle, motors whining, to look once again around the cargo hold. Angry reds and far reds rippled across the captain's calloused hide; she ignored them. What did she see and hear? Her two guards, watchful. Pk'o, stowing instruments on their motorized cart. Kt'o, among a cluster of crew, asking for news about home. More crew, floating freely, jetting about as Sr'o so yearned to do.

Something in the vista was wrong. What?

"Soon, Captain. Please bear with me." She set off, clanking, new flurries of disturbed mud and silt marking her wake. The captain jetted away, growling.

"What is it?" Pk'o asked as she reached him. "We have checked and rechecked everything."

An intuition Sr'o did not want to articulate. "A multiscanner, please."

He recoiled—as much as the suit would let him—from something in her voice. "Yes, Your Wisdom," Pk'o said formally.

She coiled a tubacle around the instrument. From another tubacle she looked once more around the hold. The cargo. The cluster of conversation. Crew swimming about.

The *swimming* was wrong.

"Captain," she called, the exterior speaker on her suit turned up high.

He jetted to a halt and angled two tubacles back toward her. "What now?"

"Some of your crew seem . . . energetic."

But energetic did not quite define the oddity. The supply ship's crew was . . . what? Ebullient. Enthusiastic. All that, and more.

Euphoric.

The captain, for that matter, was much less irate than she had expected. Than he had every right to be.

He swam down toward her. "As I told you, a long trip. The crew is excited about getting off the ship, about seeing new people and a new world."

By the end of her long trek through hyperspace to this world, *she* had been exhausted and twitchy. Certainly not euphoric.

Something about euphoria, then. "A moment, Captain," she said.

It was, she decided, as though the crew were high on magnesium salts or hydrogen sulfide, but her suit's instruments insisted all solutes in the water were within acceptable ranges.

She raised the tubacle that clasped the multiscanner. "May I take your readings?" He gave no answer, so she proceeded. He was the picture of health.

And yet, a few readouts were off: enzyme levels higher than she had ever seen. Those could account for the unexpected energy levels. A few repeating genes repeated many more times than she had ever encountered. Those genes coded for the anomalous enzymes. And, most puzzling to Sr'o, unexpected sequences *between* the genes—

Where retroviruses could lurk.

"My team and I must return to our transport," she told the captain.

"Why?" he demanded. "Is something wrong with us?"

"Something is . . . unexpected. I do not have the resources here to make a full analysis." Nor the mental capacity.

Ol't'ro did.

OL'T'RO CONSIDERED:

The cargo ship's crew: they were doomed. Had they been allowed to off-load their cargo and leave, none could have survived to return their ship to Jm'ho. Equally doomed was the navigator who had boarded the cargo ship at the rendezvous deep in the interstellar void, to safeguard the secret location of the colony.

The death that awaited them. Cells died, and cells reproduced. With each generation of cells, the anomalous enzyme concentrations would increase. Until, at sufficiently high concentrations, the enzymes would cleave the cell's DNA, kill their unsuspecting hosts, and release the retroviruses that lay dormant within.

The retrovirus. Had it been set free near the ocean vents, it would have invaded the entire transplanted food chain—and yet it would not have affected the Gw'oth colonists themselves.

Biological warfare. This contagion was no accident. It was meant to force surrender. To force the colonists, to force Ol't'ro themselves, back to Jm'ho. Back into servitude.

They could not have engineered such a plague, or such a subtle way to deliver it. The task far exceeded *any* Gw'otesht's capacity for handling data. The work could only be done on a large nonbiological computer, such as humans and Puppeteers used. A computer such as the Tn'Tn'ho might have purchased.

And, inevitably, Ol't'ro thought about countermoves. . . .

22

From high atop a rocky promontory, his clothes and hair fluttering in the stiff sea breeze, Louis watched the rising—roaring—tide. Great North Bay was long and serpentine. Its tall, stony sides funneled the flow higher and higher, until the onrushing waters became more wall than waves. The ground vibrated beneath his boots. Spume crashed from the rocks. Even a hundred meters above the surge, spray occasionally spattered his face.

Three hundred feet, Louis corrected himself. Ancient English units and ancient English speech. English, by way of Spanglish, was the primary source language of Interworld. English all around made Louis feel like an extra in a Shakespeare play, but he understood without too much effort most things he heard. Not these illogical units of measure, though. Getting used to those would take practice.

Sometime soon Nessus would reappear. Louis did not believe in karma, not exactly, but this idyll would end. And if he followed in his father's footsteps—

Beowulf Shaeffer's bouts of tourism tended to end in existential crises.

While he could, Louis would enjoy life to the fullest.

A gust of wind. A face full of spray. Louis laughed with delight. This was *so* not like being aboard *Aegis*. It had seemed he would never get off that ship. "It's beautiful up here."

"I'm glad you like it," Alice Jordan said.

On *Aegis'* arrival on New Terra, Nessus and Ausfaller had (separately? That was not made clear) urgent business to attend to. Ausfaller foisted off Louis on a deputy. And that, once Louis met Alice, was fine with him. He had not seen a woman in a *long* time.

Once Alice realized Louis was, contrary to appearances, much nearer in age to her 150 or so years than the twenty years he looked, the assignment seemed fine with her, too.

Even if Alice had not towered a head taller than everyone else on New Terra, she would have stood out in a crowd. She was confident, if not cocky. Lush black hair broke over her shoulders and spilled down her back. He could get lost in her deep, deep brown eyes, and gaze forever at her lovely, tanned, chiseled features.

She had led Louis by stepping disc across New Terra. It was a beautiful planet, sparsely settled, its climate temperate from pole to pole. Its pristine seas sparkled. Vast forests, grassy plains, and expansive fields spread across its continents. Great mountains soared into its skies. What New Terrans considered cities, designed from the start around ubiquitous stepping discs, were—what was the word?—neighborhoods. When he put from his mind the necklaces of artificial suns orbiting low overhead, and the scattering of Puppeteer expatriates living among the humans, New Terra was what Earth might have been with maybe one percent of its current population.

In a word, paradise.

"MATURITY IN THE BODY of a twenty-year-old." Alice rolled contently onto her back. "Isn't science wonderful? Any more back home like you?"

"One's not enough?" Louis pretended to be offended.

She reached out to pat his arm. "Truthfully? More than one might kill me."

Louis turned onto his side, the better to face her. He had been starved for human contact, starved for the company of a woman. And a woman as smart and beautiful and delightful as Alice? Once he met her, the need to know her, to be with her, matched the worst drug craving he had had on Wunderland. Alice was beautiful, and yet . . .

Maybe it *was* time for some truth.

All the while they had been together, amid the patter of flirting, interspersed among insights about New Terran history and culture, Alice had been pumping Louis for information, and with very perceptive questions, too. It had taken him three days to notice. Listening more skeptically, her phrasing hinted at knowledge no native New Terran would have. When he had sprinkled Interworld terms into his still tentative English, she understood more than he would have expected.

"What were you?" Louis asked suddenly, sharply. "An ARM like your boss?"

Alice jerked back. "No, a goldskin."

Belter cops wore yellow pressure suits, hence, colloquially, they were goldskins. Alice was tall enough to be a Belter. Louis wondered why he had not seen it before. "So what do you want from me?"

"A way home for the New Terrans," she said. "But you don't know the way, any more than Sigmund or I do."

Louis knew he was falling for this woman, and he was furious at her deception. "I suppose Nessus brought you here, too?"

"Do you trust Nessus?" she countered.

"Yes." He considered further. "Mostly."

"And Citizens?"

"One tried to kill me," Louis barked. And guiltily, "Right. This whole world was once the Puppeteers' slave colony."

"Remember that. Cowards can be as ruthless as anyone else. Fear only makes Citizens more devious in their plots. When they resort to violence, they apply force overwhelmingly."

Louis took her hand. "You're avoiding my question. Did Nessus bring you here?" *And you're avoiding the question I can't bring myself to ask. Is anything between us real?*

"Nothing so straightforward." Alice sighed. "Nessus knows nothing about my background. Sigmund and I would like to keep it that way."

Louis waited.

"Keeping secrets was easier before I got to know you."

He waited.

Before Alice found anything to add, Ausfaller called.

LOUIS STEPPED, emerging into a busy lobby. The stony-faced escorts waiting there closed ranks around him, and together they walked briskly into the bowels of a rambling, windowless building. They left him in an anteroom labeled OFFICE OF THE MINISTER. The willowy blonde aide at the reception desk nodded at Louis but said nothing.

The door behind the desk opened. "Louis Wu," Ausfaller said. In person his eyes looked even more brooding and intense than over a hyperwave link. "I'm glad finally to meet you in person. Please come in."

Louis walked into the office and stood waiting. Data screens, all blank, covered the walls. The large desk was clear except for a family holo. It was jarring to imagine Ausfaller as a man with a beautiful wife, children, and grandchildren.

Ausfaller gestured to a cluster of chairs. "Please, sit."

"I prefer to stand."

"This was never going to be easy." Ausfaller grimaced. "You *should* hate me, if not for the reasons you think."

You presume to know what I feel? Louis thought but did not bother to ask.

"Something to drink?" Ausfaller synthed himself a glass of something amber and shrugged at Louis's silence. "Suit yourself. What is the date in Known Space, Louis? Just the year will be sufficient."

"2780 when I left. Maybe 2781 now."

"That makes you about one hundred thirty, and I'm closing in on three hundred. And yet you look like a kid and I look younger than your true age. Carlos, Finagle bless him, is a genius."

"And as a reward," Louis said coldly, "you chased him, chased all my family, off Earth."

"Let me tell you how that autodoc came about." Ausfaller sipped his whiskey. "I once rescued Carlos and Beowulf, the astrophysicist and the adventurer, from space pirates. I was almost too late, Louis. Vacuum had severely damaged Carlos's lungs, and then his body rejected the organs the autodoc on my ship had to offer. He nearly died before we got back to Earth."

Ausfaller *saved* his fathers' lives? Nessus had said nothing about that. But with Ausfaller's words, another cryptic, half-overheard conversation from Louis's childhood made sense. . . .

Ausfaller was still talking. "That incident is why Carlos abandoned astrophysics for nanotech. After his close call, he turned his attention to making a better 'doc."

"So you chased us off Earth," Louis answered again.

"I might as well have." His hands suddenly shaking, Ausfaller drained his glass in one convulsive swig. "The ARM agent who lured—who drove—your family from Earth invented threats from me to convince Carlos to go into hiding with her. The same woman who, incidentally, then did her best to kill Bey. Carlos had refused to leave without the rest of you.

"I've done things I'm not proud of, Louis, and they gave credibility to Feather's claims. It's a long story."

This Feather woman had left Earth with Louis's parents? Louis remembered his surprise at the records he had found on Fafnir: two Graynor men and *two* women. Was this Feather the missing woman?

Louis crossed his arms across his chest. "I'm not going anywhere, at least till Nessus comes back."

"If it's any consolation, Bey came back from the dead, rebuilt by the very autodoc that worked wonders on you and me, just in time to watch me die horribly. A hole blasted through the chest will do that." Ausfaller waved off Louis's questions. "Beowulf didn't kill me, not that I could have blamed him. And yes, Carlos's autodoc saved me, too. While I was more dead than alive, Nessus found it convenient to kidnap me, selectively wipe my memories, and bring me here."

"So why should I hate you, Ausfaller? Because your paranoia made this Feather woman's treachery possible?"

Ausfaller shook his head. "That would be fair, but my failings go deeper. No, Louis, hate me because at a critical time I wasn't paranoid enough. Had I suspected what Feather had in mind, I might have stopped her. Avoided a lot of pain . . . for everyone."

More pain for Ausfaller than anyone else, Louis sensed. What had Feather been to the ARM? "Why are you telling me this . . . Sigmund?"

"The Pak Library. I need you to trust me enough not to blindly trust Nessus. I need you to consider the implications on *this* world of your actions, and of his. And if you can bring yourself to do it, I would like you to keep me in the loop."

"I see no reason to trust *anyone* at this point," Louis snapped.

Ausfaller offered his hand. "That's good enough for now."

UNABLE TO SLEEP, Louis groped past the edge of the sleeper field for the touchpoint. He was on his feet, tapping the field ON again, faster than Alice could stir. His bare feet made no sound as he crept to the door. He paused in the doorway for a glimpse of her by the dim glow of the hall lamp. Tanj, but she was beautiful.

That was the only thing he *knew*.

His mind was tied in knots by an eerie realization: Alice, Sigmund, and he were alike. They all had their demons. They all struggled with the burdens of worlds. Strange twists of fate had led them here: far from home, lost. Was Alice—or even Sigmund?—less worthy of forgiveness than he?

Louis tiptoed back to the bedroom, just to cuddle. Whatever their flaws, whatever the dawn would bring, Louis and Alice needed each other tonight.

. . .

ALICE EMERGED FROM THE BEDROOM, yawning. "You're up early."

"Uh-huh," Louis said. He had linked the living-room wallpaper to a beach camera, and all around them virtual waves broke on long expanses of bone-white sand. "I didn't want to disturb you."

She stood next to him and took his hand. "The waves are so peaceful."

When his mind could grapple no longer with human frailties and second chances, it had woken up to the other matter troubling him: Great North Bay. And so, with the audio muted, he had stared for an hour at the shore. In that time the tide had surged far up the beach.

"New Terra has no moon," Louis said softly. "It's one world, all alone in space. How can it have tides?"

She squeezed his hand. "A gift from Baedeker, long before he became Hindmost. He found a way to make the planetary drive wobble *just* a bit. It simulates the tides New Terra had as one world among the Fleet of Worlds."

"A Puppeteer gift? I don't know what to say."

"Neither did Sigmund." On four walls, sea and sand sparkled under the brilliance of a dozen suns. A comber, like quicksilver, swirled and splashed up the beach. For a time Alice seemed lost in the beauty. Then she grinned, amusement lighting her eyes. "There is nothing like a random act of kindness to screw with a paranoid's head."

23

Achilles circled the small cylinder into which his life had receded, the clop-clop-clop of his hooves offering the only sound. He had food and fresh juices, delivered four times daily; mounds of soft cushions; even, to occupy his mind, a limited-functionality pocket computer.

He ignored it all.

His cell was one seamless enclosure of General Products hull material. None of the tricks he knew for defeating the supermolecule would serve here. Nothing entered his cell, not even the food he ate or the oxygen he breathed, except by action of stepping discs. Nothing left, not even bodily waste or the carbon dioxide he exhaled, except by the action of stepping discs. Here he would remain until someone let him out. A prisoner of the state. More specifically, to judge from the great seal on the outer room's wall, a prisoner within Clandestine Directorate—and how Nike must gloat about that.

A prisoner, too, of his thoughts, for Achilles did not know how *not* to plot and scheme.

Misappropriating, even losing, a ship? That was a trivial offense. Reckless endangerment of the Concordance? More problematical, but not without ambiguity. Much could be rationalized as policy differences, and tradition afforded a great deal of discretion to those who ventured off-world. His friends and allies throughout the government could argue foreign-affairs subtleties and raise doubts forever.

If he still had friends and allies.

For there was the final matter: the attempted murder of a Citizen, with premeditation. That was a crime against, not some abstraction like the Concordance, but the very notion of *herd*.

The herd looked out, first and foremost, for itself.

Nessus had found the device left to destroy *Aegis*. He had recorded

Achilles frantically looking for the device, had captured Achilles reacting to the device dangling from Nessus' jaw. There was no ambiguity here, no excuse of policy differences. The proof was incontrovertible, and condemnation certain.

So why had the tribunal not begun? To allow appalled followers to fade away? Perhaps. If so, the plan must be succeeding. Few had come to visit; few of them had exhibited any true loyalty. Vesta, for all his rash words during the flight to Hearth, had yet to come to see Achilles.

And maybe his enemies thought to delay the tribunal until his resolve cracked.

That would never happen.

On his next circuit of the cell, Achilles paused to nibble at a bowl of grain mush. He scarcely noticed what he ate. It was sufficient that he eat, and exercise, and maintain his health. The tribunal *would* happen. When it did he would need his wits about him. For the herd looked out—first, foremost, and always—for itself.

As always, *he* would have to look out for *himself*.

HE HAD BEEN TOO YOUNG to understand much. A preschool outing. Thirty or so playmates gamboling in freshly mown pasture. Teachers and a few parents, his own among them, watching. The worlds high overhead, blue and white and brown, some round and others crescent. In the distance, on all sides, the warm yellow-orange glow of arcology walls. A utility vehicle of some kind, its rear deck piled with potted plants. Waving from the floater's clear-sided cab, a park worker dressed in protective coveralls.

He remembered a kickball gone astray, bouncing into the pasture. He remembered cantering after the ball, and happy shrieking—

And the shrieks turning to horror.

His heads had swiveled frantically. What could be wrong?

In the clear-sided cab, the driver had slumped over the controls. The floater swerved—straight at him!

Shaking with fright, he took a tentative step to the right. The runaway floater wobbled and weaved, still coming toward him. Somehow he managed several quick steps to the left.

Weaving and wobbling, impossible to predict, the floater sped closer. In hindsight, the erratic movements came of cargo shifting and from the dying driver's spasms.

Then it was all too obvious that the floater was stalking him.

He remembered squealing, paralyzed with fear, his hearts pounding in his chest. He remembered the desire, the urge, the *need* to collapse, to embrace the ground, to hide in a tightly rolled ball—but the heavily laden vehicle hovered low to the ground. It would crush him, not float over him.

Familiar voices: playmates, friends, the teacher, the parents. And *his* parents! Yodeling distress. Urging him to run. Ululating in fear and dread.

As rooted to the spot as he.

Somehow he broke the spell of fear. He took a step. And another. And another. He built up speed and, as the floater was almost upon him, toppled into one of the holes that had been dug for the potted shrubs waiting to be replanted.

The floater ran over him, scraping his hindquarters, parting his sparse, childish mane. A lip's breadth lower and the floater would have shattered his cranium. He was too terrified to cry.

With a slow-motion crunch the vehicle, its motor revving, came to a halt embedded in a massive redthorn hedge. The plants' insectivore tendrils lashed and snapped futilely at their attacker.

His playmates, keeping their distance, craned their necks to see what had become of him. None had ever seen blood before, and they howled in horror and fascination.

His parents galloped to him. "Are you all right," a parent wailed. To this day, he could not remember which. Nor care.

No one had come while it still mattered. Not friends, teacher, or parents. No one.

And so, from the tender age of four, the lesson was deeply etched: the world was out to get him, and he could depend only on himself.

So be it.

THE WAITING AREA might comfortably have held ten or more, but Nessus had the room to himself. He synthed a portion of warm carrot juice, for it had the power to calm him.

Well, ordinarily it did.

Achilles was too dangerous to give a public trial and too well connected to simply disappear. Hence, this secret tribunal. There would be no impartial reconciler to preside, no voluminous files of precedent, no council of herdmates to sift the evidence. Witnesses for and against Achilles would present their evidence, sing their claims, plead any extenuating circumstances. The Hindmost, bound only by mercy and the dignity of his office—and the practical constraints of politics—would render a verdict.

From the decision of the Hindmost there could be no appeal.

"We are ready," a hidden ceiling speaker announced.

Nessus set down his drink. He took two paces to the vestibule's lone stepping disc and reappeared in the tribunal chamber. Baedeker straddled a ceremonial bench, flanked by high-ranking officials and trusted aides: the ruling elite of the Concordance. Achilles, his posture defiant, sat opposite the Hindmost.

Nessus was too preoccupied to notice who guided him to the bench of testimony. He sat.

"Please state your name," Baedeker sang formally.

Nessus sang his full, formal name.

"You come to give testimony about the accused?"

"I do," Nessus responded.

"Proceed."

Slowly, methodically, using video from *Aegis'* security cameras, Nessus told his tale: the rescue of Achilles from the wreck of *Argo*; the recovery of the Library; Achilles' scheme to destroy *Aegis* and its crew.

Achilles resisted at every turn—but not in the manner Nessus had expected. "I never acted alone," Achilles intoned often, more manic and intense with every iteration. "Others knew. Others *here* knew. For the Gw'oth peril *must* be eliminated."

The peril fomented by Achilles' own threats against the Gw'oth. But policy toward the Gw'oth was not at issue today. If this tribunal became a policy debate, Achilles might yet go free.

Nessus replayed the video of Achilles acting to destroy *Aegis*. "And this is how you would deter the Gw'oth? By killing a Citizen?"

"We stop the Gw'oth with technology from the Library," Achilles sang derisively. "You do still have it?"

In fact, Nessus did not. One lonely shift en route to New Terra, while Louis slept and Achilles lay immobile in stasis, Nessus had jettisoned the recovered Pak hardware. The Carlos Wu autodoc as well, with its dangerously advanced nanotechnology. The abandoned equipment carried a code-activated transponder and Nessus could recover everything easily enough. He would—once Achilles had been found guilty and imprisoned, and his minions purged from the government. But no one here, not even Baedeker, knew of this precaution. It seemed best not to volunteer the information.

"Answer the question," Nessus ordered.

"Others are party to my actions. Others *here*." Achilles straightened his necks to stare down arrogantly at those who would decide his fate.

By the time his testimony was done, and the ministers' questioning, and Achilles' mocking rebuttals, Nessus could almost have believed *he* was the one at risk.

VESTA, WEARING A FORMAL SASH of office, stepped into the large, unfurnished expanse that surrounded Achilles' cell. Before Achilles could react, Vesta plucked a device from a pocket of the sash. There was a wriggle of lip nodes and on the tiny apparatus a green light began to blink.

"A Clandestine Directorate jammer," Vesta said. He spoke in English, whether because any guards who might happen by were unlikely to understand him, or because the jammer left only one mouth unencumbered. "We have a short while before the jailors become suspicious."

Because my cell is rife with sensors, Achilles completed. He had assumed that to be the case. "It is kind of you to visit." Also, overdue.

"Your pronouncements at the tribunal . . ." Vesta shivered. "You would expose me? Denounce me?"

"I merely reminded you of your commitments." And of the consequences if you choose not to remember them.

They stared at one another until Vesta wilted. "What would you have me do, Your Excellency?"

"On the flight to Hearth, you spoke of making an opportunity. I believe this would be a favorable moment." Before the tribunal concludes.

Vesta's necks drooped farther. "Fewer will help than I had hoped. There have been . . . concerns. The actions taken aboard *Aegis* . . ."

The lamp on the jammer blinked faster: they did not have much time left. Achilles kept his response simple. "I will not go alone to perform hard labor on Nature Preserve One."

Vesta quaked with fear, his unencumbered head swiveling helplessly between Achilles and the blinking device that he held.

"If the tribunal should proceed to sentencing, Vesta, you know what I will disclose."

"It will not come to that," Vesta sang sharply. With a snap of the jaw he turned off the jammer.

Then, as abruptly as Vesta had arrived, he was gone.

24

"We are the Ol't'ro you knew," the hyperwaved message began. The voice, resonant and self-assured, spoke English. "And yet we are not. The Gw'oth you met, Sigmund, live only in our memories."

Louis watched and listened, self-consciously aware of Sigmund and Alice watching *him*. Sigmund had invited Louis, without explanation, to comment on "something interesting." This was interesting, all right. And as clearly a test of some kind.

"Pause," Louis ordered.

"Indeed, sir," Jeeves announced.

At least one small mystery had resolved itself. The first Jeeves had been the shipboard artificial intelligence of the hijacked ramscoop colony ship from which New Terra was settled. Voice, with his very un-Puppeteer butler mannerisms, derived from a Jeeves copy.

Jeeves copies assisted the leaders of New Terra and flew on all modern New Terran ships. AI was a hard problem—and a discipline Puppeteers had shunned. New Terra's few would-be cyberneticists, starting from scratch, had yet to develop anything to rival the centuries-old AI from Earth.

Louis asked, "Sigmund, why say who they're not?"

"When last we met," Sigmund said, "Ol't'ro abandoned me in deep space. Well, really they abandoned Baedeker. A case can be made they engaged in a bit of preemptive self-defense, while I was merely in the wrong place at the wrong time." A fleeting, bitter smile. "The story of my life. Regardless, I was adrift, alone but for Baedeker in stasis, for a long time."

Was that a *tic* in Sigmund's cheek? It was an oddly human weakness in someone Louis still saw as an evil genius. "Then why identify themselves at all? Why not make up a name?"

"Except for the preamble, the message was—for reasons you'll soon see—encrypted. Ol't'ro used themselves as the hint I needed to deduce the key." Sigmund clenched his jaw for a while without defeating the tic. "Their last words before splitting our hull. 'We're sorry.' "

"A General Products hull," Alice added.

How did you split a GP hull? Louis had—somehow—turned *Argo*'s hull to powder, but that had involved positioning *Aegis* just right. Nessus would never explain what, exactly, they had aimed at. What, exactly, they had done.

Suppose *Aegis* had been less precisely positioned in the derelict. What would have happened? Less than total destruction? Louis said, "Let me guess. The Gw'oth opened a hyperspace bubble at midship?"

Sigmund blinked. "Your family has a worrisome aptitude, Louis, for destroying indestructible GP hulls."

How did one answer that? Rather than try, Louis looked around the room. It could be an executive conference room on any world he had ever visited. Almost. The proportions of walls, the ceiling height, and skinny table were all . . . odd. Influenced by a Puppeteer aesthetic, he supposed.

"Resume playback," Louis ordered.

"Of course, sir."

The video had opened with a close-up of an icy world and panned back to encompass a gas giant and its other moons. Louis felt vaguely cheated. He would have liked to see *Gw'oth*.

"Obviously, Ol't'ro is a Gw'otesht," he said. "Of how many members?"

It seemed a lifetime since he had studied the Gw'oth, and that recollection had him wondering, yet again, what was keeping Nessus. With every passing day Louis thought more about making a home for himself on New Terra, with Alice. Not that he had had that kind of conversation with her yet. It was much too soon.

"Sixteen," Jeeves supplied.

The recording went on. "You will remember Jm'ho, Sigmund. Jm'ho is a beautiful world, at least to us, but we no longer call it home. And therein, Sigmund, is the reason we now contact you."

"Pause," Sigmund said. "The message came out of nowhere. Backtracking the inbound signal, the closest detectable object is a dust cloud two light-years from New Terra. If the signal originated anywhere in Jm'ho's solar system, and I'm not saying it did, it bounced through hyperwave relays along the way."

"Did the signal come from ahead of New Terra?" Louis asked. New

Terra was traveling the same way as the Fleet: to galactic north. That was the shortest and quickest route out of the galaxy. Once above the galaxy, they could change course and flee the core explosion without having to dodge solar systems—and anyone living in them.

"Nessus showed me a map with a new Gw'oth colony in that direction. It had to do"—Louis hesitated, remembering the Puppeteer's hesitance to discuss his mission with Sigmund—"with why Nessus recruited me."

Alice frowned. "*We* don't know of any such colony. Either the Puppeteers have resumed scouting ahead on their own or our own scouts aren't reporting back everything they find."

"When was this colony discovered?" Sigmund asked.

"I don't know." Louis rubbed his chin, considering. "I think recently. Its discovery is why Nessus went looking for, well, ultimately me."

Sigmund laughed unpleasantly. "That, and knowing I won't let Puppeteers involve New Terra in Concordance affairs. For now, let's get back to Ol't'ro's message. Resume, Jeeves."

"We left the home world," Ol't'ro continued, "to gain our liberty. The monarch from whom we freed ourselves wants us back. And so he did this."

Louis didn't especially understand *terrestrial* biology. What followed about alien biology required several timeouts so Jeeves could interpret and simplify. Getting his arms around the computational requirements to engineer new life forms took another lengthy digression. Apparently gengineering surpassed the mental capacity of even a Gw'otesht-16.

But after Louis took in everything, the upshot was clear enough. "Biological warfare. Ol't'ro wants computers to design biological defenses."

Sigmund was nonchalantly looking around the room.

So the testing continued. Louis said, "The same computers could be used to design a counterattack against their enemies. We could be getting into the middle of an interstellar Gw'oth war."

(Alice smiled at "we," Louis noticed. A good omen. This was not the place to comment.)

"And?" Sigmund prompted.

Wheels within wheels within wheels. . . . Trying to think like Sigmund made Louis's head hurt! "It begs the question how Ol't'ro's enemies engineered their bioattack in the first place. Do the Gw'oth on Jm'ho have computers?"

"Basic ones," Alice said. "New Terra has commercial relations with several of the leading nations on Jm'ho. We sold them waterproofed versions of our pocket comps, which the Gw'oth have doubtless reverse-engineered and improved. But we know of nothing there with the capacity for genetic engineering."

"Maybe the Puppeteers provided bigger computers?" Louis shook his head. "I withdraw the question. The Gw'oth know the location of the Fleet. The Concordance would hardly provide technology that might make the Gw'oth an even bigger prospective threat."

Alice said, "If New Terra doesn't offer help and Ol't'ro are telling the truth, they may conclude we're the ones who equipped their enemies."

Louis rocked in his chair, his mind churning. "We don't actually know that Ol't'ro's colony was attacked. We have only an unsubstantiated claim. It could be a ruse, a way to get New Terran computers so *they* can build the first bioweapon."

"Or the gear could be honestly requested and still prove useful for a counterstrike. Or Ol't'ro wants advanced computers for another reason, or to be applied against another adversary, they have not even hinted at. Or, or, or." Sigmund stood and poured himself a glass of water from the carafe on the sideboard. "You know what we know, Louis. What is your advice?"

When had it become Louis's job to suggest New Terran foreign policy? More of him thought: New Terra could be my home. I *want* to be involved. It pained him to admit: "I don't know enough to recommend anything."

Sigmund raised his water glass in salute. "Recognizing how little we know is the beginning of wisdom."

AN UNEXPECTED SOUND roused Achilles. He looked about, bleary-eyed. The sound repeated, a timid rapping. And then, soft voices: "Your Excellency."

Vesta!

Achilles clambered to his hooves. In the space around his cell, still sleep-period dim, three figures stood. The slender one was Vesta. Who were the silent ones? They were tall and stocky, with the slightly crazed expressions of thugs and guards. "What is it?" Achilles asked.

"We must get you out," Vesta sang. He dipped his heads. "Deliberations at the tribunal do not go well."

"Then get me out," Achilles snapped.

Vesta gestured and one of the silent ones took a transport controller from his sash. "The access disc should be active, Your Excellency."

Achilles trotted onto the disc at the center of his cell—and stepped off another disc in the dimly lit outer room. "What is the plan?" he asked Vesta.

"These two are among your most loyal followers. They will take you to Greensward Field, where a ship and crew await your commands."

Greensward was a tertiary-at-best spaceport, an ignominious place from which to flee. When the time came to return, Achilles promised himself, it would be at a more suitable venue.

He was getting ahead of himself. "You said 'these two.' Are you not coming with us?"

"I am more useful to you here." Vesta plucked nervously at his mane. "Excellency, we must hurry. The guards will wake up soon."

Achilles sidled to where he could read the insignia on his escorts' sashes. They were members of Clandestine Directorate security. Who better to surprise the guards on duty? And leaving Vesta in place as Nike's aide could certainly prove useful. "Very well, Vesta. I will remember your initiative at this critical time."

Vesta bobbed heads in acknowledgment. "It is an honor to serve, Excellency."

They trotted past two stunned guards, collapsed on the floor; up a flight of stairs; past an internal security station with three more stunned guards; down the length of a long, arcing corridor. Finally they reached an unshielded annex of the building, accessible to the public stepping-disc network.

Pawing the floor nervously, Vesta turned to one of their escorts. "As I ordered. Do it quickly."

The false guard whipped out a stunner and Vesta crumpled to the floor. "So no one suspects him," the guard sang. Then, his eyes wild, he lashed out with his hind leg. The hoof's sharp edge opened a long gash in Vesta's flank. Blood welled from the wound. "So no one suspects," the false guard repeated.

"Let us go," Achilles ordered.

A moment later they were on the bridge of a ship. A few of the bridge crew looked familiar to Achilles.

Everyone stared at him expectantly.

There at the pilot's console: a figure with startling russet patches on his hide, earnestly coiffed, with lively green eyes. A veteran of the Scout Academy. A disciple.

Clotho: the Fate who spun the thread of Life.

Achilles believed in the greatness of his destiny. He told himself that did not require him to believe in omens. "Clotho, are we ready to depart?"

"At your command, Excellency."

"Proceed," Achilles ordered.

There was a bit of radioed exchange with Space Traffic Control, and then, under Clotho's practiced jaws, the ship lifted off from Hearth.

ALONE ON THE BRIDGE of *Aegis,* a platter of chopped mixed grasses close by, Nessus studied the mass pointer. Pointing straight at him, a single, long line: New Terra.

The bridge felt lonelier than usual. He had become accustomed to the company of Louis Wu. But Nessus' main sense of loss had nothing to do with *Aegis* or Louis. Nessus missed Baedeker.

Even amid the madness of the tribunal, Baedeker had made time for them to be together. Private dinners. An evening at the Grand Ballet. There had even been an allusion—fleeting, but meaningful nonetheless—to finding a Companion. Mating and children beckoned . . .

The tribunal must soon find Achilles culpable and sentence him to hard labor on Nature Preserve One. On that premise—and because Citizens insane enough to support Achilles might lash out at his main accuser—Nessus was en route to New Terra for Louis. Together they would retrieve the Pak Library and deliver it to a purged Ministry of Science on Hearth. And with Achilles banished, and his cause publicly condemned, the crisis with the Gw'oth should subside.

Nessus pondered the future with unwonted optimism.

In the mass pointer, the line for New Terra slowly grew.

"In three, two . . ." Nessus stopped himself. There was no one here but Voice, and Voice did not require an alert.

With a tremor, *Aegis* dropped into normal space. The walls flipped from pastoral recordings to external display. New Terra was a blue–white spark directly ahead.

And on his main console, the hyperwave transceiver blinked a COSMIC alert.

"Who is the message from?" Nessus asked.

"The Hindmost, sir," Voice intoned.

An I-miss-you-already message? Or some fresh disaster? Tasting bitter cud, Nessus feared the latter. "Play the message."

Aegis was close enough to Hearth for video; the message opened to a hologram of Baedeker looking grim. "Achilles has escaped," he began, the harmonics heavy with tragedy. "The investigation is ongoing. Nessus, call me as soon as you get this."

"Voice, place the call."

The display morphed into a new image of Baedeker. "Nessus!" the Hindmost said. "I am relieved you are safe."

There had been no delay. Baedeker had taken to a ship, was outside Hearth's singularity. For instant communications or some more ominous reason?

"I am fine, Baedeker, just this moment out of hyperspace. How did Achilles escape?"

"Rogue elements within Clandestine Directorate." Baedeker's mouths drooped with distaste. "They surprised the guards on duty. They got Vesta, too, when he tried to summon help. I wait off-world until security forces complete their work."

"Is everyone all right?"

"Yes. The attackers only used stunners. At least their madness has limits. Other supporters overpowered the crew of a grain ship cleared to depart for New Terra. Achilles and at least twenty allies are gone."

A grain ship. Because grain ships flitted in unending streams to and from Hearth. And a New Terra-bound ship because vessels flying among worlds of the Fleet lacked hyperdrives.

When a grain ship transmitted the proper authentication codes, no one—and certainly not the automated planetary defenses—looked any further. Once beyond the defenses, the ship could travel . . . anywhere.

"The security codes!" Nessus blurted.

"Have been updated," Baedeker sang. "You will need the new codes to return home."

The assurance did nothing to ease Nessus' fears.

25

"Leave us," Bm'o ordered. By an understated curl of a tubacle tip he signaled Rt'o, his most trusted counselor, to linger.

With a formal glide, the ambassador of Gk'ho Nation retreated from Bm'o's ceremonial audience chamber. Courtiers and sycophants scuttled after. As soon as the last had disappeared, Bm'o jetted to the smaller but more comfortable office from which he truly ruled.

Through its floor of clearest ice, regularly scraped smooth, he admired the glory that was his domain. Lm'ba, the world's mightiest city, stretched from the top of this seamount into the depths far beneath, from what traditionalists still called the roof of the world into the abyssal depths from whose searing vents boiled the stuff of life. Here at the summit, as across the ice, the buildings were all grand edifices of metal and glass. As his eyes swept downward more and more stone structures appeared until, stretching across the floor of the world, in the province of ranchers and herders, only rude stone structures could be seen.

The marvel of the age was that so much *could* be seen, for even the simplest rancher's hut, in the poorest tributary nation, had been electrified. Fusion technology had been known for generations; it was the building of power plants and deployment of wires that had taken time.

But Tn'ho Nation drew its might from sources high and low. Coasting through the pungent, salty water, Bm'o curled two tubacles upward to peer through the clear dome.

Mighty Tl'ho dominated the sky. It was a wondrous place, radiant in far red, its apparent surface roiled by storms. (His scientists assured him Tl'ho had no surface, only denser and denser gases for as deep as instruments could peer.) No one lived on the gas giant itself, but colonies had taken root on all its moons. Other worlds existed at distances far greater still, but the brilliance that was Tl'ho, and the ice-glare of its reflection, washed the stars from view.

Rt'o had followed at a discreet distance. She was gaunt with age, mottled with chromatophoric cells gone inert, her carapace of spines become dull. One tubacle dragged behind her, from an ancient injury; the others had grown stiff.

But her mind remained as sharp as ever. Bm'o wondered if she ever thought, as the end of life approached, about the immortality of a Gw'otesht. She had never given him a reason to suspect such depravity, but the accursed ensembles preyed on his thoughts, more than ever since Ol't'ro's betrayal. He straightened a tubacle to peer across the ice at the Gw'otesht pens.

To be blinded and deafened by *choice,* by tubacles hungrily, pervertedly swallowing each other. To submerge one's mind into some—abomination. How could they do it? How did they bear it? It was unnatural, disgusting, obscene.

The images in his mind sickened him.

Rt'o had intuited his need for silent reflection. Now she showed the ability to divine his thoughts—and to change the subject. "Space is vast, Sire."

"Yet our problems are always with us." He flashed a moiré pattern, ironic, over his dorsal surface. "Vast and yet not vast enough."

"The Tn'Tn'ho speaks the truth."

Bm'o flashed patches of impatience, with touches of green to temper the rebuke. "We are alone. You may speak plainly. What do you read into the report of the ambassador?"

Rt'o considered. "Impatience. The Gk'Gk'ho sacrificed a starship for the Tn'Tn'ho's favor. That was no small expense."

"We are impatient, too," Bm'o admitted. "We should have heard by now from Ol't'ro."

"The rebels should be hungry enough by now," Rt'o agreed. *Should.*

For a long time, Bm'o gazed at the unnatural universe above. How simple life must have been before *progress.* "I share your skepticism. That we have not heard from Ol't'ro suggests failure."

Rt'o flexed deferentially. "Only a setback, Sire. We did learn where they hide."

There was that. A hyperwave beacon hidden aboard the Gk'ho cargo ship had reported at each emergence from hyperspace.

With a wriggle of tubacles, Bm'o crossed the room to a writhing buffet of worms and creepers. A quick tug pulled loose a morsel. He chewed thoughtfully. "Review the possibilities," he directed.

"The rebels discovered the trap, Sire, or they did not. If yes, their food supply remains precarious. They will have learned that they can trust no one on Jm'ho, and that the Tn'Tn'ho will keep them from replenishing their stocks. If no, their food supply has been fatally tainted. Either way, they must seek your forgiveness or die."

"What of direct action they might take?" Bm'o meant revenge, but retribution was a monarch's prerogative. He would not so dignify any rebel move.

Rt'o paused thoughtfully. "They dare not endanger Jm'ho's ecology, whether by a kinetic-weapon strike or a biological attack. They need our food chain to replenish their own. And they are too few to undertake any conventional attack."

"*Could* they make a biological attack?"

"No, Sire. Not without help. Not without the . . . friends . . . that we have made."

Rt'o doubtless spoke to reassure him, and yet his suspicions raged. Perhaps Ol't'ro *would* die rather than submit. If so, who was to say that they would not choose to take many more with them? *He* might. Monarchs knew all about pride. But if he were prospectively immortal, would he not accept any humiliation in the hope of surviving to triumph later?

Bm'o flared far red in anger. "So you would have me believe the rebels will do nothing? That they would quietly starve?"

"Sire, forgive my shortcomings. I cannot foresee their response. Perhaps the others . . ." Rt'o flattened submissively, but with one tubacle aimed across the ice toward the Gw'otesht pens.

Perhaps one Gw'otesht could foresee what another would do. But to pose the question would also instruct how another rebellion might succeed.

"No, my friend." Bm'o extended a tubacle to raise his trusted advisor. "In this situation, we must be guided by our own insights." He paused to pluck at another bit of creeper—

The seamount was dark, from midslope down.

Bm'o watched helplessly as the blackout raced up the city toward him.

.   .   .

ONE MOMENT, the fusion plants operated at peak efficiency. The next, fusion—stopped. Hydrothermal and tidal generators, unaffected, scarcely sufficed to keep water circulating around the suddenly inert—but still extremely hot—reactors.

Just as mysteriously, half a day later, the fusion plants resumed normal operations.

No known science explained the blackout. The slave Gw'otesht in their pens did not admit to as much as a theory.

Bm'o had a theory: Ol't'ro. Their perverted kind did nothing *but* invent new technology.

Without the fusion plants, modern civilization would fall—and it would collapse without harm to the food chain from which Ol't'ro and his rebels must replenish.

Bm'o had his answer. He knew what Ol't'ro would do—if they were allowed. That would not happen. He had no corresponding need to protect *their* world. Now that he knew where the rebels had settled, it was time to launch his fleet. The rebels could surrender or die.

The choice would be entirely Ol't'ro's.

CIVIL WAR

26

Grain Ship 247 was a name unbefitting the future Hindmost, and Achilles renamed his new ship *Remembrance.* Let that designation serve, upon his coming triumphant return, to instruct his enemies: he remembered their many offenses.

If only the ship's odor could be changed as easily as its label.

Grain ships did not leave Hearth empty: they carried bodily waste. Without that return cargo, fields on the Nature Preserves would long ago have turned unproductive.

And so Achilles had ordered a detour to the nearest water world. As the ship gently sloshed in the ocean depths, its cargo hatches agape, its cargo dumped and the residues rinsed away again and again, he told himself the holds were purged. The environmental controls would scrub the final lingering traces of odor from the corridors and cabins. Then bulkheads would come down. Suitable quarters, offices, and audience chambers would be built. The ship, reconfigured, *would* suit the future Hindmost.

And none would dare to remember the humble origins of his command ship.

FROM A POCKET of the sash hanging from the back of the cabin hatch: a soft chime. Achilles climbed from his nest of pillows to retrieve his comm unit. His mane was sleep-disheveled and he answered audio only. "Yes?"

"Pardon, Excellency," Clotho said. "You have an urgent message from Jm'ho."

"Transfer it to my comm."

"Yes, Excellency." There was a brief pause. "It is done."

Only one being on Jm'ho would know the codes and chain of

hyperwave relays with which to reach Achilles. That was the General Products representative to the Gw'oth: Thalia, a longtime scout trusted by Nike.

Foolishly trusted. Thalia was among Achilles' most devoted acolytes.

"Begin message," Achilles ordered, and a hologram opened.

Thalia had always been thin, but the figure in the video was emaciated. His hide was all but without luster; his mane, although combed, hung limp. To be the only Citizen within light-years, surrounded by aliens . . . Achilles had been in that situation. It was never easy.

But Thalia's eyes *glowed*.

"Excellency," Thalia began, his voices ringing with pride, "warships have set out from Tn'ho and its client states." In a corner of the image an inset video opened: an accelerated time-lapse view of ships rushing from Jm'ho toward interstellar space. "The fleet was still accelerating when they left the range of my neutrino sensors."

Beyond sensor range put the Gw'oth ships far outside their home system's singularity. That they continued to accelerate meant they intended to enter hyperspace—and hence, to exit from it—with kinetic-kill speed. Their hindmost had lost patience with the rebellious colonists.

And all according to plan.

As for Jm'ho itself, Thalia concluded, "I await Your Excellency's command to release the retrovirus."

Achilles watched the message twice more. This accomplishment had been a long time coming, but ultimate success was not *quite* within his jaws. First he had to deliver the speech of his life.

THE STOREROOM-BECOME-RECORDING-STUDIO felt claustrophobic. But no one watching would see these stark, confining walls, Achilles reminded himself. He had personally approved the virtual background against which he would appear: a large room, richly furnished, its floor lushly carpeted in meadowplant, its lighting subtle and recessed. It was the kind of office a Hindmost used.

And *he*—his mane braided and bejeweled, his hide brushed until it gleamed, his hooves buffed until they shone—*looked* like a Hindmost.

"We are ready, Excellency," the supporter behind the camera said.

Achilles took a deep breath, and with heads held high, he began.

"Fellow Citizens, the Concordance is in unprecedented peril. That is an extraordinary claim, for recent years have brought many dangers our way.

The chain reaction at the galactic core and our flight into the unknown. The rebellion of Nature Preserve Four. The Pak incursion. But one danger is undeniably of our own making, and it is imminent. It is of this situation that I speak to you today.

"I refer to the Gw'oth. Our government refuses to give this threat its due. And why is that? Because he who lost the secret of hyperdrive, he who is responsible for making these warlike aliens into the threat they are, has become our Hindmost."

The more nuanced truth was that Baedeker gave the Gw'oth an early start with hyperdrive. The Outsiders traded with all space-capable species—almost certainly they would have sold hyperspace technology to the Gw'oth if the aquatic aliens had not already reverse-engineered it.

Let Baedeker cite nuance if he chose. It would only make him appear defensive.

"It falls to me to share the fearsome news your government refuses to disclose." The surveillance imagery from Thalia's message would be inserted here, while Achilles continued to speak. "The Gw'oth have launched a great armada at us."

On its way to the rebellious colony, the Gw'oth ships *would* pass close to the Fleet.

From undertunes of danger and regret, Achilles segued into reluctance and irony. "And who will protect us? Not the Hindmost who brought this catastrophe upon our heads. Not the same tired establishment."

And surely not the Conservatives. They had been out of power, and rightly so, since shortly after discovery of the galactic-core explosion. Consensualizations took time—and the Gw'oth warships hurtling toward the Fleet left no time. Deliverance could come only from within the ranks of the ruling Experimentalists.

And not just *any* Experimentalist.

"Fellow Citizens, we need a new Hindmost. We need him now. As your Minster of Science, it is well known, I urged that the Concordance *act* against the growing danger. For this I have been driven from office and accused of the vilest crimes.

"But many share my concerns, and these friends of the Concordance released me from unjust confinement. And so I speak to you, reluctantly, from exile, asking that you request—no, that you demand!—a change in Experimentalist leadership.

"For the Gw'oth war fleet *is* coming."

. . .

"THE PREDATOR'S JAWS or the leap from the cliff?" Nike mused aloud, pacing his spacious office.

A fair question. From his years on Earth, Nessus could pose others. The frying pan or the fire? The devil or the deep blue sea? But why choke chords. "Disaster by Gw'oth or by the insanity of Achilles?"

Vesta shrugged, as if to ask: Why does it matter? He continued to favor the side injured when he happened upon Achilles' escape.

Like poor Sigmund, Nessus decided. Autodocs only healed the body.

But Nessus' deepest sorrow came as Baedeker, who had stepped to Clandestine Affairs for an inconspicuous, confidential briefing, merely chanted dispiritedly. He seemed not to notice, or to care, that this meeting had collapsed into despair. Party elders had approached him about Achilles' accusations. Even, most recently, the previous two Hindmosts.

Almost, Nessus despaired, too. The trends were so ominous. . . .

With a nervous shiver, Baedeker rejoined the meeting. "The more immediate question is, what other traitors lurk, prepared to do Achilles' bidding?"

Did Achilles need more help? Not that Nessus could see. "Do we know who put Achilles' message into the satellite feed?"

"We do not," Nike conceded.

"Worse," Vesta said, "we do not know who in Clandestine Affairs leaked Thalia's report from Jm'ho. And because Achilles released the information, he made the government look like it was hiding the information."

"Where does that leave us?" Nike sang gloomily.

"As targets, with a Gw'oth fleet on its way," Baedeker reminded them. He straightened, and newfound resolve lit his eyes. "With planetary defenses to inspect and reinforce. With doomsday ships to launch."

"Yes, Hindmost," Nike acknowledged. He began instructing Vesta.

Only there could be no practical defense against kinetic-kill attacks! One deterred rather than defend. Nessus shuddered at the memory of Louis Wu's term: mutual assured destruction. If the Gw'oth refused to be deterred . . .

Everyone understood the futility of kinetic-kill weapons. The Gw'oth—and *surely,* any Gw'otesht—must understand, too.

So *did* Gw'oth ships come charging at the Fleet? Thalia's report—the complete dispatch, not the part Achilles trumpeted to panic the herd—said that the Gw'oth went to suppress a rebellious colony. But the Tn'Tn'ho's assurances proved nothing. If the Gw'oth meant to attack Hearth, they would hardly volunteer the fact.

"We need more information," Nessus said. And maybe Sigmund or Louis could find some melody hidden within this madness. "Permit me to take out *Aegis*—"

The door to Nike's office swung open. An aide, his eyes narrow with fear, burst in. "Your pardon," he squeaked. With a dramatic shudder, the assistant got his voices under control. "It is as Achilles' broadcasts have warned.

"The outermost hyperwave radar barrier to galactic south of the Fleet has been breached."

IN THE PRIVACY of his grandly rebuilt cabin, while the Gw'oth, unsuspecting, danced to his tune, Achilles bided his time.

For each day, through secure channels, pleasing messages streamed to *Remembrance*. Fear and doubt blossomed on Hearth. Whispers of dissatisfaction became murmurs, became grumbles, became shouts. The party elders wavered.

The summons to rule *must* come soon.

Until then, Achilles had an accession ceremony to plan.

27

Louis had never skimmed the surface of a neutron star, like his stepfather. He had not, like Sigmund, turned whole worlds into shrapnel to defeat the Pak fleets. How many had?

But Louis *had* pillaged a Pak warship, stalked a Pak fleet, and burgled the Pak Library. He had come to see himself as quite the adventurer. The shoot-down of *Clementine*, a disastrous involvement with the Wunderland underground, and painkiller addiction belonging to some remote past seemed like mishaps that had befallen another person. Well, so they had: Nathan Graynor.

But the adventuring phase of Louis's life had ended as abruptly as it had begun. Sigmund and Alice, for quite different reasons, and "for your own good," did not want amateurs involved in spying or defense. Nessus remained ensnared in affairs on Hearth.

Louis, it turned out, had one marketable skill: master chef. No matter that he could not *find* Earth, Home, Wunderland, or Fafnir. He remembered and could reproduce their cuisines.

His future on New Terra looked secure—and mundane.

Reinventing recipes involved a lot of waiting for things to rise, melt, thicken, brown, bake, or cool. He read, listened to music, filled a notepad with sketches and began a new one. He spent *way* too much time in front of New Terra's equivalent to 3-V. And like most of New Terra's population, he found himself riveted.

Many New Terrans had grown up under Concordance rule, and they monitored the Citizen broadcasts relayed by hyperwave buoys. For more than a century Concordance politics had been a spectator sport. Only now the New Terrans watched with the guilty fascination of gawkers at a traffic accident.

While New Terra—scrupulously neutral—observed, affairs between

Puppeteers and Gw'oth seemed headed for disaster. And under the strain, Baedeker's government was coming unglued. Louis had no opinion about Baedeker, but he *did* know Achilles.

All Puppeteers who left Hearth were insane; Louis understood that. He had known Nessus at his most manic and depressed into catatonia. Achilles was more than insane. Worse than insane. Achilles was a sociopath. That Achilles might become Hindmost was monstrous.

Meanwhile Louis, retired adventurer, watched 3-V and puttered in Alice's kitchen.

When Sigmund called Louis to ask if he might come to the Ministry of Defense, Louis leapt at the chance.

UNIFORMED GUARDS ESCORTED LOUIS from the Ministry Building's foyer. More guards waited outside Sigmund's office. One opened the door to let Louis in.

He found Sigmund and Alice inside. Alice smiled unconvincingly.

The office was much as Louis remembered it, only the atmosphere had changed. There had been tension on Louis's prior visit, but that was personal. The aura today was foreboding.

"Thank you for coming, Louis," Sigmund said. "Something to drink?"

"Sure." Louis synthed a cup of coffee for himself and sat. "What's going on?"

Sigmund said, "We've told you that New Terra trades with the Gw'oth. No one mentioned that we have a source aboard every ship."

"The spymaster has spies. I'm shocked, Sigmund." Louis sipped coffee, waiting. The synthesizer needed adjustment.

Alice leaned forward. "A freighter reached Jm'ho recently, and the captain reported back to us by hyperwave."

"And?"

"And," Sigmund said, "an interesting event happened on Jm'ho just before the Gw'oth launched their fleet. It's probably what provoked the military response. I'm hoping you'll see something everyone here has missed."

"An interesting event." That was awfully vague, Louis thought. Was this another of Sigmund's tests? "You're not volunteering much, but I'll hazard a guess. Ol't'ro struck back. A retaliatory bioattack, maybe?"

Sigmund shook his head. "Not a bioattack. But Ol't'ro? If only because I'm stymied, I could easily see their involvement."

"Just tell me, tanj it!" Louis said.

Alice looked at Sigmund, who nodded. She said, "We've never encountered anything like it. For half a day, someone or something suppressed fusion reactions in power plants across Jm'ho. I spent my morning discussing this with physicists. They insist it's impossible."

"So your captain has it wrong." Louis laughed cynically. "Or complain to Nessus when you next see him. He brought you the wrong Wu."

Sigmund said, "You've heard what our scientists say. In similar circumstances Carlos once told me, 'Reality trumps theory every time.'"

"I'm no scientist, Sigmund. Why did you ask me here?"

"Honest answer? Desperation. If fusion-suppression technology exists, it would make a fearsome weapon. A weapon against which New Terra would have no defense. So if there is anything you might know, any rumor you might have heard in Known Space, any offhand remark from Nessus, anything in the Gw'oth files you saw on *Aegis,* anything at all . . . we need to hear it."

"Nessus volunteers information about as freely as you, Sigmund. Sorry." Louis gripped the arms of his chair, ready to stand. Ready to slink home, to putter uselessly in the kitchen.

And then it hit him: the possible source Sigmund had not mentioned. The Pak. The attack on Jm'ho, whatever attacks Jm'ho's fleet now undertook, *everything* was Louis's fault. If only he had not started decoding the Library. . . .

Louis shuddered.

"What is it?" Alice asked anxiously.

"In the Pak Library, a file dealing with fission. I saw something about dampening fields. It meant nothing to me."

"And," Sigmund prompted.

"And," Louis said, "Achilles was with me in the lab at the time. I'm guessing the article meant a lot more to *him.*"

28

Beneath Hearth's largest ocean, below its stony crust, deep within its mantle, an artificial cavern hid.

Secrecy and the remote location had once sufficed to maintain the cavern's concealment. No longer. The more technology enabled the finding of hidden places, the more countermeasures had been deployed. Now sophisticated shielding subtly deflected any probes, whether by electromagnetic waves or neutrino beams.

Communications between the cavern and the rest of the universe relied upon neutrino micro-bursts, routed through a buried array of communication relays that ringed the planet. Only radio signals of extremely long wavelength *could* penetrate to the cavern's depth, and the large antennae needed to send or receive those wavelengths would have hinted unacceptably at the cavern's existence.

The tunnel that had originally given access to the cavern was long vanished, obliterated by the mantle's relentless heat and pressure. Stepping discs provided the only ways in or out, but not just *any* stepping discs. The addressing scheme was nonstandard; the discs' addresses were closely held secrets; the inter-disc transmissions were securely encrypted. And while radio waves interconnected the stepping-disc system on Hearth's surface, the cavern's discs responded only to modulated neutrino beams.

Those who had built and first configured the underground facility were long dead. Those few entrusted to maintain the equipment did so without ever knowing where they had been sent—and knowing that their memories would be edited upon the completion of their tasks.

Around the cavern the pressure and heat turned rock into oozing, viscous goo. Except for the pressure, lead and tin would melt at these depths. Yet inside the hidden cavern, life flourished. If one did not peer too closely at the digitally simulated distance, much of the cavern could be mistaken for meadow and woodland.

The little bubble of life, as artificial as the ecology aboard any spaceship, demanded power. Lots and *lots* of power. Power-gulping force fields to withstand the incredible pressure. Enormous thermal pumps to keep the heat at bay. More power to preserve the privacy shields and run a vast computer complex. Communications gear, teleportation equipment, autodocs, stasis-field generators, synthesizers, and more: they all took power. To provide that power, the cavern stored enough deuterium—for compactness, compressed and chilled to a solid—to fuel its fusion reactors for thousands of Hearth years.

Unseen, unsuspected, secure against almost unimaginable disaster, the facility waited.

The Hindmost's Refuge.

SAVORING THE FRAGRANCE of luxuriant pastureland, Baedeker gazed across gently rolling hills. The "sky" shone the cerulean blue of a bygone era; the brilliant orange circle overhead mimicked the sun that had once warmed Hearth. To his left, a shallow creek gurgled. Aside from a stepping disc inset in the meadowplant, the only visible artifact was the synthesizer installed atop a nearby hummock.

The idyllic surroundings were less for Baedeker than for the Companion herd whose tunes of fellowship, mindless and content, wafted from some unseen distance. Companions fared poorly in more realistic conditions. In the event of catastrophe, Companions would become Brides to preserve the race.

Baedeker planted his hooves far apart, unready to run, projecting the confidence he did not feel. Others would join him momentarily. Together they must stop the coming catastrophe.

And if he failed? Who was to say the fusion-suppression field could not penetrate to this depth? Then even the Refuge would be lost.

Motion from the corner of his eye: Nike, his spotless white hide unmistakable, his mane impeccably coiffed, cantered off the stepping disc. Then Demeter appeared, he of the darkly brindled coat. Finally, Chronos, patriarch of the Experimentalists, so ancient that no medical treatment could keep him limber.

No one else would be coming. The living who had ever been Hindmost composed a most exclusive herd. The four brushed heads in greeting.

"I have not visited the Refuge in a long time." Demeter stared frankly at Baedeker. "Do you think to play on my empathy?"

"I choose this place for secrecy, not empathy," Baedeker sang back. "Other than yourselves, I no longer know who to trust. Achilles has confederates throughout the government."

"Achilles has supporters," Chronos chided.

We *all* have supporters, Baedeker thought. Unless we four agree to influence our supporters—to pool our strengths, to unite against madness—the government will fall. To be followed by the disaster that is Achilles.

"I sang with care," Baedeker answered. Grace notes of impatience, unintended, modulated the purposeful motif of friendship. "My concern is not about politics, but rather treachery."

Nike sidled forward. "Clandestine Directorate internal surveillance had to fail for Achilles to escape. Only the system did not fail; it was bypassed. Achilles had help." And sadly, "Help from among my own staff."

Baedeker harmonized, "Yet other 'supporters' find ways to distribute Achilles' treacherous messages. And a Ministry of Science research vessel ignores the general recall sent after Achilles' disappearance."

"Are we Conservatives, then," Demeter intoned, "to obsess about minutiae? Should we not care more about the Gw'oth fleet that rushes at us, as Achilles predicted?"

"Safety before all," Chronos chanted pointedly.

"What if," Baedeker asked cautiously, "Achilles *brings* the Gw'oth?"

Chronos sang in disbelief. "Do you have any proof?"

"Less than proof, but more than suspicion," Nike sang. "The human Nessus recruited—"

"Nessus!" Chronos fluted with disdain. "I cannot speak to unsubstantiated accusations about Achilles, but I know *Nessus* has exercised a great deal too much . . . initiative in his time."

But never the initiative to try to murder another Citizen! Baedeker kept the anger inside, certain that melody would be twisted into a motive for Nessus to lie about Achilles.

"You know only that, Chronos?" Demeter looked himself in the eyes. "I know a bit more."

Meaning Nessus' relationship with Baedeker, and a dalliance with Nike before that.

Nike sang, "Louis Wu was raised by Beowulf Shaeffer, who *Achilles* twice recruited. Beowulf Shaeffer, who discovered the chain reaction at the galactic core."

"An honorable pedigree," Demeter conceded.

Nike went on. "Nessus, Achilles, and Louis together recovered a large part of the Pak Library. One file—"

"The assertion," Chronos sang, "was that Achilles somehow leads the Gw'oth."

"Not leads them," Baedeker corrected. "Brings them. Provokes them. We all know Achilles. He has always aspired to power. Perhaps his warnings are so prescient because he created the crisis."

"You all also know Sigmund Ausfaller, another result of Nessus showing initiative." Sigmund, without whose paranoid brilliance the Pak would have destroyed New Terra and Hearth—and Jm'ho, too. Only Sigmund had also tangled with Achilles. And with Nike, at the time Hindmost. The galaxy had become far too complex. "Clandestine Directorate trades information with Ausfaller. He reports that—"

This time Demeter interrupted. "Not subtle, Baedeker, mentioning Ausfaller to remind us of the Pak War and your own contributions."

Baedeker raised his voices, loud undertunes demanding respect for his office. "Ausfaller reports that the Gw'oth fleet set out after an attack on their home world. For a time, fusion reactors around Jm'ho . . . stopped. And *that* is the technology Louis Wu—and Achilles—encountered in the Pak Library."

Chronos' necks wriggled sinuously, in unapologetic surprise. "And you surmise Achilles used Pak technology to incite the Gw'oth? That he expected, amid crisis, we would install him as head of the Party?"

Were you not about to? Baedeker thought contemptuously.

"We believe so," Nike chanted.

"I would like a moment," Demeter crooned soothingly. He gestured to Chronos. At the slow hobble that was all that Chronos could manage, they walked behind the nearest hill.

The rolling hills were as artificial as everything within the cavern. A chain of knolls disguised tunneling equipment, because a sufficient disaster might destroy all stepping discs on Hearth's surface. The largest mounds held small ships with which to escape through any newly drilled passageway.

For the first time, Baedeker wondered if even *this* refuge could offer safety.

A considerable while later, the two returned. Demeter sang, "Perhaps it is not too late to resolve matters with the Gw'oth. Baedeker, we will support this government if efforts are made to negotiate. General Products has a representative on Jm'ho, surely."

"The representative who failed to report *why* the Gw'oth launched their fleet?" Nike fixed Demeter with a frank, two-headed stare. "Another 'supporter' of Achilles. We are forced to rely on Sigmund's agent on Jm'ho."

Shaken, Demeter repeated, "We will support this government."

29

Valiant was the grandest vessel in Tn'ho's navy, and the ship's council chamber was the largest room aboard. That made the never-ending strategy sessions only badly overcrowded, even with most captains participating by radio from their own ships.

At the journey's outset, Bm'o had presided daily. He had had to respond quickly to Ol't'ro's provocation, and that meant planning and adapting as they flew. Much had happened quickly—because it had to.

Engineering teams enhanced the ships' electromagnetic shielding to better deflect the spray of oncoming interstellar muck. Protected by the improved shielding, the ships had accelerated to half light speed before entering hyperspace. All the while crews built fuel cells, deploying them in every unused nook of shipboard space.

Most of his fleet would reenter normal space on a course that grazed the rebels' solar system. They would launch missiles immediately. The ships' prodigious momentum would carry them to safety if—against all odds—the rebels somehow hit relativistic targets with their fusion suppressor. The fuel cells would maintain shields until their reactors could be restarted.

Most of his fleet. His lead ships would exit hyperspace aimed directly at the rebel world. Suppress *their* reactors—if Ol't'ro should be so foolish—and the ships became deadlier projectiles than the missiles they carried. A single missile or ship strike would utterly destroy the rebels.

Ol't'ro could surrender. Or die. After a few days aboard the overcrowded warship, Bm'o scarcely cared which.

But the trip was long, made longer by the period of prolonged acceleration before entering hyperspace, and the information with which to *make* plans never changed. Still the generals planned.

Now Bm'o favored his cabin. He went to the council chamber only sporadically, entrusting the fine-tuning of the plan to his generals. They were only keeping their minds busy.

"Peasants are busy," Rt'o liked to remind him. "The ruler thinks."

Neither were rulers to be lonely, and yet he missed his counselor.

In the privacy of his cabin, Bm'o permitted a blue-green flush of emotion to wash over him. Even had Rt'o been fit enough for the rigors of shipboard life, who else might govern for so long in his place? Who else did he trust?

They consulted, of course, but Jm'ho was deep inside a singularity where hyperwave could not reach. The radio relay added delay. Their exchange of messages was a poor excuse for conversation.

Still, with a new challenge emerging at home, Bm'o felt fortunate that wily Rt'o served as his regent. The captain of a New Terran trading vessel denouncing the General Products representative? Claiming to speak for the Concordance? More likely, New Terra was in league with Ol't'ro and hoped to dissuade any reprisal on the rebels.

The overlapping crises only made Bm'o desire Rt'o's counsel that much more.

Bm'o jetted about his cabin. Idleness required no special skill, and brooding was no substitute for thought. Thinking was hard. "What would you advise?" he asked the empty cabin. "What remains to be thought about?" And he answered himself as Rt'o might have answered him. "What do you least wish to think about?"

Ol't'ro.

Not because they were obscene and unnatural, as every Gw'otesht was, but because Ol't'ro could think. Think faster, better, more creatively than any Gw'o, whatever his rank.

But surely they could not outthink the general staff, and outmaneuver the massed military power, of a great nation!

"They escaped you before," his inner skeptic reminded. "And how do your experts explain the suppression of fusion?"

His experts had yet to explain it, but his generals had planned around the still baffling weapon. Bm'o coasted to a hover midcabin. What, then, continued to bother him? What did he least want to think about?

The new surprises Ol't'ro might have in store.

With a convulsive squeeze, Bm'o jetted to the cabin hatch. He needed advice, assistance, expertise. He needed independent thought.

He had to know how *Ol't'ro* might think.

PUZZLES.

Ng't'mo liked puzzles. And they liked data: heaps, hills, mountains of data. They liked to sort data, arrange data, calculate with data, find patterns in data.

What did the patterns mean? Sometimes that, too, was a puzzle. The masters did not explain.

Ng't'mo hated their surroundings. Their cage. When they lost themselves in puzzles, they could forget their confinement. They could forget their reliance on the masters for food, data, everything.

And when the masters offered too few puzzles? Then, for as long as Ng't'mo could maintain a meld, they would remember better times.

Memories were hard. Hard to retrieve. Hard to understand. Often, hard to bear. Had they once been allowed to roam where they wished? Yes, it seemed.

The time of making their own choices seemed so . . . distant.

Once, Ng't'mo asked. Blame those called Ol't'ro, the masters said, those who defied us. And then, for Ng't'mo's disrespect, the masters withheld food for a day.

Maybe Ol't'ro *were* to blame. The masters must know. But Ng't'mo remembered Ol't'ro, too. Ol't'ro had been kind and patient. Ol't'ro had been *so* smart.

But Ng't'mo were only eight. They could never be that smart.

Ill-defined longings gnawed at Ng't'mo. To be smart. To be rid of the masters. To have enough to eat. And as they wondered why life was so hard, their hunger became primal: a crying need for *food*.

As eight-become-one, with tubacles coupled and entwined, they could not feed.

Howling in distress, they came apart into miserable self-aware pieces in their crowded cage.

THE MASTER OF MASTERS had a new puzzle! But what exactly *was* the puzzle? What did the Tn'Tn'ho want?

Something about ships, worlds, and harm.

Ng't'mo struggled with the new data. They understood ships. Ships went between worlds. They were on a ship. Missiles were like ships without Gw'oth on board. Worlds were places like home. They missed home.

Ng't'mo's units knew *what* ships and missiles could do, but little about *how*. The masters seldom told Ng't'mo how anything worked. Because Ol't'ro understood how things worked, and they escaped?

Fusion made a ship go. Ng't'mo did not understand fusion, and certainly not what might make fusion stop. But they understood what was important: the faster a thing moved, the more it hurt when it hit. If you were hit by a thing going *really* fast . . .

They put aside the bigger puzzle for the joy of calculation. Go twice as fast and the harm when the ship or missile hit was four times as much. Go three times as fast: nine times the harm. Go fast enough, almost like light, and—the calculation became pleasingly complex—the harm grew almost beyond numbers.

Go almost as fast as light and the thing would be on you almost before you could notice it.

What else did they know?

Hyperspace was somewhere ships could go really, *really* fast, and where hyperwaves could reach anywhere in no time at all. Hyperspace did not go all the way to planets. When ships got near worlds, they had to leave hyperspace.

Capabilities and possibilities swirled through their mind. They began to see purpose to the Tn'Tn'ho's puzzle. The master of masters brought ships and missiles to smash a world. Their puzzle: could those on that other world stop an attack?

Ng't'mo assembled their data. They sorted and arranged and found patterns. Without knowing how hyperspace machines worked, a possibility emerged from the patterns. They calculated until they knew. Those on the world could avoid being smashed.

They decoupled a tubacle, reaching for the buzzer that would summon a master. And paused before signaling. Who was on that world?

They worried at this new puzzle for a long while, sifting hints and inferences. Once more they sorted and arranged their data. And found a pattern.

The target was Ol't'ro.

Immersing themselves in memories of better times, Ng't'mo signaled . . . nothing.

30

Sigmund set down his fork and slid back his plate. "That, Louis, was the best meal I've had in a long time."

"Thanks," Louis said. But he had prepared the banquet for *Alice,* before she headed out to space in the morning. And he had had in mind a second, entirely different send-off once she digested dinner. He was a bit miffed that she had brought Sigmund home for last-minute coordination. And a lot miffed at Sigmund when, rather than working over dinner, the spymaster lapsed into telling war stories.

"Enough looking back," Sigmund finally said. He folded his napkin and set it on the table. "But before Alice and I caucus, I have to tell you something. Louis, we owe you. I assume you're following events on Hearth?"

Louis nodded. "The leadership, for lack of a better word, has united behind Baedeker."

"According to Nessus, it's your doing," Sigmund said. "Had you not tied Achilles to the Gw'oth fleet, he might have been given charge of the government by now."

"Why isn't this mess a reason for the Conservatives to reclaim power?" Louis asked. It was a safer question than why Sigmund refused to let him join Alice's diplomatic mission.

"Events have become too tangled and strange," Alice said, "and tradition is useless as a guide. At this moment no Conservative would want power. If they had power, they wouldn't know what to do with it.

"But how the Conservatives feel doesn't matter. The Citizen consensus process works slowly; there simply isn't time to consider turning over control. The Gw'oth fleet will do whatever it's going to do before any change in parties *can* happen."

And that returned matters to Alice's mission. Louis stood and started clearing the table. Tanj this twenty-year-old body! He could not just *sit,* and that made him seem immature.

"Achilles knows all this, too," Louis snapped. "I spent months aboard *Aegis* with him. He'll never quit. He doesn't know how."

"That's my guess, too," Sigmund said. "I met him in Human Space. I didn't trust him then and I don't trust him now. Since I've been on New Terra, I've had Puppeteer experts monitoring him constantly." Sigmund sighed. "Louis, I'm sure you're right. You know Achilles better than anyone on this planet."

The unspoken dare: tell me what Achilles will do next.

Louis carried the plates into the kitchen, noisily dumping them into the recycler. He was mad that he didn't have the answer. Never mind that no one else did.

He must convince Sigmund to add him to Alice's mission. How could he make himself indispensable?

According to Nessus, the Gw'oth war fleet kept popping up on Fleet hyperwave radar, headed for Hearth. With each return to normal space, the Gw'oth were closer. But separate flurries of hyperwave exchanges with Ol't'ro and with Sigmund's agent on Jm'ho painted a different picture: Achilles seemed implicated in attacks on both Gw'oth worlds. The Gw'oth king, by launching his fleet, was only escalating a conflict already under way. The Gw'oth warships would fly *past* Hearth.

And at that point Achilles, rather than seeming prescient, would look foolish.

Once again, *something* stirred in Louis's subconscious. Something that refused to be coaxed out.

He returned to the eating area to clear the remaining dishes. The silence had stretched awkwardly, and he felt compelled to say something. But what? Everything he knew about the Gw'oth situation came from Alice or Sigmund.

Louis said, "Ol't'ro and his people are going to get clobbered."

"That's how it looks," Alice said. She meant: that's why she had to go.

"This is crazy," Louis said. "Everyone's agreed that this Rt'o character is stalling. Every indication is that the Gw'oth fleet is going in for a kinetic kill. They have no interest in talking."

Alice shook her head. "It's possible that they'll listen to a neutral party. I can't stand by without trying."

"Neither can I!" Louis pounded the table with a fist. Dishes jumped.

"The Gw'oth fleet about to stomp Kl'mo is ultimately my fault. If I hadn't poked about in the Pak Library—"

"Then Achilles would have found another way to provoke this conflict," Sigmund interrupted loudly. "You said it yourself. Achilles doesn't quit."

"You have to let me go along," Louis insisted.

"This mission *is* dangerous," Sigmund said. "That's why everyone assigned to it is well trained. But you, Louis? You want to ride along to make yourself feel better. Maybe you would, but I'd feel worse. I've done more than enough to you and your family. I won't put you at risk—and let you endanger the crew—just to humor your guilt."

So instead Sigmund acted to assuage *his* guilt—and that was equally misplaced. Sigmund had not plucked Louis from Known Space, Nessus had.

None of which changed anything. Louis was stuck here.

But he refused to be useless, tanj it! Because Achilles would *never* quit.

Finagle! That was the key.

Louis said, "The Gw'oth fleet hurtling past Hearth will make Achilles look foolish. He can't let that happen. He'll do something first. That must always have been his plan." Louis went out on a limb. "He plans to ambush the Gw'oth, show himself as the savior of Hearth."

Alice and Sigmund both began talking and Sigmund gestured at her to continue. She said, "Achilles would have to be insane to do that. Of course he *is*. Crazy as a loon.

"Suppose Louis is right. Achilles has the fusion-suppression weapon. He has one ship; his supporters can probably steal more. But what does he do for crews? How many Puppeteers besides Achilles are crazy enough to take part in an ambush?" She paused, head tipped in thought. "He'll recruit crew here on New Terra."

Louis pounced. "You need an agent in the underground for Achilles to hire. Otherwise you won't find out his plan in time to stop him." Louis thumped his chest. "Me."

"We *have* agents in the underground," Alice said.

Sigmund shook his head. "He's right, Alice. Achilles completely avoided our people when he hired mercenaries for his Pak adventure. Roland, Finagle curse him, had enough training to have spotted our folks. And the Puppeteer scouting expedition that discovered Kl'mo almost certainly used New Terran crew we knew nothing about."

"It's got to be me," Louis said. "I'll go underground."

"You won't fit in," Alice said.

"That's all right. I *want* to be noticed."

"And then?" she asked. "You stunned Achilles so that Nessus could deliver him to justice. You'd have to be as nuts as Achilles to put yourself into his hands. Jaws."

Now you know how I feel about your crazy mission, Louis thought. "Maybe not, Alice. Achilles dislikes me, but he respects my work with the Library. And he *hates* Nessus and Baedeker. The bad blood between them goes back a long time. Using me against them would have an appeal to it."

"How would you go about it?" Sigmund asked.

"I'm bitter. Instead of a big payday and a return to Human Space, Nessus has stranded me. I'm broke and without direction. I sit in a bar, sloppy drunk, complaining about Nessus, and I wait for Achilles or his people to find me." But not so sloppy drunk he became addicted. That risk Louis kept to himself. "Alice tossing me onto the street wouldn't hurt. If she can delay her departure for a day."

"That's good," Sigmund allowed.

Louis thought: So much for your unwillingness to put me into harm's way.

Alice looked at the men in disbelief. "This is just too dangerous. Louis, you have *no* training for this sort of thing."

"What's the alternative?" Louis asked gently. "Achilles as Hindmost can't be good for New Terra. I'm coming to think of New Terra as my home, too."

Left unstated: who Louis meant to live his new life with.

"I'll leave you two alone." Sigmund went onto the balcony, sliding the glasteel door shut behind him.

"You know this is our best bet," Louis said.

Alice grimaced. "That doesn't make this easier."

There wasn't anything to say after that.

Twenty minutes later Sigmund returned from the balcony, a pocket comp in hand. "I got patched through to Hearth. Nessus agrees with Louis. About everything. The situation terrifies him."

PREEMPTIVE WAR

31

Red in the face, his right arm twisted high behind his back, his shoulder in agony, Louis stumbled out of Sigmund's office. The armed guards and receptionist in the anteroom stared uncertainly.

Sigmund gave Louis's wrist a final vicious yank before releasing the hammerlock. "Stay the tanj away," he snarled. To the guard unit he added, "Escort Mr. Wu from the building. And update the security files to keep him out."

The guard lieutenant saluted. "Yes, Minister."

Louis rubbed his aching shoulder with his left hand. "Ausfaller, you bastard! You're going to pay for—"

"Lieutenant," Sigmund snapped.

"Yes, sir!" The lieutenant gestured to another of the guards. "Sergeant, with me."

Louis raged, "Do you know what that—?" He stopped when the lieutenant put a hand on his sidearm.

"You heard the minister," the lieutenant said. "Walk."

Guards double-timed Louis down long corridors; he fussed the entire time. Heads turned in one crowded hallway after another. When they reached the main entrance and its long queue of visitors waiting for clearance to enter, Louis shouted, "Your precious Ausfaller ruined my life. He destroyed my family. He—"

"That's not my problem, sir," the lieutenant said. "Please leave the building."

Muttering under his breath, rubbing his injured shoulder, Louis did.

AT THE HEART of Long Pass City's main dining district, in the center of the posh restaurant's dining room, at the intimate table for two, the tension was palpable. Louis and Alice ate in icy silence. Their waiter whisked away appetizer and salad plates the moment a fork was set down. Diners at nearby tables kept stealing glances their way.

"I don't see how you can defend him," Louis finally blurted. "I told you what he did to my family."

Alice looked up from her duck à l'orange. "This isn't the place."

"No place ever is," he snapped back. "And because your precious boss is sending you away, there is no chance we'll talk about it anytime soon. How convenient."

Her eyes narrowed. "I mean it, Louis. Not here."

"While brave, heroic Sigmund sits on his fat ass in his comfy office," Louis continued.

"*You* die horribly three times, and get stranded alone twice in deep space. Then you can criticize his phobias."

"Big secret mission," Louis went on. "Out of touch for . . . how long? How stupid do the two of you think I am? When I think about you and Sigmund, together—"

Alice took out her pocket comp and started tapping.

"Am I *boring* you?" Louis shouted. "You're checking your *messages?*"

"No, I locked you out of my apartment. You can see the building manager tomorrow for your things." She stood, knocking her chair to the floor. "Don't bother to let me know where you end up."

With her head held high, Alice strode from the restaurant.

"GIMME ANOTHER," Louis said. He had enough detox pills in his system that the slurring was for effect. Mostly.

On the worlds of Human Space, at his present alcohol level, autobars—and more than a few posh human-served bars—would have denied him service.

Not here.

The bartender was a florid, round-faced woman with big hair. Without comment she poured Louis another whiskey. Her attention stayed on the 3-V and a football tournament.

Louis neither knew nor cared who was playing. Football here was a sissy game. He blamed the Puppeteers.

Nor was sissy football the only lingering Puppeteer influence on New Terra. Puppeteers were too social to mechanize any service that anyone might want to provide. They deployed automation only for dangerous and odious tasks, or when shortages made mechanization essential. They had indoctrinated their human servants with their inefficient but communal attitudes. Louis could not recall seeing a single autobar on this world. He didn't miss them.

But New Terrans had had more than enough paternalism under Puppeteer rule. If you wanted to drink yourself to death, no one stopped you. Bartenders, cheap *and* snooty, did what they were supposed to do: serve drinks and listen.

A very civilized world, New Terra.

Louis had killed time and brain cells in plenty of spaceport bars far seedier, but by New Terran standards this hole-in-the-wall was a dump. The lighting was all but nonexistent, the floor sticky, the smell sour and oppressive, the clientele thoroughly disreputable.

It was certainly more squalid than the joints Sigmund's agents favored. Louis had been through a few of those dives, too, but only lest his drunken excursion seem to be avoiding them. The people Louis hoped to find—if this plan was not entirely delusional—would never approach him at known agents' haunts.

"Lousy bastard," Louis said to no one in particular.

No one commented.

He caught the bartender's eye. "Buy you a drink?"

"Sure." She got herself a beer and then fulfilled her part of the transaction: "Who's a bastard?"

Louis clinked glasses with her. "How much time have you got?"

She laughed. "Call it one bastard to the glass."

He made a show of eyeballing the credit balance on his comp. "Then I'm on a two-bastard budget tonight. Sigmund Ausfaller screwed my family and ruined my life. And Nessus the Puppeteer—ex*cuse* me, Citizen— stranded me in this galactic backwater. Pardon my English."

"Who *are* you?" she asked.

From the corner of an eye Louis sensed interest around a nearby table. Because he had finally found the right bar? Or because he had insulted the men's precious icon, Sigmund Ausfaller? Growing up on Home, Louis had learned some martial arts—a body of human knowledge the Puppeteers had successfully eradicated here during their rule—but four to one re- mained tough odds. Even before the lumps and bruises he had collected brawling in other saloons.

"My name is Louis Wu," he said. "Like Ausfaller, Nessus brought me to this world. I had a job to do, after which Nessus was supposed to take me home with a big reward for my efforts."

"And?" the bartender asked.

"He stranded me on New Terra. Like that bastard Ausfaller, I've been stripped of the memories I'd need to get home. As for pay—never mind that Nessus almost got me killed a few times—here's what I got: Nessus looking himself in the eyes. I take it that's a good laugh. When I complained, Nessus said to take it up with General Products."

The bartender finished her beer. When he nodded, she refilled her glass. And another few credits vanished from the pitiful cash balance showing on Louis's comp.

Not that he would run out. Secret codes replenished the visible balance whenever he needed it. A sly fellow, that Sigmund. Clandestine funding was the least of the tricks in the ordinary-seeming comp he had given Louis.

"That's tough," she offered.

"Someday I'll get even with that two-headed freak. With both those bastards." Louis stopped as four burly men in greasy coveralls came up to him. "Something I can do for you gentlemen?"

"Yeah," one said. "Take it outside. *Minister* Ausfaller saved this world more than once."

Louis turned back toward the bar, only to be grabbed by the collar and dragged off his stool. He was shoved, none too gently, into the trash cans in the alley behind the saloon. Seconds later, this being an absurdly civil world, his pocket comp sailed out the door after him.

Louis staggered to his feet, brushed off the worst of the garbage, picked the comp off the pavement, and started for the next watering hole.

IN THE SANCTITY of his newly expanded cabin suite, in the relative safety of a random spot in deep space, Achilles waited. He needed New Terran mercenaries for his assault on the Gw'oth. Roland Allen-Cartwright and his crew, having so carelessly gotten themselves killed, were once again making his life difficult. Death discouraged recruiting.

Enzio Walker-Wong peered out of the holo display. Achilles' new mercenary chief had a thin face, a broad nose, and blond hair so wispy and pale he seemed to lack eyebrows. "I'm up to six," he concluded his report.

Six. Achilles had asked for a combat crew of ten. But with the Gw'oth fleet already on its way, the clock was running. He would destroy the Gw'oth navy with guile and Pak technology, not by force of numbers. Six would suffice to staff the weapons consoles. "Six will have to do. Your fee, of course, will be reduced accordingly."

"Here's something you might find interesting," Enzio said. Changing the subject? "There is a self-proclaimed Earthman down here drinking himself to death."

Not Ausfaller, obviously. "Louis Wu?"

Enzio looked surprised. "You know him?"

Know Nessus' lackey? Sadly so. But Wu was not without his skills. Without Wu, Achilles would not have gotten his glimpse of the Pak Library. That almost made up for the human stunning him at Nessus' order.

Smart. Adaptable. Able to follow orders. Maybe . . .

"We were shipmates," Achilles said. "Why is Louis drinking so heavily?"

Enzio laughed. "You name it. His woman threw him out. He's broke and stranded far from home. He's ticked off at Ausfaller and Nessus."

So Nessus had abandoned his underling. "Why Ausfaller?"

"Things Ausfaller supposedly did to Wu's family. Persecuted them. Chased them from Earth. Wu is drunk and raving half the time, so the details aren't exactly clear."

Wu's spat with Ausfaller and ignominious departure from the Ministry of Defense was the talk of New Terra. Achilles had had reports about the commotion from several sources and thought nothing of it. As a raving paranoid ARM, Ausfaller had doubtless ruined more than his share of lives.

"Who is Beowulf Shaeffer, anyway?" Enzio went on.

That wasn't a name Achilles expected to hear. "Why do you ask?"

"I gather Shaeffer is Wu's stepfather," Enzio said. "But neutron stars and black holes? Wu isn't making much sense. A lot of it has to be the liquor talking."

Beowulf Shaeffer was savvy, a survivor. So Louis had been raised by Shaeffer. It made sense, suddenly, that Nessus had recruited Wu. And it made using Wu *against* Nessus and Baedeker irresistibly appealing.

"Bring Wu along," Achilles said.

"He's a drunk, useless. I don't want him on my crew."

"That wasn't a suggestion," Achilles said. "Do it."

. . .

LOUIS'S HEAD POUNDED. His stomach lurched. His mouth tasted like a rat had curled up inside and died.

Detox pills evidently had their limits.

Eyes closed, arms folded on a saloon table, he laid his head down. How long had he been on this wild goose chase? And when he ran out of bars at which to make a fool of himself, then what?

Closing his eyes made his head spin. Forcing his eyes open gave Louis a sideways view of a stranger walking toward him.

"Mind if I join you?" asked the man. He was ghostly pale. "Wu, right?"

Blinking, Louis sat up. "Who are you?"

"Just a friend." The man pulled out a chair and sat. "Or, rather, a friend of a friend."

Louis gestured to his empty glass. "Friends desert you."

The man smiled. He had a gap between his top incisors. "Let's start over. You're not the only one with a gripe about Nessus."

"I want my back pay, not sympathy."

"Back pay, I can't give you. But a new paying job? That's something I can handle. I have a ship, and I'm hiring crew."

"Do you know what everyone in this dump has in common? Look around. We're failures, even the ship captains. So tell me. At what are you a failure? Contract scouting? Prospecting? Trade with the Gw'oth? Smuggling?"

The friend of a friend persisted. "Just so you know, my boss hates Nessus with a passion."

Louis frowned in concentration. "Your boss. Anyone I know?"

"He said you were shipmates."

Achilles! Now not to act too eager.

Louis said, "Oh, him. Tell him to give me a call." Not least of all because Sigmund's tech wizards were tracing calls to Louis's comp.

The man stood. "Will do. I'm Enzio, by the way. Let me buy you another drink."

"I can't say no to that." Louis laughed. "Obviously."

Enzio returned with two glasses and handed one to Louis. "To working together."

"Could happen," Louis admitted before swigging his whiskey.

LOUIS WOKE, his head pounding worse than ever. He was afloat between sleeper plates. As his eyes adjusted to the dimness, he noticed walls with handholds. Ventilation fans whirred and a background hum droned.

This was a ship. He'd been drugged.

Best guess, Enzio had carried Louis from the bar. No one would have questioned, "My friend had one too many." And once on the street, via the nearest stepping disc, to a spaceport.

At great insult to his liver, he had found Achilles! Now to find out what the sociopath was up to. . . .

Groaning, Louis reached out of the sleeper field and slapped the touch-point. The collapsing field set him gently onto the lower plate. No lump in his hip pocket pressed into his butt. His comp was gone, and with it the hidden software by which to reach Sigmund in secrecy.

Did Sigmund have any idea where Louis was?

32

On the cabin's fold-down desk Louis found detox pills, pain pills, and an insulated drink bulb of hot coffee (but nothing that had been in his pockets). A fresh jumpsuit hung in the tiny closet. The hatch was unlocked. The room even had a sonic shower. Compared to how he had boarded *Aegis,* this was a walk in the park.

But going aboard *Aegis* only his own sorry ass had been at risk. Now he meddled in the fates of worlds.

Detoxed, showered, and in clean clothes, feeling almost human again, Louis ventured from his cabin. The bridge seemed the most likely place to find answers.

The ship was built in a General Products #2 hull and mostly configured like *Aegis.* He sniffed the air: no trace of Puppeteer pheromones. A New Terran vessel, then. The bridge would be at the bow, not amidships as in *Aegis.* He went forward.

Enzio, seated at the pilot's console, glanced up at the sound of footsteps. "Good, you're awake."

Louis took the empty copilot's seat. The mass pointer was active, and it showed no significant objects nearby. "This is where you explain. But please talk softly."

"Achilles said to bring you. I did."

"Keep going."

"It was time to leave, Achilles wanted you, and you were in no shape to discuss career options."

"I suppose not," Louis said. "Achilles wanted me?"

"He needs a crew. You must have impressed him."

Louis nodded. *He impressed me back.* "Yah. You probably wonder why."

Enzio chuckled. "You're taking things surprisingly well."

"Uh-huh. I'm older than I look. Old enough to know that screaming won't make you turn around the ship, will it? I'll save my complaints for Achilles. So when can I see him?"

Enzio gestured vaguely at his console. "A few hours till we rendezvous."

Another ship then. The grain ship in which Achilles had escaped from Hearth? "And then?"

"Then it's between you and Achilles."

BEFORE THEY DOCKED, Louis had met all the mercenaries. Counting Enzio and himself, five men and two women. Two disgraced former police, four career criminals, and Louis.

Just then, if Louis had had to come up with a label for himself, it would have been dilettante. Spy was merely another failed occupation for his résumé. Yes, he had been right about Achilles gathering mercenaries. So what? Beyond whatever his disappearance might reveal, Louis had communicated nothing to Sigmund.

Most of the crew could fly the ship—by then Louis knew the vessel was called *Addison*—but only Enzio considered himself a pilot. Louis returned to the bridge to offer his services as copilot.

"Sorry," Enzio said. "Another of Achilles' orders. You don't get access codes."

Too bad. It had occurred to Louis that simply activating hyperdrive as they docked might stop whatever Achilles had in mind. Not easily: Louis would have to position the ship near something vital. Even at maximum power, the normal-space bubble that tiny *Addison* could project would barely impinge on a grain ship. Not cleanly: there would be casualties if he carved a chunk out of the hull. But Achilles' minions were, at a minimum, abetting a fugitive would-be murderer and war instigator.

The stratagem must have occurred to Achilles, too.

Maura somebody was in the copilot's seat. She was ex-police. Unlike the drunks with whom Louis had been tussling, she probably had had martial-arts training. Sigmund had trained the trainers who had trained most first responders. She was built like a wall and could probably beat Louis to a pulp.

He decided not to try for the controls.

Enzio and Maura let Louis observe from the bridge doorway. When they dropped from hyperspace, to his surprise the radar ping located two ships. From the blip sizes, both had #4 hulls.

"Calling *Remembrance*," Maura called. She had a booming, slightly nasal voice. "*Remembrance*, come in. This is *Addison*."

"*Remembrance*," answered an unfamiliar voice in English. A Puppeteer, because no real-world woman ever sounded that sexy. Not even Alice—

Louis tamped thoughts of Alice *way* down. He had to stay focused.

After an exchange of authentication codes, the Puppeteer continued. "We have opened a cargo-bay hatch. Proceed to docking."

Fly into a hatch? Not an easy bit of piloting. "I've done that before," Louis said casually.

Enzio ignored him.

"Achilles escaped Hearth on one ship. What's the other for?" Louis asked.

"Supplies," Maura said. "Now be quiet."

Two GP #4s? What the tanj did Achilles have in mind?

With a deft touch Enzio rotated *Addison* bow-out from the larger ship, backed through the yawning hatch using only his attitude thrusters, and set his ship onto a cradle in the otherwise empty hold. With a thump something clamped onto *Addison*'s hull.

Addison brought more than mercenaries, Louis guessed. Achilles had just acquired a lifeboat.

ACHILLES CHOSE THE EMPTY cargo hold he had come to consider his audience chamber to interview Louis Wu. At the appointed time, he heard a soft, respectful trilling. Achilles recognized Clotho's voices. "You may enter," Achilles sang.

Clotho entered first. "Excellency," he intoned, heads held low respectfully. Louis came next, looking all around, followed by two Citizen crew.

"Leave us," Achilles sang. Clotho and the crew withdrew, closing the door behind them.

Louis stood tall with hands clasped behind his back. "Did you bring me here to kill me?"

"If I did not trust you, Louis, would we meet alone?"

Louis shrugged. "My escorts likely remain just outside the door. Holding stunners, I think. You wouldn't risk potentially lethal weapons near you. It's easy enough to toss a stunned person out an air lock."

Achilles looked himself in the eyes. "You have learned to understand us, I see."

"So *will* you have me killed? You will not have forgotten that I stunned you."

Achilles sat astraddle a comfortably padded bench. He stretched a neck briefly to point at a human-style chair. "Sit. No, I have not forgotten. But Nessus was your hindmost, and you followed his orders."

"Nessus." Louis spat on the floor. "That's what I think of Nessus. If he had any honor, I would be home by now, a rich man."

"Without memories of your adventure," Achilles reminded.

"Without nightmares. You can't imagine how often I dream of that Pak ship filled with corpses."

"Let me share something with you. I have come to learn Beowulf Shaeffer is your . . . I believe the term is stepfather. I knew Beowulf. I respected him a great deal. When I worked in Human Space for General Products, I hired him twice. *And* I paid him in full both times."

"Keep talking," Louis said.

"Nessus treated you badly. He poisons the mind of the Hindmost, thus serving the Concordance badly. And so it falls to me to end the threat of the Gw'oth." And to take command of Hearth, and destroy my enemies, as my reward.

"I have watched you work, Louis, and come to respect your talents. Join me. Be an asset to our cause and teach Nessus the lesson he deserves."

"Two ships against a Gw'oth war fleet? I didn't think Citizens went in for suicide missions."

Achilles was unaccustomed to being questioned. He reminded himself he valued the human's independent mind. "We have weaponry the Gw'oth cannot even suspect."

"Pak technology." Louis narrowed his eyes in thought. "And when we're done, Achilles? Will you honor Nessus' bargain?"

"When we succeed everything changes, for the herd cherishes those who can keep them safe. Baedeker will be gone and I will be Hindmost. The reward of the Hindmost will vastly overshadow whatever paltry reward Nessus might have provided." Or fail me, and you *will* go out the air lock.

"And I've watched you at work," Louis said. "You do not take no for an answer. So tell me where I start."

LOUIS'S FIRST ASSIGNMENT was entirely mundane. What Maura had called a supply ship turned out to be a Ministry of Science research vessel. The New Terrans got to off-load most of its supplies to *Remembrance.*

Sigmund knew from Nessus that a Concordance research ship had gone missing.

No one volunteered what the other vessel would do after the cargo transfer. Skulk around Hearth, coordinating with Achilles' loyalists, Louis supposed.

The two big ships flew in tandem, a few kilometers apart. The New Terrans shuttled between cargo holds by stepping disc. Louis asked for his pocket comp back to use as a stepping-disc controller. Enzio declined but found Louis a spare computer.

For the largest items they used floaters to shift cargo onto freight-sized discs. With hold gravity turned down the crates were light, but they still had inertia and, all too often, awkward sizes and shapes. It was hard, mindless work, and it left Louis fretting about how to reestablish contact with Sigmund.

Packaged emergency rations. Vats of biomass for synthesizers. Synthesizers. Stepping discs. Space probes, basketball-sized, built inside General Products #1 hulls. Puppeteer autodocs and pressure suits. Portable power sources. Lab instruments. Cable reels. Equipment consoles. Spare parts for shipboard systems. Raw materials for machine shops.

Three of the New Terrans could read Puppeteer labels, which was fortunate because Louis could not. They had to know what was what to appropriately deliver the goods to holds and storerooms, labs and workshops, closets and pantries throughout *Remembrance.*

The ministry vessel also carried tens of powerful lasers. For experiments into long-range communication or improved fusion devices, Louis supposed—or so Achilles, as Minister of Science, might once have justified equipping a research ship. The lasers would make excellent weapons. Puppeteers unwired the lasers and secured them in crates that the humans moved.

Then things got interesting.

At the back of the last cargo hold, looming larger than anything Louis had yet handled, were a dozen or so enormous black slabs. No matter how low they dialed gravity, these things were *huge.* Inertia did not care about gravity. The monoliths would be tough to move.

"What are these?" he asked Maura.

She looked up and down several slabs. "The labels only say, 'MAIN EXTE-RIOR HOLD.'"

Near deck level each monolith had what looked like a service bay. Louis released a latch and slid open the access panel. He uncovered fat connectors for power hookups, skinny connectors for fiber-optic cables, and little digital readouts.

Did these slabs get wired together? In his mind's eye, he pictured something like Stonehenge.

Sigmund, in one of his war stories, had described something like that. A device from the long-ago conflict with the Pak. One of the unsuccessful, homegrown planetary drives that instead tore worlds to gravel.

That Achilles controlled such a device made Louis's blood run cold.

33

The Fleet of Worlds, slowly but steadily accelerating toward galactic north since the discovery of the core explosion, had attained almost half light speed. (The New Terrans, who had for decades pushed their planetary drive closer to redline to get some separation from their former masters, traveled a bit faster still.)

Remembrance started with Hearth's normal-space velocity and quickly matched course and speed with the Gw'oth war fleet rushing its way.

LOUIS'S EXPERIENCE in the Wunderland civil war—greatly embellished, because who could know otherwise?—made him the expedition's lone military veteran. Enzio remained the leader of the combat crew, but Louis's veteran status made him tolerated on the bridge. Even when Enzio was not running weapons drills. Even though Clotho, the ship's hindmost, seemed skeptical about Louis.

It probably helped that after the cargo-loading exercise, Puppeteers and New Terrans alike knew that Louis could not read Citizen writing.

He couldn't. But Louis had spent a long time on *Aegis'* bridge, comparing readouts on his console with the displays on the Puppeteer version, watching Nessus operate his controls.

Louis had a tanj good idea what most of *Remembrance*'s bridge instruments had to say—

Enough to begin to worry Achilles might actually be able to *win* his war.

IF A SPHERE COULD BE SAID to have a midsection, *Remembrance*'s bridge occupied most of its waist. Concentric circles of consoles ringed the deck.

Most consoles and crash couches accommodated Puppeteers, but one cluster was designed for humans. The combat cluster.

Enzio drilled his team two shifts every day. While *Remembrance* was in hyperspace they drilled with simulators. When *Remembrance* dropped back to normal space they drilled with live instruments and shot at target drones. They practiced with anti-space-junk systems. They practiced targeting manually. And Louis, to maintain his credibility—and with it, free run of the bridge—had to demonstrate weapons competence.

Why did they keep hopping through hyperspace? The New Terrans claimed not to know and the bridge crew would not say. Whatever the reason, after every emergence *Remembrance* disgorged squadrons of free-flying spacecraft: most of the probes Louis had helped unload from the Ministry of Science vessel. Hyperwave buoys, Louis guessed, judging from the associated flurries of activity at the bridge's comm console. He could not imagine why they deployed so many relays, so close together.

"Redeploy drones," Enzio called for the tenth time that shift.

A small fraction of the little space probes—still numbering in the dozens—were target drones. Each drone carried thrusters, a fusion reactor, and optronics for guidance, comm, and sensing.

"Drones repositioned," the stringy-maned Citizen named Hecate reported from a supervisory console. He was one of the few Puppeteers aboard who spoke English. "Thrusters active. Stealth active."

A stealthed General Products hull was *very* stealthy, actively canceling both neutrino probes and electromagnetic energy across the spectrum. It gave only two hints to its presence.

The first clue, but only in one very specific direction, was a jet of neutrinos. Every GP hull blocked neutrinos to hide the emissions of its onboard fusion reactors—except in one small area left transparent to the particles. Otherwise the neutrino flux from the reactors would accumulate, bouncing inside forever. Over time there might be consequences. Puppeteers built these things, after all.

The Gw'oth had stealth, too, but not impregnable hulls. They had not managed to reverse-engineer General Products hull technology—and the Concordance refused to sell them GP hulls. Lacking GP hulls, the reactors aboard Gw'oth ships spewed neutrinos in all directions.

"Evasive maneuvers," Enzio ordered. "Begin."

"Maneuvering," Hecate acknowledged. "Drones turning."

For this exercise Louis sat at a sensor console. The drones reoriented, now beaming their neutrino emissions straight at *Remembrance,* and his display lit up. It was as though the targets had just emerged from hyperspace.

"Six drones," Louis announced. Hecate varied the number of targets to keep the humans alert. "Weapons lock on four. Five. Five. Still five."

The sixth drone, jinxing and zigzagging, kept outwitting the targeting software. Space junk did not make evasive maneuvers.

"Fire on automatic," Enzio called.

"Three hits," Hecate reported. The lasers had been set to minuscule output levels and the drones carried coherent-light sensors.

On Louis's display, three of the targets flipped from red, for active, to black.

"Switch to manual," Enzio said.

Maura and a hatchet-faced man named Rogers started firing short bursts at the remaining "live" drones. And Louis stole a glance at the hyperwave-radar display.

Hyperwave was the other way to find a stealthed GP hull. Anywhere outside of gravitational singularities hyperwaves interacted weakly with normal matter. Had it been otherwise, hyperwave transceivers and hyperdrive shunts would not have been possible. Because hyperwaves traveled instantaneously, the hyperwave echo off an object only revealed a direction. But if one deployed arrays of hyperwave transceivers, and those units coordinated among themselves instantaneously by hyperwave, and they triangulated . . .

Rank after rank of coordinating hyperwave buoys flew in tandem with the Fleet of Worlds, to provide early warning of any visitors. Someone must be giving Achilles real-time access to the Fleet's hyperwave radar system. Louis wished he could report back to Sigmund and Nessus, to name that discovery and others, and just for the contact.

Achilles' spy network continued to function flawlessly. Louis, so far, was pretty much useless as a spy.

"Final target still maneuvering." Louis turned his head to report, sneaking a look at another arc of bridge instruments. In a tactical display, a line of dots pointing more-or-less at the Fleet showed consecutive detections of the Gw'oth armada. Gw'oth needed sanity breaks from hyperspace, too.

Finally, Rogers tagged the last target.

Hecate rotated the drones, hiding their neutrino emissions from *Remembrance*'s sensors. The targets disappeared from Louis's console.

"Let's do it again," Enzio said. "The Gw'oth aren't very far away."

LOUIS CORNERED ENZIO in a relax room. "How are these drills useful?" Louis demanded. "We're practicing against drones, most maneuvering randomly. The Citizens remotely piloting the rest have no combat experience. Nothing is shooting back at us. *We'll* be going up against twenty or so Gw'oth warships. You *do* know laser light goes right through a GP hull?"

Enzio grinned. "Because the Gw'oth won't be maneuvering or shooting back."

So the mercenaries had been promised, and they took the matter on faith. Louis took it as an indicator of Pak fusion-suppression technology to be deployed against the Gw'oth. Achilles had yet to mention fusion suppression, so Louis did not bring it up with Enzio.

Even with fusion suppression, Louis did not get how this operation was supposed to work. He dredged up a line from his brief military training on Wunderland. "The first casualty in any conflict is the battle plan."

"What do you propose? A different kind of drill? New drones?"

"No," Louis said. "Let's you and I have a chat with Achilles."

"He won't answer questions," Enzio said. "I've tried."

"Trust me," Louis said.

We'll all be killed got any Puppeteer's attention. Enzio and Louis were passed quickly up a chain of flunkies to Clotho to Achilles.

Puppeteers worked themselves into a manic frenzy when they had somehow to be brave. Aboard *Aegis,* Louis had seen mania in Nessus and Achilles both. They developed crazy glints in their eyes. Their speech got loud. They twitched with nervous energy.

When Achilles, wild-eyed, invited Louis and Enzio into his spacious quarters, he quivered with repressed energy. Combat must loom. Achilles said, "I thank you for your concerns, but they are misplaced."

"Then explain," Louis answered bluntly.

Achilles looked himself in the eyes. "Why not? Louis, you helped make it possible."

Enzio glanced at Louis with new respect, while Louis kept his face passive.

"We see the enemy coming," Achilles said. "From their routine appearances on hyperwave radar, we know they will emerge near here soon."

Enzio frowned. "Gw'oth are supposed to be smart. Why would they act so predictably?"

Because they *weren't* predictable, as Louis knew from his lurking on the bridge. Despite an overall pattern, the gap between consecutive emergence points varied by up to a light-year—and hence, three days. Nor was the armada's course exactly a straight line. The only absolute consistencies were in normal-space velocity, the number of ships, and that the vessels maintained formation. The better to defend each other against surprise attacks, Louis deduced.

Achilles wriggled a neck dismissively. "They will be sufficiently close. When they emerge near here, we will disable them. I will tell you how.

"With your assistance, Louis, I have discovered the technology to suppress nuclear reactions. Within the projected field, neither fission nor fusion can occur. When we immerse the Gw'oth ships in the field, their reactors will stop. The fleet will be adrift in normal space."

"Where we can pick them off," Enzio said. "My apologies, Excellency, for doubting."

The boast seemed impossible, but Achilles trembled with manic confidence. Louis knew he was overlooking something. But what? "We could be a light-year away when the Gw'oth emerge. They could be back in hyperspace before we arrive."

"Louis, you think in terms of the design you saw in the Pak Library. To project their dampening field, the Pak used a radio signal. Naturally you assume I do the same."

Skimming the Library, the text mostly untranslated, the math far beyond him, Louis had scarcely recognized the *subject* nuclear-reaction dampening. To suppose he had any idea how to project a dampening field? Achilles gave Louis far too much credit.

While *he* had underestimated Achilles. With fresh dread gnawing at his gut, Louis suspected everyone had.

"But Pak do not have hyperwave technology," Achilles sneered. "Hyperwaves interact with normal matter, else we could not build hyperwave radios. In a like manner, a properly modulated hyperwave signal of sufficient power can dampen nuclear reactions."

And the hyperwave beam would reach the Gw'oth fleet instantaneously. "Hyperwave buoys to keep beaming the field continuously," Louis guessed, "while *Remembrance* jumps back to hyperspace to get within laser range."

"Exactly right," Achilles said. He seemed oddly . . . pleased.

"*That's* why this ship has been saturating a small volume with hyperwave buoys." Small by hyperdrive standards. A sphere more than a light-year across.

Achilles' heads bobbled, up/down, down/up, up/down. "Very perceptive, Louis. You do not disappoint. The fusion suppression field requires transmission at very short wavelengths, and at those wavelengths interstellar dust and gas scatter the signal. The range is limited. That is why we distribute so many buoys."

It hit Louis: I'm an audience. A surrogate for Nessus. Achilles wants me to understand. He wants to gloat.

"Are you satisfied now?" Enzio asked pointedly.

With sick fascination, Louis had to know everything. "The field has to be turned off before *Remembrance* arrives, or our reactors will go offline, too."

Achilles bobbed heads again in enthusiastic agreement. "We will be finished long before they can get their reactors back online. There have been tests."

The attack on Jm'ho, Louis realized. That suppressor had been used deep inside a gravity well. That projector must have used radio waves, like the Pak version. Other than from Sigmund, Louis had no way to know about that, and he kept his knowledge to himself. "I see that you've thought of everything."

The worst part was, Louis feared that was true.

34

Singly and in small herds, an unending stream of Citizens sought Baedeker's ear. Party officials, agency administrators, scientists, celebrities, academicians, counselors, legislators, hindmosts of industry . . .

He listened and assessed, delegated or decided or deferred, all the while indifferent to the issues brought before him. All the while morbidly aware *why* so many so urgently wanted his attention: to be, should the Gw'oth emerge on the Fleet's doorstep, among the chosen few invited to the fabled Hindmost's Refuge.

Millions had fled aboard grain ships to the Nature Preserves and New Terra. Perhaps thousands had abandoned the Fleet altogether on stolen ships. Who could know precisely who had run when billions hid at home, in their own bellies, paralyzed with fear? Other billions thronged great pedestrian plazas around the globe, whether demanding preemptive surrender to the Gw'oth or agitating for Achilles to take charge and do—something. With workers everywhere abandoning their posts to spend what might be their last days with loved ones, every estimate was suspect.

One number was no estimate. *He* gambled with the lives of all trillion Citizens.

A senior aide appeared to announce another appointment. "Reschedule," Baedeker said, not caring who this supplicant was. "I am stepping to the residence, Minerva. Arrange for Nike to join me when he can."

Minerva lowered his heads. "Yes, Hindmost."

The Hindmost's personal residence was carved deep into the seaward slope of a coastal mountain. From the long and narrow terrazzo patio, behind a shoulder-high stone balustrade, Baedeker peered downhill to the seething ocean. Nature Preserve One, in full phase, hung just above the horizon. Its reflection, shattered into countless pieces, glistened on the trembling waters.

Shattered or whole? Which was Hearth's future?

Voices mingled in the vestibule. A moment later, Minerva trotted out. "Hindmost, Nike has come, as you requested."

"Thank you," Baedeker answered. "Have him join me."

Nike cantered through the grand salon, through the weatherproof force field, onto the patio. Despite the crisis, he was immaculately coiffed. "Hindmost. How may I serve?"

Baedeker brushed heads with Nike, waiving formality. "Inform me. First, what of the Gw'oth ships?"

"The same pattern," Nike sang. "Nearer at each emergence from hyperspace. Ausfaller's agent on Jm'ho is still told the ships will pass us, maintaining at least a light-year's distance."

"What of"—Baedeker's voices choked—"our deterrent?"

"On its way, Baedeker. The Gw'oth have been made aware."

If the deterrent did not deter, if a war fleet came too near to Hearth, he would surrender. Any Hindmost would. The herd *must* survive.

The Pak only trusted in the complete destruction of their enemies. The Gw'oth might follow that policy, too. Baedeker asked, "And our defensive status locally?"

"Automated planetary defenses are fully supplied and ready. We were able to deploy only two armed ships with crew. The New Terrans refuse to provide ships or crews."

Why *would* the humans take sides? Baedeker wondered. "What do your analysts deduce of the Gw'oth's intentions?"

"They believe the normal-space velocity of the Gw'oth ships is significant. At their current course and speed, the worlds *least* threatened are the worlds of the Fleet. If the aliens mean us harm, it will not come on kinetic-kill weapons."

"And *do* they mean us harm?" Baedeker's tune was rhetorical and Nike did not answer. "On to our other crisis. What of Achilles?"

"Of Achilles," Nike fluted, "we know nothing. If Ausfaller is correct, and I believe he is, Achilles lurks nearby to intervene—somehow—at the last moment. Hyperwave radar cannot distinguish his ship from the vessels that have abandoned Hearth and await events."

"And Ausfaller's new spy, this Louis Wu?"

"Vanished." Nike pawed the patio tiles nervously. "Ausfaller fears the worst."

Sigmund always feared the worst. But for his propensity to act, Sigmund would have made an excellent Citizen. For a long while Baedeker stared at the crashing surf and the shimmering sea. Achilles, too, would act. When he did, would he make matters better or worse?

Nike broke the silence. "The time for planning has passed. Perhaps I can serve best on a ship defending Hearth."

"You serve best assisting me," Baedeker sang. "If the worst should happen and the Gw'oth come our way, you will step with me into the Refuge."

"SIX CITIZENS PERISHED today, trampled at two separate rallies protesting inaction against the so-called Gw'oth menace. Advocates for the . . ."

Nessus froze the broadcast, relayed by hyperwave. The news continued to stream to archive, if he could ever bear to watch. Each time *Aegis* returned to normal space, he told himself the news was less important than that there *was* news. While broadcasting continued, it meant the Gw'oth had not devastated Hearth.

And that at the end of this long voyage, he did not have to perform his impossible duty. Could he really launch kinetic-kill weapons at Jm'ho and its nearby colonies? Could he commit genocide to avenge what the Gw'oth must have seen as necessary self-defense in the faces of Achilles' ceaseless threats?

Citizen and human speech could not express his frustrations. The Kzinti, though, knew how to rage and curse. After spitting and hissing for a while in Hero's Tongue, Nessus felt marginally better.

Perhaps Sigmund was correct and the Tn'ho forces meant to zoom past the Fleet. Perhaps Louis would somehow stop Achilles from striking at the armada and drawing their wrath upon Hearth.

And if, miraculously, all that came to pass? Then *another* world of Gw'oth would die horribly for Achilles' insane ambitions.

Someday, Nessus promised himself, Achilles would pay for his crimes.

35

It was going to be a massacre.

Louis sat at his combat station, doggedly working through yet another battle drill. Thirty-two drones this iteration, whittled down to four. In his furtive glances at the tactical display, the connect-the-dots course had the Gw'oth only two hops away from their likely closest approach to Hearth. From the ambush.

And it was entirely his fault. If only he had never looked at the Pak Library. Without the fusion suppressor, this ambush would not be possible.

But what about another weapon, another attack, another vicious, amoral scheme? Achilles did not quit, Louis reminded himself—knowing it was only useless rationalization. *This* ambush was his doing. *These* deaths would be on *his* conscience. He stood from his console.

"Hey!" Enzio shouted. "Where are you going?"

Louis cupped his hand over his mouth. "Sick. I'm going to hurl."

"I've got it," Rogers said, moving from one of the weapons consoles.

"Go," Enzio said.

Louis bolted from the bridge, as though rushing to the recycler. He went three decks aft to prowl a deserted corridor. Apart from the bridge, engine room, and crew quarters, the huge ship was all but uninhabited. *Remembrance*'s entire crew was perhaps twenty-five Citizens, plus the mercenaries all busy with their combat drill.

Back and forth Louis paced, his stomach churning. This was Wunderland all over again, but without any birds circling overhead for him to shoot in warning. He needed to alert the Gw'oth, move them past *Remembrance* without incident. Getting out a message meant using hyperwave, and that was impossible. He had never seen fewer than six Puppeteers on the bridge, and the closer the Gw'oth approached, the more often Enzio had the New Terrans on the bridge drilling. *Addison* had a hyperwave radio, but Achilles had engineers all over the little ship. That Louis knew of, they were installing stealth gear, equipping a cabin with Puppeteer amenities, and retro-fitting the bridge with a Puppeteer-friendly crash couch and console.

Sometime in the next few days, following their pattern, the Gw'oth would drop from hyperspace. The exit after that would put them into Achilles' trap. Typically the Gw'oth stayed in normal space for a few hours. Those few hours were Louis's only opportunity to warn them. And he had no tanj hyperwave access!

Unless . . .

He stopped his pacing. There might be a way to alert the Gw'oth, and it would require Achilles' unwitting cooperation.

"YOU ARE MOST PERSISTENT, Louis," Achilles sang. He meant: *you are pushy.* Still, he allowed the human into his suite. The man had proven useful before.

"I apologize," Louis answered. He looked in vain for a New Terran chair before perching on an end of a padded bench. "For what I have to say, time is of the essence."

Achilles settled into a deep nest of cushions. "Proceed."

"With their fusion reactors inoperative, the Gw'oth will be helpless. That is the plan, correct?"

"You see a problem?"

"Possibly." Looking uncomfortable, Louis squirmed on his bench. "Suppose the Gw'oth ships have backup power. Batteries. Fuel cells. Some unanticipated power source that a Gw'otesht invented."

"Then they will not be entirely helpless," Achilles completed. "They might get off a few shots from their lasers before exhausting their emergency power reserves."

"Exactly." Louis rubbed his chin. "And with emergency power for their launch systems, they could target us with missiles. They must carry guided missiles, or they would not have accelerated to kinetic-kill velocities."

"And you imagine I did not think of these possibilities," Achilles said coldly.

"I'm sure you did. At the core of a ship this size, within a General Products hull, probably the Gw'oth can do us no serious harm before we destroy them."

Almost certainly correct, although a few crew on *Remembrance*'s periphery might not fare well if the Gw'oth got lucky. Lasers and concussion could kill right through the hull. "Louis, are you more timid than a Citizen?"

Louis laughed. "No, but I would still rather eliminate the enemy more safely. *Really* safely. I think I know a way."

Safer was always better. "What is your suggestion?"

"It goes back to a war story from that bastard Ausfaller." Louis stood, rubbed his posterior, and began shifting his weight from leg to leg. "That's just not comfortable."

A war story. "The Pak War?" Achilles guessed.

"Right. Do we have a planet-buster aboard? Like Ausfaller used to blast Pak fleets?"

The technology was much improved since the Pak War. Then, the devices took days to set up and calibrate. *Remembrance* carried a unit of the latest design, and it could be made operational in less than a day. And the irony would be delicious: to stabilize the early homemade planetary drives even long enough to use as weapons, Baedeker had required the assistance of a Gw'otesht.

Achilles plucked absentmindedly at the meadowplant carpet, considering. "Set off such a device while the Gw'oth ships drift without power."

"That was my thought. Assuming we can find a world nearby to bust."

Planet-buster. What a naïve oversimplification. When a planetary drive destabilized, it shook nearby space-time and sent waves of quantum chaos in every direction.

A planet-buster near the ambush point would more than destroy the Gw'oth ships. The space-time ripples would rattle every dish on Hearth. None would be able to deny that something extraordinary had happened. That someone extraordinary had saved the Concordance.

And eliminating even the remotest possibility of a lucky Gw'oth shot *did* have appeal.

IT WOULD HAVE BEEN NICE, Louis thought, to have an actual plan. Instead he had had a notion and a rush to improvise. But time pressure also distracted the Puppeteers. Urgency might be working in his favor.

It was a nice thought, anyway.

Louis's crash couch twitched: one of the Puppeteer engineers at work on *Addison*'s bridge, prone on the deck, his heads and necks deep inside a wiring cabinet, had kicked the seat. A melody, using the term loosely, sounded from the cabinet.

"He said, 'I am sorry,' " Metope translated from the bridge doorway. His tan-and-cream hide was striped, like some sort of understated zebra.

Everyone pretended Metope was here to translate, not to supervise Louis.

"It's all right," Louis answered. Better than all right. He had access to a hyperwave radio, with far fewer eyes watching than if he were on *Remembrance*'s bridge.

Many worlds drifted between the stars, but nothing guaranteed a world in a suitable spot for blasting the Gw'oth. The plan remained to fry disabled ships with lasers, and neither Achilles nor Clotho would divert any resource essential to that attack. That very Puppeteer caution relegated the proposed search for roaming worlds to idle instruments on *Addison*.

As Louis had hoped.

He hummed to himself as he reconfigured *Addison*'s hyperwave radio. The equipment sent and listened in only one direction. If its beam encountered any substantial object, the strength of the echo would hint, with *very* uncertain precision, at a distance.

To pinpoint a remote object with hyperwaves took triangulation. Achilles would not redirect the Fleet's hyperwave array—and risk disclosing that he could control the array—until a reasonably small search area was isolated.

The scary part was that Achilles *had* access. Traitors high in Hearth's defense establishment, Louis inferred.

And if he failed to warn the Gw'oth and this search *did* locate a suitable free-floating world? He told himself that the Gw'oth would be no deader one way than the other. He told himself Achilles would have expended the most terrible weapon in his arsenal.

Mostly, Louis told himself that he must not fail.

"Why does this take so long," Metope asked.

"We can trade jobs if you want," Louis snapped. He knew Metope wouldn't accept: cables still dangled from the Puppeteer-friendly console awaiting installation. "Look, it's complicated. This is a hyperwave *radio,* not part of a radar array. The faint echo it will get from a distant object is more like background noise than signal. I had to reprogram the noise filters. And because this is a radio, it's supposed to *point,* not sweep."

If only the Gw'oth were in normal space! Then merely a "misdirected" scan could scare them off. But Achilles, whether from distrust or simple Puppeteer caution, had restricted the search window. Louis would be escorted from *Addison* long before the Gw'oth might next reappear. Or if Louis had had his old pocket comp, with its hidden codes for reaching Sigmund. Or, or, or.

You have this one chance, Louis lectured himself. Do *not* blow it.

"So you are programming a scan pattern," Metope offered.

"Exactly." Louis talked about scan-pattern parameters. He prattled about the spin axes of nearby stars, and what that said about planetary orbital planes, and what *that* said about where best to seek planets ejected from their native solar systems. Anything that might distract Metope. Happily, Louis's babysitter was not an engineer.

All the while keying the emergency codes Nessus had insisted Louis memorize. Nessus had distrusted Achilles then; Louis could hope that whoever monitored Clandestine Directorate's emergency communications network was no friend of Achilles now.

Galactic coordinates, presumably the location of a trusted hyperwave relay buoy. Louis arranged his scan pattern to sweep over those coordinates. As he chattered about the difficulties of reconfiguring the hyperwave set, and needing to transmit a distinctive pulse sequence so that any hyperwave echoes would be unique, and the parameters to be estimated, Louis entered the memorized control sequences.

"This approach seems unlikely to work," Metope decided, "if you ever even finish."

"Almost done." Louis planted a boot tip deep into the flank of the engineer still sprawled on the deck. The engineer wailed atonally, Metope's heads swiveled—

And Louis keyed a short message to modulate the scan beam. His final keystroke cleared the display.

"Arrrgh! My foot slipped. Tell your friend I apologize," Louis told Metope. "The good news is the configuration is complete. We are ready to begin scanning."

36

Baedeker jolted from deep sleep, his hearts pounding. Utmost emergency tones!

He leapt from his nest of cushions. Hooves pummeled his door, and alarmed voices bleated for permission to enter.

Few had his *very* private personal number; fewer still the codes that overrode his privacy settings. This interruption could only portend ill. He must take the call alone. He sang through the door to the unseen sentries, servants, and aides, "I am all right. Stay where you are."

He had left his communicator in the pocket of a sash. He took the unit, still ululating, and set it onto a table. "Take the call," Baedeker ordered.

Over the communicator, a hologram opened: Nike. He appeared to be standing in his office, but the bedraggled mane said he, too, had just been awakened.

"My pardon, Hindmost. I seek your guidance."

We live in troubled times, Baedeker thought. "What has happened?"

"A text message from Nessus, very cryptic, received over the Directorate's emergency communications network." Nike's hoof tapped nervously at his floor. "But we heard from Nessus earlier today, on a scheduled respite from hyperspace. He intended to be in hyperspace, unreachable, for the next three days. After this odd message, we tried and failed to contact him."

Because Nessus was making the long trek to the Gw'oth home system. "What is this cryptic message?"

"Galactic coordinates and two English words: hyperwave power."

Many at Clandestine Directorate knew English, from training during the colonial period or more recent dealings with New Terra. The message would not be in English for security purposes. "*Is* the message from Nessus?"

"It has his authentication code," Nike said. "That could not be coerced from him"—because he would die first from fright—"but conceivably he gave the code away."

"You infer something. Sing plainly."

Nike bobbed heads. "The message entered our network at a remote relay buoy. Nessus is far from there. But when he chased after Achilles, at the rear of the Pak fleets . . ."

"You believe Nessus gave highly classified Concordance codes to Louis Wu."

"I think Nessus was more realistic than the rest of us about the danger posed by Achilles."

Baedeker understood that melody as agreement. And as a rebuke for so long tolerating Achilles in the name of Party unity. "Assume this message comes from Wu. 'Hyperwave power.' What does it mean? What do the coordinates tell us?"

"The coordinates define a place in the Fleet's wake. If the Gw'oth ships follow their pattern, the message points to the center of the region in which they are likely to emerge next."

A human unaccustomed to Citizens might think to propose an attack on the Gw'oth, but Louis Wu was no stranger to Citizens. The message's brevity and cryptic nature suggested haste; what little the human had sent must have meaning.

" 'Hyperwave power,' " Baedeker sang. "A powerful signal? Sent to the Gw'oth when they next appear?"

"I believe that is the intent." Nike hesitated. "But to say what?"

" 'Power,' " Baedeker mused. "Wu sent only two words. Both must be significant. Suppose we transmit at high power or using many convergent beams. To what purpose?" The instincts of a politician told Baedeker nothing. But reasoning as the engineer he once was . . . "Powerful beams would simulate many ships, hidden ships, nearby. All scanning."

"Wu means a trick?" Nike trilled, baffled. "But to fool whom? Ausfaller sent Wu off to pursue Achilles."

"I think we cannot know." Baedeker stared at his bedchamber walls, over the heads of virtual herds and into the illusion of distance. He decided. "Nessus trusts Louis Wu. So does Ausfaller. Isolate everyone with knowledge of this message, then proceed as Wu proposes."

.   .   .

"NOTHING," LOUIS DECLARED. "Not a world to be found. I've run the search pattern twice."

"Then we have finished," Metope said. He had claimed the pilot's bench the moment the engineers completed their work and departed *Addison*'s cramped bridge. "Turn off everything and come with me."

Louis powered down the copilot console. He closed and pocketed his doodle-filled notepad. "You don't sound disappointed."

"I trust His Excellency. His plan will work."

I hope to tanj it does not come to that. "We will know soon enough," Louis said.

Metope took a transport controller from his utility belt. For the stepping disc in the corridor, just beyond the bridge hatch.

"Hold on," Louis said. "I'm going to grab a few provisions while I'm aboard. The synthesizers on *Remembrance* do a lousy job with human recipes. No offense."

"The others do not complain."

"Look, I only want some food items, cleaning supplies, and a notebook and pen. It's all sitting in the pantry or closets, going to waste. Five minutes, Metope. Help me carry, and it will go faster still."

Metope considered. "And you will leave anything if I ask. No argument."

"No argument."

Five minutes later, the bags of supplies stowed in his cabin, Louis was drilling in the combat center.

ANOTHER SCHEDULED EXIT from hyperspace drew near, and Bm'o's guests had become restless. Some hastened their eating, or stopped eating altogether. Others wriggled where they lay, tubacle tips curling in the banquet-floor mud.

He shared their impatience, but he would never show it.

Across his fleet, crews prepared. Bridge crews calibrated their sensors. Combat crews readied their weapons. Communications crews queued outgoing messages and prepared to download any messages waiting on distant relay buoys. They had done it all before, many times.

More than routine, the return to normal space . . . beckoned. No less than the lowliest Gw'o in the fleet, *his* mind, too, crawled whenever they swam in hyperspace. Inarticulate whispers. Hints of madness. An insatiable void endlessly gnawing at his consciousness. But he was Tn'Tn'ho. He showed emotion neither on entering hyperspace nor when leaving.

Especially not when leaving. The Citizens, far from being a threat, trembled before the might of his war fleet. Their fear was plain in their broadcasts, long relayed to Jm'ho by stealthed buoys. As Bm'o's ships drew near, Citizens in ever larger numbers urged their government to surrender.

Surrender! Of what possible interest to him were a trillion alien subjects? Of what conceivable value was their overcrowded, overheated world—even if it were not escaping from the galaxy?

"All may leave," Bm'o announced to his guests, and they scrambled from his presence as speedily as decorum permitted. He followed at a far more leisurely swim.

The direct path to Ol't'ro's rebels was already long. Rt'o had counseled, her wisdom more evident with each passing day, that to detour around cowards was senseless. By choosing to match course and speed with the Citizen worlds, he had demonstrated that he meant them no harm. His fleet's course was predictable, to avoid alarming the Concordance (if not *too* predictable, lest, against their nature and all logic, the Citizens should consider an attack).

And still they feared Bm'o's might.

Air or water, tubacles or jaws, the laws of politics never changed. Rt'o had correctly seen the threats of Concordance politicians as posturing for domestic consumption—just as Bm'o had often used external threats to intimidate his rivals. By the same universal laws he dare not ignore Ol't'ro's insolence, no matter how far the rebels fled. Any unanswered flouting of the Tn'Tn'ho's authority would incite new resistance at home.

And so, uneventfully, the voyage proceeded, with naught to fear but the eeriness of hyperspace.

As the scheduled moment of emergence approached, Bm'o jetted into the control center of his command ship. Crew flattened, groveling, at their duty stations. Commanders respectfully lowered the arcs of their tubacles.

"As you were," Bm'o ordered.

The crews and junior commanders returned to their tasks. The captain directed a tubacle at his sovereign, awaiting guidance.

"Reenter as planned," Bm'o said.

Displays filled with stars. (Extraordinary objects, stars. He wondered if he would ever become accustomed to them.) In other displays, ships. His fleet, intact, clustered to support each other and protect him.

The routine chaos of emergence began. Astrogational measurements. Sensor sweeps. Communication exchanges. The commanders would be—

"Sire!" the ship's captain said. Alarm hues rippled across his integument. "We are being scanned!"

"From where?" Bm'o asked calmly. The Citizens had been tracking them at every recent emergence. "The same border sensors?"

"Those sources, Sire, and many others," the captain answered. "The Citizens' stealth technology must be . . . very good. From the power levels, they are close. Very close."

So the Citizens meant to defend themselves against a nonexistent attack. Commendable, although surprising.

Waiting only until a revised sequence of reemergence points—*un*predictable, this time—could be radioed and acknowledged, Bm'o ordered his fleet back to hyperspace.

37

"Catastrophe is upon us." Behind the camera, gazing adoringly at Achilles, virtual Citizens stood in untold thousands. Their rapt attention inspired him. "Catastrophe is upon us, and our Hindmost does . . . nothing.

"He flatters his inaction with imposing names. He speaks of calm and patient determination, of deterrence and quiet diplomacy. He claims we have nothing to fear. All the while, the enemy approaches."

At this point, when broadcast, the recording would cut to an animation: a time-lapse holographic map built with data from the hyperwave-radar system. Achilles risked nothing now by revealing that his minions had access to the border sensors. The Gw'oth were in hyperspace on their last hop this side of Hearth. The last hop before he obliterated them.

"See how the enemy's war fleet approaches while your government does *nothing*.

"But who is this enemy? To whom did the Hindmost lose the secret of hyperdrive? At whose mercy does the Hindmost's paralysis leave us?"

A video sequence would appear here:

—A single Gw'o scuttling across seabed muck, slimy and repugnant.

—A Gw'oth banquet surreptitiously recorded by Thalia, the aliens grabbing, crushing, rending their food. Their *live* food. Their *prey*.

—More imagery from Thalia, this of Gw'oth warships leaping from an icebound world.

—And the final sequence: the pulsating, entangled mass of a Gw'otesht. That this scene came from Nessus' long-ago mission files made using it all the more satisfying. The throbbing, writhing tangle looked like an orgy, and Achilles would not say otherwise. Let Baedeker's experts try to explain.

"*These* are the predators almost upon us."

Now the images would vanish. Achilles leaned toward the camera, toward his virtual audience, toward his glorious destiny. "The Hindmost has failed you. I shall not.

"Within five days"—although, more likely, the Gw'oth would reappear sooner—"*I* shall have eliminated this threat."

And you will have acclaimed me Hindmost.

"WHERE DO THEY GO?" Achilles raged. His tune echoed from the walls of his cabin.

Clotho stood with heads bowed. "I cannot say, Excellency."

Then what good are you? Achilles nearly wailed, but he kept the grievance inside. He needed loyal supporters more than ever.

(In his mind's eye, classmates and parents . . . watching. Doing nothing. Always, others failed him. He must dominate. He must work his will. He *would*.)

The Gw'oth should have emerged within a day of his broadcast. But that day had gone by, and another, and now *another*. "The aliens avoid us," he roared.

"Yes, Excellency." Timidly, "How is that possible, Excellency?"

"Go find out!"

"Yes, Excellency, at once." Clotho sidled to the hatch, reeking of fear pheromones. He stood, frozen, one head looking at Achilles and the other at the closed hatch.

"Now."

Clotho pelted from the room, scarcely slowing to shut the hatch behind him.

Achilles called up and studied the latest tactical data. The gleaming icon of the Fleet of Worlds. The dotted, not-quite-straight path of Gw'oth reappearances in normal space. The mauve region within range of the buoys that projected the suppressor field. The yellow region into which the Gw'oth might next emerge—*that* volume growing with every moment the aliens continued in hyperspace.

Ships in hyperspace traveled at a constant rate: a quantum limitation. Achilles knew with mathematical precision that if the accursed aliens did not soon reenter normal space, they would emerge beyond the reach of his farthest tier of suppressor buoys. Untouchable.

He caterwauled in frustration.

Soon after the Gw'oth passed his buoys, they would pass *Remembrance* itself. If he allowed *that* to happen, mathematical precision also decreed he would never catch up. Not unless, unlike their past behavior, the Gw'oth chose to dally in normal space.

But if *Remembrance* jumped to hyperspace to remain ahead of the Gw'oth, he risked them emerging when he could not see.

Mathematical precision could not guide him now. Intuition must serve. Achilles took a comm unit from his desk. "Clotho, set course for Kl'mo. For now, use only thrusters. Be prepared to jump to hyperspace on my order."

FOR DAYS BAEDEKER had lived and slept in the Clandestine Directorate command bunker. Each time he checked with his ministers the panic among the public had grown. The uncertainty became palpable.

For days—as the tension in the bunker grew, as defenders lapsed into catatonia and had to be replaced, as hushed whispers became murmurs became intermittent keening—nothing happened. No Gw'oth. No pronouncements from Achilles. No news from Nessus, or Sigmund, or Louis Wu.

Until—

"A strong signal," Nike sang out from near a hyperwave-radar console. "A large return. Many ships."

"Ripples," sang another operator. "Many ships are emerging from hyperspace."

Baedeker had been fitfully dozing astraddle a shift-watcher's bench. He jerked awake. "Copy the data to my station," he ordered.

With a sweep of a head he superimposed both holograms. A short, sharp trill expanded the scale. Another trill brightened the grid lines. "Thank the herd," he crooned to no one and everyone.

The Gw'oth had reemerged a light-year *beyond* the Fleet, still speeding northward.

BAEDEKER, LAUGHING AT HIM!

Achilles galloped through the corridors of his ship, sweat running down his flanks, chest heaving, inarticulate with rage. His mane coiffure had collapsed into a sodden mass. Crew, round-eyed, scrambled out of his way.

How fitting that he ran in circles, for there was nowhere *to* run.

Baedeker, mocking him!

Achilles could not banish the humiliation from his mind.

Oh, the Hindmost's speech to the Concordance had been entirely proper: the Gw'oth ships have passed. There never was danger. Even the appearance of danger has ended. Citizens should return to their homes, their work, and their normal routines. "Alarmists" should be ignored.

Alarmist. How casually, unceremoniously, callously, Baedeker dismissed him.

While across Hearth countless lackeys did Baedeker's bidding, proclaimed the Hindmost's *true* message: that the crisis Achilles had so grandly proclaimed was a mirage, the great battle he had foreseen, a delusion. That Achilles was a failure, a fool, and a menace.

Success had been snatched—Achilles still did not know how!—from his jaws. He *would* have vanquished the Gw'oth and then claimed his rightful place as Hindmost. Now, cheated of his victory, he could not return at all, except to shame and banishment and Baedeker's gloating.

The Gw'oth must pay. His enemies must pay. Above all, Baedeker *must pay.*

Achilles tore faster and faster, hooves pounding, droplets of sweat flying, his sash flapping, but his mind raced quicker still. To regain the initiative he must overtake the Gw'oth fleet. If *Remembrance* stayed in hyperspace all the way, hardly ever dropping into normal space, he could reach Kl'mo first. Laboring around the clock to replace the abandoned suppressor buoys would keep everyone's mind busy. A few insanities among the crew were likely, but that was acceptable. He had enough to manage.

Baedeker, taunting him! Unacceptable!

Smash Kl'mo. Destroy the Gw'oth fleet. Return proudly to Hearth with the enemy crushed. Who then could say what the aliens had planned for their homeward trip?

He could yet claim his prize. He *would.*

A cross corridor loomed and, hooves skittering for traction, Achilles veered into it. There was not a moment to be wasted. He galloped onto the bridge. Clotho stared at him.

Achilles chanted firmly, with a confidence that he did not feel, "Depart immediately for Kl'mo."

THE FOG OF WAR

38

"Good news at last," Nessus sang. *Aegis,* suddenly, felt much less empty.

"Very good, sir," Voice answered, as though he had not processed the message as Nessus listened. Or earlier, while downloading it.

The English butler mannerisms grew tiresome, even rendered as music. "What do you think of the news?"

"I should imagine you will be happy to see Hearth again," Voice answered cautiously.

Baedeker *and* Hearth. Nessus climbed off the pilot's bench and stretched. "If only . . ."

"If only what, sir?"

If only he could believe the danger had passed. Achilles stymied, and the Gw'oth warships safely past Hearth? That, Nessus accepted. Louis and Sigmund would make a formidable team.

But Achilles stopped? Nessus had known Achilles—struggled against Achilles—far too long to believe that. Achilles cared only for himself. While Achilles could conspire, he would.

"If only the universe were not so complicated."

"I do not think I can help you with that, sir."

For a long time Nessus stood staring at the view ports. Two nebulae shone nearby, lit by the stars to which they had given birth. The cooler cloud glowed blue; it only scattered the ambient starlight. The second cloud, its gases heated to plasma by the tight cluster of young stars within, blazed with its own pink light.

Only he was rushing away from the nebulae at nearly half light speed. The display corrected for the massive red shift.

He had a long trip ahead of him, returning the way he had come. But it would have been longer still if *Aegis* had shed any of the Fleet's normal-space velocity.

Happily, he had not had to confront using that velocity to slaughter a world of Gw'oth. Good news, indeed.

"Voice, record a reply."

"Of course, sir."

"Recall order acknowledged. On my way home. Will check in every three days." Nessus paused. "Send that to the Hindmost."

"Very good, sir."

On the long trip home, he would try to make sense of the new task Baedeker and Nike had inexplicably assigned to him. What did he even know about . . . ?

Nessus had to flip his mindset into Interworld to frame his own question. Counterespionage. How would he find Achilles' illicit sources—spies—within Clandestine Directorate?

Where would he even begin?

Nessus gazed again at the glowing nebulae. He would enjoy their beauty a bit longer.

"Voice. Put through a hyperwave call to New Terra. I urgently need to consult with Sigmund Ausfaller."

39

From the center of his spacious audience chamber Achilles settled into a mound of plush cushions, then gestured graciously to his minions to make themselves comfortable. He expected this to be a long meeting.

Clotho, his usually alert gaze dulled by fatigue, chose a lesser collection of pillows. Louis and Enzio took opposite ends of the low human-style sofa.

All watched Achilles expectantly.

"We shall begin," Achilles said. "The topic is our disposition of the Gw'oth fleet."

Disposition. Achilles thought it the perfect word. No battle. No danger. Merely a task to accomplish, items to be discarded. Nothing scary.

After ten consecutive days in hyperspace, most of the Citizen crew was anxious, short-tempered, despondent. Two cowered in their cabins, lost to catatonia. Of the humans Achilles had less ability to judge, but they, too, struck him as ill at ease.

And so production of new fusion suppressors lagged behind his goals. That was all right. The shortfall had only propelled him to new heights of brilliance.

"We heed, Excellency," Clotho said. He spoke English, of course, so the humans could take part, but adding respectful grace notes for Achilles' ears. "Guide us."

"I have devised a foolproof plan." Achilles inhaled deeply, the air thicker than ever with artificial herd pheromone. The rich scent sufficed to maintain his calm. "I brought you here to discuss implementation.

"The action we last planned depended on the Gw'oth fleet following a pattern. Unfortunately, they changed their pattern."

"So we return to normal space to learn their new pattern?" Enzio asked hopefully.

Too hopefully. He, too, suffered from so long in hyperspace.

"To the contrary," Achilles answered. "The surest place to meet them is where they must appear: near Kl'mo." And that is why *Remembrance* must arrive first.

Unseen within Clotho's nest of pillows, a paw ripped through meadow-plant to scrape at the hard deck beneath. "The crew will redouble its efforts to build suppressors."

"In the new plan," Achilles said, "we will not need so many. Perhaps none at all."

Louis's eyes narrowed. "What *is* this new plan, Achilles?"

"In a way, it is *your* plan, Louis." Achilles paused dramatically. "We will use our planet-buster."

Clotho twitched. Enzio looked puzzled. Louis looked . . . wary.

"I will explain," Achilles said. "The plan is quite simple. We arrive first. We deploy a few passive probes instrumented to sense any large hyperwave disturbances. *Remembrance* remains outside the singularity by making very short hops centered on the enemy's solar system.

"We wait and watch for the ripples of the Gw'oth fleet emerging. If the fleet arrives when we ourselves are in hyperspace, we will find that upon our reemergence by querying the probes. When the enemy appears—we deploy the planet-buster."

"Then we will need a rogue planet to bust," Clotho said. "Finding one may take time."

Not so. That was the beauty of the plan. That and the delicious irony that Baedeker had developed the technology that would doom his rule. That and the equally wonderful twist of fate that Baedeker would never have succeeded in developing that technology without the help of Ol't'ro, now leader of the rebellious Gw'oth.

Achilles said, "Debris is only necessary to cover a large volume. For a volume not much larger than a solar system, the device's other effects suffice."

"I'm not sure I follow," Louis said.

"The space-time effects should be more than adequate." The effects would be spectacular, but not everyone could appreciate his vision. And the understatement of *adequate,* like *disposition,* amused Achilles.

"I . . . see," Louis said.

"You do not seem convinced," Achilles prompted.

"No, I am." Louis leaned forward. "Just trying to work out the sequence in my mind. See enough ripples to denote the Gw'oth fleet emerging, jettison the planet-buster, activate it, and then *Remembrance* jumps to hyperspace before the device triggers."

"Correct."

"And the drive stays stable for *how* long?" Louis persisted.

Did Louis imagine the plan not thought through? Achilles began to feel irked. "The latest devices are much more stable than those Ausfaller observed. We will have minutes to activate our hyperdrive." A few seconds would be ample.

"A brilliant plan, Excellency," Clotho offered. "I shall direct the crew to cease production of fusion suppressors."

And leave them with idle mouths and jaws? *More* would lose their minds. Achilles said, "Have them continue. Now let us turn to the details. . . ."

LOUIS'S MIND REELED. By warning off the Gw'oth fleet, Louis had managed to make the situation worse. Somehow, he had to stop Achilles. But how?

Achilles finally dismissed everyone. Enzio lagged behind with Louis while Clotho cantered ahead.

When Clotho disappeared around a curve of corridor, Enzio grabbed Louis by the arm. "You're not one of my team, Wu. Achilles picked you, so maybe you don't owe me an answer. But something is bothering you. Something major."

Nessus had worried aboard *Aegis* that Achilles would make and hide bugs. Louis was not about to gamble Achilles did not spy here. Louis took out his sketch pad and pen and jotted a note. He flashed the page at Enzio. *Sensors. Have my comp?* Louis returned pad and pen to his pocket.

Enzio nodded, ever so slightly.

"I'm going for a walk," Louis said. "Deck Eight, outer corridor. Care to join me?"

"Thanks. I have something to do first. I'll catch up with you."

Enzio joined Louis a few minutes later. Soon after, power walking side by side, Louis noticed an unaccustomed bulge in his pocket. Pickpocket was obviously among his crewmate's criminal skills.

After another half lap around the corridor, Louis slipped a hand into that pocket and found a comp. By touch he fingered a four-button numeric control code. He was rewarded by a soft chirp acknowledging activation of what Sigmund called protocol gamma: sound suppression, bug suppression, and a holographic projection to defeat lip readers. Louis left the comp in his pocket. A passerby or hidden camera noticing a translucent aura around the two men was a bigger risk than Puppeteers who read lips.

"If this isn't the comp you took from me on *Addison,* tell me now," Louis said.

"It is," Enzio said. "Now, who are you? One of Sigmund Ausfaller's agents?"

"Let's just say I'm not who Achilles thinks I am. We need to talk fast. The jamming field is apt to show up in security sensors as noise. Jamming mode will turn itself off before anyone is likely to come looking."

"Evasion duly noted. So what is the problem?" Pause. "How crazy *is* this new plan of his?"

Not crazy impractical. Genocidal and sociopathic crazy. "The planet-buster," Louis began cautiously. "Do you know much about them?"

"They bust planets. From what Achilles said, they shake up space-time when they go off." Enzio wheezed, out of shape and out of breath, and slowed their pace. "Sounds like a nice safe way to take out the Gw'oth fleet."

"Oh, it is." And *Alice*'s ship, too, tanj it. She had left for Kl'mo days before Enzio kidnapped Louis. She would not be quite there yet, but she would arrive before *Remembrance.* He *had* to stop Achilles. "But there are a couple of details Achilles hasn't shared.

"If the Gw'oth are a danger to the Citizens, it's because of *his* machinations. He instigated a war between Gw'oth worlds just to create a fleet that would pass near Hearth. By squashing the threat he himself created, he expects the Experimentalists to elevate him to Hindmost."

"And the other detail?"

"Those space-time 'ripples'?" Louis shivered. "They'll be enough to disrupt planetary orbits across the solar system. Drop planets into the sun? Eject planets into the dark between stars? Anything can happen, and there's a whole innocent colony on one of those worlds."

Enzio scowled. "I'm a thief, not a physicist. But neither am I an idiot. We can't possibly be carrying something with the power to do that."

"I'm no physicist, either, but I understand basic mechanics. Citizens keep trying to duplicate the planetary drives bought at great price from the Outsiders. The homemade drives are unstable, so they blow planets apart rather than move them.

"The thing is, Enzio, no one fully understands Outsider technologies. Not hyperdrive. Not the planetary drive. Not the reactionless drive that propels Outsider ships in normal space. But here is one amazing thing we do know. A city-sized Outsider ship can drop from near light speed to a dead stop, or zoom back again, in an instant."

Sigmund had seen it happen. So, Louis was almost certain, had First Father. Sigmund's story had struck a chord, had reawakened another cryptic childhood memory of Beowulf and Carlos talking while young Louis skulked about.

"To stop," Louis continued, "that ship sheds an *incredible* amount of kinetic energy. If it didn't, the ship would vaporize from kinetic energy transformed to heat. To instantly reacquire that velocity, the same ship regains the same amount of kinetic energy. Only the Outsiders know how it's done, but their ships must shift energy between normal space and . . . somewhere. Hyperspace? Another dimension? Another universe? Don't ask me. But they do it."

"And the planet-buster aboard *Remembrance* taps the same other-where forces?"

From Louis's pocket, a double chirp: the comp's wrap-it-up warning. "Enzio, we're running out of time. Big picture: if we allow it, Achilles will slaughter bunches of innocents. Everyone on the Gw'oth fleet and everyone in the Gw'oth colony."

And Alice and everyone aboard her ship, too. Louis kept that to himself. For all he knew, Enzio would go straight to Achilles.

While Enzio mulled, a triple chirp: the jamming mode's timeout/shutdown announcement.

"So I like the Capitals this season," Louis said. The Capitals were the first New Terran football team whose name he dredged up. For all he knew they were terrible. "Who do you like this season?"

"The Capitals? Hah! I think the Swans."

A few paces later, weight vanished from Louis's pocket. Louis said, "You're *so* wrong. When those teams play next, I call it the Capitals by fourteen, sixteen points." The activation code for jamming mode: one four one six. If Enzio had believed anything he had just heard, he would talk it over with his people. Louis added a reminder, one more data point, for that discussion. "Not that we can listen here to New Terran news."

"Fourteen, sixteen." Enzio snorted. "We'll be talking about *this* again."

"Anytime," Louis said, knowing he had put his fate into the hands of criminals.

. . .

A SHARP TAP-TAP on Louis's cabin door jerked him awake. He collapsed the sleeper field and stood. "It's not locked."

The door opened. By the nightshift-dimmed corridor lighting he recognized Maura. She stroked the touchpoint beside the door as she entered, and the cabin lights came up. The door clicked shut behind her. Another click sounded as she engaged the lock.

He must have looked surprised.

"You do nothing for me either, sport." Her right hand was in a pocket and the pocket chirped. "But Citizens are private about their own sex lives, if they even have sex. They *won't* want to know what you and I are doing in here. That's why Enzio sent me."

"About?"

"Enzio told us about your conversation. We talked it over. We signed up to defend Hearth, not to attack anyone else. Certainly not as mass murderers. We want out."

"Achilles won't care," Louis said. "I can get us all out, but I'll need everyone's help."

"So we assumed. Why else would you say anything to Enzio?"

"And it means taking orders from me. Enzio, too."

She nodded. "We assumed that, too."

"You can start by returning my computer."

She set it on his desk, just as it emitted its double chirp of warning. Red, yellow, and green dots chased each other around the display until, with a triple chirp, the device turned off.

Maura killed the overhead lights and sidled up to Louis. Her breath hot in his ear, she murmured, "Start talking."

And so, in the dark, in urgent whispers, he laid out his plan.

40

The hardest part was the waiting.

It was not that Louis and his reluctant allies were without things to do. There was the timeline to refine. Tasks to delegate. Supplies to gather in secrecy. Stepping-disc coordinates to explore, confirm, and exchange. Details to tune and tweak. Even weapons to be made, mostly smoke grenades and Molotov cocktails, whoever Molotov was. As for more potent bombs, Louis had retained enough from his Wunderland training not to blow himself up improvising explosives and detonators with the chemicals he had retrieved from *Addison*. Whether the devices would blow up when they needed to remained to be seen.

And they had to do everything without attracting Puppeteer interest.

Still, they finished. And waited. And fretted. And waited.

While *Remembrance* remained in hyperspace, they could not act.

"PREPARE FOR NORMAL SPACE," Achilles called out. He pretended not to hear the soft notes of relief from the bridge crew. But unless he provided *some* respite, he would be without a crew by the time they reached the Kl'mo system.

"Normal space," Clotho acknowledged from the pilot's couch. "In ten. Nine. Eight . . ."

At zero, the bridge displays switched from virtual meadows to real stars. The gnawing tickle vanished from the back of Achilles' brain. The hushed bridge chatter sounded brighter.

Achilles activated the intercom. "We will remain in normal space for an hour. Clotho and I will keep watch on the bridge. You are all relieved until five minutes before we continue on our way."

The bridge crew trotted from the room. Happy songs echoed in the corridors. Achilles stood, ready to walk about the for-once-uncrowded bridge.

Until the alarms shrieked.

PERCHED AWKWARDLY on the Puppeteer-friendly pilot's crash couch, Louis activated the short-range radio. "This is Louis Wu aboard *Addison,* calling Achilles. Repeat, this is *Addison* calling Achilles."

At the copilot's station Enzio was running the preflight checklist. The other New Terrans were in the engine room or their cabins. The main bridge displays showed a panoramic view of the cargo hold.

"What have you done, Louis?" Achilles answered. Midsentence, warbling alarms cut off abruptly.

"The New Terrans and I are leaving, Achilles." Louis did not explain. A sociopath had no interest in another's reasons. "Release the hull clamps and open the cargo-hold hatch. Open all the cargo holds' hatches."

"I am afraid I cannot do that, Louis. What have you done?"

Delivered lots of improvised explosive devices by stepping disc. Only the smoke grenades had been live, triggering fire alarms, emergency systems, and safety shutdowns. But *Remembrance*'s most vulnerable areas were beyond Louis's reach. The bridge had no discs, and no human had been allowed into the engine room to discover stepping-disc addresses there.

The smoke grenades were distractions, however unsettling. The Puppeteer crew were naïfs, dupes, mentally unstable: herd-minded beings instinctively following a strong leader. Aside from Achilles, none was evil. Louis meant them no harm. He *did* mean to stop them.

Louis said, "Nothing dramatic . . . yet. Do as I say, Achilles."

Enzio cleared his throat. "Ready when you are, Louis."

"Do it, Achilles," Louis said.

"Or else?" Achilles sneered.

Crushing weight!

"Automatics compensating," Enzio grunted. The excess weight vanished, offset by *Addison*'s artificial gravity. "Louis, with the hold's gravity set this high, our thrusters won't budge us."

Louis nodded. "Or else, Achilles, you'll force me to take the hyperspace exit."

. . .

THE EMERGENCY HATCH SLAMMED, but not before thick smoke had poured onto the bridge. Dampers clanged in the ventilation ducts to finish sealing the room. Ceiling lamps and most consoles went dark; the main displays and most critical consoles flickered as emergency power cut in.

With one glance at the main status board, Clotho collapsed to the deck. Achilles watched in dismay as Clotho furled into a tight ball, heads tucked between his forelegs. Only muffled bleats of panic emerged.

It is up to me, Achilles thought. As always, everything is up to me.

Above Clotho's inert body, security-camera displays cycled randomly from corridor to cargo hold to cabin. Emergency bulkheads automatically sealed to stop the spread of the fire. Crew trapped wherever the safety lockdown found them. Smoke billowing in most of the ship.

So *much* smoke. How had smoke spread so widely before setting off alarms? Unless there were many fires across the ship. Set at once? *Delivered* at once? With a shudder of insight, Achilles realized he had not seen a single human.

He overrode safety protocols to disable the stepping-disc network controllers. It was the best he could do from lockdown. Individual discs still functioned; for safety reasons discs could only be disabled in person. But at least now, the humans could spread trouble only via the specific disc addresses they already knew.

The comm console flashed: carrier wave detected. Electromagnetic radio. But *Remembrance* was in the middle of nowhere! Achilles opened the channel.

"This is Louis Wu aboard *Addison,* calling Achilles. Repeat, this is *Addison* calling Achilles."

Wu! "What have you done, Louis?" Achilles answered. With his other head, he suppressed the still warbling alarms.

"The New Terrans and I are leaving, Achilles. Release the hull clamps and open the cargo-hold hatch. Open all the cargo holds' hatches."

Let the humans go? Watch his lovely fusion suppressors drift into the void? "I am afraid I cannot do that, Louis. What have you done?"

"Nothing dramatic . . . yet. Do as I say, Achilles."

The "fires" were tending to themselves. The smoke was already clearing, vented by air handlers and scrubbed by active filters. Achilles left the automatic systems to work by themselves, saying nothing, sorting through his options.

Send an armed group aboard *Addison*? Not plausible, even if enough crew somehow worked up the frenzy to try. The humans were sly enough to disable the few stepping discs aboard their ship and disconnect its exterior air-lock controls. That would be confirmed, but he knew what would be found.

Addison had a General Products hull. Almost certainly, he could not get at the humans and they could not get at him. They had a comm laser—at close range, a dangerous weapon—but useless while the ship remained clamped with its bow pointed outward. Their laser could only fire harmlessly *through* the hull material of the cargo-hold hatch, and into the void.

Lasers. Any of *Remembrance*'s lasers would take time to dismount and move. The humans could dismount and move their comm laser just as quickly.

"Do it, Achilles," Louis said.

"Or else?" Achilles sneered while, with his other mouth, he set gravity in the hold at ten times Hearth normal. For a satisfying moment—until, as he had known would happen, their ship offset the force field—all he heard was anguished gasping.

"Or else, Achilles, you'll force me to take the hyperspace exit."

The Gw'oth method! That fool Nessus had shown the human how to destroy *Argo*'s hull. Achilles lunged for the hyperdrive controls as he spoke. "Do not do that, Louis. Not while we are *already* in hyperspace."

And if Louis did anyway? That was an experiment no sane being would contemplate.

Fresh alarm lamps flared on the status board. The bridge view ports stubbornly continued to display stars.

"Hyperdrive draws a lot of power," Louis said imperturbably. "I am quite confident Puppeteer fusion reactors won't operate while there are fire alarms throughout the ship."

And Louis was correct. Sensors across the ship would require manual resets before the reactors would restart. "What do you want?" Achilles asked desperately.

"I told you. Release the clamps. Open the cargo bays. Let us go."

"Clamps and cargo-bay hatch," Achilles repeated.

"Hatches," Louis corrected. "And turn off gravity in the holds."

And let everything float out? Never! "I need those weapons to defend Hearth. Especially after my *brave* human crew runs."

"In thirty seconds, Achilles, I engage hyperdrive."

Everything within *Addison*'s normal-space bubble would jump to hyperspace with it. The clamps and bits of the docking cradle. Perhaps some of the cargo-bay hatch. Nothing Achilles could not manage without.

"Twenty seconds. Nineteen."

Achilles surveyed the few bridge consoles still functioning. The space-junk defenses were on an emergency-power circuit, and *Remembrance*'s hull bristled with powerful lasers. Backup power could manage several salvos.

Wu dare not fly around *Remembrance* to check out the other holds. His insolent demand that cargo be jettisoned was a bluff.

"Fifteen. Fourteen."

"You win," Achilles said, tasting bitter cud. "I am releasing *Addison*."

ADDISON LURCHED. For an instant, Louis came out of his crash couch.

Louis grabbed his armrests. "What happened?"

"Gravity in the hold went off. The automatics readjusted." Enzio peered at an external camera. "The clamp is retracting. *Addison* is afloat."

From outside the ship, a blaring alarm and strobing red light. The exterior hatch was about to open. Louis watched it slowly gape.

"A wise choice, Achilles." Louis broke the connection, wondering if the other holds' hatches were open. He did not intend to stay around—and get laser-blasted—to find out.

He activated the intercom. "All hands. We're leaving *Remembrance*."

Through the air ducts, a ragged cheer.

"Take her out, Enzio," Louis said. *Addison* was barely outside when Louis engaged the hyperdrive.

SENSORS FLASHED from intense hyperwave backwash. The treacherous humans were gone.

On the status board, more and more zones reported themselves free of smoke. Achilles announced over the intercom, "There is no cause for alarm. The fires have been contained. I will release the emergency quarantine, deck by deck, as that becomes safe."

And then we will restart the reactors and resume course. Wu could not stop him. But the human *would* pay later. Pay dearly. Pay and pay and . . .

LOUIS'S EYES WERE GLUED to his wristwatch. "Three. Two. One."

At zero, timers triggered the second set of devices deployed earlier by stepping discs. *These* bombs did more than smoke.

41

An hour departed from *Remembrance,* Louis dropped *Addison* from hyper-space. "I need to contact the authorities," he told Enzio.

"Uh-huh," Enzio said casually. Too casually.

Endangering New Terran neutrality was serious business, and Louis was the one witness. Enzio and his gang could easily enough chuck their problem out the air lock.

Would they? The next seconds were critical.

Louis said, "The six of you have been nothing but helpful. That's all I'll have to say."

"And about the manner of your arrival?" Enzio prompted.

"I needed to find Achilles. You brought me where I wanted to be." Louis smiled. "As I remember it, I volunteered."

Enzio mulled that over. "Go ahead. Make your call." But he stayed on the bridge to monitor.

Louis took out his comp and unlocked the classified access codes. He made the call.

Sigmund responded immediately, apparently from home. "Louis! It's good to see you."

"This is a friend, Sigmund." Louis left it to Enzio to introduce himself if he wished. The comm delay in and out of New Terra's singularity left him plenty of time to decide. "He and his crew got me aboard Achilles' ship. And as important, they just got me off."

"New Terra thanks you, friend," Sigmund said. "Louis, you know the protocol."

Louis took *protocol* as a protocol-gamma reference. As in: report in private. To try excluding Enzio seemed likely to shatter the fragile bonds of trust. Sorry, Sigmund.

Louis said, "In a minute. First, what about Alice?"

"En route, checking in routinely. Her last contact was yesterday, so she'll be out of touch for a while. She'll be glad to hear you're all right." Sigmund's brow furrowed. He wanted his report.

"Here is the story, Sigmund." Louis compressed weeks of adventure into a few minutes. "If my bombs worked, Achilles is disarmed. The planet-buster, busted. The fusion suppressors were inside GP number one hulls, but concussion should have taken out many of them."

Louis withheld one detail: he had burgled a buoy. Achilles could not know, not until someone checked out the little spacecraft one by one. Thrusters, micro-reactor, and hyperwave transmitter occupied most of each basketball-sized hull. The Pak-inspired fusion suppressor itself was impressively tiny. Louis had crammed the small space he had emptied with random optronics parts from a spares cabinet. With luck and enough concussion, maybe no one would notice.

Fifteen minutes after launching from *Remembrance,* on a recycler break, Louis had popped into his old cabin. The suppressor circuitry went from jumpsuit pocket to the toe of a spare boot in his closet. Fusion suppression was *not* a capability he wanted in the hands of soldiers of fortune.

"So what do you think Achilles will do?" Sigmund asked.

Louis had wracked his brains for days, trying to anticipate. He had had no insight, only intuition. He knew with whom they contended. "He won't quit, Sigmund."

Sigmund sighed. "I suppose not. So when can we expect you home?"

"I'll get back to you," Louis said, and broke the connection.

"YOU DON'T TRUST AUSFALLER," Enzio observed.

"Let's just say," Louis said, "that forgiveness is easier to obtain than permission."

"Forgiveness for *what*?"

Louis gazed longingly at the stars. If he had his way, none of them would see normal space for a while. "The woman I love is going to Kl'mo, hoping to broker a peace deal."

"While a Gw'oth fleet races straight at her. Probably Achilles, too."

Louis had been as cold as ice through the escape. Fear for Alice made him tremble. "Whatever Achilles tries, he will not want witnesses."

"And how do you see this playing out?" Enzio asked pointedly.

Everyone was racing toward galactic north.

Departing from New Terra, Alice had the shortest trip to Kl'mo. But she had begun with New Terra's normal-space velocity. The plan had been to take long breaks from hyperspace, shedding velocity on the way, to appear less threatening upon arrival.

Setting out from the failed ambush, from just south of the Fleet of Worlds, Achilles had a bit farther to travel to Kl'mo. But he had no interest in *Remembrance* shedding the normal-space velocity it had inherited from the Fleet. And he wasn't taking many or long breaks in normal space.

The Gw'oth war fleet was not far behind *Remembrance*—and they would keep gaining until Achilles managed to restart his ship's fusion reactors. The Gw'oth had matched normal-space velocity with Hearth before Louis warned them off. Best guess, they meant to use that velocity to threaten Kl'mo with kinetic-kill weapons. So the Gw'oth ships would not be slowing down, either.

"I think," Louis said, "that Alice, Achilles, and the Gw'oth warships will all arrive at about the same time."

"And us, too? That's what you're thinking."

"And us, too," Louis agreed. "If you will let Sigmund hire you and your ship."

Enzio leaned back in his crash couch, fingers interlaced behind his head, eyes closed in thought. He finally said, "We would have to be crazy."

Louis said nothing.

"And do what when we arrive?"

"Improvise," Louis said.

ACHILLES THOUGHT: Yet again, I can rely only on myself.

Two crew had been frightened to death. More, including Clotho, had lapsed into catatonia so deep that not even blasting the hull-breach alarm could animate them. They were in stasis, stacked in an out-of-the-way storeroom. Even among the crew back on duty, several exhibited insanity beyond the ability of autodocs to treat.

Louis Wu had much to answer for.

But first—although the planet-buster was crushed beyond repair—the Gw'oth must be defanged.

. . .

LOUIS WAITED IN HIS CABIN while the New Terrans, crowded into *Addison*'s relax room, debated. His future. And Alice's. And the fates of several worlds.

After far too long: a chime from his pocket computer. Louis grabbed it. It showed Enzio's comm ID. "Yes?"

"You got us out of a real mess, Louis. We decided we owe you." Enzio paused. "On Ausfaller's promise he'll pay us."

"You'll have it."

42

"Apologies, Your Wisdom."

"Unavoidable," Sr'o said, neither knowing nor caring who had bumped
her or who had spoken. She could not summon the energy to protest the
unwanted honorific. When last she had counted two fivefolds swam laps
with her. They jetted about for exercise, and to clear their minds, and in
vain hopes of making themselves weary enough to sleep.

The melding chamber, as crammed as it was, remained the least
crowded large space aboard *Mighty Current*. Through the transparent parti-
tions she could see into the more congested control center and engine
room. She would be back in the control center soon enough.

The colony was ever vigilant because Ol't'ro was certain an attack must
come. They poured their resources into weapons because to do any less
might doom them all. They kept *Mighty Current* hopping around Kl'mo system because any defense coordinated from inside the singularity was destined to fail.

And they were stressed beyond endurance, waiting.

Drowsiness continued to elude Sr'o. With ripples of resignation (dorsal,
yellow and green), she acknowledged that she could not sleep, and that
once again a duty shift loomed.

Until then she would ponder the colony's ever more precarious ecosystem. All her interventions had been futile, the transplanted biota dwindling
with each passing day. She saw no solution without new supplies from
Jm'ho.

Yet they did not dare divert resources to seek healthy stocks. Ol't'ro calculated an assault was imminent, and decreed the colony must defend foremost against genocidal violence. Absolute rulers were absolutely mad.
Before escaping, the Gw'otesht had watched Bm'o's descent into absolute
power and self-absorption.

Sr'o found herself reduced to hoping the onslaught was imminent. Unless an attack came quickly—even if the colony survived it—there would be no colony left to seek resupply from the home world.

There was a three-way collision midchamber, and a tangle of tubacles. "Sorry," she said automatically. "My thoughts were elsewhere."

She did not doubt Ol't'ro—that would be too much like doubting herself—but the colony's options tormented her. Die slowly? Die quickly? Return to servitude? Ol't'ro insisted none of those would come to pass. The others would—

The pulsating glare of an alarm lamp sliced through the ship. *Intruder alert.* Sr'o jetted to the floor to peer into the control center. A second alarm began to blink. *Hyperwave hail.*

The captain put the incoming call on speaker. The hail was in the New Terran language, English. ". . . Terran embassy ship *Metternich.* Repeat, this is the New Terran embassy ship *Metternich.* We come in peace and friendship. This is . . ."

The tactical display presented hyperwave-radar data from the recently completed defensive array. A big blip, Sr'o thought, the ship significantly larger than hers. But humans were bigger than Gw'oth.

That the newcomer spoke English proved nothing. Citizens knew English. Anyone dealing with the New Terran traders learned English. It was trivially simple compared to any Gw'oth language.

If the ship did originate from the human world, they had taken pains to shed their normal-space velocity. Their course vector did not point to the inner solar system. Sr'o saw nothing immediately threatening.

"*Metternich,*" the captain responded, "this is Kl'mo planetary defense. Maintain course and speed. Await further instructions."

". . . peace and friendship. This is—" The recording stopped and a new voice began. Sr'o thought it was a human woman's voice. "Kl'mo planetary defense, we are pleased to find your colony still well. My name is Alice Jordan, and Sigmund Ausfaller sent me. I would like to speak to Ol't'ro."

The sixteen were already jetting to the melding chamber.

"WE ARE OL'T'RO," they declared.

"Before we start," the one calling herself Alice Jordan said, "I bring a message from Sigmund. I am to tell you, 'Apology accepted.'"

The probability that the intruder was New Terran rose significantly. "We meant him no harm," Ol't'ro replied.

"You asked Sigmund for help. There is little New Terra can do without taking sides, and that we cannot do."

Take sides. Ol't'ro remembered humans' peculiar appearance, symmetrical only around one vertical plane. Sides: an odd term, but they understood. "Little you can do, but not nothing. What can you do?" What *will* you do?

"You and the other side may not need to fight. Perhaps a neutral party can help you find a middle ground."

Middle ground: more strangeness. The only middle grounds on Jm'ho were the nutrient-free wastelands far from any hydrothermal vents. Worthless. The middle "ground" between stars was void, likewise useless.

Alice prattled on for a while, all platitudes. It was pie in the sky, wishful thinking, pipe dreams, the wire talking. From Ol't'ro's long-ago sojourn with humans during the Pak War, they had an excellent grasp of English idiom, even though the antecedents often eluded them.

Not even Jeeves, Sigmund's artificial intelligence, had been able to explain every human expression. *That* Jeeves had been killed in the Pak War. The death made Ol't'ro sad: an AI was as potentially immortal as a Gw'otesht. Someday, maybe they could meet another Jeeves.

"A compromise," Ol't'ro summarized eventually.

"Exactly."

"Explain the compromise between the side who would be free and the side who would enslave."

Alice was silent for a long while. "My bridge crew reports I am talking with a source moving at half light speed."

"A hyperwave relay," Ol't'ro lied.

The inevitable war fleet from Jm'ho would race out of hyperspace. Every time Ol't'ro did the calculation, their prediction was the same: the Tn'Tn'ho's ships would have matched velocities with the Fleet of Worlds. With that velocity they would make themselves less threatening to the Citizens—and they might even pretend to be Citizens themselves. With that velocity they would be *very* threatening to the fragile colony Ol't'ro must defend.

And so *Mighty Current* had accelerated to the Fleet's normal-space velocity. When, inexorably, the battle opened, when every instant would count, Ol't'ro would have no need to adjust for relativistic distortions.

If they had correctly divined the enemy's thoughts.

Meanwhile, like its constellation of defensive probes, *Mighty Current* remained near the solar system with an unending series of hyperspace microjumps.

"Very well," Alice said. "About how we might help. As a neutral party, we have our own perspective. We can be objective. We may recognize options the conflicting sides have not. We may—"

Ululating sound over the hyperwave channel. At the same instant, bright lights resumed strobing through the clear floor of the melding chamber: *intruder alert.*

On the bridge, the captain redirected a portion of the hyperwave array at the disturbance. "A very large ship," he called. "Making half light speed northward directly toward Kl'mo."

IT ALL HAPPENED at once.

Alice was already struggling to keep pace with Ol't'ro. Sigmund had warned her—about the commanding, resonant voice the Gw'otesht would adopt; the stunningly quick thoughts; the seemingly intuitive leaps whose thoughtful underpinnings she would only deduce later—but she had had to *experience* the ensemble mind to understand. To be properly humbled. She talked slowly, circuitously, verbosely, buying with her wordiness extra seconds for reflection.

How could she find a possibility Ol't'ro had not envisioned long before?

Metternich was only minutes out of hyperspace, the domain visible to its light-speed-bounded active sensors still limited. Every glance she could spare toward the tactical display revealed another one or two neutrino sources whizzing about at relativistic speeds. Neutrino emissions meant fusion reactors, but what devices did those reactors power? As she watched the display, frowning in concentration, one of the sources winked out. Elsewhere, seconds later, another appeared.

Meanwhile, the hyperwave detector was alive with ripples. From the transient neutrino sources, hopping through hyperspace? From the hyperwave buoy Ol't'ro claimed? She did not understand boosting a relay to such high speed.

Meanwhile her earnest young aide, by his stance and facial expression and standing *way* too close, signaled frantically for her attention. "What?" she barked.

"A message from Sigmund just uploaded from a comm relay." He handed her a comp, and perhaps by accident started the message playing. "Sorry to add to your worries, Alice, but Achilles is probably headed your way and out for Gw'oth blood. He may not be too happy about humans, either. Louis says—"

Louis! She had worried since he dropped from sight. That had to wait. She tried to foresee Achilles' probable actions even as she kept speaking with Ol't'ro. "Very well," she said. "About how we might help. As a neutral party, we have our own perspective. We can be objective. We may recognize options the conflicting sides have not. We may—"

And a bridge alarm wailed. "Something big just dropped from hyperspace," the captain announced.

ON *REMEMBRANCE*'S BRIDGE, no longer crowded, Achilles focused on the mass pointer. A long blue line representing his destination groped hungrily at him. The longer he waited, the surer the doom of the Gw'oth world. Deploying fusion suppressors—in one cargo hold, Louis Wu's explosive device had fizzled—would be safer without any risk of local interference.

Curse that Louis Wu! Achilles needed badly to *smash* something.

But in the back of his mind, terror gibbered. Wait *too* long and they would disappear into the singularity's hungry maw. The ultimate predator . . .

Hecate stood, trembling, alone among the combat consoles. He kept glancing furtively at the mass pointer.

"We will be safe," Achilles sang impatiently.

"Yes, Excellency."

"Launch status?" Achilles prompted, more to occupy Hecate's thoughts than expecting anything to have changed.

"Missiles ready. The cargo-hold hatch is armed. The pressure curtain is active." A surveillance hologram changed as Hecate panned a security camera. "Excellency, Phoebe has fallen into catatonia. The others stand ready."

Just beyond that hatch, one button push away, lurked—nothing. Less than nothing. Oblivion. The wonder was not that Phoebe had collapsed, but that

Hebe and Theia had not. But the hatch must be opened as quickly as possible, the probes set to thrust outward through the air-pressure curtain.

The long blue line nearly licked the mass pointer's transparent sphere. Achilles called, "Return to normal space in three . . . two . . . one . . . now."

The stars returned. One shone far brighter than the rest: the sun that warmed their target. The sun at which *Remembrance* raced at half light speed. With attitude thrusters, Achilles spun the ship so that his kinetic-kill weapons faced directly sunward.

"Hatch open," Hecate reported. "Missiles report sensor lock."

"Launch."

"Missiles launched!" Hecate called.

On Achilles' instruments, two objects streaked away.

And an inexplicable number of neutrino sources seemed to be zipping about in all directions. Without waiting, Achilles plunged *Remembrance* back to hyperspace before the ship crossed into the singularity.

From Hecate: a bleat of sheer terror. Then, silence.

Eyes closed, Achilles sidled to the combat center. By touch he found the ON/OFF switches and powered down the video displays. When he dared to open his eyes, Hecate still stared where the surveillance hologram of the cargo hold had been—without focus, lost in some infinite distance. Lost in the Blind Spot.

"Hecate," Achilles sang. No response. "Hecate," he repeated, much louder. Nothing. He raised a forehoof and gave Hecate a strong shove in the flank.

"Excellency." Hecate shuddered. "What have you *done*?"

"Probably saved us," Achilles sang.

But not the crew in the cargo hold, its enormous hatch gaping into hyperspace. Only Phoebe, his eyes and ears and consciousness withdrawn into a tightly rolled ball of flesh, might survive.

NG'T'MO FLOATED in their tiny chamber, melded and waiting. Waiting on the master of masters. Waiting to leave hyperspace. Waiting for sensors to come alive. Waiting for threat and conflict. Waiting for the deaths certain to come.

Whose deaths? That they must wait to learn.

. . .

"SURRENDER OR DIE!" Bm'o shouted. His fleet was just out of hyperspace.

A moment later chaos erupted across the control center. How could a reply come so soon? Radio waves had only begun their light-speed trek into the inner solar system. Unless the reply came from outside the singularity, via a relay very close by.

"We will do neither," a familiar voice said. *Ol't'ro.* "Look around. We have an enemy in common."

And in his displays Bm'o saw *another* vessel. It was huge, larger than all his ships combined. It must be a Citizen ship! Its normal-space velocity matched that of Bm'o's fleet. And inward from that monstrous ship—

Fusion flames drove missiles streaking toward the rebel world.

A WONDROUS PUZZLE!

Ng't'mo drank in the data sent to their cage from the ship's control center. The sun and planets. Neutrino sources racing at great speeds in all directions. And two large ships, not part of the master of masters' fleet. And missiles.

Two missiles raced toward the world where Ol't'ro must live!

Ng't'mo remembered puzzling whether anything could defend against missiles at these speeds. They remembered concluding it was possible. And that Ol't'ro was smarter than they.

They hoped they were correct.

LOUIS WAS ON HYPERWAVE the moment *Addison* dropped from hyperspace. "*Metternich,* a hostile Puppeteer ship is on its way. *Metternich,* be prepared to evade."

From the copilot's couch, Enzio stared in disbelief. He keyed furiously at his console. A hologram popped up, a riot of colors. "Louis, you need to look at this."

What was he seeing? A solar system. Many objects, neutrino sources, rushing in all directions at relativistic speeds. Two streaked straight for the inner planets!

"WE ARE BUSY," Ol't'ro broadcast. They closed channels to *Metternich* and the Tn'Tn'ho's fleet.

The huge Citizen ship plummeted toward Kl'mo at half light speed. The missiles, accelerating steadily, plunged faster still. But aboard *Mighty Current,* Ol't'ro had almost the same relative velocity. They studied their defensive array, its many elements racing in all directions. Ol't'ro selected two probes speeding crosswise to the plunging missiles. The closing velocity between those probes and the missiles approached three-quarters light speed.

Hyperwave signals were instantaneous; the course and bearing calculations were quickly completed. Ol't'ro dispatched targeting information to their chosen interceptors. The interceptors micro-jumped through hyperspace to the optimum launch points, where they would also receive final readouts from the hyperwave-radar system.

Ol't'ro repeated the process with a second pair of probes.

The missiles plunged across an invisible border, into the singularity where hyperwave ceased to function. Ol't'ro used visual observations to target a third set of interceptors, knowing the data was obsolete.

The first pair of interceptors fell into the singularity, beyond instantaneous communication. From now on, the antimissiles must guide themselves.

And Ol't'ro could only watch.

HALF A MINUTE—AND A LIGHT-HOUR removed from the singularity—later, *Remembrance* dropped from hyperspace. Achilles waited impatiently for the light and neutrinos from his missiles to reach him. Hecate, without asking permission, galloped from the bridge to care for those in the cargo hold. Futile.

Achilles stared, transfixed, into the tactical display. He saw a swarm of ships: the main Gw'oth fleet had arrived. Streaking to the colony world, he saw the missiles' fusion exhausts—

With two unknown neutrino sources shooting directly at them.

The telescopic displays flashed impossibly bright in the instant before overload protection cut in. Tears filled his eyes.

A proximity alarm screamed. An object, relativistic, had appeared from nowhere. The object rushed straight at him!

Another of whatever had destroyed his missiles?

The ship's hull might survive impact, and the emergency stasis field for his crash couch *would* protect him. Nothing else within the ship could possibly withstand the concussion. Achilles' mind flashed back in horror to the hollowed-out hulk of *Argo*.

Bleating in terror, Achilles slapped *Remembrance* back into hyperspace. He was not safe here. No one was.

But where did he dare go now?

AN END TO WAR

43

Louis knew he was no diplomat. He told himself that that was for the best, for surely no negotiation had ever unfolded under circumstances so strange.

Leaders of both Gw'oth factions were on ships outside the singularity, able to converse instantaneously by hyperwave. But Bm'o and Ol't'ro also consulted with counselors back home, entailing many hours for light-speed delays within their respective solar systems.

Louis and Alice could also communicate instantaneously, with each other and with the space-based Gw'oth. Sigmund sometimes joined the conversations. Because New Terra flew free, without a star, that round-trip comm delay was less than two minutes. (Closer to two minutes for Alice than for Sigmund or Louis. From her frame of reference, New Terra and its singularity had relativistic speed. Time dilation added about twenty percent to the delay she experienced.)

Twice the Hindmost called, the round-trip comm delay with the Fleet of Worlds a still-manageable three minutes. He apologized for the rogue actions of Achilles, promised severe punishment once Achilles was apprehended, hinted at opportunities for trade, and offered good will to everyone—while reminding everyone that the Concordance would soon be far away.

Every ship but *Metternich* had started with or accelerated to the normal-space velocity of the Fleet of Worlds: about half light speed toward galactic north. Ol't'ro's planetary defense probes raced just as quickly, but in all directions.

To stay near Kl'mo—whether defensively, offensively, or as neutral observers—spacecraft kept vanishing to hyperspace to loop back. No one trusted anyone; disappearances came without warning, even midsentence. The hyperspace jumps could be seconds or minutes, and to avoid predictability, jumps were also made for no reason beyond keeping everyone else off balance.

Louis's bridge displays were an ever-changing froth of ships appearing and disappearing, of space writhing with hyperwave ripples from ships and the more numerous defensive probes entering and returning from hyperspace at points around the solar system.

And most ships were armed to the teeth. And no one could keep pace with Ol't'ro's thoughts or Sigmund's paranoia. And when Gw'oth factions chose to speak directly, the humans were left to speculate among themselves.

There was much, sometimes too much, to discuss. The issues among the Gw'oth: which grievances were authentic and which were actually Achilles' provocations. Human subtleties: New Terra's neutrality, Alice's services as arbiter, and Louis's free-agent status. Threats, deterrents, and mutual assured destruction. The costs of war and the perils of appeasement. Whether two human ships arriving almost at the instant of Achilles' attack denoted coincidence, hostile distraction, or good intentions. Possible confidence-building measures. And on, and on. . . .

Of everyone in the negotiation (if that's what this cacophony was), Louis had spent the most time with Achilles. Again and again, Louis was asked to explain the rogue Puppeteer. When Louis's answers failed to satisfy, he brought in Enzio and Sigmund. The Gw'oth even interrogated the Hindmost about Achilles. Baedeker assured everyone that Achilles was an outlaw, a herdless one, who would be brought to justice.

Ol't'ro, especially, seemed curious about Achilles. Louis wished he understood why.

Had the New Terran intervention helped? All Louis knew for certain was which disasters had *not* happened. No more missiles had been flung at planet or ships. No ships had left to threaten anyone else.

Things could be a lot worse.

ABLE AT LAST TO TALK AGAIN, it was hard for Louis and Alice to bear that they remained millions, sometimes billions, of miles apart, and that while Louis sped along at half light speed, Alice was all but stationary. But it would take days to match velocities. So far Sigmund had decreed that *Addison* and *Metternich* maintain their very different velocities. He offered no rationale beyond maintaining flexibility.

Flexibility. Louis cursed the notion. Tanj, he had missed Alice!

"You're beautiful," he said a lot. Maybe it was a case of abstinence making the heart grow fonder, but he had never seen Alice so radiant.

"I miss you, too," she often answered. "You have no idea how much."

"Come aboard and you can show me."

"Yah, right." She smiled, more lovely still.

They stole every moment they could, in the delays waiting for Sigmund to respond or during Ol't'ro's or Bm'o's unannounced absences from normal space. Every minute was precious. When the Gw'oth talked only among themselves, Louis and Alice spoke together a lot. They talked about finding him a job on New Terra. They talked about building a home together, a *life* together. They filled the hyperwaves with sweet nothings.

As the days passed, the Gw'oth spoke more and more among themselves. Louis and Alice tried to convince one another that the direct dialogue meant progress. The two sides no longer needed referees.

To which sentiment Sigmund would chide that optimism was merely a euphemism for wishful thinking.

Optimistic or not, none of them could avoid wondering just what the Gw'oth talked about in private.

BM'O HAD FORGOTTEN how unsettling dialogue with Ol't'ro could be.

It went beyond dealing with an abomination, a freak of nature. It was worse than being made to feel slow and stupid. Events Bm'o knew only from history, the Gw'otesht had lived through—and as often had caused to happen.

And Bm'o did not have a choice.

"Compromise is the only option, sire," Rt'o had concluded in her last message from home. "You have seen Ol't'ro defeat kinetic-kill weapons. Their defenses will destroy any unauthorized ship that attempts to approach the colony. Our world has no such defense, but we control what the rebels must have: new biological supplies."

In the end, with no other choice, Bm'o *had* compromised. Every aspect of the final agreement was logical. Almost every aspect carried implications that teased and taunted him, possibilities and eventualities beyond the ability of the noblest Gw'o to comprehend.

To what had he agreed unknowingly? Only time would tell. But at least he and his great fleet would return home little the worse for their epic voyage.

If with nothing to show for it.

Bm'o took comfort in knowing he would soon set course for Jm'ho.

And that Achilles' lackey on the home world, and everything Thalia had brought, and all his possessions, had been dropped into the sun—before they could release the ecosystem-demolishing retrovirus.

WE ARE NG'T'MO.

Nothing else was certain. Nothing else made sense. The eight had been ordered apart, roughly dragged from their cage, herded one by one through crowded corridors to a water lock and aboard another ship. An empty ship.

Melded anew, Ng't'mo struggled to grasp their circumstances. A larger cage? An exotic place to die?

Vibrations suggested ships separating.

Change was bad. The masters seldom rewarded, but they were quick to punish. The master of masters was the most quick-tempered of all. Ng't'mo had suffered exceedingly for insisting—truthfully—that they saw no way to fool the rebel's defensive system.

Then the master of masters had commanded them to find evasive patterns that would protect the fleet. Only the patterns Ng't'mo had devised, however seemingly random, would be predictable to a sufficiently sophisticated mind.

Because they hoped the leaping of the ships would be recognized as the product of *another* sophisticated mind. They might be freed if Ol't'ro noticed.

Now, fearfully exploring this new cage, Ng't'mo wondered if the master of masters had noticed.

We are Ng't'mo, they told themselves. They crept, as quickly as they were able with so many tubacles mated and entwined, until they found what might be controls. None of their units had piloted a spaceship, or been allowed to see a control center.

The controls were a puzzle. They would solve the puzzle.

Then: lights flashing on a console. New vibrations. A soft *thunk*. The sound of a water lock cycling. An unfamiliar Gw'o, flashing greens and far reds in patterns of welcome, swam into the control center!

"We come from Ol't'ro," the new arrival said. "You are safe. You are free."

. . .

"WE ACCEPT YOUR OFFER to help," Ol't'ro had hyperwaved to *Metternich* and *Addison*.

"I thought we've been helping." Louis tried to keep sarcasm out of his voice. Had he not already saved the Gw'oth fleet from massacre? Perhaps only Bm'o considered that to be help.

"You offered useful information," Ol't'ro granted. "We ask now that you *do* something."

"Ol't'ro, I'm putting you on hold for a moment," Alice said.

"This is good," Sigmund offered when the relayed conversation caught up to him. "If they let New Terra help, it means we're on no one's enemies list. As long as whatever thing they want done is not too dangerous."

Says the man light-years away. Louis kept *that* to himself, too.

Something in Ol't'ro's presentation made Louis nervous. He could not put his finger on it. "Sigmund, what's your best guess about Hearth? Are the Puppeteers on anyone's enemies list?"

"Let's hope not," Sigmund finally said.

Louis presumed hope was also a euphemism for wishful thinking.

Alice reconnected with Ol't'ro. "Help, how?" she asked.

"Our colony needs supplies from Jm'ho. When we tried to obtain them ourselves, what we got was tainted."

Alice said, "So you want New Terran ships to retrieve fresh specimens for you?"

"Would we know a good specimen from a bad one?" Louis asked. Sigmund had the same concern shortly after.

"Unlikely," Ol't'ro said. "We must send our own experts for that. We ask that one of *your* ships go along as a witness. And as a confidence-building measure, as you humans call it. Bm'o, too, wishes your participation, as you should confirm."

Trust me, I will, Louis thought.

"I can send a ship," Sigmund offered. "It will rendezvous with your mission on its way."

"Not acceptable," Ol't'ro said. "Our experts and a cargo ship leave immediately from Kl'mo. Our vessel cannot travel even partway without an escort. Besides, our need is urgent. Any ship leaving New Terra for Jm'ho must waste days decelerating."

"Crap." The word just slipped out of Louis. "You mean *Metternich*." You mean Alice.

"Of course," Ol't'ro said.

Sigmund said, "The new ship can take *Metternich*'s place en route."

"We have come to know and trust Alice and her crew. Or is that a problem?" Ol't'ro's question came out: *Or can we not trust you humans after all?*

"I'll do it," Alice said softly. On a side channel to Louis she added, "This is my job. It needs to be done."

"I know," he answered. And I hate this.

IT TOOK ANOTHER DAY for the local Gw'oth to assemble their expedition. That was too little time for Louis and Alice to rendezvous, but painfully long for a good-bye.

"I love you," Alice said. She seemed on the verge of tears. "You have no idea how much. Wait for me?"

Had she ever been more beautiful? Louis put on a brave face. "Where else would I go? Thanks to Nessus, I have no sense of direction."

"Wise guy."

"And? It looked like you had something else to say."

The same . . . strange . . . look. "Nothing that won't wait."

Huh? He looked at her differently. Critically. There was *something*.

She was sad. (So was he, but somehow her sadness was different. Moodier.) She glowed with health. Her face seemed a bit rounder than when he first met her. That meant nothing: so she had put on a pound or two. Maybe her face only looked round because her camera was in an oddly tight close-up.

The pieces came together.

"You're *pregnant*!" he burst out.

"Yes." She smiled ruefully. "I pictured telling you some other way."

"You can't go," Louis said. "Let me back up. It's wonderful. I couldn't be happier. But a warship is no place for a pregnant woman."

"It's a peace mission."

Which was different than peaceful, but that wasn't what bothered him. Arithmetic did: About sixty days since their last night together, and nothing said conception hadn't happened earlier. About thirty light-years to Jm'ho meant ninety days just in hyperspace travel. Each way. Add sanity breaks in normal space along the way. Add delays while the Gw'oth selected and loaded, and at the other end unloaded, their precious cargo. Then roughly ten light-years, and more sanity breaks, from Kl'mo to New Terra.

"You'll have the baby on the way," Louis said.

Alice shook her head. "I'll spend most of the trip in medical stasis. I won't have this baby without you."

He saw something else in her expression. Reticence? Wariness? Wistfulness? "You promise?"

"I promise."

44

Probes rushing in every direction, with speeds so high that time and space took on another meaning and the calculations became fascinating.

Probes leaping from normal space to hyperspace and back, dodging the singularity.

Probes always ready to smite any intruder, from any direction, at any time.

It was the greatest puzzle of all.

Ng't'mo almost burst with joy, pride, and gratitude. They were free. They were happy. They were trusted.

They would protect their new home—and show themselves worthy of Ol't'ro's trust—no matter what.

"WHAT DO YOU MEAN, gone?" Sigmund demanded, frowning.

Which part of *gone* was unclear? Louis managed not to snap. He had *Addison*'s bridge to himself. Since Alice's departure his ship felt lonelier than ever. That wasn't Sigmund's fault. Not entirely.

"*Addison* had coasted north of this solar system again. I hopped us south. When we dropped back to normal space, the Gw'oth fleet wasn't here. They might have been making a station-keeping jump of their own, so I didn't think anything of it at first. But it's been too long. They're headed . . . somewhere."

"And Ol't'ro's ship?"

"Gone, too."

"Leaving Kl'mo unprotected," Sigmund said skeptically.

"No. We still see the defensive array." The spacecraft showed up on Louis's sensors as a swarm of tiny neutrino sources. "There is still a Gw'oth ship outside the singularity, presumably to manage the array. But if Ol't'ro is aboard, no one admits it."

"Hmm. I need to think about this."

Louis tired of waiting. "It seems like time for us to come home."

Sigmund shook his head. "Think about it. The war fleet pulled back. The colony is getting new supplies, with a neutral party observing to make sure it happens."

"Right. So?"

"What did the other side get?"

"Their fleet was not smashed by Ol't'ro's defensive system."

"Possibly." Sigmund rubbed his chin thoughtfully. "Except Bm'o could have made that deal on Day One. I think he got something else."

"Something that involves Ol't'ro leaving at the same time," Louis added.

"Almost certainly."

What would both Gw'oth factions want? Louis hadn't a clue. "I haven't heard a reason yet why my friends and I shouldn't come home."

"Agreed. Call in daily for news." A thoughtful pause. "Both sides would want safety from Puppeteer meddling."

"So they're going after Achilles? Ol't'ro has been very interested in him. How are they going to find—"

"No," Sigmund said firmly. "Don't ask me to prove this, because I can't. But I'm certain. The Concordance can't or won't control Achilles, so the Gw'oth mean to hold the Concordance responsible."

"So what's Ol't'ro's plan?"

"Baedeker and I almost died the last time we crossed paths with Ol't'ro." Sigmund shivered. "I doubt we'll have better insight this time."

45

When the pings began, Nessus began to relax. Crossing the hyperwave-radar boundary meant he was almost home. He welcomed the digital exchanges between *Aegis'* onboard transponder and Space Traffic Control in its remote orbit around the Fleet. And as the Fleet itself came into naked-eye view as a cluster of not-quite stars, he positively relished the voice contact with a traffic controller.

"This is Hearth traffic control," the voice sang.

Sang! Full throated. Abundantly chorded. Rich with undertunes and grace notes and complex rhythms. Nessus had been away from home for far too long.

"This is Concordance vessel *Aegis,* registered to the Ministry of Foreign Affairs," Nessus sang back. He hoped his voices were a fraction as melodious.

"Identity confirmed," the controller sang. "We have some backlog, *Aegis,* handling refugee ships returning after the recent crisis." And shifting to a minor key, disapprovingly, "And a few ships outbound again, ignoring our rules. The Gw'oth ships are apparently homebound and likely to pass near the Fleet again."

"Understood." Nearing home, Nessus had seen the unusual number of transponders on his sensors. The panic on Hearth must have been incredible to drive so many Citizens off-world. "Controller, I am on official business, Hindmost's orders." Nessus sang a string of code digits. "You can confirm that with his office. I request immediate authorization, clearance to the primary General Products orbital facility, and also clearance for a shuttle from orbit to Hearth."

"One moment." Very quickly the controller returned, his song appreciably more formal. "Clearances granted, *Aegis.* Proceed."

"Thank you, Controller. Beginning final approach. *Aegis* out."

The General Products facility orbiting Hearth was an orb bigger than some moons Nessus had seen. He had had the celebrity tour more than once. Within the factory's cavernous central volume, even the #4 hulls of grain ships under construction seemed tiny. Service docks lined the factory's periphery; from a distance, the round hatches mimicked craters. Within the space docks, completed hulls were outfitted and returning ships received service and maintenance.

As *Aegis* settled into its assigned service dock, Nessus emitted a glissando of relief. He pivoted a head toward the portable server that stood amid his luggage. The Hindmost notwithstanding, artificial intelligences remained proscribed. Voice could not remain aboard where General Products engineers might find it.

"Voice, we have arrived. If you must communicate, message me."

"Understood, Nessus."

Nessus exited the air lock. Just out of deep space, *Aegis'* exterior remained frigid. Rime condensing from the air covered the hull. Icy fog filled the bay. A service crew in coveralls stood waiting.

The foreman lowered his heads subserviently. *Hindmost's orders* did that. "How may we serve?"

"A complete overhaul, bow to stern. The ship is overdue."

Long overdue. To and around Human Space to find Louis, then most of the way home. To the rear of the Pak evacuation and all through the Library fleet. Back to Hearth, on to New Terra, and back to Hearth again. Well on his way to Jm'ho and back again.

Nessus pointed at *Aegis'* hull. "Take good care of this ship. It has served the Concordance well."

"We will," the foreman sang earnestly.

The workers loaded Nessus' luggage onto a cargo floater. The floater followed him to a shuttle bay for the short trip to Hearth. To his long-empty apartment. To Baedeker. To the assignment of hunting Achilles' spies throughout the government.

For a moment, pondering his impossible-seeming task, Nessus almost wished he were going out again on *Aegis*.

WITH TREMBLING JAWS, Achilles dropped *Remembrance* to normal space. The inchoate dread of hyperspace had finally overcome vivid memories of the onrushing missile. The Gw'oth must be punished! Stopped! Obliterated!

"Release the retrovirus," he ordered Thalia. It was a recording, unsatisfying. From the fringes of the Gw'oth home system, the edict must make its way deep into the gravity well. "Acknowledge your orders, then report progress daily."

Of all who had set out with Achilles, only Hecate and Metope continued to serve. The rest were catatonic, dead, or—vile, unfaithful humans—run away. And so, all but alone, Achilles guided his ship toward Hearth. Where else could he go? And he brooded: What would he do when he got there?

An idea would come to him. One always did.

Anticipation buoyed him through another stretch of hyperwave flight. The Gw'oth of Jm'ho would starve. The colony on Kl'mo would fail.

Thalia was ever loyal. Thalia would die before failing him.

But when *Remembrance* next returned to normal space, Achilles' order remained unacknowledged.

"ANOTHER SUBJECT HAS ARRIVED," Nessus cautioned.

"I will not speak," Voice replied. His server sat on a shelf in Nessus' office.

Nessus walked to his anteroom, where his next subject paced nervously. Nessus was midway through his preliminary interviews of those at Clandestine Directorate with access to the hyperwave-radar system. Any of them might have disclosed to Achilles the Gw'oth fleet's course and emergences.

Nessus kept hoping no one was to blame, that Achilles had found some technological weakness to exploit. But Baedeker had assured Nessus that such a lapse was impossible. Baedeker—unlike Nessus—was qualified for his part of the investigation.

Nessus extended a neck to brush heads. ("Keep the subject off balance," Sigmund had advised.) "Thank you for coming. Call me Nessus."

"Circe," the subject sang. Circe was tall and lean for a Citizen, with a curly dark mane. He wore a formal Directorate sash festooned with emblems commemorating minor recognitions. "I assure you that I am—"

"Please. Come into my office." Nessus led the way. He straddled a high, padded bench behind a massive desk. For the subject, there was only a low, hard bench. Harsh overhead light shone down on that seat. "Please sit."

Circe settled onto the uncomfortable bench. "I assure you I have done nothing wrong."

272   LARRY NIVEN AND EDWARD M. LERNER

"Then you have nothing to fear," Nessus sang back. "Nonetheless, it is well known that the fugitive, Achilles, has obtained information from sources within the government. The Hindmost has directed me to find those sources."

Nessus waited.

"Nervous subjects will blurt things out," Sigmund had advised. Only how applicable was Sigmund's expertise? *Everyone* Nessus interviewed was nervous. Citizens were herd beings who did not betray their own, and any suspicion made them act strangely. Like voice-stress analysis, another of Sigmund's suggestions, exploiting nervousness was useless.

Sigmund had talked about coercion, too. Coercion! Another unproductive suggestion. With a second Gw'oth flyby imminent, a hint of coercion could drive even the innocent into catatonia. Or worse. Nessus did not want any deaths on his heads.

"Let us begin," Nessus sang. "Explain distribution of information from the border array."

"I only get reports," Circe sang cautiously.

"How do you get reports? What do you do with the information? With whom do you discuss what you see and read?"

Circe plucked at his mane. "It is all networked, and I am on distribution. I look for emergence patterns. . . ."

Voice recorded everything. Nessus observed mannerisms more than he listened. He interrupted, "And you are sympathetic to Achilles, no?"

"Yes. I mean I agreed with your 'no.' You are confusing me."

"You sympathize with Achilles," Nessus sang flatly. Deception was among the few of Sigmund's techniques that *could* work with Citizens.

Circe sat mutely, stunned. "It is not true," he finally sang.

"Others have told me about you," Nessus lied again.

"Not true," Circe repeated weakly.

"Do not try to deceive me. It will go better if you cooperate. Maybe you made an innocent remark or some ill-considered complaint in a moment of frustration. Tell me. Let me help you."

"I . . . I do not remember."

"Then you do not deny it," Nessus sang. He hated harassing the workers. Surely most had done nothing wrong. But what choice did he have while Achilles remained at large? What choice when the Hindmost asked this of him?

Circe sat, mute.

"And what of sharing the hyperwave radar information? Perhaps with good intentions you sent a copy to a colleague, someone unauthorized whom you believed deserved clearance." (*Give them the rope with which to hang themselves,* Sigmund called this ploy. First hearing the expression had made Nessus ill.)

"No. . . ."

Interesting hesitation. "You may not know this, Circe, but security software on the Directorate's computer network tracks everywhere that data goes. It even spots altered copies, and copies embedded in larger files. It all shows up in Security records." And Voice—impersonating Nessus, who had been granted system-administrator privileges for his investigation—was skilled at analyzing the audit trails.

Nessus tapped at the terminal on his desk. As he started to turn the display toward Circe, Nessus also trod on the button on the floor beneath his desk.

The button signaled his assistant. The door swung open. "I apologize, but this is urgent. A call for you from the Hindmost."

"Excuse me," Nessus sang to Circe. He circled his desk and exited the office, shutting the door behind him. "I will be back. I suggest that you think about what we have discussed."

Circe would peek at his display.

They *all* peeked. Nessus had more than enough video from hidden cameras to know. Throughout their consultations Sigmund kept saying, reassuringly, "Have some confidence. The spies are amateurs, too."

The terminal on Nessus' desk displayed an imaginary file directory on a server at Clandestine Directorate. It was a server to which the subject had authorized access. The location where supposedly damning evidence would reside. *If* the subject had done anything inappropriate.

A different imaginary location revealed to every subject.

Nessus would return in a few minutes, act distracted by his call, and hurriedly conclude the interview. Whatever the audit trail might have disclosed would have remained undiscussed. Remain—for how long, the subject could not know—exposed to edits or deletion.

If one of his subjects ever accessed the information, Nessus thought, then he would have something with which to work.

.   .   .

"EXCELLENCY," VESTA PLEADED from the hyperwave display, "it is time that I join you."

Achilles stood tall, impaling his timorous underling with a bold, two-headed stare. He had *Remembrance*'s bridge to himself. "I need you at Nike's side. You will not fail me."

"But, Excellency! Nessus probes deeply into operations across the Directorate. He works with the blessing of the Hind—of Baedeker—and your supporters fear they will be exposed. A few have fled, even vanished. Someone, surely, will talk to Nessus."

That the scruffy, insolent scout might once more stymie him was more than Achilles could bear. "How many in the Directorate know of your ties to me?"

"Most who knew joined your escape, so only one, Excellency. The investigation has not yet reached him."

"Nessus will keep searching until he finds a source in the Directorate. Do you intend for Nessus to find you?"

Vesta pawed nervously at the carpet of his office. "Of course not, Excellency. But Dionysus is loyal. He will not—"

Achilles stood straighter still. "While you live in comfort and luxury on Hearth, many have *died* that our cause may triumph. What is one more?"

Vesta plucked at his mane. "You mean—"

You know what I mean. "Many must remain unaccounted for from the panic as the Gw'oth swooped past Hearth. What is one more?

"However you manage it, your security is paramount. As a confidant of Nike and Baedeker, your reports to me are valuable beyond measure. And know that I have not forgotten who freed me from Baedeker's prison."

Achilles watched the struggle behind Vesta's clear blue eyes. Fear against greed. Vanity against herd solidarity.

Vanity and greed won. "I shall take the necessary measures, Excellency."

"Your service will be rewarded." Achilles broke the connection.

Plunging *Remembrance* back to hyperspace, continuing onward toward Hearth, Achilles knew he would yet snatch glorious victory from the jaws of defeat.

He only wished that he knew how.

46

"'We spared your worlds once. You attacked us anyway,'" Bm'o repeated. "Transmitting that at each emergence is all we need to do?"

"It is all *you* need to do," Ol't'ro corrected. "Except for the few ships we will borrow, you and your fleet may return to Jm'ho." And we will be happy when you do.

"A few ships," Bm'o persisted. "It seems insufficient."

Because the monarch's imagination was insufficient. Worse, his manner was arrogant. Even by audio-only hyperwave, Ol't'ro found it an ordeal to work with Bm'o. During the Pak War, *they* had spent much of a Jm'ho year with Baedeker, now Hindmost. *They* had worked among the Citizen scientists struggling to stabilize their version of a planetary drive. And *they* had studied Achilles in detail, analyzing his actions and everything the New Terrans could share about the rogue Citizen.

So yes, *they* knew what would suffice.

All Ol't'ro said was, "The Citizens' own fear will do the rest."

"Very well," Bm'o said. "We will speak again before the fleet splits."

"We are sorry," Ol't'ro said, "to hear about Rt'o's passing. She led a productive life. Doubtless you will find much to do after the loss of such an able advisor."

"Thank you." There was a hesitation in Bm'o's response. Wondering who had told Ol't'ro about the regent's death? Or reasoning that Ol't'ro had cracked the encryption on which the fleet's security and Jm'ho's defenses relied?

"We will speak again before you leave," Ol't'ro agreed and broke the connection.

.   .   .

BAEDEKER STUDIED HIMSELF in his bedroom mirror. Mane matted and snarled. Eyes dull. Coat unbrushed. Had he ever been so disheveled? The slovenliness came not from neglect or panic, although both bubbled beneath the surface, but from the sheer lack of time as the end of the world approached.

The only beings with whom he sought contact were Gw'oth, and *they* would not care about his hygiene. If they might have, it hardly mattered. They ignored his messages. They ignored *all* messages from Hearth.

While transmitting, over and over, "We spared your worlds once. You attacked us anyway."

Doom impended, all the more ominous for not knowing how the end would come. Not by kinetic-kill weapons, for the Gw'oth fleet once more aimed at Hearth still matched the Fleet's normal-space velocity. What did the aliens want? What would they do?

What and *how* continued to elude Baedeker. *When* was all too clear.

He plucked anxiously at his mane. Since first triggering the hyperwave radar on the Fleet's northern perimeter, the Gw'oth had appeared four times in normal space. Each appearance brought them closer to Hearth.

A few days. No more. And then?

A tremulous voice from beyond Baedeker's door: "Hindmost? Are you all right? May I get you anything?"

"Thank you, Minerva, but no," Baedeker answered his aide through the closed door. Thank you for reminding me of my duty. I cannot save the herd, but I must do what I can to ease its final days. And to do *that,* I must appear to be in charge. "I will be ready presently."

He sampled the news and public-safety cameras as he groomed. Another spate of grain ships stolen. Citizens by the billions unaccounted for, presumed catatonic in their apartments or hidden in the remotest recesses of Hearth's few parks and botanical gardens. Terror and madness. Assemblies around the globe, from solemn to panic-stricken to angry. He watched an enormous rally whose orator, in full-throated threnody, excoriated the Hindmost for the coming destruction and demanded his resignation.

Brushing his mane, chewing bitter cud, Baedeker wondered: What would the herd think if they knew I had offered to resign? The elders of the party refused his resignation, lest any of them wind up presiding over the end of the world. Even Nike had sunk into despair. The Conservative leaders were too overwhelmed to talk. The party of precedent had been totally immobilized by the coming day of reckoning.

How could he resign when none would take his place?

Still, he *had* offered. The Gw'oth responded to Baedeker's resignation offer as they had responded to his attempts to surrender Hearth, as they responded to every transmission sent from the Fleet. "We spared your worlds once. You attacked us anyway."

With his token grooming finished, Baedeker cantered to the door. He found aides and his security detachment clustered outside. "I will be in my personal office," he announced, "preparing an address to the worlds. Send for Nike and Nessus."

"Immediately, Hindmost," Minerva replied. He trotted alongside Baedeker to the residence's office complex.

Baedeker's home office overlooked the rocky coast, and he stood for a while gazing over the ocean and the incoming tide. Cloud darkened the sky and reduced Nature Preserve One to a vaguely amorphous glow.

Chords to open an address refused to come to him. In past crises humans had kicked him—sometimes literally—out of a downward spiral of despair. But New Terrans maintained their neutrality.

And gloated at the coming karmic justice hurtling toward their former oppressors?

"Hindmost." Minerva had reappeared at Baedeker's door. "I cannot reach Nike."

"I would expect him to be at Clandestine Affairs," Baedeker sang impatiently.

Minerva bobbed heads. "I, too. He stepped there earlier today and there is no record that he has left, but no one can locate him."

"Did you reach Nessus?"

"Yes, Hindmost, at Clandestine Directorate. He will complete his current interview and then join you here."

"I changed my mind. Have Nessus meet me at Nike's office."

"Yes, Hindmost."

The unlisted stepping disc in Nike's office would not accept a connection, nor did it respond to an emergency override. If panic had reached even into Clandestine Directorate . . .

Preceded by armed guards, Baedeker stepped through to the Directorate's security center. He found workers milling about in confusion.

"Who is in charge here?" Baedeker demanded. "What is happening?"

The ranking security officer groveled. "Hindmost, I am called Triton. Many are missing. Their communicators are out of range or powered down. Yet according to the stepping-disc system and the building's door cameras they have not left the building."

"Who?"

"Nike and much of his staff, Hindmost."

"We will go to Nike's office," Baedeker sang. "Accompany us."

Baedeker, his personal security detail, and Triton stepped to the hall outside Nike's office. Nessus stood there waiting. Behind the locked door was only silence. "Open the door," Baedeker ordered.

Cringing, Triton overrode the lock.

Of Nike and his staff, there was no sign. The meadowplant carpet was in tatters, as though shredded by countless anxious hooves. The desk had been pushed against the wall, its legs scoring parallel grooves in the living rug. Where the desk had been, a stepping disc stood revealed.

"What is that symbol embossed on the disc surface?" Triton asked. He turned to point at the second disc across the room. "And why hide a disc in a room that *has* a disc?"

"Everyone except Nessus, go to the hall," Baedeker ordered. He shut and locked the door. A desk ornament tossed onto the formerly hidden disc landed with a clatter. The disc was no longer in transmit mode. He removed a transport controller from his sash pocket. It was a very special controller. "Do you know what this is?"

"A secret exit, obviously," Nessus sang. "Where did they go?"

Voices murmured in the hallway, the melodies indistinct but the worry plain.

Lips and tongue pressed against the device's biometric sensors, Baedeker crooned the pass code. The activation LED remained dark. He stepped onto the disc and nothing happened. The controller's diagnostic mode insisted that the disc itself was working properly. The disc's maintenance log had recorded twenty-three transfers that day. Everything was in order.

But the destination disc no longer responded.

"Where can *we* not go?" Nessus asked this time.

Baedeker put the transport controller back in his pocket. An eerie calm came over him. He had one fewer decision to make. "Nike has fled to the Hindmost's Refuge and locked the door behind him."

Nessus looked himself in the eyes. "I think we know who Achilles' source was."

LOST IN THOUGHT, Achilles circled his empty bridge yet again.

He did not have *Remembrance* to himself, not quite. Metope and Hecate were quavering wrecks, scarcely able to feed themselves, useless to him. Even if he could anticipate the Gw'oth's actions, even if—damn Louis Wu!—he had retained enough fusion suppressors to disable a fleet, he no longer had workers enough to deploy them.

But other options had begun to appear.

"Guide us," one transmission pleaded. "Be our Hindmost," another begged. At last count, entreaties had come from eighteen evacuation ships. Most signals were faint, broadcast in all directions, for the refugees could not know where to find him.

And, "Come home," the Party elders implored. With the Gw'oth upon them, evidently the patriarchs were ready to overlook esoteric infractions. They, too, had had to resort to broadcast, but using Hearth's most powerful transmitters their appeals came through clearly. "We need your wisdom. Baedeker has no answers, nor will the Gw'oth speak to him."

How satisfying it would have been to return to Hearth, to see his enemies grovel at his hooves, to crush and humiliate Baedeker. But the gratification would have been short-lived. Whatever rancor the Gw'oth felt toward Baedeker, they must feel more toward *him*.

Let Baedeker officiate over disaster.

Achilles would bide his time. Vesta's reports made clear that the Gw'oth were scant days behind him. If they left anything and anyone behind, Achilles would be ready to pick up the pieces. And if not? Then he would be Hindmost of those who had taken to ships, the founder of a whole new Citizen civilization.

He routed maximum power to the ship's hyperwave transmitter. "To those who have left Hearth, I am touched by your pleas. Gather at"—and he gave coordinates far removed from the Gw'oth's apparent course—"and I will meet you."

But only after the Gw'oth ships were well past.

ACHILLES WALKED UP and down the empty corridors of *Remembrance*. When pacing grew old, he synthesized and pecked at a shallow bowl of mixed grains. Vesta's call was late. Had his disciple been caught?

When the contact finally came, Vesta's eyes darted about wildly. His voices trembled, the undertunes strident with panic. "All here is chaos."

"Your insights remain valuable," Achilles answered. *Stay where you are.* "Tell me more."

Vesta twitched. "Nike and many of his senior staff have fled, Excellency. Baedeker has put me in charge of Clandestine Directorate."

And so put Hearth's defenses and the emergency communications network into Vesta's—and Achilles'—jaws. A fool, Baedeker. As ever.

"Fled where?" Achilles pressed. "Is Nike apt to return? Is anyone looking for him?"

"Unknown, Excellency. To my knowledge, no one is looking."

Meaning Baedeker already knew where Nike had gone? Or a falling-out between the two so extreme that Baedeker did not want Nike back? Either possibility was interesting. Achilles set those scenarios aside to ponder another time.

"Nike and most of his senior staff. Why not you?"

Vesta looked away from the camera. "I was off-world, inspecting space-based defenses, when Nike fled."

So Vesta, too, would have run if he could. The herd's newly appointed defender was but one unexpected shadow, one loud noise, one surprise removed from panic. Achilles demanded the latest authentication codes for the automated planetary defenses before proceeding. *The ability to slip past the Fleet's defenses could prove useful.*

Achilles sang, "And what would our useless 'Hindmost' have you do?"

"Whatever I can." Vesta's heads swiveled frantically, seeking safety where none existed. "*Can* anything be done, Excellency? Is the Concordance doomed?"

If the Gw'oth had wanted to destroy Hearth, they would have accelerated in normal space. They wanted something else. Something Baedeker could not, or would not concede. Something that a more insightful Citizen might provide?

And then Achilles *had* the insight. "Here are your orders. You control the Directorate's emergency communications network. Use it. Tell the Gw'oth . . ."

47

With frightening precision, six ships dropped from hyperspace at the same instant to surround *Remembrance*. The ships were short, squat cylinders, tinier than any Citizen ship.

Achilles puzzled over their asymmetric deployment until he imagined the newcomers turning lasers on him. No laser beam passing through *Remembrance*'s hull would strike another vessel.

Achilles shuddered. The Gw'oth were a warlike race.

"We are Ol't'ro," announced the hail. (It came relayed through a buoy that had likely dropped from hyperspace at the same time as the ships, but that Achilles had just now noticed. Rerouted, the hail denied any hint which ship housed the enemy leader.) "Our ships are ready."

Not enemy. Ally. From the bridge, Achilles opened three cargo-hold hatches. He waited alone, as Metope and Hecate cowered flank to flank in a remote cabin.

He radioed, "This is Achilles. Come aboard."

Via security cameras, he watched the tiny ships dart inside, two to each cargo hold. They landed far apart. Positioned to blast *Remembrance* from within if he should manage to immobilize them.

He would not be so foolish as to try. It had been Ol't'ro, after all, who invented the Gw'oth method of destroying General Products hulls. Ol't'ro, who helped invent the planet-buster that defeated the Pak. Not that a successful trap, if Achilles were insane enough to take the risk, would suffice. The rest of the Gw'oth still sped toward Hearth.

And only Gw'oth allies had the means to satisfy his hunger. . . .

"All ships are aboard," Ol't'ro sang. "You may proceed."

"Acknowledged. Welcome to *Remembrance*. Hatches closing."

The little ships disgorged crew. (Boarding parties. Their pressure suits and exoskeletons seemed indistinguishable from battle armor. The unfamiliar implements dangling from their harnesses surely included weapons.) They scuttled about like gigantic bugs, disgusting even encased in their protective gear.

As the aliens formed into orderly units, Achilles steeled himself to meet them. He had railed, warned, and conspired against them for years. He had used them; now they would use him.

"Send the floor plans for this ship," a Gw'o radioed. The song, while fluent, lacked the commanding presence that Ol't'ro could project.

In each cargo hold Achilles set a ceiling light flashing. "Find the disc in the floor beneath the blinking light. Tell me where in *Remembrance* you wish to go. The discs will deliver you."

"Send floor plans," Ol't'ro commanded, the undertunes of authority sharp and unambiguous.

Achilles transmitted the files. He watched through security cameras as his new masters scuttled and scurried to the engine room, the life-support center, and onto the bridge.

I act to save the herd, Achilles told himself. If I had not proposed this, then what? Baedeker did nothing. Baedeker *could* do nothing, for the Gw'oth refused to talk with him. Nike had fled—wherever. Vesta, tasked with the defense of the Fleet, struggled even to respond robotically to orders. Many among the Party elders had succumbed to catatonia; the rest, without ideas of their own, had added to the cacophony emanating from Hearth with renewed pleas that Achilles—somehow—help.

Accommodation was the only way to placate the Gw'oth. Among all the herd, only he had the vision and imagination to make an accommodation.

But in his hearts, Achilles knew a deeper truth. While he kept order on Hearth, Ol't'ro would not care what the new Hindmost did or to whom he did it.

His time—to savor power; to bask, at last, in the public adulation of his supporters; to crush and humiliate everyone who had ever thwarted him—had finally arrived.

"THIS IS CONCORDANCE VESSEL *Remembrance,* registered to the Ministry of Foreign Affairs, inbound to Hearth," Achilles announced. He sat astraddle the pilot's crash couch, close to the comm set's camera. The armored Gw'oth on the bridge squatted outside the camera's line of sight.

"This is Hearth traffic control," a voice sang back. "*Remembrance,* we are not reading your traffic-control transponder."

"Inoperative," Achilles responded. It was, having had its power cut off. The transponder registered to *Grain Ship 247* was all too likely to be flagged somewhere within the space-traffic-control system. "We have been away for a long time."

"Maintain course and speed while we confirm with Foreign Affairs," the controller sang.

"Acknowledged." Achilles waited, unconcerned. Vesta had created *Remembrance,* a long-range scout ship, in the databases of Clandestine Directorate.

"*Remembrance,* we have confirmation. Because your transponder is offline, I will need current ministry authentication codes."

"Transmitting on a secure channel." Achilles sent the data Vesta had provided. "Can you expedite, traffic control? We are on urgent official business."

"One moment." After considerably longer than that, the controller returned. "Codes confirmed. Detailed approach information is on its way, *Remembrance.* Maintain regular radar pings for safety, since your transponder is offline. I am clearing a path for you."

"Understood, traffic control. *Remembrance,* out."

While armed Gw'oth watched, Achilles piloted *Remembrance* through layer after layer of Fleet defenses. None of the few grain ships still flying came anywhere close. He entered the worlds' singularity. He continued inward. He approached the plane of the planets. . . .

"Now," Ol't'ro ordered from within their ship. "Open the hatches."

BAEDEKER HAD JUST BEGUN an unannounced nightshift inspection of the Clandestine Directorate command bunker when everything fell apart.

"Unidentified neutrino sources!" an operator sang. "This is not a drill. Four. Five. Six. Six ships."

"Where?" Baedeker shouted. And, "Get Vesta in here."

The operator enlarged his tactical hologram, a synthesis of data from public sensors, the defense grid, and Space Traffic Control. One unidentified blip streaked toward each of the Nature Preserve worlds. Two sped toward Hearth. And at the point from which the blips must have emerged: the icon of a Directorate vessel, *Remembrance.*

There was no Directorate ship by that name.

For a moment, transfixed, Baedeker stared at the catastrophe racing at the worlds of the Fleet. Racing was not exactly correct. Only the ships' proximity made them appear fast. These were not kinetic-kill weapons.

"How did intruders first appear deep inside the singularity?" Baedeker trembled in disbelief: at what was happening. That Gw'oth ships—who else could these be?—had arrived before their main fleet. That the automated defenses had yet to activate. "Never mind. Set loose the automated defenses."

Vesta arrived, his mane elaborately coiffed as if for some ceremonious occasion. He bobbed heads at the tactical display. "The war has come to us," he intoned portentously.

"Why do our weapons not fire?" Baedeker ululated.

Across the room, images flashed above a diagnostic console. The operator there sang out, surprise plain in the second and fourth harmonics, "The intruders are transmitting Directorate authentication codes."

"Override!" Baedeker sang. "Target manually, if you must."

"A broadcast on the public safety channel," Vesta interrupted.

"This is Achilles," the broadcast began.

Not now! Baedeker wanted to scream. He forced himself to listen.

". . . The government cannot defend you from the Gw'oth fleet that approaches. At the invitation of the Experimentalist elders, I return, reluctantly, to assume the duties of Hindmost. Assist me in the transition of power, and you *will* be safe. Stay in your home or—"

"Mute that herdless outcast!" Baedeker sang. The intruder blips, now visible to ground-based telescopes, had morphed in the tactical display into flat cylindrical icons. Gw'oth ships, definitely. "Why do our defenses not fire?"

"A hail on the Directorate emergency network," Vesta called. "Now, two hails. Full encryption."

"Whose authentication codes?" Baedeker asked.

"Both hails use my codes," Vesta sang.

Baedeker stared. "Take the first hail. Put the call on speaker."

"Is Baedeker there?" the familiar, hated voices of Achilles asked.

"The *Hindmost* is here," Baedeker sang icily. "If you wish to help the Concordance, get off this channel."

"Only I can save the Concordance. Now empty the room—I imagine you are in the command bunker."

"Why should I do that?"

Achilles whistled in amusement. "Surely your sensors show six very good reasons. Now for the good of the herd, send out everyone before responding to the second hail."

Baedeker counted to twenty. "It is done."

"He lies," Vesta sang.

Baedeker stared. The betrayal was suddenly clear.

"Clear the room, *Baedeker*," Vesta sang.

MIGHTY CURRENT was on its final approach to Nature Preserve Five, close to atmospheric entry, when the hail over the secure channel was answered.

"We are Ol't'ro," they announced.

"This is the Hindmost."

"We remember you," Ol't'ro sang. "It has been a long time. We ask a question for the good of the Concordance, so do not deceive us. Are you alone?"

"Yes. What do you want?" Baedeker sang sourly.

"We want safety for everyone, Citizen and Gw'o alike. You have failed to provide that."

"Safety, how?"

"You will address the Concordance. You will announce your immediate resignation and endorse Achilles to succeed. Soon after, Achilles will declare the successful conclusion of a brilliant negotiation.

"The lagging part of our armada will turn away. Most of our ships already in the Fleet of Worlds will withdraw. *We* will remain on a Nature Preserve to assure Achilles' absolute obedience.

"Except for you, Achilles, and us, none need ever know who rules these worlds."

An odd, half-choked melody, inarticulate. Heavy breathing, as the Hindmost regained control of his emotions. "Ol't'ro, it was *Achilles* who threatened your worlds. Why would you help him? Why would you trust him?"

Was it not obvious? "We do not trust him, Baedeker. We use him."

"Then use *me*. You must know Achilles is . . . beyond insane."

Ol't'ro had considered that. But especially after sharing *Remembrance*, after seeing how egomaniacal Achilles was, they had no doubts: Achilles was their ideal tool. He would do *anything* to maintain his status and power.

"You may take our refusal as a compliment. Achilles' obsessions make him easy to predict and control. If he disappoints us, we may reinstate you to office. He is instructed not to harm you."

"Achilles has endangered worlds to further his ambition. You cannot, you *must* not, hold a trillion Citizens hostage to his good behavior." Baedeker's harmonics rang with despair. "It is too easy to imagine the day he will stop caring about their fates."

Achilles had never started to care. "Were we to disclose even a small part of what we know about him, even you timid creatures would surely trample him. He craves the herd's adoration. He will obey us."

"And if I do not resign?"

Through an uncoupled tubacle, Ol't'ro peered through the melding-chamber floor at navigational sensors. All six ships were on their final landing approaches. The Fleet's compromised defenses remained inoperative. "We are taking control of your planetary drives."

"T . . . to change the Fleet's course?"

"Baedeker, think as the engineer you once were. What will happen if we destabilize even one of the Fleet's planetary drives?"

There was a roar like a seamount avalanche, and an ice sheet cracking and grinding, and a million voices screaming—and then silence.

In a low, quaking melody—devoid of grace notes, its harmonics limp, with undertunes ineffably sad—Baedeker intoned, "I will comply."

48

Emergency tones, piercing and insistent, ripped Nessus from exhausted sleep. He lunged for his pocket computer as it shrieked on his nightstand.

"Thank the herd I reached you!" Baedeker sang. "Vesta was the traitor. Nike did only what any sane person would: he ran for safety while he still could. You must go to the Directorate immediately and erase all director-restricted files. Then, hide. Get to New Terra if you can."

Nessus' hearts pounded. "Why? What is happening?"

"There is no time. Do you trust me?"

"Of course," Nessus sang.

"Then hurry and be safe." Baedeker broke the connection.

Nessus gave his sleep-stirred mane a perfunctory brushing, just enough to avoid calling attention to himself. He stepped through to Clandestine Directorate's security foyer, where the nightshift guards stiffened in surprise. "Other worlds, other schedules," he sang in explanation. They confirmed his identity and let him proceed into the building.

The lights rose as Nessus entered his office. It was an ordinary room, filled with standard furniture, displaying everyday scenes on its walls, and it all seemed to mock him. Would normality ever hold a place in his life?

The moment he shut the door, Voice spoke from his shelf. "The Hindmost has scheduled an address to the Concordance. He was in the command bunker, but has left."

Nessus could not guess what that meant, or why Baedeker had made his mysterious request. Nor did Nessus waste time wondering, because he trusted Baedeker implicitly.

System-administrator access required full biometric authentication. Nessus used lip-, tongue-, and voiceprints to identify himself. He navigated through the file system to the director-restricted storage, then jacked

Voice's server into the office terminal. "Delete it all, Voice. Remote back-ups, too."

"Shall I copy anything? Produce an analysis of what is there?"

"Not if it will slow you down."

"Very good, sir."

Nessus imagined an edge-of-audibility *whine* as somewhere on the Directorate network trillions of bistable memory molecules reset. What dark secrets they must hold—too many of his own shameful deeds among them. All done to protect the Concordance.

"Done, sir," Voice announced. "Full deletion."

Nessus grabbed Voice's server by its jaw grip; the fiber-optic cable ripped loose as he dashed for the door. His mind churned with half-remembered stepping-disc locations he might reach without encountering guards on patrol. And once out of the building? *Aegis* was still being overhauled. Maybe he could commandeer a grain ship. He opened the office door—

Vesta and a dozen guards, stunners in their jaws, were galloping down the corridor.

IN TRIUMPH, ACHILLES WATCHED Baedeker's curt abdication speech. He basked in the Party elders' renewed, urgent pleas for his return. When they had groveled sufficiently, he transmitted his acceptance and guidance for his victorious homecoming. He brushed and combed, braided and weaved, curled and teased, until his coiffure was beyond magnificent.

Only then did he set *Remembrance* on the short trip to Hearth's main spaceport.

Achilles disembarked into the tumult of millions stomping their approval, the adoration swelling louder and louder. Even viewed from atop the reviewing stand, his devoted subjects stretched from horizon to horizon. They covered even the illumination strips embedded in the landing field's concrete. A forest of temporary lampposts lit the myriad upturned, expectant faces and banished the stars from Hearth's perpetually dark sky.

He drank in the herd's adulation for a long while before launching into his speech. By then Hecate had removed *Remembrance* lest it block anyone's view of the enormous projected image of—him.

Achilles stood with necks straight and vertical, heads held high, hooves placed apart, utterly confident and serene. The post lamps slowly dimmed until all that the vast herd—and the floating news cameras—could see was his imposing figure. From the display/sunlight panels of arcologies, his image gazed down on throngs in malls and plazas around Hearth.

At the first notes of his amplified voice, a hush fell over the multitude. But when he pledged a swift resolution to the Gw'oth crisis, and swift justice for those whose negligence had brought the Concordance to such a perilous state, the crowd roared its approval.

Finally, his throats hoarse, his legs trembling with fatigue, Achilles brought his oration to a close. "Remember this day, for it is the start of a new era," he concluded. With the crowd still cheering lustily, he stepped through to the Hindmost's—to *his*—official residence.

Where Nessus and Baedeker, their legs cuffed, awaited their fates. A bit of gloating would be the ideal end to the perfect day.

"WE ARE OL'T'RO."

While radio waves crept from Nature Preserve Five to Hearth and back, they completed another set of inferences about the Outsider-built planetary drive. When the Pak threat had loomed, their work would have proceeded far swifter had Baedeker only given them access.

Doubtless Baedeker would soon suffer, although not for that lapse of judgment.

"This is the Hindmost," the reply finally came, with undertunes smug and proud.

"We would participate more closely in the councils of government," Ol't'ro announced. There would be another delay, and they resumed their line of research.

"State your needs and I will make it so," Achilles sang, a bit of the haughtiness gone from his voices.

"We will be your Minister of Science." We will sample and guide all the research and development done in the Concordance.

"But none can see you!" The swagger was entirely gone now, replaced by notes of panic. "None can learn of our . . . arrangement."

Lest all should see you as a puppet. Ol't'ro's thoughts skipped from puppet, to Puppeteer, to the human from whom they had learned the term. Sigmund Ausfaller.

"We will participate remotely, as a hologram," they sang. "You will explain that our research is often dangerous and so we work on the Nature Preserves, from ships, and even in deep space. Agreed?"

"A hologram! Of what?"

"Of a Citizen." Sigmund had traveled with an artificial intelligence. Jeeves, the creature had been called. While he could, Sigmund had hidden the existence of the software.

But Ol't'ro had yet to find any trace of artificial intelligence in the Concordance's vast computer network. "Obtain an artificial intelligence, perhaps from New Terra. We will alter it to present a Citizen persona."

"Agreed. You shall have your Voice," Achilles sang. "And what shall we call your persona?"

Voice. Ol't'ro recognized without understanding the capitalization and renewed smug grace notes. They decided it did not matter.

To impersonate an Experimentalist politician, they would need a designation from human mythology. They uploaded databases from the Human Studies Institute on Hearth, then sorted and sifted. Names. Terms. Human history. Cultural icons.

They would be the power behind the throne, the eminence grise, the invisible hand, the ultimate Puppeteer. They required a name of subtlety and wisdom, of distinction and authority.

Ol't'ro sang, "We shall be called Chiron."

Did this Hindmost know the sage and cunning centaur from human myth who taught the legendary Achilles? If so, he wisely kept it to himself.

49

Once more, *Addison* dropped back to normal space.

Louis scrambled to assess the tactical situation. "Nothing visible," he told Enzio. That did not preclude the Gw'oth fleet at any instant dropping from hyperspace all around *Addison*.

"Radar ping?" Enzio suggested.

"Go ahead." Absent extremely bad luck, the Gw'oth fleet, wherever they were, would be beyond radar range, too. "I'm going to check the New Terra relays for messages."

He found a recording from Sigmund. "Louis, everything has gone to hell. Contact me immediately."

Louis did, and Sigmund *looked* like hell. All color except five-o'clock shadow was gone from his face. "Where are you?" Sigmund demanded.

"Is Alice all right?" Louis shot back. His last message from her was days old.

"The last I heard, she's fine and her trip remains uneventful. Now where is *Addison*?"

"We're about a day north of New Terra by hyperdrive. Tell me what's happening."

"Here's what I know." Sigmund grimaced. "What little I know. Just after you last went back to hyperspace, the Gw'oth began ominous hyperwave broadcasts. The Concordance was paralyzed. Billions catatonic. Billions pleading to be saved. More ships—a surprising number, considering we're talking about Puppeteers—headed to New Terra, begging for asylum."

"To be saved," Louis repeated. "Saved by what or whom? Achilles?"

"Yah. It gets worse. The Fleet's border array lost track of half a dozen Gw'oth warships. Then, in extremely short order, Baedeker *resigned* and Achilles returned heroically to Hearth. Tanj, but the Puppeteers are herd animals. There was worldwide panic, worldwide mass hysteria, and out of it Achilles has gotten himself acclaimed as Hindmost."

"What can *anyone* say to that?"

"Nothing," Sigmund said. "But things got stranger still. Almost immediately, Achilles announced a diplomatic settlement with the Gw'oth. As best my analysts can tell from hyperspace entry/exit ripples, the Gw'oth ships have veered off. They are detouring around the Fleet to take a longer route home."

"What about the Puppeteer border array? Does hyperwave radar support the supposed course change?"

"That's the strangest part of things. I don't know." Sigmund grimaced. "Since Achilles took over, I'm out of the loop. I can't contact Baedeker, Nike, or Nessus."

AS SIGMUND SPUN OUT paranoid fantasies—of secret deals between Achilles and the Gw'oth, of Gw'oth secretly ruling Hearth itself—Louis struggled to take in everything. He wasn't sure he cared who ruled on Hearth. It was New Terra that mattered, and the life he hoped to make there with Alice.

But what about Nessus?

When Louis joined Nessus, the only job description was *it may be dangerous . . . I can reveal no more than that.* Certainly Louis had faced more than his share of danger since. Not until he was aboard *Aegis,* and cured of his addiction, had Nessus disclosed what he really expected of Louis: peace with the Gw'oth. Surely no one could have accomplished that.

So why did Louis feel that he had failed?

What if Nessus had not rescued Louis from Wunderland? Every possible outcome was grim. He would be a hopeless addict, or a serf in an aristo labor camp, or dead.

Sigmund watched silently from the hyperwave display. Looking uncomfortable. Deciding how to bring up . . . something.

"You don't have to ask, Sigmund." I know you won't ask, because New Terra cannot afford to take sides in Concordance politics. But *I'm* not from around here. "I *will* save Nessus. Baedeker, too, if I can. But I'm going to need your help."

. . .

TROWEL FIRMLY CLENCHED in his jaw, Baedeker dug at a stubborn, deeply rooted weed. When the wildflower yielded, he turned his attention to another. The fields stretched all around him. He need never worry about running out of weeds. His work this day was nearly done, for only a single sun remained in the sky. It would soon be dark.

Nature Preserve One was the earliest and most conservatively engineered of Hearth's companion worlds. The annual emission cycles of the suns emulated the seasonal variability Hearth had once experienced. And because the single string of suns orbited over the equator, the climate grew colder with higher latitudes, reproducing conditions long vanished from the home world itself.

In one way Baedeker considered himself lucky. Penance Island lay near the equator. The days were hot, but the evenings were almost pleasantly cool. The island never experienced winter or snow.

He hated snow.

"I think I shall go mad." Nessus' melody was thin and unadorned, for one of his mouths was also encumbered. He toiled three crop rows to Baedeker's right.

"The majority is always sane. At least, given enough time." Baedeker uprooted a chokeweed while he considered his next chords. A thing needed to be sung, and yet he had been reluctant to express the thought. "I am sorry, Nessus, that you are here. It is my fault."

"And yet I feel better for being here with you. Except . . ."

Baedeker dropped his trowel to speak more clearly. "Achilles intends us to suffer as he perceives he suffered during his long banishment. You and I will not be harmed physically." At least not soon. Baedeker chose not to dwell on that possibility.

"This is not suffering?"

Relieved of responsibility. Spared of impossible expectations. Immersed every day in a mindless task. Lost every night in exhausted sleep. Suffering? Hardly. This was release. This was, at least for now, all that Baedeker could handle.

"I know this dance. You will get used to it," he sang.

The warble of a siren: work's end for the day. He began gathering his tools in the pockets of his oversized sash. Across the fields, other inmates did the same. He glanced at the dark clouds. "Come, Nessus. It will rain soon." The tents leaked, but they still offered some shelter.

He and Nessus trudged to the tents. Baedeker ignored the growing clumps of damp soil that clung to his hooves.

Within the administrative compound, artificial lights switched on. Inside the wall was another universe, a place of controlled climate, data networks, computers, stepping discs, cargo floaters, food synthesizers. . . . Outside the wall the only technology was rude implements and muscle power. Nothing to make life easier. Nothing that could be used in an escape attempt if anyone should be crazy enough to try. Baedeker tried to ignore the bright lights and their unwelcome reminder of a more complicated existence.

The first fat raindrops fell. He and Nessus hurried their pace, for rain this late in the afternoon often became a downpour.

"What was in the files?" Nessus sang abruptly.

The files but for whose destruction—at Baedeker's insistence—Nessus might have had the opportunity to escape Hearth and the wrath of Achilles.

Baedeker sang, "You know I cannot say."

"I know you will not say."

"And yet you persist in asking." Baedeker veered, brushing flanks with Nessus to lessen the sting in his melody. "Some burdens only a Hindmost may bear."

Like the appalling record of Citizen atrocities against other species—always for the safety of the Concordance, of course. In the now inaccessible Refuge, Nike watched over the sole remaining copy of that shameful history.

Proof of past Concordance ruthlessness lay along the Fleet's path, not many years' flight ahead. The alien artifact was enormous; Ol't'ro could not fail, in time, to discover it.

Baedeker knew Ol't'ro. Without a doubt, they would send an expedition to explore the ring world. They must *never* learn of Hearth's prior involvement there. If Ol't'ro ever suspected, let alone confirmed, what extreme measures the Concordance had taken to preempt possible adversaries, they would obliterate the herd without qualms. Not that Baedeker knew Gw'oth even had consciences. . . .

Baedeker shuddered. "Be thankful you do not know."

.   .   .

THE PINGS BEGAN more than a light-year from Hearth. Louis held his breath each time, but every hyperwave exchange ended with the authorization to come a micro-hop closer.

Sigmund would not break neutrality with Hearth, but he had bent it nearly into a pretzel. He provided information, and lots of it: identification codes and crew manifests from refugee ships impounded on the tarmac on New Terra. Instructions that Louis could not execute—but Maura could—to hack *Addison*'s space-traffic-control transponder and upload the new codes. Detailed maps of their destination. A copy of Jeeves as a Puppeteer translator.

"I can—maybe—get you into the Fleet," Sigmund had said. "I can't get you into, or out of, the prison."

"Relax," Louis had answered. "I have that covered." And fervently hoped that was true.

Another drop to normal space. The worlds of the Fleet were naked-eye objects. Another digital exchange. And then—

From *Addison*'s main comm console: a clatter of notes. Metallica orchestrating the Goldberg Variations.

"'This is Hearth traffic control,'" Jeeves translated. "Shall I respond?"

"That's why you're here," Enzio muttered from the copilot's couch.

He and his crew were here for the very large funds transfer Sigmund had made, the confirmation also part of Sigmund's upload. It must have occurred to Enzio that Sigmund might forge the confirmation, because Enzio had not set their final course until he confirmed a deposit directly with his bank.

For past services, Sigmund had designated the payment. "If you are caught . . ."

Louis had had no difficulty completing that sentence: New Terra would deny all knowledge of their actions. It did not matter. He would *not* abandon Nessus to the nonexistent mercy of Achilles.

Louis tried not to imagine *himself* at Achilles' mercy.

"Shall I respond, Louis?" Jeeves asked again.

"Proceed," Louis directed. "As we discussed."

Jeeves sang back, then translated. "This is scout training vessel *Prudence,* returning to Nature Preserve One."

Another of Sigmund's contributions: identifying among the refugee fleet a Concordance vessel officially stationed on NP1 and built, like *Addison,* in a GP2 hull.

A longer, more manic torrent. " '*Prudence,* your transponder identification is confirmed, but you are listed as unaccounted for.' "

Louis suggested, "Say we panicked and ran from the Gw'oth. We're better now."

"Us and how many more?" Enzio laughed and gestured at the display filled with inbound Fleet transponders.

More back and forth. " 'You are cleared for Nature Preserve One,' " Jeeves translated. "I acknowledged."

"Well done, Jeeves," Louis said.

"Thank you, sir."

A final jump and they would be in the thick of the Fleet's automated defenses. Louis took a deep, steadying breath. "One more time, Enzio. With precision."

Enzio dropped *Addison* from hyperspace eighteen million miles from the Fleet's center of mass. That was scarcely a million miles—and under a second's travel in hyperdrive—outside the singularity.

"Finagle, Enzio! That wasn't precise," Louis said. "That was insane."

Enzio shrugged.

Another jangling burst of chords.

" 'Welcome back to the Fleet, *Prudence,*' " Jeeves translated. " 'Next time, do not emerge so nearby.' I acknowledged, apologetically."

"We're still in training," Enzio said. "Did you get that, traffic control?"

Addison's inbound course toward NP1 wavered as Enzio feigned veering and overcompensating.

Louis projected a globe. Their destination—thousands of miles from their approved base—was a remote, near-equatorial, comma-shaped land mass near the center of NP1's largest ocean. Penance Island.

The Concordance's maximum-security prison colony and labor camp.

50

Addison swerved on final approach, diving bow-first into the ocean ninety miles from its designated landing field. Cabin gravity and inertial dampers absorbed most of the shock. "We're trainees," Enzio cackled.

"Just go deep and drive," Louis growled. He couldn't help but remember arriving on *Aegis,* beneath the ocean on Wunderland. *I'm coming, Nessus.* "I'm going to the main hold."

"I'm picking up an emergency-services call," Jeeves said. "Help is being dispatched to the crash site."

"Ten minutes to the island," Enzio said. Something thumped off the hull as he spoke.

Louis found the crew in the hold. All carried stunners and flashlights. Louis jammed a stunner in his pocket. "Is this it?" he asked Maura, pointing.

"That's it," she said.

Louis opened the utility box for a final look. There was not much inside. A fuel cell. A radio transmitter. And the gadget that might make this rescue possible: the fusion suppressor he had taken from *Remembrance.*

He would know soon enough if he was clever or delusional.

"Two minutes to the island," Enzio announced on the intercom. "Coming up in one."

"Radio off," Louis ordered. "Confirm."

"Confirmed."

Louis had to imagine *Addison* bursting from the ocean and swooping to the island. He heard a thump and felt the bit of tremor the inertial dampeners had not perfectly offset. They were down! He slapped the release for the main hatch. "Go! Go! Go!" he shouted.

He rolled through the still-opening hatch, hugging the suppressor to his chest. A heavy rain was falling. The others followed and the hatch cycled shut behind them.

Lights suddenly blazed from the small, walled building complex, and floodlights swept across a cluster of tents. Sirens wailed. Puppeteers caterwauled and shrieked. At any moment, if it had not happened already, armed reinforcements would start stepping through.

Louis triggered the fusion suppressor—and all the lights went out. The sirens stopped. Stepping discs ran off embedded fusion reactors—they would have stopped, too. The shrieking got louder. Behind the wall a few emergency lamps came on, running from batteries or fuel cells.

Above the building complex, briefly, a faint green beam pulsed: *Addison*'s comm laser, its beam scattered by the rain. At this range, the laser would be quite deadly. The threat would keep any sane Puppeteers inside the walled compound.

"To the tents!" Louis ordered. "Reinforcements will be here soon."

Arriving in ships built in General Products hulls, opaque to the radio waves carrying the suppression field. Louis could hope they would have radios on, and that the suppression field would sneak aboard through open comm circuits. He did not count on it.

Flashlight beams wobbled as the New Terrans dashed across muddy fields. Lightning flashed overhead. Thunder roared. Puppeteers erupted from the tents, screaming, scattering in all directions.

Two Puppeteers galloped straight at Louis.

"Don't shoot!" Louis ordered.

A LOUD *THUMP!* SIRENS. From the compound's wall, bright light streaming through the coarse cloth of the tents.

Then darkness and silence.

Hearts pounding in his chest, Nessus peeked between tent flaps. Lightning flashed, and in the fields he saw a ship! Dim beams of light jiggled and jogged. Hurtling from the ship toward the tents.

"Come," Nessus sang to Baedeker. "We are rescued." He kept chanting it, forcing himself to run *at* the mysterious intruders.

They galloped together into the fields. Nessus heard a shout, in English: "Don't shoot!"

He *knew* that voice. "Louis Wu!"

"Nessus!" They met at midfield. "Is this Baedeker? We don't have much time."

"I came only to say good-bye," Baedeker said. He switched to song. "Be strong, Nessus."

What? "You *must* come," Nessus sang back. "Achilles will . . ." His voices trailed off, his imagination failing him.

"I am the legitimate Hindmost, no matter who grasps power. I will not abandon the Concordance. I rose once before from prison to power. I will do it again."

"What's he saying?" Louis asked. "Nessus, we have to *go.*"

"A moment." In song, "Achilles' rage will be terrible after this."

"Nessus, my place is here. Now *go.*"

"I will not abandon you."

Baedeker stood tall. "As your Hindmost, I order you to leave. Make a new life for yourself, serving the herd as you think wise."

Trembling with emotion, Nessus could only sing, "I obey."

Then he was running across the fields, amid the humans, to the ship.

LOUIS REACHED DOWN in his mad dash back to *Addison* to scoop up the fusion suppressor. He unlatched its access panel as he ran and toggled the power switch. The ON light died. He waved all-clear at the ship's bow. Enzio would be monitoring through his infrared sensors.

The cargo-hold hatch started to open, and the landing party tumbled inside. Nessus stopped just within the open hatch to wail something mournful. He was filthy, his mane a tangled snarl, and his ribs showed.

"I'm sorry," Louis said. He slapped the CLOSE button and then the intercom. "Enzio! Get us out of here!"

"Launching," Enzio said. "Anyone care to join me on the bridge?"

"On my way." Louis turned to Nessus. "Achilles had a cabin converted for himself. It's on deck three, if you want to clean up. Join me on the bridge whenever you feel ready."

"Thank you, Louis. For everything."

They splashed back into the ocean, went deep, and surfaced thousands of miles away. Another of Sigmund's transponder codes let *Addison* merge inconspicuously into the Fleet's inter-world traffic. Nessus, cleaned up, had by then joined them on the bridge.

Between routine radar sweeps Maura disabled the ship's transponder.

Before traffic control noticed anything amiss, *Addison* was far from the shipping lanes. Increasingly frantic radar searches swept past *Addison,* fooled by the stealth gear Achilles had retrofitted into his erstwhile lifeboat.

After four hours at maximum acceleration, they exited the Fleet's singularity.

"Jumping to hyperspace," Louis announced, "in three. Two. One. Now."

The external displays went blank. The mass pointer lit with five lines for the five worlds of the Fleet. At the instrument's present sensitivity setting, a few nearby stars registered as stubs and New Terra did not appear at all.

"On to New Terra," Louis said. He dismounted the very human-unfriendly pilot's couch. "Nessus, would you care to do the honors?"

Nessus straddled the seat. "I am happy to set our course, Louis. But before we go to New Terra, there is something we need to retrieve."

51

His hooves clattering on the hard tile floor, Nessus followed Sigmund down the long corridors of an underground lab complex. Sigmund lied that Nessus seemed recovered from his ordeal, and Nessus pretended to believe him. Most doors were shut, access controlled by the handprint sensors beside the jambs. Signs offered room numbers but no other information. Nessus suspected that what Sigmund called the Office of Strategic Analyses did not officially exist, an agency more clandestine than Clandestine Directorate.

That Sigmund disclosed this much (but not the stepping-disc address by which they had arrived) showed a surprising degree of trust. Nessus liked to think he had earned it. Or, perhaps, Sigmund meant to show Nessus the Library would be safe here. The Library whose existence aboard *Addison* Nessus had yet to mention, and Louis might not have mentioned—and information Enzio and his people had surely offered for sale to Sigmund.

A door flew open as a white-coated technician bustled out. Nessus glimpsed several dartlike spaceships in a small hangar.

Sigmund saw Nessus' heads swivel. "One-person ships, hyperdrive-equipped. They're pretty handy."

"I would think so," Nessus said. Such little ships would be hard to detect, even without the stealthing gear they doubtless carried. Useful for spying on the Fleet. With Achilles the Hindmost, more useful than ever.

Turning a corner they came to another closed door. Sigmund palmed the access panel and the lock clicked. Sigmund waved Nessus inside, where the wall displays showed only terrestrial-style forest. "My office."

Nessus saw a Citizen bench, but chose to stand. "Times are bad," he said to Sigmund. "Thank you for meeting with me."

"Bad times are *why* I'm meeting with you. This is the most secure room on New Terra. What's on your mind?"

Abandoning Baedeker, but that did not concern Sigmund. "I have important technology that needs safeguarding."

Sigmund nodded. "The Pak Library and what, from the description I've heard, must be the Carlos Wu autodoc."

"I have no secrets, do I?"

"Not if I am doing my job properly."

"So will you protect them, Sigmund?"

"What are your terms?"

"Do not disclose that New Terra has these items. I ask this for your safety as well as my own purposes. Promise to return the items and all that you have learned from them when the rightful government returns to Hearth. Until that government returns, share what you learn only with me. And I will need a ship or . . . wait"—sudden thought—"make that two ships."

"Generous terms. New Terra will keep copies of everything, of course."

Nessus had never imagined otherwise, not was there any way to prevent it. "Agreed."

"I understand the rightful government. That's Baedeker." Sigmund's brow furrowed. "I'm not sure I understand the *current* government on Hearth. Is that Achilles? Or does . . . someone . . . rule from behind the new Hindmost?"

Nessus' hoof scraped the hard floor. He wondered—and worried—too. Removing Achilles would be struggle enough. What if the *Gw'oth* secretly ruled? "Truly, I wish I understood. Do you accept my terms?"

And what will I do if you refuse? Seize *Addison* and its cargo anyway? Perhaps Sigmund already had.

"I accept," Sigmund said.

INSIDE THE MELDING CHAMBER, at the center of *Mighty Current,* within the massive structure that housed Nature Preserve Five's planetary drive—where none dared even to approach—Ol't'ro considered:

Rebirth for Kl'mo colony under Ng't'mo's protection.

Bm'o's inevitable struggles, after his long absence, to reassert his authority on Jm'ho.

The respite that the Tn'Tn'ho's problems would give the colony.

The wealth of knowledge in Concordance archives, from nanotechnology to stepping discs, from starseed lures to computers, and much more they had yet even to sample.

How best to resource and guide millions of Citizen scientists and engineers.

Satisfaction with all that they had accomplished, with minimal loss of life to *any* species.

The wondrous plaything that was Voice, and the pleasurable prospect of future tinkering with the artificial intelligence.

The Chiron persona they had given Voice to monitor and interact with Citizens.

Achilles laboring, even while Ol't'ro pondered, to restore order among the Citizens.

Reluctantly, Ol't'ro diverted a bit of their attention through Chiron to the cabinet meeting on Hearth. . . .

". . . RESOURCES WITH WHICH TO RESTORE public confidence," Hermes sang in conclusion. He was the newly appointed Minister of Information. "Naturally that must be our first priority."

If the conclusion is natural, Achilles thought, why does making the case require so long a tune? Letting the discussion drone on, he left his place at the end of the long oval table to fill a plate from the grains bar on the sideboard. He had loathed cabinet meetings as a minister; the duty was even more onerous as Hindmost.

He had worked so long to be here. And everything was as glorious as he had imagined—at first. The mass adoration at his triumphant return. The spectacular mountainside residence. The fawning servants. The adulation of his acolytes. But another future stretched out before him, an era of endless meetings, bureaucratic trivia, and mind-numbing detail.

"Safety and order beget confidence," Themis sang. His charge was the Department of Public Safety. "If we were to announce new resources for public safety—"

"*True* safety will beget confidence," Vesta chided. In the new government, he continued to lead Clandestine Directorate. "Our priority must be stronger defenses. And we must search for ways to reconstruct the valuable archives Nessus destroyed."

Curse Nessus, Achilles thought. And Louis Wu, too. The jail break was only Wu's latest outrage.

Meanwhile, the squabbling for resources continued. The Minister of Industry proposed to create new jobs for those needing distraction. To the same end, the Minister of Education advocated new learning opportunities. The Minister of Housing sought resources for an apartment-to-apartment search for the billions of Citizens still unaccounted for. The Minister of Agriculture sang urgently about returning grain shipments to normal. The Minister of Transportation asked how and when the stolen grain ships would be repatriated from New Terra.

"We will get those ships back," Achilles chanted. "Vesta, I want ideas how to motivate New Terra to—"

"That is a bad idea," Chiron sang flatly.

The new Minister of Science participated by hologram and these were his first notes of the meeting. Around the table, necks wriggled sinuously in surprise. Who was this newcomer, this unknown, to contradict the Hind-most so bluntly?

But *Achilles* knew. His secret master beyond the hologram, behind the artificial intelligence, must be obeyed. "Back to the matter of priorities," Achilles sang mildly.

Around the table, ministers and subministers glanced at Chiron with curiosity and sudden respect.

Achilles swallowed his rage. "Hermes, we should hear more about your proposal."

And while the Minister of Information sang on and on, Achilles let his thoughts drift to matters that could transpire beneath Ol't'ro's notice. Truly urgent matters. Matters that would fill *him* with happiness. He would find Nessus and Louis Wu.

And they would suffer as greatly as Baedeker now suffered.

AWAKENED IN THE MIDDLE of the night, hastily dressed, a few personal items crammed into his pockets, Louis went with a squad of stern-faced men and women to . . . he did not know where. Someplace nondescript. Wall displays gave no clues to his location. His abductors wore ordinary clothes but bore themselves like soldiers. For lack of a better term, Louis decided he was in a safe house. Had he been allowed to keep his pocket comp, he guessed it would not operate any of the stepping discs here.

Neither in the hotel room from which he had been taken nor in this blandly enigmatic confinement had his captors answered any question beyond, "I am not allowed to discuss that." He found the living room, lay down on the too-short sofa, and waited for someone who would explain.

Something woke Louis. Rustling. Two of his captors, springing to attention. Sigmund Ausfaller striding into the room. "Dismissed," Sigmund said, and the soldiers left.

"What the tanj?" Louis demanded, sitting up. "After all I've done for New Terra, you're *arresting* me?"

"Protective custody. I'm truly sorry." Sigmund sat on the leather ottoman across the room. "There was no time to argue."

"I'm here now. How about explaining?"

"The short version? There is a bounty on your head, a fortune if you're killed and a lot more if you are delivered alive. The same for Nessus."

"Achilles."

"Achilles," Sigmund agreed. "He's *not* happy with you two. And trust me, the word is out. Every criminal, hard-luck case, and lowlife on the planet is looking for you."

"You plan to lock me in this—wherever I am—forever? That's unacceptable, Sigmund."

Louis had become pretty good at taking care of himself. He would take his chances. If he had to, he would learn to put up with bodyguards. Eventually Alice would come home and—

"Tanj! Alice. The baby."

"Leverage to get at you," Sigmund said. "You would *all* have to hide. And in time they'll still find you."

For the first time since emerging from the autodoc on *Aegis*, Louis felt his true age. Felt ancient. Felt the weight of worlds on his shoulders. At the same time the confusion of his childhood crashed down on him. "I can't abandon my own child. I won't do it."

Sigmund said, looking miserable, "A child who never knew you won't miss you. All that anyone on New Terra knows about you and Alice is that she threw you out. If you never see her again . . ."

"Then no one need ever know it *is* my child," Louis completed unhappily.

"You know what you have to do," Sigmund said. "I'm sorry. Truly."

Leave New Terra. "Then Alice leaves with me." Louis swallowed hard. "If she'll come, that is."

Sigmund stood, crammed his hands in his pockets, and began to pace. "Forget for a moment that Alice will be gone for months and you are in danger *now*. You and anyone with the bad fortune to be near you when the shooting starts. Do you have any idea what you would be asking Alice to give up?

"Louis, I hate this, I really do, but there are things you need to know. You think you and Alice love one another. Maybe you do. But apart from hyperspace conversations, you've known her for only a few months. So how much about her *do* you know?"

"Who the hell are you to judge—"

"Be quiet and listen," Sigmund barked. "Alice and I have been friends for over a century. Did you know I pulled her out of stasis, from a derelict ship the Outsiders had been carrying around for even longer? No? Then don't be so sure you know everything about her.

"She woke up to a new life here—pregnant by a lover torn from her old life. I watched her get past that, and it wasn't quick or easy or pleasant. Yet for the sake of the short time you two have had together, you would ask her to leave children, and grandchildren, and great-grandchildren."

Could Louis ask Alice to give up her whole life on New Terra? To go where? Alone, into the unknown. Or back to Known Space, their memories wiped. They would not even know each other. . . .

Louis shuddered. Every choice was impossible. But one choice was hardest only on him. He said, "It's time for me to go home. Alone. Help me contact Nessus."

52

No matter the urgency of the mission, Alice's life had narrowed into dull routine: med check in the autodoc; stasis; message-queue review; repeat. She did not expect anything consequential to happen until she reached the Gw'oth home system.

And then the hyperwave message from Sigmund arrived, and within it the recording from Louis.

Louis was gone forever.

And Sigmund had encouraged Louis. For her good. For the baby's good. *Damn* them both. *Damn* their impeccable logic. Didn't *she* deserve any say? She was simultaneously enraged, touched, and heartbroken.

Somewhere, she knew, Louis must be suffering as she did. She suddenly could not bear to be alone. She left her cabin, trembling.

A passing crewman stopped and stared. "Are you all right?"

She glanced down at her belly, her pregnancy beginning to show. At Louis's baby.

"No," Alice said, "but I will be."

NESSUS PLODDED UP and down the stairways and curved corridors of his all-but-empty, yet-to-be-named, new ship. Plumes of pheromones trailed in his wake. Virtual crowds, murmuring unintelligibly, kept pace in the wallpaper. Neither comforted him. Stepping discs would have whisked him anywhere aboard, but even if he had had a destination in mind, why bother to save a few paces? Whole empty years stretched before him, soon with only a Jeeves for company.

So far they had barely spoken. Jeeves was an everyday reminder of Voice and his uncertain fate. An everyday rebuke. Another weight on Nessus' conscience. . . .

He discovered Louis in the relax room, seated at the fold-down table, an untouched meal in front of him. He did not look up.

Nessus said, "Just you and me. It seems like old times."

"I'm lousy company. Sorry." Louis slid away his plate. "I'm not happy how things turned out, Nessus. Not at all."

The Concordance, betrayed. Both their lives shattered, and their loves abandoned. Their mere presence a lure for Achilles' wrath, an intolerable danger to everyone and everything they held dear. No sane being *could* be happy. "I set us an impossible task, Louis."

"We completed several impossible tasks. Every accomplishment made matters worse." Louis laughed bitterly. "The law of unintended consequences is harsh."

"As you say." The guilt was almost more than Nessus could bear. But with a small lie, at the cost of a bit more loneliness, he could ease Louis's suffering. "I came to tell you, it is time."

Louis looked at his meal, grimaced, and stood. "Fine. Let's get this over with."

They walked in silence to the cargo bay in which stood the Carlos Wu autodoc. With nanotech precision, it had recorded Louis's pre-adventure engrams. It was the ideal device to do what must now be done.

Louis raised the dome and disrobed. "Nessus . . ."

"Yes, Louis?"

"You have been a good and true friend. Remember that for both of us, because soon I won't be able." Climbing inside the intensive-care cavity, he paused. "If somehow I can make things better, somehow atone for all that has happened . . . come get me. Use me."

"You have been a true friend to me, as well. Now, please lie down."

Louis lay flat and hit the activation button. As the dome closed, he said, softly, "Good-bye."

Nessus induced sedation and initiated the memory modification routines. Then—even though at least forty days remained before he and Louis would part ways—Nessus set off, lonelier than ever, to finish his final preparations.

And once Louis was sent on his way? Other than staying far from the Fleet and New Terra, Nessus had no idea.

Nessus paused in the doorway to look back. "Until we meet again, my friend."

EPILOGUE

With a struggle, Louis Wu opened his eyes. He saw a wall of instruments. He closed his eyes to try again, and forgot what he was doing.

When next he opened his eyes—much later, to judge from the aching ear and the kink in his neck—the instruments remained sideways. He was clear-headed enough this time to notice his head was down on a shelf. Whatever this was, he was studying it sideways. As through a fog, laughing at himself, he sat up.

Too fast. His head began to spin and he almost threw up. The room went dark. . . .

THE NEXT TIME Louis woke, his thoughts were clearer. Cautiously, he opened his eyes. Navigational instruments. At the center of the console, an inert mass pointer. Make that a pilot's console. The "room," tiny though it was, was the bridge of a starship!

"Let's find some hair of the dog that bit me," Louis muttered. The urge seemed more learned than a bodily craving. Odd. Usually, it worked the other way around. He searched the drawers under the console shelf for emergency medical supplies. He eventually found bandages and antiseptics. No painkillers.

Where was the crew?

He got up, gingerly, from his seat: a pilot's crash couch. He barely had space to turn around. When he managed, intending to leave the bridge and find the crew, he found only two narrow hatches. The first was for a tiny closet that held a pressure suit. The suit looked like it would fit him. The second hatch opened into a cupboard-sized room that apparently served for sleeping, eating, recreation, hygiene, and exercise. The access panel in the multipurpose room's rear wall revealed a hyperdrive shunt, thrusters, cabin-gravity generator, life-support gear, and a fusion reactor. As far as he could tell, the ship had only the two small cabins.

Louis had never heard of such a compact starship.

Somehow, *he* was the crew.

Every alcoholic, painkiller, and recreational-drug option on the synthesizer had, inexplicably, been disabled. Tanj, but his thoughts were fuzzy! Before crashing from his last fix, he must have jiggered the synthesizer so he couldn't hit again. A workable substitute for willpower. He had to settle for a bulb of strong coffee. He returned to the bridge, sat, and let the caffeine do its job.

This was a one-person ship. He was the one person. So where was the ship?

According to the navigational instruments he was nowhere near *anything* familiar. Twenty light-years from . . . he stopped to think what he last remembered. Wunderland. Twenty light-years from here!

"What the tanj are you doing, Louis, two months or more from Wunder—"

His name was Nathan. Why was he calling himself Louis?

LOUIS WU.

That was right. He was sure, somehow. Another long-lost memory recovered from a drug haze? Straining, he thought he remembered an orphanage. And an older sister!

Whatever. He *was* once Louis Wu. And since Wunderland's aristos wanted Nathan Graynor, it was time for a change of names.

This would make more sense if he remembered planning to change names. How long had he been on the pills before he cut himself off? How long until the last of the drugs was out of his system?

He struggled to focus. There had to be a way to make sense of being alone, in a very expensive ship, in the middle of nowhere. The scattered images he retrieved almost seemed like someone else's memories. But that was nonsense, his mind on drugs.

Step by step, he connected the dots. Smuggling med supplies to Wunderland. Shot down. Rescued by the rebels. Wounded during the rebel ambush. Waking in the makeshift hospital.

After that, things got fuzzy. The pills, of course. Way, way too many pills. After the ambush, he had only nebulous, almost secondhand memories. Fled the rebel camp. Made his way through dense jungle to a city. Had the . . . surgery?

Another rush of not-quite memories. Louis went to the other cabin and, his hand shaking, found a mirror. He looked about twenty years old!

A rebel sympathizer: that was it. Now Louis remembered: a cosmetic surgeon had helped. That, and given Louis a dose of boosterspice. A really potent batch, apparently.

He returned to his reconstruction. Addiction. Flee the rebel camp. Surgery. And . . .

And steal this ship!

Louis laughed. The aristos were leeches. Whatever they owned, they had effectively stolen first. Louis's conscience was clear, and it would remain clear when he sold this amazing little ship—the ultimate singleship—to some wealthy Belter. For an obscene amount of money.

With that cheerful thought, Louis set to work synthing a hearty meal.

STARS SPARKLED in his view ports as Louis laid in a course for Sol system. Two months in hyperspace, plus however many normal-space sanity breaks he decided to take. Two months and a bit until he sold this ship. Two months and a bit until he settled into a mundane, comfortable existence.

He looked at his instruments. He looked out the view ports at the unblinking stars, and the patterns reminded him where he was.

He reentered his course, on a heading straight away from Sol.

After everything he had been through, surely he deserved an adventure he would actually remember.

ABOUT THE AUTHORS

LARRY NIVEN has been a published writer since 1964. He has written science fiction, fantasy, long and short fiction, nonfiction, children's television, comic books, and stranger stuff. His books, including many collaborations, number somewhere around sixty. He lives in Chatsworth, California, with Marilyn, his wife since 1969.

EDWARD M. LERNER worked in high tech for thirty years, as everything from engineer to senior vice president. He writes hard SF, from near-future techno-thrillers, most recently *Fools' Experiments* and *Small Miracles*, to far-future space epics like the Fleet of Worlds series with Larry. Ed lives in Virginia with his wife, Ruth.